A KILLING OF INNOCENTS

ALSO BY DEBORAH CROMBIE

A Bitter Feast

Garden of Lamentations

To Dwell in Darkness

The Sound of Broken Glass

No Mark Upon Her

Necessary as Blood

Where Memories Lie

Water Like a Stone

In a Dark House

Now May You Weep

And Justice There Is None

A Finer End

Kissed a Sad Goodbye

Dreaming of the Bones

Mourn Not Your Dead

Leave the Grave Green

All Shall Be Well

A Share in Death

A KILLING OF INNOCENTS

A NOVEL

DEBORAH CROMBIE

𝓌𝓂
WILLIAM MORROW
An Imprint of HarperCollinsPublishers

A KILLING OF INNOCENTS. Copyright © 2023 by Deborah Crombie. All rights reserved. Printed in the United States of America. No part of this book may be used or reproduced in any manner whatsoever without written permission except in the case of brief quotations embodied in critical articles and reviews. For information, address HarperCollins Publishers, 195 Broadway, New York, NY 10007.

HarperCollins books may be purchased for educational, business, or sales promotional use. For information, please email the Special Markets Department at SPsales@harpercollins.com.

A hardcover edition of this book was published in 2023 by William Morrow, an imprint of HarperCollins Publishers.

FIRST WILLIAM MORROW PAPERBACK EDITION PUBLISHED 2024.

Title page art © Aleksandr Faustov/Alamy Stock Photo

Library of Congress Cataloging-in-Publication Data has been applied for.

ISBN 978-0-06-299347-2

23 24 25 26 27 LBC 5 4 3 2 1

For Caroline Todd
Mentor and dear friend, you are sorely missed

ACKNOWLEDGMENTS

The Thomas Coram Hospital and its staff in Guilford Street are entirely products of my imagination, as are the gallery in Museum Street and the nightclubs Bottle and Bottoms Up (although researching those fancy cocktail recipes kept me very entertained during the long months of Covid isolation).

I owe many thanks to Alex Macias, potter extraordinaire, for allowing me to get my hands in the clay and for answering endless questions about ceramics, and most of all for the inspiration provided by her beautiful work. Thanks also to Minda Macias, queen of glazes!

Steve Ullathorne took photos of Bloomsbury and provided lots of local London tips when I couldn't be there myself. Barb Jungr introduced me to the famous jazz club at Pizza Express Dean Street.

Gigi Norwood and Diane Hale read the manuscript in progress—I am as always enormously grateful for their insight and advice.

My Jungle Red blog sisters, Hallie Ephron, Hank Phillippi

Ryan, Rhys Bowen, Lucy Burdette, Julia Spencer-Fleming, and Jenn McKinlay, gave me daily support and encouragement, as did Frances Ballweg, my sister-from-another-mother.

One of the greatest pleasures of writing this series is working with illustrator Laura Maestro, and her map for *A Killing of Innocents* brought the story to life in the most charming way.

Thanks to my agent, Nancy Yost, and all the terrific team at NYLA, for your patience, support, and encouragement.

And many, many thanks to all the team at William Morrow, and especially to my editor, Carrie Feron. I am so fortunate to have the privilege of working with such talented and dedicated folks.

Last but not least, thanks to my family. Kayti, Wren (when you are old enough to read this!), Gage, and Rick. Love you bunches.

A KILLING OF INNOCENTS

A
Killing
of
Innocents

(Staffordshire Ceramic Dogs)

Sid, at home in Notting Hill

Toby rehearsing as a Nutcracker mouse

Wallace (Quirk's terrier)

ALBANY TER.

REGENTS PARK

Gordon Square Garden

GOWER ST.

GOODGE ST.

TOTTENHAM COURT

GOODGE STREET

NEWMAN STREET

CAVENDISH PLACE

MORTIMER ST.

CAVENDISH SQ.

REGENT STREET

Oxford Circus

OXFORD ST.

OXFORD ST.

OXFORD STREET

DEAN ST.

SOHO SQ.

Snow's "Cholera" pump

WARDOUR ST.

POLAND ST.

Pizza Express

Carlisle St.

Chowdhury's flat

SOHO

GREAT MARLBOROUGH ST.

BROADWICK ST.

John Snow's pump

Silver

Lexington St.

Camisa

St. Anne's Church (SOHO)

St. Anne's Church

Golden Square Area

Beak St.

Brewer St.

Bridle Lane

Warwick St.

Golden Square

Bottle-

WARDOUR ST.

DEAN ST.

Great Windmill St.

SHAFTESBURY

THE W

REGENT STREET

PICCADILLY

SAVILE ROW

Illustrated map by Laura Hartman Maestro © 2022

CHAPTER ONE

She stood looking down at her daughter, sleeping, damp hair tangled, her duvet kicked half off. The child had never slept easily. But those nights of walking and rocking, walking and rocking, were too distant now, a memory she struggled to grasp, just as she struggled to recall the warm weight of her baby in her arms. Now the half-light from the open bedroom door made hieroglyphics of the unicorns dancing across her rumpled pajamas, as if the beasts were dancing in scattered moonlight.

How could she bear to leave her little girl, perhaps for months? But she must, she knew she must. She needed to be herself, needed room to breathe, room to think, room to make decisions without the constant weight of his displeasure.

She felt his presence even before she heard his footstep in the hall and his shadow blocked the light behind her. He grasped her shoulders. "You won't go."

She didn't turn, tried to stop herself flinching. "I have to. You know I have to. I can help—"

"That's your God complex, my dear," he said softly. "Your place is here. A mother. A wife."

"Yes, but——" Her protest died away as his fingers bit into the soft flesh of her upper arms.

His voice was a whisper now, a breath in her ear. "If you do this, you will regret it. I can promise you that."

———

Duncan Kincaid stretched the paperwork-induced kinks from his neck and took an appreciative sip of beer. The Victorian pub in Lamb's Conduit Street was beginning to fill up with Friday happy-hour drinkers, most of whom seemed to be refugee staff from Great Ormond Street Hospital across the street. Kincaid himself was on his way home from Holborn Police Station but had agreed to meet his detective sergeant, Doug Cullen, for a quick debriefing on an interview Doug had taken that afternoon in Theobalds Road. The team was tidying up a few loose ends from a case, the knifing of an elderly Asian shop owner during the robbery of his corner shop. The assailants had been vicious but not too bright—balaclavas had covered their faces but not the distinctive tattoo on the knife-wielder's hand, caught on the shop's CCTV. The pair had spent the meager proceeds of the robbery on six-packs of lager bought in a shop in the next road, this time maskless.

Idiots. It was the sort of senseless crime that made Kincaid feel weary. Taking another sip of his pint, he glanced at his watch. Doug was late. The young woman sitting alone at the next table seemed to mimic him, checking her own watch, then her mobile, with a frown of irritation. In spite of the blustery November evening, the room was warm from the fire and she had shrugged off her fur-trimmed anorak to reveal hospital scrubs. Their pale green color set off her dark skin and the dark twists of her hair. A doctor, he thought, as the nursing staff were usually in uniform, and he revised his guess at her age up a few years. When she tucked her mobile back in her bag, he looked away, aware that he'd been staring.

The door nearest the fire swung open, bringing a blast of cold, damp air and a flurry of brown leaves. The young woman looked up, her face expectant, but it was Doug Cullen, his anorak and fair hair beaded with moisture, his cheeks pink from the cold. Oblivious, Doug slid into the chair opposite Kincaid and pulled off his spattered glasses. "Bugger of a day," he said, wiping the lenses with a handkerchief. He nodded at Kincaid's glass. "Whatever you're drinking, I could use one."

"Bloomsbury IPA. My shout," Kincaid told him, standing. As he made his way to the crowded bar, he saw the young woman begin to gather her things. When he turned back a few minutes later, pints in hand, she had gone.

———

With her back to the warmth of the pub, she hesitated. She checked her mobile once more, then sent a quick text.

Turning, she glanced back inside. The nice-looking white bloke who'd been studying her was at the bar. She'd have taken him for a cop even if she hadn't glimpsed the blue lanyard tucked into his suit jacket. And married, too—she'd seen the glint of the ring on his left hand. Figured, she thought with a grimace. Turning away from the lamp-lit window, she crossed the street, huddled into her coat, and headed north.

She'd turned into Guilford Street when her mobile pinged with an answer. *The usual? Give me 15, yeah?*

Sending a thumbs-up in reply, she tucked her mobile back into her bag and quickened her step. She could just make it to the café if she cut across Russell Square. When she reached the Fitzroy, she jogged around the corner and entered the square from the north-east corner.

It was fully dark now, the lights of the splash fountain obscured by the after-work crowd, all heads-down and hurrying. Shivering, she remembered summer evenings spent lounging on the grass or sipping wine on the patio at Caffè Tropea. As if to mock her, a gust of wind splattered her with droplets of water from the trees along the walk.

A cyclist zipped past her, so close she felt a breeze from the disturbed air. She spun round, meaning to shout at him, but he was gone. Mad bastards, all of them, cyclists, and God knew she'd mopped up enough of them in A and E.

As she turned back, someone bumped her hard from the front, gripping her shoulder as she staggered from the force of the impact. Before she could protest, the dark blur of a figure was gone, swallowed in the crowd as quickly as the cyclist.

Her heart gave an odd little skip. "What the—" she whispered, but the words died in her throat. Then the edges of her vision blurred, and she was falling.

—

"Mummy." Trevor tugged at the hem of her coat.

Lesley Banks gave a sigh of exasperation and kept her eyes fixed on the screen of her mobile. "Honestly, Trev," she snapped. "Amuse yourself for one minute, can't you? You're a big boy now." One of her staff at the hotel had just sent her a text saying she couldn't come in for evening shift and Lesley had got to sort it out straight away. The walk across the square was the only time she didn't have to keep her eye—and her hand—firmly fixed on her five-year-old.

"But Mummy—"

"Trev, just look at the pretty fountain, okay?" she said, scrolling through her contacts for someone who might be willing to fill a shift at short notice.

"Mummy." Trevor's tug was more insistent. Something in his voice made her look away from her screen. "Mummy, I think that lady isn't well."

"What lady is that, love?"

Trevor pointed. "That lady over there, by the tree."

Lesley made out a dark shape beneath the trees just beyond the illumination cast by the fountain's lights. She shook her head. "Not our business, love."

"But Mummy." Trevor scuffed at the leaves. "She walked funny. And then she fell down."

"Look, baby, it's probably someone who's just had a bit too much—" Lesley stopped. Why teach your children to be kind if you weren't prepared to be bothered yourself? With a sigh, she pocketed her mobile and grasped Trevor's hand. "Okay, let's have a look." Taking a few steps closer, she called out, "Miss? Are you okay, miss?"

There was no movement from the shape. Her eyes had adjusted and now she could make out legs, and the outline of a boot. Lesley hesitated. There was something about that stillness that struck her as wrong. Even drunks weren't usually completely unresponsive. She glanced round, suddenly hoping for a supportive fellow Samaritan, but the crowd had thinned while she'd been dithering.

She could call 999, of course, but she'd look an idiot if it were a rough sleeper merely the worse for wear. And if the woman really was ill, well, she'd had first-aid training—you had to these days in the hotel business, didn't you?

Loosening Trevor's hand, she put him behind her and said, "You stay right here, baby, while Mummy checks on the lady."

Taking a deep breath, she crossed the intervening ground and knelt. "Miss," she said.

When there was no reply, Lesley put tentative fingers on the woman's shoulder and gave it a gentle shake. The figure, loose as a jelly, rolled face-up. The flopping arm brushed Lesley's knees.

Lesley jerked back, her hand to her mouth. "Oh Christ," she gasped. Behind her, Trevor began to cry.

CHAPTER TWO

Lesley was aware of her son crying, and of people beginning to gather, but she couldn't tear her eyes from the young woman's face. There was no tension in the features, and the eyes stared blankly upwards. Tentatively, Lesley reached out, felt the woman's neck for a pulse. Nothing. But it hadn't been five minutes since she had fallen. Maybe it wasn't too late. Swallowing against the blood pounding in her ears, Lesley glanced back. "CPR," she said, but it came out a hoarse whisper. She tried again. "Does anyone know CPR? She needs help."

The couple hovering behind Trevor shook their heads and the woman took a step back, looking frightened.

Trevor's wails had subsided and he was inching towards her. "Trev," Lesley said as gently as she could. "Stay behind Mummy, okay? I'm going to help the lady." To the couple, she added, "Ring 999. Tell them to hurry."

—

The call came as Kincaid and Doug were putting on their coats, preparing to brave the windy damp for the short walk back to Holborn Station. Kincaid's heart sank when he saw the name on the screen—Simon Gikas, his team's efficient case manager. Hopefully, it was just paperwork. He'd promised Gemma he'd make the tail end of Toby's ballet rehearsal.

"Simon, what's up?" he asked, stepping out onto the pavement, Doug on his heels.

"Guv, I wasn't sure if you'd gone for the day. But we've had a call, a knifing in Russell Square. I thought you might want to take this one yourself."

"A fatality?"

"Yeah. A young woman, near the café. A passerby thought she was ill, tried to help."

"Bugger," Kincaid muttered. Doug looked at him questioningly.

"Guv, I can route it—"

"No, no, you did the right thing, Simon. Where's Sidana?" Detective Inspector Jasmine Sidana was his second in command.

"She's on her way. She'd already left for home, so she might be a few minutes. I'll just ring Cullen—"

"No need. He's with me. We're just down Lamb's Conduit."

"Should I send a car?" Simon asked.

Kincaid deliberated. It was a short enough walk, but still, a car would be faster. "Yes. We'll meet them at the station. Make sure uniform seals off both entrances to the square, will you?" When he'd rung off, he met Doug Cullen's inquiring glance. "Looks like we've got ourselves a murder."

—

The car dropped them at the north corner of the square, nearest the Caffè Tropea. The blue flashing lights of the emergency vehicles lit the ornate facade of the Fitzroy Hotel and cast an eerie glow on the glistening leaves of the trees at the square's edge. Thanking the driver, Kincaid got out, then studied the scene for a moment. The two PCs manning a hastily strung tape at the gate had their hands full keeping the evening commuters out. Kincaid showed his ID to the female officer.

"Sir," she said, looking relieved to see him.

"Anyone giving you a hard time?" he asked.

"Just the usual. Some curious, some just want to get home and this is their normal route."

"Backup?"

"On the way, sir."

"Good. If anyone volunteers information, get their names and addresses. Radio the same instructions to the other gate, would you?"

"Yes, sir." She stepped aside, keying her shoulder mic as Kincaid and Cullen ducked under the tape.

They followed the central pathway, passing the Tropea, where lights still shone merrily through the large windows. The outside terrace, however, was empty, the chairs tipped in against the moisture-slicked tabletops. A solitary smoker stood huddled under the awning, mobile to his ear.

Once they reached the fountain, Kincaid saw people clustered to one side of the path. Two uniformed officers separated the onlookers from the ambulance crew in their safety-green jackets. Beyond the medics, Kincaid saw a dark shape against the base of a tree.

When they'd identified themselves to the PCs, Kincaid approached the medics. "I'm Detective Superintendent Kincaid," he said, "and this is Detective Sergeant Cullen, Holborn CID."

"Chris Burns." The older of the two men gave them a nod of greeting. "This is my partner, John Ho."

"Mind filling me in on what we've got here?" Kincaid asked.

"Female, mid- to late twenties in my estimation. A puncture wound to the chest. My guess is that it nicked her aorta. The pathologist will be able to tell you. A passerby"—he tipped his head towards a woman who stood some distance away from the other onlookers, a small boy at her side—"saw her fall and administered CPR, but there was no response. No joy for us, either, so we had the supervisor call time of death."

"She's wearing scrubs, by the way," put in Ho. "And a Coram lanyard." This was the small hospital just down Guilford Street from Great Ormond Street Hospital.

Kincaid felt the first prickle of unease. Frowning, he switched on his mobile phone torch and crossed to the body. She lay on her back, her coat open to the pale green of her hospital tunic. Her face was turned away slightly, but he recognized her instantly.

"Oh, Christ," he muttered, stepping back and nearly treading on Doug's toes.

"What is it?" Doug moved closer and Kincaid heard the sharp exhalation of his breath. "Shit. Isn't that the girl from the pub?"

"I'm afraid so." Kincaid squatted in damp grass, frowning as he studied her. "And this can't have happened, what, more than a quarter of an hour after she left? She must have walked straight here." He tried to wrap his mind round the idea that this young woman had lain dying while they were sipping their pints.

"Who would do such a thing? Surely it's not a gang knifing?"

Kincaid pulled a pair of nitrile gloves from his coat pocket and slipped them on. The woman's lanyard had been pushed to one side when the medics cut open her tunic. Carefully, he lifted it by the edge and examined it. Her face stared back at him from the photo, her lips curved in a friendly half smile. "Sasha," he said quietly. "Her name is Sasha Johnson. SpR." He looked up at Chris Burns, the medic, who had come to stand beside them. "What's that?"

"Specialty registrar. It means she was a trainee doctor."

So he had been right, Kincaid thought without satisfaction. He moved the focus of his torch from her face to her torso. The medics had pulled her tunic up, but the wound was barely visible. "There's not much blood."

"No," replied Burns. "Most of the bleeding would have been internal."

Just as Kincaid straightened up with a sigh, his phone pinged with a text from Simon Gikas. *Rashid Kaleem on the way.*

"We're in luck," Kincaid said to Doug. "Simon's got Rashid." The young pathologist was, in Kincaid's opinion, the best in the city now that Kincaid's friend Kate Ling had left the service. He'd met Kaleem during an investigation in the East End more than a year ago. That had been the case that brought Kincaid and Gemma their foster daughter, Charlotte.

Kincaid thanked the medics, then turned to Doug. "Make sure the SOCOs are on their way, and have uniform start setting up a perimeter. I want to have a word with our Good Samaritan so we can release her." The little boy had begun to whine and tug on his mother's hand. "And where the hell is Sidana? Find out, will you?" he added over his shoulder as he turned away.

The witness stood, gathering her son into her side. She was white, slender, with mousy-fair hair pulled back from a high forehead. "I'm Detective Superintendent Kincaid," he said, extending a hand. Her fingers felt icy in his, and her face was pale and pinched with cold.

"Lesley Banks," she answered. "And this is Trevor." The boy's hair was as straight and white-blond as Toby's, but he looked closer to Charlotte's age.

Kincaid leaned down to the child's level. "Hi, Trevor. What a good boy you are to take care of your mum. I'll bet you're"—Kincaid make a show of thinking—"six."

"No, I'm five!" Trevor puffed up his chest and peered at Kincaid. "And a half. Are you a policeman?"

"I am. And I need you and your mum to tell me what happened to the lady."

"Mummy says she'd dead," Trevor told him. "Our budgie died. He fell over in his cage. The lady fell over, too."

"Did you see her fall over?" Kincaid asked, with a quick glance at the boy's mother.

Trevor nodded. "She walked funny. And then she fell down. I told Mummy."

"You're very observant, Trevor. Did—"

"I told Mummy the lady looked ill but Mummy said she had too much—"

"Hush, Trev," put in Lesley Banks, looking embarrassed. She gave Kincaid an apologetic shrug. "Well, you'd think that. But Trev said she looked fine and then she collapsed, so I thought I'd better have a look." She shivered. "But she was too still. I couldn't find a pulse."

"So you started CPR?"

Lesley nodded. "I've had the training. I manage a hotel and we have to be prepared."

"Who called 999?"

"I'm not sure. I just shouted for someone to ring. It seemed like forever before they came, but I kept up the compressions."

"You were counting, Mummy," Trevor said helpfully.

"Yes, I was." She gave him a squeeze. "And you were very brave."

Kincaid bent down to the boy again. "Trevor, I want you to think very hard, okay? You said the lady was fine and then she fell down. Did you see anyone with her before that?"

Trevor screwed his face into a frown. "There were lots of people. They were hurrying. I think maybe a man bumped into her."

"And she fell down after that?"

Trevor nodded.

"Can you tell me what the man looked like?"

The boy glanced up at his mother.

"Go on, love," she said. "Tell Mr. Kincaid what you told me."

"He had a hood."

"You mean like a hoodie?" Kincaid asked. "A sweatshirt?"

Trevor shook his head, his blond hair flopping on his brow. "No. It was a big coat. Like mine, but bigger." He touched the front of his ordinary winter anorak.

"Was it blue, like yours?"

"No . . . I don't know. It was dark." Trevor's voice quavered a bit.

"One more question, okay, Trevor? Did you see which way the man went, after he bumped the lady?"

"That way." Without hesitation, Trevor pointed towards the square's north entrance.

"Thank you, son. You've been a big help." Kincaid turned to Ms. Banks again. "Did you see this man as well?"

Lesley Banks sighed. "No. I was on my mobile. A work problem. Trev was bored, and he notices things when he's bored. And"— she paused, then shrugged—"he has an active imagination. That's why I didn't think there was anything wrong at first. If I'd been quicker . . ."

"I don't think there was anything you could have done," Kincaid told her.

With a glance at her son, she said quietly, "I heard the ambulance men say she was"—she mouthed the word—"stabbed. Is it true?" Tightening her grip on Trevor, she glanced round at the now almost-empty square. "I'd never have thought it wasn't safe here."

"I promise we'll do our best to find out what happened. If you'll give my sergeant your information, someone will be in touch to take a formal statement. And if you think of anything else, don't hesitate to ring me." He handed her his card. Before he turned away, he touched her arm lightly. "And thank you for what you did. Not everyone would have stopped."

—

Gemma James sat on the floor, watching half a dozen children wearing oversized mouse heads prance across the floor of the rehearsal room in the Tabernacle Community Center in Notting Hill. The boys all wore identical white T-shirts and black leggings, but even with his face hidden by the slightly moth-eaten mouse head, she could easily pick out her seven-year-old son, Toby. There was something just a bit more precise in his movements, something that was definitively Toby.

The ballet school had started rehearsals for the Christmas production of *The Nutcracker* a month earlier, but tonight was the first time the children had tried the battle scene between the mouse army and the Hussars while wearing the awkward costumes. Cues had been missed, tears had been shed, and several of the little mice had blundered into one another.

Gemma had long since decided that the ballet master, Mr.

Charles, had the patience of a saint. He was dancing the part of Herr Drosselmeyer as well as directing the production, and yet he never seemed to get ruffled. Wishing she had half his calm, she stretched her aching back against the rehearsal-room wall. Her legs had gone all pins and needles, and if she didn't get up soon she was going to be paralyzed. The few other parents on the sidelines looked equally fidgety. And just where the hell, she wondered, was Duncan?

He'd promised he'd be there to see Toby's first appearance in the mouse head. Toby was also dancing in the opening party scene, but for him that paled in comparison to the thrill of wearing the mouse costume and wielding a plastic sword. He was the youngest of the Mice, cast because he'd progressed so rapidly in the short time he'd been dancing. Mr. Charles said Toby was a natural, and Gemma's feelings about her son's potential talent kept her swinging wildly between pride and dread. She had an idea just how demanding a serious commitment to dance could be, thanks to their friend Jess Cusick. A few years older, Jess was dancing the part of Fritz, the Stahlbaums' mischievous son, but Gemma knew he had his heart set on dancing the Nutcracker Prince in the next season or two.

The rehearsal-room door inched open, its squeak disguised by the thump of the piano, and Gemma's friend MacKenzie Williams slipped through the gap. Wearing dancer's leggings and an oversized T-shirt, and looking much more limber than Gemma felt, MacKenzie sank down to the floor beside her. "How's it going?" she whispered.

"Interminably," Gemma answered with a roll of her eyes, but she grinned. MacKenzie's good humor was infectious. She was also the most persuasive person Gemma had ever met, but not even MacKenzie at the height of her powers had been able to talk

Gemma into dancing one of the grown-up partygoers. MacKenzie, however, was none other than Mrs. Stahlbaum, Clara and Fritz's elegant mother, and she'd talked her husband, Bill, into taking the part of Mr. Stahlbaum.

"Did you see Kit and Charlotte?" Gemma asked.

"In the café. Kit's helping Stephanie with her homework."

"I'll bet he is." Kit's recent willingness to come to ballet rehearsals had little to do with interest in the production and everything to do with the pretty fifteen-year-old ballerina dancing Clara.

On the floor, the scene was nearing its end. The Mice, overcome by the Hussars, fell dramatically to the floor, waving their feet in the air as they expired. Gemma checked her mobile again—still nothing from Duncan. Well, it was a good thing that she, at least, had been able to get away early.

Her new job tracking and identifying knife crime in Greater London had at first sounded glamorous but had turned out to mean mind-numbingly dull days spent at a computer terminal at the new Met headquarters, poring over reports.

Gemma missed the CID team at Brixton, as well as boots-on-the-ground investigating. Most of all, she missed the easy camaraderie she and her friend Melody had shared when working on a case. Melody hardly spoke these days, and seemed to conveniently disappear whenever it was time for lunch or a break. Gemma guessed it was due to the spectacular breakup with her boyfriend on their recent long weekend away. Every time she thought she might ask, Melody had an excuse not to talk.

Gemma must have sighed aloud, because MacKenzie gave her a concerned look. "You okay?"

"Just thinking about work."

MacKenzie shook her head. "More likely thinking about giving

Duncan a bollocking, would be my guess. Will Toby be dreadfully disappointed?"

"Oh, no. Cops' kids." Gemma shrugged. "They know how it is. Besides, I took a video."

Just as Mr. Charles clapped his hands and called out, "Once more, positions, please," Gemma's phone vibrated with an incoming text. It was Duncan, but he wasn't apologizing for being late.

Got something for you. Russell Square, if you can make it.

———

Opening the fridge door and peering into the empty interior, Melody Talbot wondered how she had managed to make such a balls-up of her life. The bare shelves stared back at her, unhelpfully. A dried-out piece of cheese, a tub of carrot salad from M&S that seemed to be growing mold, one egg, and a crystalized jar of marmalade. It was pathetic. Not even Jamie Oliver could make a dinner out of that.

And she was pathetic as well, she thought. Home alone— again—on a Friday evening, with nothing on but a date with Deliveroo.

Just a few months ago she'd had a boyfriend, a social life of sorts, and a job that she liked. Even if the guitarist boyfriend had been touring, she'd had phone calls and video chats to look forward to. Now, nothing beckoned to her other than a cheap unopened bottle of wine on the countertop, and that was company she knew she'd regret.

Melody knew she was responsible for her breakup with Andy Monahan. She'd been stupidly jealous and, worse, she'd been untruthful. The fact that it had been a sin of omission hadn't made it any less damaging. When she'd first met Andy, it hadn't seemed important that she tell him who her parents were. After all, the fact that her father was the publisher of a major national newspaper—which her mother actually owned—was not something that she'd ever shared willingly. The longer she'd put off telling Andy, however, the harder it got, and when he learned the truth, he'd been furious.

Crossing to the bay window, she looked down at Portobello Road. Her flat was on the back of a mansion block facing on Kensington Park Road, which ran parallel to Portobello Road. The location was a nuisance on market days when the sound of the crowds started at daybreak, but tonight the road was empty and quiet, the glow from the streetlamps dimmed by the heavy mist. She should put on her coat and go out. It was only a few steps round to the Sun in Splendour. Fish and chips, a glass of crisp white wine—she'd feel the better for it. But the thought of standing out like a sore thumb as she battled the after-work crowd for a single table dissuaded her.

Suddenly, she had a better idea.

Grabbing her mobile from the coffee table, she pulled up Doug Cullen's number and tapped the Call icon. The number rang and rang. Just when she thought the call would go to voicemail, Doug picked up, sounding breathless.

"Hullo? Melody? Are you okay?"

"Of course I'm okay. Why wouldn't I be?"

"I haven't heard from you in weeks, and you haven't returned my calls, that's why." Doug sounded thoroughly irritated.

"I've been busy," she said. But he would know that was a lie, because Duncan would have told him that she and Gemma were stuck at Met headquarters pushing paper like zombies. "Look, it's Friday night. I thought maybe we could meet for a drink somewhere. How about the Botanist, in Sloane Square? I could do with a Bramble. We could—"

Doug cut her off. "I can't." There was a murmur of voices in the background. "Look," he went on. "We've got a case on. I'll ring you lat—"

But Gemma's number had popped up on Melody's screen. "Fine. Cheers," she said, a little more vehemently than necessary, and switched calls. "Boss? What's up?" she said when Gemma's icon filled her mobile screen.

"Fancy a night on the town?" asked Gemma.

———

Doug Cullen shook his head in exasperation. He'd been worried about Melody the last few weeks. He'd thought they'd at least reached a truce over his meddling in her relationship with Andy Monahan, and then suddenly she'd dropped off the map. Until tonight. But tonight he didn't have time to worry about it.

Glancing over at Kincaid, he saw that he was still talking to the woman and her child. Doug could at least make a start on getting a proper ID on the victim.

He pulled a pair of gloves from his coat pocket and crouched carefully beside her, trying to remember if he'd seen a handbag as he'd passed her in the pub. If she had been carrying one, it wasn't visible now. The hem of her coat covered her left hand. He extracted it gently. No ring. Her right hand lay across her belly, looking as natural and relaxed as if she were sleeping.

Her body seemed slightly elevated on the right side, and as far as Doug could tell, the ground beneath her was level. Carefully, he slid his hand beneath the small of her back and was rewarded by the feel of an object. It gave slightly when he pressed his fingers against it. When he eased it free, he saw that it was a small bag, tan leather or leatherette, with a shoulder strap. Had she dropped it before she fell? Snapping open the flap, he felt inside. Lipstick.

A pack of tissues. A credit card–size wallet. No mobile phone. He eased himself back a bit and used his mobile torch to illuminate the wallet's contents. She'd carried only a bank card, her national insurance card, and an identification card. There was no driving license, but the ID told him that she'd lived in Guilford Street, just behind Great Ormond Street Hospital. Her full name was Sasha Elaine Johnson and she was twenty-eight years old.

He started as a mobile phone began to ring. Instinctively, he touched his own pocket, then realized it wasn't his mobile. It was hers. Trying to disturb the body as little as possible, he felt for the near pocket of her anorak and after a fumbled attempt, retrieved a slender mobile phone just as it fell silent.

"Damn and blast," he muttered as he pressed the unresponsive screen. Of course the mobile was locked. They'd have to turn it over to the techies.

He'd risen, intending to report his finds to Kincaid, when the mobile screen lit beneath his fingers with another incoming call.

CHAPTER THREE

Sitting at the banquette in the tiny bookshop café, Tully had outstayed even the chubby bloke in the outrageously fuchsia cardigan. He'd sat at the next table, regaling his friend with malicious gossip about his coworkers. From a soft carrier beside him on the bench, a tiny dog snarled and snapped whenever the manager came close enough to refill the man's teapot. Tully had been careful not to let her coat slide too close to the dog, or the owner. Perhaps he snapped, too.

Now it was only Tully and the manager, a cheerful white woman with a boy-short haircut and full sleeve tattoos, both arms displayed by a tank top despite the drafts that swirled through the café whenever the door opened.

Tully checked the time on her mobile phone, again. The café was closing. She'd drunk much too much tea, and had pushed the remains of her slice of carrot cake around on her plate until it was unidentifiable.

"You all right, love?" asked the manager, looking concerned.

"You're a bit off-color today." Tully was a regular, as the café was just round the corner from both her job at the British Museum and the ceramics gallery where she filled in part-time.

Tully frowned. "It's just that my flatmate was supposed to meet me here more than an hour ago, and she's never late. She's not answering her mobile, either."

"Well, stay a bit longer if you like, love, as long as you don't mind me mopping around you." The manager flipped the sign on the door to Closed.

"Oh, thanks, that's kind of you," said Tully, "but I'll get out of your way." But as she gathered her coat and bag, she added, "Maybe I'll just give her one more try." Standing, she dialed the number once more.

When a man answered, for a moment she was too surprised to speak.

—

"If I could drive," grumbled Kit from the passenger seat, "I could've taken everyone home, and Melody could have picked you up here."

"You're not driving anytime soon," Gemma told him with a grin. Since the acquisition of her newish Land Rover, he had become obsessed with cars. "Although I'm sure you'll be very responsible when you do."

She hoped that by the time he was actually eligible at eighteen to take his test, the idea of getting behind the wheel of a car would have lost some of its glamour. Driving in London was not for the faint of heart, or the inexperienced. At least Duncan had managed to mothball his old MG with his father up in Cheshire, so they didn't have to worry about Kit driving that deathtrap.

Notting Hill was quiet enough tonight, however, she thought as she looped around into Westbourne Park Road, crossing Portobello Market with its shuttered stalls.

"I'm starving," Toby moaned from the backseat.

"Me, too. I'm starving, too," chimed in Charlotte, although Gemma knew Kit had bought her a snack in the café.

"I know, loveys. Kit, do you want to call out for a pizza?"

He shook his head. "I can make something. There's a pasta I want to try. It's got peas and mushrooms and caramelized onions." Kit had always liked cooking, but since the weekend in September he'd spent helping out at a pub in Gloucestershire, he was even more keen to experiment.

"Are you sure you don't mind?" Gemma asked. "I don't think I'll be long, and you can ring me if you need anything. Where's Wes tonight?"

Their friend Wesley Howard occasionally helped out with the children, but he was busy these days, between his course at business college, his photography, and working part-time at Otto's Café in Elgin Crescent.

"Working evening shift. He said they were short-staffed at lunch tomorrow if I wanted to help out."

"Okay, well, you can ring Wes, too, if—"

"Gemma, I'm not five, you know." Kit gave an exasperated eye roll.

"I'm almost five," piped up Charlotte from the back.

"You were just four. Baby. You're nowhere near five," taunted Toby as she drove round the curve of Landsdowne Road.

"Am *not* a baby," Charlotte retorted with a wail.

"Enough, you two." Gemma was glad to pull up in front of their house. "We're home. Everybody out."

The cherry-red front door was welcoming even in the rain, and she could hear the dogs' excited barking as she unlocked the door. For a moment, she was tempted to stay in for the evening. She could have a glass of wine, help Kit with his pasta, maybe even watch a film with the boys after Charlotte was in bed. But her curiosity was aroused. What had happened in Russell Square that Duncan thought she should see?

—

A few minutes later, the children settled, she found Melody pacing in front of her block of flats on Kensington Park Road. Melody wore a bright-red Macintosh but her head was bare, her short dark hair glistening with raindrops. "What on earth are you doing?" Gemma cried as she pulled up and leaned over to throw open the passenger door. "You'll be soaked."

"Forgot my brolly," said Melody as she climbed in. "And this stupid coat doesn't have a hood."

"That's what you get for being fashionable," Gemma said. "I hope I didn't spoil your evening."

"Not a bit of it." Melody ran her fingers through her damp hair, making it stand on end. "I thought Doug might be up for a drink, but he said he was busy. Serves him right if we turn up on his patch."

Glancing at her, Gemma thought she saw a hint of a smile. At least Melody and Doug were speaking, then.

"Any idea what this is about?" Melody asked.

"Not a clue. Did Doug not tell you anything, either?"

Melody shook her head. "No. He was just annoyingly self-important. What a surprise."

Gemma was tempted to ask Melody if she'd heard anything from Andy Monahan, but the silence that had fallen between them as she drove through the dark streets was comfortable, and she hated to spoil it.

She wouldn't have chosen to drive through Central London on a Friday night, but she managed to avoid Oxford Street and the worst of the traffic.

"Bloody maze," she muttered. "He could have mentioned which side of Russell Square we wanted." But as she turned down Woburn Place, her question was answered by the distant flash of blue lights. When she reached the square itself, she pulled up onto the pavement behind a panda car and the crime-scene van. An enormous Victorian building loomed over them from across the street, its ornateness a contrast to the ordinary buildings surrounding it.

"Spare brolly in the door pocket," she told Melody. Then, putting a POLICE placard on the dash, she slid out and held up her ID to the advancing uniformed officer. "I'm looking for Detective Superintendent Kincaid."

"Oh, right, ma'am," said the young woman. "Just go in the entrance there and past the café. The SOCOs are setting up the lights. You'll see them soon enough."

That proved to be an understatement. As they entered the park, the glow from the portable lights drew them like a beacon. The crime-scene technicians had yet to erect a tent, so that as Gemma and Melody drew near, they saw a group of figures in an illuminated tableau. Kincaid stood in the center, holding a large black umbrella. In the sharp light, he looked tired, Gemma thought suddenly, as he often had since his accident in September.

In the shelter of his umbrella knelt Dr. Rashid Kaleem, the handsome young Home Office pathologist. A white coverall hid what she guessed would be one of his signature pathologist-joke T-shirts. Slightly to one side, under a separate umbrella, stood the detective inspector on Kincaid's team, Jasmine Sidana. She was watching Kaleem intently, but without the frown that usually marred her expression. Gemma made out a prone shape on the ground. Two white-suited crime-scene officers moved like ghosts beyond the circle of light.

Glancing up, Kincaid caught sight of her and smiled. "Gemma. And Melody. Glad you could make it."

Rashid looked up as well. "I think you'll find this interesting."

"Hello, Rashid," said Gemma. "Inspector," she added, acknowledging Sidana with a nod. Joining them, she saw that the victim was a young Black woman with a delicate, strikingly pretty face. "Oh. What a shame," Gemma murmured with a pang of dismay. This moment, when the puzzle became a person, always came, and she never felt it any less. "What happened to her, Rashid?"

"She was stabbed." He shined a small torch on an area just below the victim's left breast. "See here? It doesn't look like much of a puncture, but the weapon must have been very sharp and the blow delivered with a great deal of strength. It penetrated her coat and was still forceful enough to kill her."

"She was stabbed here, in the square?" Gemma asked, looking around.

"Just there." Kincaid gestured a few yards farther along the path to an area the SOCOs had already cordoned off. "According to our only witness, who happens to be all of five years old."

"I won't know for certain until I get her on the table, but I suspect your witness is correct," said Rashid. "If the blade nicked her aorta, she'd have died almost instantly."

Melody was frowning. "No one else saw anything?"

"The boy's mum was on her mobile, so she wasn't paying attention," Kincaid told her. "The boy thinks he saw someone knock into her, but no one has come forward. The other witnesses at the scene only gathered because they heard the boy's mother calling for help."

Gemma shivered, feeling suddenly cold and damp, even sheltered by her umbrella. Had the girl realized what was happening to her?

"We'll be appealing to the public," put in Sidana as she turned away to speak to a constable, and Gemma imagined she was already writing the press release in her head.

"Do we have an ID?" Gemma asked.

"Sasha Johnson. She was a junior doctor." Kincaid hesitated for a moment. "Funny thing is, Doug and I saw her earlier. She was in the Perseverance. She left right after Doug arrived."

"Where is Doug, anyway?" Melody asked, looking around as if she expected him to materialize out of thin air.

"Gone to meet the victim's flatmate."

———

The conversation had been awkward, to say the least.

When Doug answered the ringing mobile, his "Hello" had been met with a moment of surprised silence.

Then a female voice had said, hesitantly, "Sasha? I'm sorry, have I got the wrong number?"

"This is Sasha's mobile," Doug replied, only just then realizing the difficulty he was facing. "Um, my name's Doug Cullen. I'm with the Met—the police."

"The police?" The question ended on a squeak. "What's happened? Is Sasha okay?"

Doug did not want to give the news to this friend—or perhaps family member—over the phone. "I'm sorry, would you mind identifying yourself?"

"I'm Tully. Tully Gibbs. I'm Sasha's flatmate. Look, what is this about? Sasha was supposed to meet me ages ago. Has something—"

"Miss Gibbs, can you tell me where you are? It would be better if we spoke in person."

"I'm—I'm at a coffee shop, near the museum. But they're closing." Tully Gibbs sounded less startled now, more shaken. "But the gallery where I work is just round the corner. I can open the studio next door." She gave him an address in Museum Street.

"Give me ten minutes," he said. "I'll meet you there."

"But—Look, if Sasha's in some sort of trouble, I want to—"

"Miss Gibbs, it's better if I come to you."

———

Doug peered at the numbers on the shops, trying to work out what he would say to this Tully Gibbs. He knew the drill, of course. He'd had to deliver bad news often enough when he was in uniform, and he'd done it as a detective as well. But every case was different, and she had sounded young and, from what she'd said, on her own.

It was the display in the shop on the other side of the street that caught his eye. Although the Closed sign was up on the door, a single long table in the window held ceramic pieces in various shapes, their colors glowing in the soft lighting. Crossing the street, Doug saw that the room held other display tables, and white shelving along the walls held books and more striking ceramics. It all looked clean and spacious.

Seeing no sign of anyone inside the shop, he checked the street number, then found the door to one side. This one was unmarked and looked as though it might lead to the redbrick flats above. He pushed the ground-floor buzzer and waited. After a moment, the door swung open to reveal a plain carpeted hallway and a flight of stairs. A door at the back of the hall opened, revealing a woman's silhouette.

"Are you the police?" It was the voice from the phone, soft, with a hint of West Country accent.

"Yes. Detective Sergeant Cullen." Doug held out his ID. "Miss Gibbs?"

Nodding, she said, "You'd better come in." She was young, he saw, probably near Sasha Johnson's age, white, with chin-length light-brown hair and trendy, heavy-framed glasses.

Doug followed her into the studio. A low, triangular table housed what he assumed was a potter's wheel. Beside it stood a stool and a bucket of murky water. A long worktable held sponges, bits of towel, and strange implements he didn't recognize. They were all liberally streaked with white clay. As was the floor. He hesitated, unsure where to put his feet.

His discomfort must have shown, because Gibbs said, "I take it you've never been in a potter's studio before. Don't worry, nothing will bite you. Just don't touch the things that are drying." Following her glance, he saw metal shelving along one wall, filled with pieces in various stages of production.

Marveling that the elegant work he'd seen in the display window next door had come from what looked like a mud bath, he mumbled, "It's a bit chaotic, isn't it? This is part of the gallery?"

"Yes. There's a kiln in the back garden, too, hard to come by in Central London. Look, is Sasha okay?" With a quaver, she added, "I've been so worried."

Doug hesitated. There was never an easy way to do this, but he knew it was better to get it over quickly. "Miss Gibbs, I'm afraid there's been an . . . incident. I'm sorry to tell you that your friend is dead."

Tully Gibbs stared at him, her face going even paler against the dark frames of her glasses. "No," she whispered. "There must be some mistake."

"I'm afraid not. She was wearing her hospital ID. I really am very sorry."

With a whimper, Gibbs put a hand to her mouth. Behind the glasses, her eyes filled with tears. "Oh no." She swayed where she stood, and Doug was suddenly afraid she might faint. He should have asked her to sit down. Spying a chair tucked in beside the shelving unit, he swung it over and, taking her by the elbow, guided her into it. Tully Gibbs sat, unresisting.

Shivering, she managed to croak, "What—What happened?"

Doug glimpsed a kettle and mugs on a shelf near the back door. "I'm going to make you some tea, okay? And then we'll talk."

He found teabags in a battered tin caddy beside the utility sink. When the kettle boiled, he filled a mug, plopped in a teabag, and, without asking, stirred in a couple of heaping teaspoons of sugar. He carried the mug to her, wincing as he turned it so that she could grasp the handle.

"Th-Thanks." Her teeth were chattering. If the studio had heating, she hadn't thought to turn it on. Gingerly sipping from the mug, she grimaced. "Don't like sugar."

"It will do you good. Drink it, please." He found a second chair and sat down facing her, hands on his knees.

When she'd sipped a little more, she wrapped her hands round the cooling mug and, swallowing hard, said, "Tell me what happened. Was it an accident? Sash is always so focused on getting where she's going, sometimes she doesn't look—"

But Doug was shaking his head. "I'm sorry, no. She was walking across Russell Square. I'm afraid she was . . . stabbed."

"What? That's mad. Why would anyone stab Sasha?"

"Do you know anyone who might have wanted to hurt your friend?"

"She was a junior doctor, for God's sake. Everyone loved her. You can't think it was someone she knew—It must have been some random nutter—"

"That's possible," Doug said. "But until we know more, we have to look at all the possibilities," he continued. "Did Sasha have boyfriend problems?"

Gibbs shook her head emphatically. "Sasha was too focused on her work. Her mum was always telling her she was missing her chance at—" She gasped, sloshing her tea. "Oh God. Her mum. Her parents. They'll be gutted. Someone will have to tell them—" she began, but Doug cut her off.

"Don't worry, we'll take care of that. Do you feel up to giving me their contact information?"

After a moment, Gibbs nodded. "Her dad's a school headmaster. Her mum's a psychologist, NHS. I've been to their flat, but I don't remember the exact address—I was with Sash. It's in Westbourne Park, across from the Union Tavern."

"I'm sure we can find them," Doug told her. "I'm afraid we'll need to have a look through Sasha's things, if you could help us with that as well."

Tully Gibbs cradled the cooling tea. "Could you—could we do that now? It's just that—I'm not sure I can bear to go in the flat on my own . . ."

"Of course," Doug assured her. "But first there are just a couple more questions, if you're up to it." When she nodded, he went on. "You said Sasha was supposed to meet you at the café. Would she normally have walked through Russell Square?"

"From our flat, yeah, it was the shortest way."

"And that's in—"

"Guilford Street, next to Coram Fields."

"Did anyone else know she was meeting you?"

Frowning, Gibbs said, "Well, my boss, obviously. When Sash texted, I had to leave him to close the gallery on his own. He was that annoyed. And . . ." She hesitated. "My brother. I texted him a bollocking. He was supposed to have met her for a drink. He didn't show up."

Doug raised an eyebrow. "They were friends?"

For the first time, Tully Gibbs didn't meet his gaze. "Um . . . not exactly. She just said she needed to talk to him. And that it was urgent."

CHAPTER FOUR

"You saw her in the pub?" Gemma asked, surprised. "When?" They had stepped away from the body while Rashid finished up his examination.

"Doug and I met up for a pint after work—" At her expression, Kincaid added hastily, "I was going to get the tube from Russell Square—I'd have been in plenty of time for Toby's rehearsal. She"—he nodded towards the victim—"was there before Doug, alone. She kept checking her mobile, and I remember thinking she was going to be seriously annoyed with whoever was making her wait. But Doug came in then, and she must have left while I was getting his drink."

Gemma tipped the pooling rainwater from her umbrella, getting a splash in the face in the process. "Had you seen her before this?"

He shook his head. "I don't think so, but it's not unusual to see staff from the area hospitals there."

Studying him more closely, Gemma saw the strain around his eyes. She touched his arm. "Must have been a dreadful shock for you, finding her here."

Kincaid looked away, and when he spoke his voice was tightly controlled. "Someone bloody stabbed her while Doug and I were sitting over our pints. It can't have happened more than twenty minutes after she left the pub."

"You didn't see anyone waiting for her outside? Or talking to her?"

He shook his head. "I wasn't paying attention. If I'd—"

Gemma cut him off sharply. "You know there's nothing you could have done, love." More gently, she added, "But I can't blame you for feeling . . . odd. Bad enough that it's on your patch. Has there been anything similar?"

"Stabbings? A few domestics and the odd drink-related scuffle. No fatalities."

"But the case you've been working, the shop robbery—"

"Those two little thugs are on remand. And besides, they had a history of petty thievery. Although before this robbery, they'd only *threatened* people with a knife. The shop owner charged at them with a broom handle and got stabbed for his pains—otherwise this incident probably would have gone the same way as their previous attempts. This"—he looked towards the victim again—"this had to have been done with intent."

"And by someone who knew where to aim." Gemma looked back at the body. Rashid had finished and was on his mobile, probably notifying the mortuary. "She wasn't robbed? The purse snatchers can be pretty ruthless."

"Her mobile and her little bag were still on her. Trevor saw no sign of a scuffle."

"Trevor?"

"The little boy who saw her collapse. But he was more credible than plenty of adult witnesses."

Gemma tried to imagine Toby or Charlotte seeing someone killed that way, and shuddered. She hoped Trevor's mum was giving him some extra care tonight.

"Besides," Kincaid went on, "the snatchers are usually slashing, not stabbing. Rashid says this was a narrow-bladed weapon, not the sort of thing you'd use to slice through a bag strap. He'll know more after the post—" Kincaid's mobile rang. Glancing at the screen, he mouthed, *Doug* to Gemma as he answered.

Doug's voice came to her faintly as Kincaid listened, nodding.

Melody walked over to stand beside them, murmuring, "What's going on?" but before Gemma could answer, Kincaid finished the call.

"Doug's seeing the flatmate home," he told them. "The place is nearby, just behind the hospital. I'll meet them there. I want to speak to the woman myself, see if there's any indication someone had a grudge against Sasha Johnson."

"Some grudge," said Melody with a grimace. "Isn't it more likely—"

This time they were interrupted by Gemma's mobile ringing. "I think we're playing musical phones." She shrugged an apology as she juggled holding her umbrella with fishing the mobile from her bag. But when she saw the ID, she frowned and turned away to answer. "Kit? What's up?"

"Sorry to bother you, Gemma, but you said to call . . ."

"It's fine, love. Is everything okay?"

Still sounding hesitant, he said, "Yeah, well, sort of. It's just that—Well, I got Char down, but then she woke up with a bad dream, and I can't get her to settle again. I've tried all the usual things; Horlicks, a story, a cuddle, but she wants you."

Gemma felt a wash of guilt. "Oh, Kit, I'm sorry." Glancing at the time on her mobile, she was surprised to see how late it was. "Look, I'm on my way. Tell her I'm coming, will you? And don't worry about getting her back to bed. Let her watch something nice on the telly with you, for a treat, and I'll be home soon."

Ringing off, she saw that Kincaid had gone to give more instructions to Jasmine Sidana. "I've got to go," Gemma told Melody. "Kit says Charlotte's having a bad night."

"Oh, dear. Is she okay?" asked Melody, who knew Charlotte's history.

Gemma sighed. "Nightmare, Kit says." Belatedly, she realized that she was Melody's transportation. "I can drop you, of course."

"Um, I think I'll stay," said Melody after a moment's consideration. "I can get the tube home. I'd like to have a look at the victim's flat." She turned to Kincaid, who'd rejoined them. "If you don't mind me tagging along, of course."

"Not at all." Kincaid turned to Gemma. "What did Kit say? Is everything all right at home?"

When Gemma had explained, he shook his head, frowning. "Dammit. She's been doing better. I thought—"

"All kids have nightmares," Gemma reassured him. "Don't worry. I'll text you when I've got her settled."

———

Melody slipped into the back of the panda car beside Kincaid. He was on his mobile again, now talking to his team's case manager. "Who's available as FLO?" he asked, then nodded as he listened. "McGillivray? Good. Tell her to stand by until we get an address for the family."

Of course, they would need a family liaison officer to inform the next of kin, and Melody didn't envy whoever had caught the rota on that job. Dealing with bereaved relatives had never been her strong suit, and she'd often envied the easy way Gemma seemed to connect with the families they interviewed.

As Kincaid continued organizing his team, Melody realized that her feet felt like blocks of ice. She hadn't been prepared for standing in puddles in the park and her ankle boots were soaked. Beside her, Kincaid's coat gave off the distinctive aroma of wet wool as it steamed in the blast from the car's heater. She thought of Gemma, going home to a warm, dry house, and wondered if she'd been a bit hasty in asking to tag along on this interview when she could be home and dry as well. But the rain-blurred streets zipped by and in moments the car was pulling to a stop, just as Kincaid ended his call.

Glancing out, Melody saw the bulk of Great Ormond Street Hospital rising on the south side of the street. On the north side was a rather grim-looking building in dark brick, its color indistinguishable in the gloom. Kincaid scrolled through his mobile, apparently checking the address. "Let's see if Doug is here yet," he said, and tapped out a text.

Melody realized this was the first time she'd been alone with Kincaid since the weekend in Gloucestershire when she'd made such a hash of her life, and felt herself coloring with sudden awkwardness. Kincaid, however, seemed oblivious, and when his mobile pinged with a reply, he put it away and leaned forward to speak to the driver. "If you could wait, I don't think we'll be long. And then we'll need a run to the station." To Melody, he added, "Doug says he'll buzz us in."

Melody followed him as he slid out of the car and crossed the street, picking her way around the rivulets running in the gutters.

The fanlight-topped black door buzzed open as they reached

it, and they stepped into a dingy hallway with a scuffed linoleum floor. The door to the ground-floor flat opened, framing Doug Cullen. His eyes widened as he took in Melody. "What are you—" He shook his head. "Never mind. You'd better come in."

He stepped back to allow them into a sitting room. The place was furnished in student chic—including the rice-paper globe covering the hanging ceiling bulb—but looked clean and relatively tidy. A rolling rack filled with women's clothing had been positioned in front of the window, providing a curtain of sorts. There were a couple of squashy armchairs and a futon covered with layers of Kantha throw blankets and some sequined pillows. The flat smelled faintly of curry.

A high, shallow shelf above the futon held a row of the oddest dolls Melody had ever seen. They had distinctly individual clay faces, some with hats, some with molded hair, and they were dressed in random scraps of colorful cloth. Melody had the uncomfortable feeling that they were watching her.

"She's just having a wash," Doug said quietly, glancing at a door in a short hallway that appeared to lead to a bedroom and a kitchenette. "She's a bit upset." He looked as if he were about to say something more, but the door opened and a young woman came out of the bathroom.

Her pale face was damp, as if she'd splashed it with water, but it was still pink and blotchy about the nose and eyes. She wore heavy-framed glasses that obscured her features. Her chin-length hair was light brown and looked to Melody as if it had been hacked with nail scissors. "I'm sorry," the woman said, looking at Kincaid and Melody. "I just needed a minute."

"It's we who are sorry." Kincaid stepped forward and took her hand briefly. "I'm Detective Superintendent Kincaid, and this is Detective Sergeant Talbot. I know this must be difficult for you, but we'd like to ask you a few questions about your flatmate."

The young woman sniffed and nodded, then seemed to collect herself. "Oh, sorry, I'm Tully Gibbs. But then you know that, don't you? I guess we should sit down or something." She looked round vaguely, as if unsure how exactly they might do that. Doug guided her to the futon, then perched on the edge so that he could swivel to face her. Kincaid pulled over the chair from a small table that seemed to serve as a desk. This left Melody with the squashy armchairs, so she lowered herself into one of them reluctantly.

"I still can't believe it," whispered Tully. "Sasha. I keep expecting her to walk in the door."

"Had the two of you shared a flat long?" Kincaid asked.

"A couple of years. Sasha got the place when she was at college and afterwards she managed to hang on to it. When her first roommate moved out, Sasha put a notice on the board in the uni student center, asking for someone to share." Her eyes widened. "I hadn't thought—her name's on the lease. I don't know what I'll do now."

Melody noticed a small table at one end of the futon. It held a clock, tissues, a mobile phone charger, and a battered paperback copy of Phil Rickman's *The Chalice*. Looking more closely at the sequined pillows, she realized that they were slipcovers for ordinary bed pillows. She glanced again at the rack of clothes in front of the window. The things all looked what her mother would call arty—loose-fitting tops, nubby jumpers, well-worn jeans. "Miss Gibbs," she said, "I take it you and Miss Johnson didn't share a bedroom?"

Tully shook her head. "No. It's Sasha's flat, and the bedroom's barely big enough for one person. But you know how it is in Central London. I'm lucky to have a place to sleep." Her smile was tremulous. "And I can walk to work."

"And where is that, Miss Gibbs?" put in Kincaid.

"I'm an assistant collections manager at the British Museum.

Ceramics. But it doesn't pay much, so I work part-time at a ceramics gallery in Museum Street."

"Is that where Miss Johnson—Sasha—was meeting you tonight?"

"Not at the gallery, no. At the bookshop café round the corner."

"This was planned?"

"No, no. She texted me. I told the sergeant," she added, shifting in her seat. When Kincaid leaned forward, clasping his hands on his knee, Tully continued with a little shrug. "She was supposed to meet my brother, but he didn't show up."

"At the café?"

"No. At a pub in Lamb's Conduit Street. But when Jon didn't come, she wanted to talk to someone. She sounded upset."

"They were an item?"

Tully's eyes widened. "Oh God, no. They were just—friends. More like acquaintances, really."

Kincaid raised an eyebrow. "But they were meeting for a drink?"

"That's what she said. When she texted me."

"Do you have any idea why?"

"Not really. But she did say something about Ty. Her brother, Tyler."

—

Sasha Johnson's tiny bedroom was almost monastic in its simplicity. A single bed, a bookcase filled with medical books, a few Booker-shortlisted paperbacks, and a Bible. A wardrobe held a few casual things and shelves of neatly folded hospital scrubs.

Kincaid stood in the doorway, looking back into the room with a frown. He had no sense of the young woman who had lived here—

and who had died so suddenly and brutally tonight in the darkness of Russell Square. Her flatmate, on the other hand, seemed to have imprinted herself thoroughly throughout the rest of the flat, even though she was, he suspected, an illegal tenant. The sitting room was obviously Tully's domain, and the little kitchen had been filled with her handmade pottery. Sasha Johnson's space, on the other hand, felt . . . scrubbed. He wondered if she'd spent most of her time somewhere else. Then he realized what else was missing.

Returning to the sitting room, he added, "Miss Gibbs, did Sasha have a computer?"

"Oh. Yes. You mean she didn't have it with her when she—" Her fist tightened, crumpling some of the papers she'd been looking through.

"No. She only had a small bag." Kincaid returned to his seat on the desk chair.

"She must have left it at the hospital. In her locker. She must have meant to go back, after she met J—" Tully paused suddenly, as if she hadn't intended to go down that avenue.

"Your brother," Kincaid finished for her. "We'll need to contact him, of course." He glanced at Doug. "If you could give Sergeant Cullen his details."

"It's Jon. Jonathan Gibbs. He manages a club in Soho. In Archer Street. He lives in the flat above."

"What sort of club?" asked Melody, who had apparently been paying attention.

Tully gave Melody a glance of dislike. "Not that sort. It's very respectable. Trendy cocktails, some bar food. Some jazz."

"I'm sure," Kincaid said. Had he imagined her defensiveness? "We'll just have a word, in case Miss Johnson mentioned any concerns to him. She didn't say anything to you about being bothered by someone? Or followed?"

Tully paled and gave an uneasy glance at the window. "You don't think she was being . . . stalked?"

"I'm afraid it is a possibility we have to consider. You're certain there was no ex-boyfriend in the picture?"

"No. I told the sergeant. It was all career for Sasha."

That didn't mean someone hadn't been interested in her, Kincaid thought.

Tully pulled an envelope from the letters she held. "Here it is, the Johnsons' address. They sent Sasha a birthday card a couple of weeks ago."

Taking the envelope, Kincaid saw that the address was in Westbourne Grove, just on the edge of Notting Hill. He could make the bereavement visit with McGillivray, then get her to drop him home afterwards. "We'll leave you to it, then, Miss Gibbs. I know this has been difficult for you. We appreciate your help."

"Is there anyone you can ring to stay with you?" Doug asked with uncharacteristic sensitivity.

Tully shook her head. "No. But I'll be fine." She didn't sound it.

"You have my number," said Doug. "If you think of anything about Sasha—or if you just need someone to lend an ear—give me a ring."

—

Gemma slipped into the house so quietly that the dogs didn't bark. She stood in the front hall for a moment, taking stock. The house held the starchy, comforting smell of cooking pasta, and the rumble of her stomach reminded her that she'd missed her supper. Then a startled yip and the clicking of toenails on floorboards heralded the arrival of the dogs, their tails wagging in greeting. "Hello, loveys," she murmured, taking a moment to stroke Geordie's silky cocker spaniel head before hanging her coat and bag on a peg. A glance showed her an empty kitchen, dishes draining on the sideboard, so she followed the faint sounds of the television into the sitting room. An episode of *The Great British Bake Off* was playing on the television. Charlotte sat on the floor in front of the sofa, coloring a sheet of paper on the coffee table. Toby was stretched out above her, engrossed in something—ballet, she assumed—on Kit's iPad, while Kit, earbuds in, sat in the big armchair, hunched over his mobile.

Glancing up, Kit pulled his earbuds out with a startled jerk. "Gemma. I didn't hear you come in."

"Call me Ninja Mum," she said with a smile as she came into the room. Smacking Toby's feet, she added, "Shoes off the sofa, please." When he complied, she sat in the newly vacated spot and pulled Charlotte into a hug. "What's that you're drawing, love?"

"Princesses." Charlotte's candy-floss hair felt sticky and smelled of dried sweat, a sure sign of a nightmare. "With kittens. See, there's Rosie." She held up the paper for Gemma to examine. Gemma gave serious consideration to the vaguely cat-shaped outline filled with black and orange blobs of color. Really, it was quite a good rendering of their calico cat, Rose. Better than anything Toby had drawn at four. Perhaps Char had inherited her mother's artistic talent. Sandra Malik had been a brilliant textile artist and photographer. Charlotte's father, Naz, had been a successful East London lawyer. It had been more than a year since their deaths, and Gemma often wondered how much Charlotte actually remembered of them—except in her fevered dreams.

"I saved you some pasta," said Kit, getting to his feet. "I'll just pop it in the microwave." He nodded towards the kitchen.

"Oh, good, thank you. I'm starving." To Charlotte, she added,

"I'll just have a bite and then we'll get you back into bed, pumpkin."

But before she could get up, Toby prodded her with his toe. "What about Dad? Did you show him my video?"

"He was working, love. I promise I'll show him as soon as he gets home." What a motley crew the children were, Gemma thought, tousling her son's fair hair as she stood. A son of hers, a son of his, and a daughter that was only theirs by the grace of social services. Toby had never really known his natural father, who had left them when he was a baby, and he had long since called Duncan Dad.

She followed Kit into the kitchen and poured herself a glass of Pinot Grigio while he spooned pasta onto a plate. "That looks delicious," she said, sinking into a chair at the kitchen table.

"I burned the onions a bit. Gemma"—Kit turned to face her, frowning—"I'm sorry to have dragged you away from a job. I just—I haven't seen her that upset in a long time, and I think it was my fault."

"What?" Gemma, caught on a sip of wine, choked and coughed. Eyes streaming, she said, "Don't be daft. How could it be your fault?"

"Toby wanted to watch a Harry Potter film. I thought it would be okay. But then they were talking about Harry's parents being killed, and I realized she was listening." He glanced at the doorway, making sure he wasn't overheard. "I think that was what she was dreaming about. Her parents."

"Oh, Kit." Gemma gazed at his stricken face, appalled. "I'm so sorry. It's not your fault. Really. Anything could have triggered her dream." She thought how unfair it was for him to have to deal with this. Kit had enough of his own nightmares. "Don't think any more of it. I'll have a little talk with her when we go upstairs and see if I can find out what's worrying her."

—

But when Charlotte was changed into fresh pajamas and snuggled up in her little white bed with Captain Jack, their black-and-white kitten, at her feet, Gemma didn't mention the nightmare. Instead, she sat down on top of the duvet, making Charlotte scoot over. "Do you want me to read you a book?" she asked.

Charlotte wriggled closer, putting her head on Gemma's shoulder. "No, Mummy. I want you to *tell* me a story."

"Hmm." Gemma scrunched her face into a very serious expression. "But I'm not a very good storyteller."

"Tell me anyway."

Gemma gazed round the room, searching for inspiration. "Okay," she agreed, "but just a quick one, as it's very late and way past your bedtime." Her glance settled on one of the prints on Charlotte's wall, a stylized depiction of zoo animals. "There once was a little girl called Jewel," she began, "who lived in the far, far north of London, beyond the zoo, beyond the Heath, above a bakery . . ."

—

Detective Constable Lucy McGillivray was new to the team. Kincaid hadn't worked with her closely before, and he was curious about her.

In her late twenties, she was slightly stocky and almost blindingly fair, with a round face and a deceptively bland expression that he'd found concealed a sharp Scottish wit. Entering the CID room, he greeted her, then gave a few last-minute instructions to the others. "When you've finished up," he concluded, "go home, get some rest. Briefing at eight in the morning."

Gikas had a panda car waiting for them in Lamb's Conduit

Street. "Do you not have a car here, sir?" McGillivray asked when they were settled in the back.

"No. I came in on the tube, and I live not far from where we're going. You can drop me at home after. Where are you from, Constable?" Kincaid asked McGillivray as the car sped north and then west through the wet streets.

"The Highlands, sir, near Aviemore. But we moved here when I was fifteen, so I've considered myself a Londoner for a good while now. I did my training here as well."

"Have you had much experience with death notifications?"

"I did my share in uniform, sir, accidents and sudden deaths, but this will be my first in a murder case."

"Well, much the same, I'm afraid, except that we have to ask questions afterwards." Kincaid had never become inured to it, and he lapsed into silence, the acrid coffee he'd drunk churning in his stomach now. There was, he thought, no worse task than breaking the news to a parent of the death of a child.

His mind wandered back over the details of the evening. Had Sasha Johnson, junior doctor, simply been in the wrong place at the wrong time? His gut told him no. Random attacks were usually more frenzied, and this had seemed calculated in its ferocity. One blow. Who had the expertise for that? Or had the killer merely been lucky?

He shook himself back to the present. They were entering the Harrow Road now. Soon they would reach the eastern fringes of Notting Hill. The road was lined with a comfortable mix of shops and flats, most of the buildings only three stories high. When they turned left into Elgin Road, he pulled up a map on his mobile phone and asked the driver to slow. Leaning forward, he said, "It looks like it's across from the Union Tavern. See if you can pull into Woodfield Road, and we'll cross back over."

Although he knew the area relatively well, he was still surprised when he caught his first glimpse of the flats where Sasha Johnson's parents lived. The three-story block fit snugly into the angle where the road met the Grand Union Canal. The arrow-shaped roof sat atop the building like an oversized white cap, the triangle's apex pointing at the pub across the road. The walls of the structure were curved to fit into the angle as well, and the rear of the building was an odd bulbous shape.

"What a strange building," said McGillivray. "The rooms will be awkward. Nice views of the canal, though."

The Grand Union Canal curved gently through this part of London, passing Kensal Green Cemetery and the northern edge of Notting Hill. The fortunate inhabitants of the flats with canal views would look out at colorful narrowboats moored below.

When their driver had found a place to stop the car, Kincaid asked him to wait as he and McGillivray got out. The pub was still open, so it had not yet gone eleven. Kincaid hoped that the Johnsons would be up. Light spilled from the pub, and a glimpse in the windows revealed a cheerful interior, the tables still packed with diners and drinkers. No one but the most inveterate smokers would be sitting outside tonight, he thought as he turned up his collar against the persistent drizzle.

Followed by McGillivray, Kincaid crossed the road on a break in the traffic and opened the wrought-iron gate set into the wall surrounding the flats. The tiny courtyard was neat, with a few potted shrubs and a couple of chained bicycles. The building's main door was well lit and, after searching for the flat number in the labeled buttons, he pressed the buzzer. It took two tries before a male voice answered, sounding aggrieved.

"Who is it? Do you know what time it is?"

"Mr. Johnson? It's the police. May we come up?"

They found the flat easily and McGillivray had raised her hand to knock when the door swung open. A middle-aged man wearing a red paisley dressing gown stared out at them. "I thought you said you were police."

"Mr. Johnson?" Kincaid held out his warrant card. "I'm Detective Superintendent Kincaid, and this is Detective Constable McGillivray."

Peter Johnson was a large man who didn't look easily fazed. His bald head was shiny, and he wore rimless glasses that looked as if they'd been hastily shoved onto his nose. He stepped back, allowing them into a pleasant sitting room. The west-facing windows on the curved wall were fitted with slatted blinds, closed against the night. Kincaid had the brief impression of a mustard-colored leather sofa and bright wall hangings in reds and purples and the same deep yellow.

"Is your wife at home, Mr. Johnson?" he asked. "It would be best if we could speak to you both."

Johnson's frown deepened. "Doro, it's the police," he called out. "They want to—"

Before he could finish, a woman appeared from an interior hallway. She was slender, with close-cropped hair going gray, and the same high-cheekboned facial structure as her daughter. She was also, unlike her husband, plainly terrified. "Tyler," she said on a panicked breath. "What's happened? Is he all right?"

"Mr. and Mrs. Johnson," Kincaid said, "it's your daughter we're here about. Sasha. Perhaps you could sit down."

Mrs. Johnson merely grasped her husband's arm and stared at them, wide-eyed. He could see the pulse beating in the hollow of her throat.

There was no softening the blow. "Mr. and Mrs. Johnson, I'm sorry to tell you that your daughter is dead."

—

Peter Johnson's dark skin had taken on a gray tinge. His wife's legs had given way beneath her as she let out a wordless cry. Supported to the sofa between her husband and McGillivray, she'd begun to sob. While Kincaid had explained, as gently as possible, what had happened, McGillivray went to fetch water and tissues.

"You must—there must be some mistake—" Mrs. Johnson broke off, pressing her hand to her mouth. "She was working—she will have been on shift tonight—" Tears spilled over and ran unchecked down her cheeks.

"She was meeting a friend for a coffee," Kincaid said. "Her route took her across Russell Square, where she was attacked. She was wearing her hospital ID." Any doubts he might have had about the victim's identity had been laid to rest now. He'd glanced at the family photos arrayed on a console table adjacent to the curved window wall. There were three children in various stages of growth, Sasha clearly recognizable and obviously the eldest. In another she stood alone, grown now, in a university cap and gown. In another she sat with her younger sister, smiling over the baby balanced on her knee.

Of the youngest child, a boy, there were no recent photos.

"We will need one of you, however," Kincaid continued, "to make a formal identification in the morning. I know how difficult this must be for you," he said, for the second time that night. McGillivray had returned with two glasses of water, which neither Johnson seemed to see, and stood unobtrusively behind him. "Constable McGillivray here will escort you, and she'll be available to help you in any way possible. Again, I'm very sorry for your loss."

While McGillivray spoke to them about the arrangements, he

stood, drawn back to the display of photos. Something he had glimpsed niggled at him—a familiar face in an unexpected place. He found it, slightly behind a studio family grouping obviously taken when the children were younger.

This photo, however, was casual, and recent. Dorothy and Peter Johnson had been snapped at what looked like a neighborhood party, perhaps during Carnival, going by the costumes of some of the attendees in the group.

Peter Johnson stood in the foreground, smiling into the camera. He had one arm around his wife, and the other around the shoulders of the Kincaids' friend Betty Howard.

CHAPTER FIVE

The next morning, after a few restless hours' sleep, Kincaid showered and dressed while the household slept on. When Gemma stirred, he leaned down to kiss her and whispered, "Go back to sleep. It's Saturday. I'll ring you later." He tiptoed down the stairs and let himself out of the house as quietly as he'd come in the night before.

Stepping outside, he was glad to see that the rain had stopped, although at just half past six, the sky had not yet begun to lighten in the east. He walked up Lansdowne Road towards the Holland Park Underground Station, hands in his overcoat pockets against the chill. He still felt the Johnsons' grief like a weight on his shoulders, and he knew the enormity of the loss would not entirely hit the parents until they'd seen their daughter's body.

At least they had their two other children close by. The younger daughter, the Johnsons had told him, worked as a receptionist in a local health clinic and lived in Kensal Green with her husband

and baby. The son, who was the youngest child, lived in rooms at University College London.

When he reached the coffee shop just down the street from Holborn Police Station a half hour later, Doug was there before him, ensconced at one of the few tiny tables with his laptop already open. Kincaid ordered a large coffee and two toasted egg-and-bacon sandwiches at the counter, then joined him.

"She was a ghost," Doug said without preamble.

"What? Who was?" Kincaid definitely needed the coffee.

Doug angled the laptop towards him. "Sasha Johnson." Kincaid felt a little visceral shock as the girl from the pub stared out at him from a Facebook profile, vibrant and alive once more in the photo. "It doesn't look like she was ever very active," Doug went on, "but up until a year ago she had a fairly normal social presence. Family parties, birthdays, the occasional after-work drink, although she didn't post anything very personal, and nothing about relationships. Then, nothing."

"But she didn't close her account?"

"No, just stopped using it, apparently. And I didn't find her on any other platforms. She pops up occasionally on her sister's page. Baby christening, birthdays."

Kincaid took a sip of his still-scalding coffee and winced. "So she wasn't estranged from her family?"

"Doesn't look like it." Swiveling the laptop, Doug clicked the mouse a few times, then turned the screen back to Kincaid. "From her sister Kayla's page. I'm assuming these are her parents."

Kincaid recognized the Johnsons instantly. Wearing broad smiles, they leaned into the shot behind the two young women, who held between them a baby of indeterminate gender. He recognized the background of the shot as well—it was the view of the

Elgin Avenue Bridge over the Regent's Canal, taken, he guessed, from the canal-side terrace of the Union Tavern. The dusting of pale green on the trees beyond the bridge chimed with the March date of the post. They wore coats, and the baby was muffled in a blanket.

Sasha Johnson's sister was beaming with what looked like proprietorial pride. Sasha's smile, on the other hand, seemed stiff, and she looked as if she'd been drawn into the group involuntarily. "Interesting," Kincaid said.

When he returned from fetching his sandwiches, Doug had turned the laptop so that he could tap on the keyboard again. "I couldn't find a profile for either parent."

"Makes sense," Kincaid mumbled through a mouthful of hot sandwich. "They both have professional jobs that might make it awkward. What about the brother Tully mentioned?"

He popped the last bit of the first sandwich into his mouth, then consulted the note he'd made on his phone last night. "Tyler. The parents said he was at UCL."

After a moment's perusal, Doug said, "There's no Tyler Johnson in Kayla Johnson's friends list. Or in Sasha's."

"Maybe he's too cool for Facebook," Kincaid suggested. If Tyler was at university, he was only a few years older than Kit, and Kit wouldn't be caught dead on Facebook.

"I'll have a look through the other platforms, but there could be hundreds of Tyler Johnsons."

Kincaid suddenly remembered Dorothy Johnson's first response when he and McGillivray had announced themselves last night. "Maybe it's police records you should be checking, not social media."

—

On any ordinary day, Tully would have spent her walk to work gazing at the Bloomsbury streets she never tired of. When she'd first moved into the flat and had learned that Virginia Woolf and Dorothy Sayers had both lived just around the corner in Mecklenburg Square, she'd been giddy at the thought. Sasha, of course, had looked at her as if she'd gone totally bonkers. It was surprising, really, that they'd rubbed along as well as they did. At least until recently.

When she'd finally managed to drift into a broken sleep last night, Tully had still been half listening for the latch on the door. It had seemed incomprehensible that Sasha was just . . . gone.

It seemed no less so this morning. Tully couldn't bear the thought of taking her usual route across Russell Square. When she reached the Fitzroy, she hesitated, unable to tear her gaze away from the green expanse of the square across the road. Where had Sasha—no, she couldn't let herself imagine it. Averting her eyes, she trudged along Southampton Row, her head down.

Her heart sank further when she reached Museum Street and saw that the gallery's big display windows were already lit. She'd meant to slip into the shop an hour early, giving herself time to tidy anything she'd left undone when she'd run out in such a hurry yesterday evening. But David was obviously here before her, and as soon as she stepped inside she knew that he was in one of his moods.

David Pope was a tall, thin scarecrow of a man, with a sharp plane of a nose and sparse sandy hair that habitually fell over his forehead. Without turning from the shelf he was dusting, he said, "So what was the great emergency that kept you from finishing your shift yesterday?"

Usually, David's moods made her anxious, but this morning she was suddenly infuriated by his pettiness. She slammed the shop door hard enough to rattle the displays. "It was my flatmate. Sasha. I told you I was meeting her. But she—" Tully swallowed hard. Somehow she hadn't realized she'd have to say it. "She— she was—killed. In Russell Square."

David turned and stared at her. "Don't be ridiculous. What are you talking about?"

"It's true. She was coming to meet me at the bookshop café and someone—someone stabbed her. They said she just . . . died, where she . . ." The thought of the nice detective sergeant who'd given her the news almost undid her.

David shook his head, once, and glanced at the duster in his hands as if not sure what he was doing with it. "Well. I'm sorry," he said. "That's dreadful." Then he added, "I suppose you'll be wanting time off?"

Tully blinked in surprise. It hadn't occurred to her to ask. Not that she could have faced sitting in the flat all day, alone. Getting through the night had been bad enough. But now she realized that a few hours would give her a chance to get in touch with her brother, Jonathan—who'd still not returned her texts or calls—even if she had to go and pound on his door. And she would need to ring Sasha's parents, when she could steel herself to do it.

"Well, okay, yes," she said. "I could use some time today." Saturday was the gallery's busiest day and it was kind of David to offer. "But let me help you open first." When he nodded, she headed for the sales desk to make sure everything was in order. To her surprise she saw that the previous day's receipts had not been filed and the cash box hadn't been emptied. David must have been really cross with her for leaving him to close up.

A half hour later, she had everything sorted. She felt a bit better, as if she'd righted the universe in some small way. But as she gazed round the gallery, she realized that what she really wanted was to get into the studio, to get her hands in the clay, to feel as if she could bring something to life.

—

Gemma had spent the bulk of the morning making domestic arrangements. By the time she dropped Toby at ballet and pulled up in front of MacKenzie Williams's Hansel and Gretel cottage, she was already feeling knackered. "Be good, pumpkin, and do what MacKenzie tells you," she murmured into Charlotte's hair as she boosted her out of her car seat and gave her a last squeeze.

"She and Oliver will have a grand time," MacKenzie promised as she opened the gate in the stone wall that separated the small front garden from the street.

"I'll ring you when I'm on my way back. Thanks so much." Gemma gave MacKenzie a quick hug, too. "I don't know how I'd manage without you," she added, and it was true enough.

A half hour later she'd reached East London and her mood lifted as she turned into Columbia Road. Even without the color and bustle of the Sunday flower market, she loved the street with its comfortable mix of shops, pubs, and cafés. She would have to pick up cupcakes from Charlotte's favorite bakery before she headed home.

Turning into a quiet side street, she found a spot for the car. The sun, which had been spotty all morning, slipped from behind a cloud, illuminating the first-floor balcony of the building before her. Even in mid-November, it was a sight to behold, a lush tangle of color and greenery. Over the past year, however, Gemma had learned that the little elevated garden's casual appearance was deceptive. Michael, who with his partner, Tam, owned one of the two flats opening on the balcony, was a floral designer, and the placement of every plant and pot was well thought out and constantly changing.

Louise Phillips, who owned the other flat, had been Charlotte's father's law partner, and was now the executor of Charlotte's estate. The sale of Naz and Sandra Malik's Georgian house in Spitalfields had netted a substantial sum and the Maliks had left everything in trust for Charlotte.

Gemma climbed the stairs to the balcony, which was gated at the top to allow some outside space for Tam and Michael's German shepherds. But today the dogs were not in evidence and the couple's flat was quiet. Gemma let herself in the gate and tapped on Louise's door.

"Gemma. Come in. It's good to see you," Louise said with a smile as she opened the door.

Gemma had learned not to offer the customary social kiss. Louise had been diagnosed with tuberculosis the previous winter, and while she was not now considered contagious, she still insisted the people around her take precautions. "You look great," she said as she followed Louise into her cluttered sitting room, and she meant it. Louise's face had lost its gauntness and her eyes were bright. "How's the treatment going?"

"The doctors seem happy enough with me, but I've a few months to go on the antibiotics."

"Are you back in the office at all?" Gemma asked, nodding towards the piles of papers on the dining-room table that served Louise as a home-office desk.

"I've been going in for a few hours on Saturdays and Sundays, to catch up on the things I can't do here. That way no one has to share my air." Louise shook her head. "When I think of all the people who've died from untreated TB, I can't imagine how difficult it must have been. But enough of that. Come back into the kitchen. I'll make us some tea."

As Gemma followed her, she took a closer look around the flat, trying to work out what seemed different. "You've decorated," she said as she admired the sitting-room walls, which looked freshly painted in a soft sea blue.

"Tam and Michael decorated, you mean. They said there was no excuse for walls stained the color of old tea from cigarette smoke. And I have to admit it did brighten things up." Louise gave Gemma an appraising look. "But I don't think you came to talk about my interior design choices. Are you okay?"

"Oh, it's just . . ." Gemma felt uncomfortable now, burdening Louise with her worries. But knowing Louise wouldn't allow her to prevaricate, she went on. "I'm worried about Charlotte. We thought she was doing well, but she had a bad nightmare again last night. I'd gone out to meet Duncan on a case and left her with Kit. Now I'm thinking that even though I've already cut my hours, it wasn't enough. I should be home more." She wrapped her hands round the mug Louise handed her, soaking in the warmth as if it might help her say what she hadn't shared with anyone else. "You know we have another review with social services coming up soon. What if they think we're not doing a good enough job?"

They'd been fostering Charlotte for a little over a year, and were now beginning their petition for a formal adoption.

Gemma made herself sip her tea, but the worries kept popping up like the cutouts in a shooting gallery.

"I think you're making mountains out of molehills here," said Louise. "You and Duncan have provided a safe, loving environment for a traumatized child. You love her, and she loves you.

Those are the important things." Before Gemma could feel too re-assured, Louise set down her cup and added, "However. I do think you need to reconsider your childcare arrangements."

Gemma's heart sank. "But she's already in her school's wrap-around care after school, and I—"

"Gemma." Louise's voice held a command. "Listen to me. You've spent the last year running yourself ragged, cobbling together childcare by depending on Kit and on the kindness of friends. You've given up a CID job that you love. It's time you faced the facts. It's not working."

Staring at her, Gemma swallowed hard. "But—I can't—I don't want to give up my job. What would I—how could we—"

"First of all, if anyone had to give up a job, why should it be you?" Louise puffed out an exasperated breath. "But neither of you do. It's a simple enough solution. You need a nanny."

—

The team briefing had gone as well as Kincaid could have hoped, with none of the expected grousing from Jasmine Sidana when he'd asked her to attend the postmortem and the formal identification of Sasha Johnson's body at the Royal London later that morning. When he'd given her a skeptical raised eyebrow, she'd merely smiled at him. DC McGillivray would be picking up the Johnsons and escorting them to the morgue.

Sidana had prepared a press release that would go out online and on the evening news broadcasts, along with an appeal to the public for information regarding Sasha's assailant.

When everyone had been assigned actions, he and Doug made the short walk along Guilford Street to the hospital where Sasha had worked. A smaller facility than the Great Ormond Street Hospital, the Thomas Coram had been named after the great eighteenth-century philanthropist who had established the Foundling Hospital. Unlike the massive and sprawling GOSH, the Coram was a graceful Georgian building in brown brick.

Tully Gibbs had given them the name of Sasha's ward, so after checking the signage in the hospital's reception, they took the lift to the correct floor. A man in a dark-blue uniform tunic looked up from his computer at the nurses' desk, frowning at them a bit impatiently. "Can I help you?" Round spectacles gave his slightly pudgy face an owlish aspect, but his glance was assessing. His name tag read Neel Chowdhury, RN, with some other abbreviations Kincaid didn't recognize.

Kincaid introduced them and showed his identification. "We need to speak to whoever's in charge here. It's about one of your doctors."

Chowdhury frowned. "I'm the senior ward manager. But I'm short-staffed today, as one of our juniors didn't turn up for shift, so I can't give you much ti—"

"Juniors?" Kincaid broke in.

"Junior doctors. They're less than reliable, particularly this one."

"Is it Sasha Johnson you're missing?"

"What?" The sharp eyes locked onto his before light glinting on the lenses of Chowdhury's glasses obscured them. "How did you know that?"

Kincaid was aware of the whisper of footsteps and the squeak of trolleys in the corridors leading away from the nursing desk. "Is there somewhere we could speak privately?"

Frowning, Chowdhury hesitated, then stood. "I suppose we can use the staff room." He led them into one of the branching corridors and through an unmarked door. The small, cluttered room could

have been lifted straight from any similar institution. Its plain furniture looked as well used as the assortment of mismatched mugs
jumbled on a counter beside a battered electric kettle. Magazines
were scattered across a ring-marked wooden table, and one wall
held rows of metal lockers.

Chowdhury turned to them. "Is Sasha in some sort of trouble?"
He looked a little uneasy now, but still not really worried. Kincaid
had to wonder if the man thought senior detectives turned up for
shoplifting or drink-driving charges.

Kincaid sat, uninvited, leaving Doug to wander casually around
the perimeter of the room, while Chowdhury sank gingerly to the
edge of a coffee-stained armchair. "I'm afraid Sasha Johnson is
dead," Kincaid said. "She was killed last night, not far from the
hospital."

Whatever Chowdhury was expecting, it hadn't been this. His
mouth dropped open and his skin blanched, making Kincaid glad
the man was sitting. "Killed? But that's—That's—How—Was it
some kind of an accident?"

"Someone stabbed her. I'm sorry to shock you, Mr. Chowdhury. Were you friends?"

"Friends?" Chowdhury frowned. "I'm her manager. You can't
be too chummy in my position. And Sasha didn't encourage . . ."
Kincaid waited, and after a moment Chowdhury went on. "Sasha
kept herself to herself. She wasn't—" He stopped, pressing his
lips together. "As I said, I'm the ward manager. I suggest you
speak to some of her other colleagues, not that she got on particularly well with them, either. Now, I really must get back to the
ward."

As Chowdhury stood, Doug Cullen spoke for the first time. "I
see Sasha had a locker here. Do you know if she kept her laptop
in it?"

"I have no idea. If you need to look through her things, you'll have to show a warrant to administration." When he reached the staff-room door, Chowdhury held it open for them, adding, "I couldn't open her locker even if I wanted. It's locked and not even senior management will have the combination."

CHAPTER SIX

As Jasmine Sidana rode the lift down to the basement of the Royal London Hospital, she straightened her dark suit jacket and brushed reflexively at her lapel. She'd left her overcoat in her car, not wanting to be lumbered with it, but bloody hell it was cold in this place. The lift doors opened and she stepped out into a corridor that smelled faintly antiseptic. She'd attended enough postmortems, but not one in this particular hospital, and not one with Dr. Rashid Kaleem, Kincaid's golden boy. Suddenly, she felt like an awkward DC. "Get a grip," she muttered to herself, taking a breath. She followed the signs to the autopsy suite and introduced herself to the mortuary assistant, a woman with bright ginger hair put up in neat plaits like an advert for Austrian strudel. Her name tag read Heidi, appropriately enough, and she gave Sidana a cheerful smile.

"I'll just tell Dr. Kaleem you're here," the woman said. "I think he's ready for you."

Sidana hoped that meant he'd finished with the cutting-open

part of the procedure. Not that she was terribly squeamish, but she much preferred the explanatory part of the process, and she certainly didn't want to look like a ninny in front of Rashid Kaleem.

Heidi announced her over the intercom, then proffered gloves, gown, and mask. When Sidana had donned them, Heidi pressed the door release and Sidana entered the suite.

In his protective white bunny suit, mask, cap, and face shield, Kaleem resembled an alien from a sci-fi film. When he looked up, however, his dark eyes were instantly recognizable, although today they did not hold their usual mischievous glint.

"Inspector Sidana," he said, his voice magnified by the mic he wore. He nodded at her, then glanced down, drawing her gaze to the gurney before him. "I hope you don't mind if I've got the preliminaries out of the way."

"Not at all." Sidana stared, transfixed, at the body on the table. Her first thought was that she wanted to cover the woman. Her nakedness seemed an affront, stripping away her dignity, making her unfairly vulnerable in death. Her second thought was that Sasha Johnson had been, and was still, beautiful, the brown of her skin masking death's blotching and pallor. She was also glad to see the neat stitches of the closed Y incision down the woman's sternum. "Oh, what a shame," she whispered, moved to forget her resolution to be absolutely professional.

Kaleem glanced up at her, apparently surprised. "Yes," he said simply.

"What can you tell me?" Sidana asked, making an effort to recover her usual brisk demeanor.

"She was a fit and healthy twenty-eight-year-old." Kaleem used the tip of a forceps to point to the small wound below the victim's left breast. "Until someone stabbed her. Quite neatly done, too."

Sidana frowned. "A lucky hit, do you think?"

"Possibly. Her coat was open. But even so, the blow was very well placed."

"What can you tell me about the weapon? Was it a knife?"

Kaleem shook his head. "I think not. Look at the wound." He gestured again and Sidana moved closer. "It's round, not the oblong or teardrop shape you see from a knife blade. There's no tearing or slashing, and the puncture was uniform in size until it nicked her aorta. Anything long and pointed would have done the trick—a sharpened screwdriver, for instance, an ice pick, a carpenter's awl. Even a knitting needle, although gripping it might have been difficult for the assailant."

"Did she feel it?" Sidana asked, in spite of herself.

"Probably, yes. But it was very quick. Even with her medical training, I doubt she knew what was happening."

Glancing down again, Sidana had to resist the urge to step back. She wondered how Kaleem managed this physical intimacy with the dead, day after day. What sort of boundaries did that take? Glancing up at him, she realized how little she knew about the man, other than his reputation as a top-notch pathologist.

She forced herself to pay attention. "Would it have taken medical training, a blow like that?"

"It wouldn't have hurt, certainly. But anyone can study an anatomy book. As I said, he might have got lucky. Or he might have practiced."

"Practiced? You mean, on people?"

"It's possible, although I've not come across any similar deaths recently. But he could have used a ham, or a side of beef." At Sidana's expression, he added, "Don't worry. I'm not suggesting we have a mad butcher on our hands."

"I certainly hope not." Frowning, Sidana picked up another thread. "You said 'he.' You're assuming the perpetrator was male?"

Kaleem gestured to the victim with his forceps. "She wasn't a small woman—I'd say about your height—and the thrust angled upwards, so I'd say it was likely her attacker was taller. Add that to the force of the blow and the likelihood skews towards a male."

The picture he painted was vivid, animated, a far cry from the static finality of a corpse on the ground. Sidana shivered.

"Are you cold?" Kaleem asked, sounding concerned. "It does get brutal in here."

She realized that, indeed, the cold had begun to seep beneath the flimsy Tyvek gown and through her clothes. Her fingers were icy, and even with a mask, she could feel the tip of her nose growing numb. "I am, a bit."

"Let's adjourn to my office, unless there's something else you need to see here." He glanced at the large clock over the suite's double doors. "I understand the family's due here soon. We'll need to get her ready for the viewing." Returning his forceps to the instrument tray, Kaleem pulled the sheet over the body in one deft sweep. Then, to Sidana's surprise, he touched his gloved fingers gently to Sasha Johnson's forehead. It was just for a moment, and he didn't speak, but Sidana had the sense that this was a private ritual for him. Then he buzzed for the mortuary assistant and led Sidana briskly from the room.

—

Dr. Rashid Kaleem's office was a windowless room at the end of a long basement corridor, but it wasn't a clinical cubicle. Colorful graffiti covered any bare expanse of the concrete walls not hidden by bookcases. The piles of books and papers on his desk seemed to be in a pitched battle to oust the large computer monitor. One stack precariously supported an old-fashioned shaded library lamp, the warm pool of its light counterbalancing the overhead fluorescent fixtures.

Kaleem had slipped a white lab coat over a T-shirt that she thought said "Play safe or I will see you naked," but she couldn't very well ask him to give her another glimpse. She must have looked askance because he glanced at his chest and shrugged apologetically. "I don't usually see the paying customers. Pathologists' humor."

"I wasn't—" She stopped, flushing.

He nodded towards a coat stand behind the door, where a pale blue button-down shirt hung neatly on a hanger, draped with a suitably conservative red-and-blue dotted tie. "I can look presentable if necessary."

"I didn't mean . . ." Trailing off, she sank into the chair Kaleem offered her.

Before she could dig herself in any deeper, he said, "Have a coffee to warm you up. It's the least we can do." He waved a hand at the counter behind his desk, where an espresso machine and a jar of coffee pods were nestled in between more stacks of books and some very unpleasant-looking anatomical models. "There's even milk," he added, pointing out a tiny fridge below the counter. "I promise I don't keep specimens in there with it, and I run the mugs through the autoclave."

"I'd like that. The coffee, I mean." She snapped her mouth shut before she could babble on. Why did this man make her feel so bloody awkward?

"I was just kidding about the autoclave," he said as he popped a pod in the machine and retrieved a mug emblazoned with a large red heart between the words "I" and "forensics." "I wash them in the staff room." The machine rumbled and hissed as the mug filled.

When he'd added a splash of milk to the coffee and handed it to her, she said into the silence, "Dr. Kaleem—"

"Please. Call me Rashid." He sat behind his desk, looking suddenly less like a rock star and more like the expert he was.

"Rashid," she said carefully, cradling her mug, "what else can you tell me about Sasha Johnson?"

Tapping on his keyboard, he glanced at the computer monitor. "Her stomach was empty except for a small amount of white wine, so I'd say she'd hadn't eaten since lunch, or earlier. There were no drugs in her system, and no sign of chronic drug or alcohol use."

"Superintendent Kincaid says he saw her in a pub in Lamb's Conduit Street, about half an hour before she must have been killed."

Kaleem looked concerned. "He didn't tell me that. What a bugger for him."

"More of a bugger for her, I'd say," Sidana blurted, then mentally kicked herself as Kaleem's eyes widened.

"Yes, of course," he agreed, with a wariness that suggested he was now looking out for minefields. "That would be about right for the wine."

"Anything else?" Sidana asked, wishing she hadn't accepted the coffee. It made it awkward for her to take her leave, and every time she opened her mouth she seemed destined to put her foot in it. "The woman's flatmate says she didn't have a boyfriend, but if there's a possibility that this was a targeted attack, we need to consider her relationships. Was she sexually active?"

"There were no signs of recent intercourse," Kaleem said carefully. "But I think you can be certain she was sexually active." He paused, meeting her eyes. "She was pregnant."

—

Gemma stared at Louise in disbelief. "A nanny? That's absurd, Louise. We can't afford a nanny. And besides, we're not—" She'd been about to say "posh" when Louise's expression stopped her.

"Don't tell me it offends your class sensibilities, Gemma. It doesn't mean you're shirking your responsibilities. This is not like the well-to-do shuffling their kids off to boarding school before they're out of nappies. Charlotte had a nanny before she came to you."

"But that was only after her mother went missing, and Naz couldn't—"

"Manage on his own. He needed help. You need help."

"Even if you're right," Gemma said after an uncomfortable moment, "it's just not feasible. We don't have room for a live-in. The boys are squashed together as it is. And someone even part-time would cost the earth."

"You've paid Wesley."

"Yes, but Wesley's a friend. And it's only been here and there, when it was convenient for him." Wesley's help had made a huge difference, she had to admit, but he was very busy these days with his own commitments. "It was nice to have him, though," she added with a sigh. "The children love him. And he cooks."

"I'm sure you could find someone who could help out with meals."

"Kit would be offended," Gemma said. "Wes cooking, he doesn't mind, but otherwise he considers the kitchen his domain. He only tolerates Duncan and me."

"Still cooking up a storm, is he?"

"Yes, and working in the café with Wes on Saturdays, too."

"It's good experience. He's growing up, Gemma. He needs time for himself as well as the family."

"Yes, but—"

"I know you think an old spinster like me has no business telling you what's best for your children," interrupted Louise, leaning forward for emphasis, "but I do remember what it was like to be Kit's age."

Gemma had to laugh. "I've certainly never thought of you as a spinster, Louise. But you're right. Kit does need his own friends and his own interests. He takes too much on himself. There are days when I feel like he's the adult in the house."

"Then fix it."

"But—that's easier said than done. Even if we could afford it, I'd have no idea where to start."

Louise hesitated for a moment, then said, "Look, Gemma, I know you don't like taking money from the estate, but those funds are there to provide for Charlotte in whatever way is needed."

Gemma was already uncomfortable with the fact that the estate was paying the bulk of Charlotte's school fees. "The school fees are just for Charlotte. This would be different," she protested.

"Why? It would benefit Charlotte. Is it somehow against the rules that it should help the rest of the family, too?"

"No, but—"

"As for how to go about it, I suspect your friend MacKenzie Williams would have some suggestions. Or you could check the adverts in *The Lady*." Louise's grin was wicked. That venerable publication was where London's yummy mummies looked for domestic help.

"No way." Gemma was suitably appalled.

"Then speak to MacKenzie. Just think about it, Gemma, and talk it over with Duncan."

Gemma gave in gracefully. Louise in full lawyer mode was a force of nature. "Okay," she agreed. "I'll speak to him."

Sitting back in her chair, Louise said, "Now. Tell me what else has been going on. We've hardly spoken since you came back from your"—her eyes twinkled—"very posh country house weekend. How's your mum?"

Half an hour later, awash in caffeine and having promised to bring Charlotte for a visit before Christmas, Gemma prepared to take her leave. "Oh, Louise," she said as she reached the door, "you will come to Toby's performance, won't you? I'll save you a ticket."

"Today the Tabernacle, tomorrow the West End," Louise answered with a chuckle. "I wouldn't miss it for the world."

They'd reached the door when the sound of raised voices halted them. One of them Gemma recognized instantly.

"You cannae do this, lad! Is that your brain addled?" It was Louise's Scottish neighbor, Tam Moran.

The second voice grew louder, as if a door had been opened. "I told you, I've made up my mind. We've made up our minds, Poppy and me. It's off." With a shock, Gemma realized the second speaker was Andy Monahan, Melody's ex. Tam was his manager.

"But you cannae back out of a tour." Tam sounded as if he was making an effort to be reasonable. "It's been booked for donkey's—"

"We're not doing bloody spa towns at Christmas, Tam. You shouldn't have committed us."

"You cannae just stop when you've got momentum, laddie. You're risking your career—"

"Then sod it." There was a slam, and Gemma looked out Louise's front window just in time to see the back of Andy's blond head as he disappeared down the stairs.

—

"Pregnant?" Staring at Rashid Kaleem, Sidana thought of the young woman's slender form on the steel gurney in the autopsy suite, the belly smooth and flat. "Are you sure?" When he looked taken aback, she realized she'd put her foot in it again.

"I am, actually," Rashid said, his received BBC accent more pronounced. "There are marked changes to the cervix. But the lab results will confirm it."

"How far along was she?"

"I'd say four to six weeks, at the most."

Sidana considered this. "Would she have known?"

"Perhaps. A recent test probably would have been accurate." He grinned suddenly. "Although I've seen women carry to term without realizing they're pregnant."

"You're taking the mickey."

"I'm not, honestly," he said, but there was a hint of a quirk at the corner of his mouth. "Stranger than fiction."

She refused to be drawn. "Well, regardless, Sasha Johnson was a doctor, and I'm pretty sure she wouldn't have mistaken the early signs of pregnancy." And if Sasha had known, Sidana continued to herself, would she have panicked? For a single, career-driven young woman, terminating an unwanted pregnancy would have been an easy solution, with no one the wiser.

Unless she had wanted the baby. Suddenly feeling a bit queasy, Sidana set down her coffee in the only uncluttered spot on Rashid's desk and pushed her chair back.

"Are you okay?" Rashid asked, his dark eyebrows drawing together.

"I'm fine." Sidana stood. "Thanks for the coffee. I'd better go speak to the parents."

He stood as well, coming round the desk to usher her to the door. "I don't envy you," he said, all traces of his earlier teasing gone.

"No." There was no snappy reply to that. "Let me know if anything turns up in the lab work."

Rashid reached out, his fingers barely brushing her arm, and for a moment she thought he'd meant to give her shoulder a squeeze. Then he rested his hand on the edge of the door, pushing it a bit wider for her. "I will. And you'll let me know if you have any more questions?"

"Of course," she answered briskly, turning away, but she could feel his gaze on her back all the way down the long corridor.

—

Rashid didn't know what to make of the prickly detective inspector. She'd barely given him the time of day when they'd worked the scene at St. Pancras together last winter. Thinking about it now, though, he hadn't seen much evidence of Sidana being chummy with Gemma or Duncan last night, either, so maybe it wasn't personal.

Still, there had been moments today when he'd seen a hint of a thaw. She'd almost smiled more than once, and he'd realized that without the perpetual frown drawing her brows together, she was actually quite attractive.

Shaking his head, he turned back to his computer. She was no business of his, and his curiosity was inappropriate. But he'd seen that moment of vulnerability as she contemplated telling Sasha Johnson's parents that their daughter had been carrying a child. Maybe Jasmine Sidana was not as bulletproof as she appeared.

—

Kit walked down Kensington Park Road with his hands stuffed in the pockets of his hoodie. After yesterday's drizzle, the air was sharp with the sort of biting nip you only got on crisp, clear autumn days. If Gemma had been home she'd have told him to wear a coat, but no one at school wore a coat unless it was the apocalypse.

His friend Erika Rosenthal had tutted at him, however, when he'd stopped by her flat in Arundel Gardens with the muffins he'd made that morning. "You'll catch your death," she'd said. "You'd better come in for some tea."

He'd turned her down, saying he had to be at Otto's by eleven, but he'd felt a pang when she looked disappointed. He hadn't seen her much lately, he realized, and he thought she looked a little frailer. She was getting on, after all, and she had no family—they should check on her more often. He'd ask Gemma if they could invite her for Sunday lunch tomorrow.

In the meantime, he was looking forward to working the lunch shift at Otto's. The café was always busy on Portobello Market day, and Otto and Wes would need the extra help. He loved the buzz and efficiency of a busy kitchen, and he felt comfortable there, more so than he ever did at school.

Turning into Elgin Crescent, he glimpsed the cheerful blue awning of the café front. Sandwiched between the charity shop and a bar that had changed hands half a dozen times since Kit had moved to Notting Hill, Otto's Café was a neighborhood institution. Just beyond it, the hat stall set up on the pavement provided a blaze of color against the crowd thronging Portobello Road. The fine weather meant it would be a good day for the market, and the punters should be edging from morning coffees into early lunches. In front of the Duke of York, a busker was playing very good jazz guitar and a crowd had gathered to listen.

Pushing open the café door, Kit met a blast of warmth and the smell of fresh coffee. With one glance, he checked the small dining room's occupied tables. One woman, plastic shopping bags piled at her feet, was scrolling through her mobile, an empty coffee cup and a crumb-littered plate on the tabletop. At another two-top, a couple was perusing menus. The man set his down and looked round impatiently.

Kit frowned. The first table should have been cleared, and someone should have taken the two-top's orders. Where was everyone?

He crossed the room, nodding at the impatient man and murmuring, "Someone will be right with you," then clattering down the stairs to the kitchen.

He stopped dead in the entryway, staring. Wesley Howard sat on the single kitchen stool, the palms of his hands pressed to his face. Otto stood before him, flapping his apron like a rotund chicken, his bald head gleaming with sweat under the harsh overhead lighting. The smell of hot fryer fat singed Kit's nostrils.

"What's happened?" he asked. "Wes, are you okay?"

Wes's shoulders gave a convulsive heave. When he swiped his palms across his cheeks, Kit saw that his dark eyes were brimming with tears. Although a good few years older, Wesley was the first real friend Kit had made when he'd moved to London to live with his dad and Gemma. He had never seen Wes cry.

"Ah, Kit, you are here." Otto turned to him with a look of relief. "I'm afraid Wesley has had some bad news."

CHAPTER SEVEN

Kincaid understood that rules and procedures had to be followed, even in exigent circumstances, but Neel Chowdhury seemed deliberately obstructive and he wondered why.

As he and Doug followed the nurse from the staff room, Kincaid saw that Doug was already texting the warrant request to Simon Gikas. To Chowdhury, he said, "We'd appreciate anything you can do to facilitate opening Dr. Johnson's locker, once you have the requisite paperwork."

Chowdhury pursed his lips. "I don't like disruptions on my floor, but I suppose it can't be helped."

Handing him a card, Kincaid added, "If you—or anyone on your staff—think of anything that might help us in finding out who did this, please let me know. Is there anyone in particular we should speak to?"

"Well, I'm not one to gossip . . ." Once again behind the nursing station desk, Chowdhury hesitated. The ward doors swung open and a man wearing a consultant's white coat over his scrubs charged through.

"Neel, I need Mrs. Slocum's chart. Why the hell wasn't it updated first thing this morn—" The consultant stopped, staring at Kincaid and Doug. "Visiting hours are restricted on this ward," he snapped.

"Ah, Owen." Chowdhury turned to Kincaid with a little smile. "This is Dr. Rees, Superintendent. He might be able to help you. He's the senior consultant on the ward."

Kincaid thought the man was young for the position, perhaps in his late thirties or early forties. But he radiated a nervous energy, and his whip-thin physique and the dark circles under his eyes made Kincaid think he might work hard enough to overcome the deficit.

"What's this about?" Rees asked, frowning, his fingers hovering over the tablet he carried. His accent, Kincaid noticed, was faintly Welsh.

"These are detectives from Scotland Yard," Chowdhury said. Before Kincaid could correct him, Chowdhury added, "They're here about Sasha Johnson. She's been killed. Murdered."

Rees stared at them. "Is this some sort of a sick joke?"

"I'm sorry. I'm afraid it's true." Kincaid held out his Metropolitan Police warrant card. "I'm Duncan Kincaid and this is Detective Sergeant Cullen. Do you think we could have a word?"

He saw the shock ripple down Rees's face then, his eyes dilating and his lips blanching. "I-I can't believe it. Murdered?"

"Yes." Kincaid glanced at Chowdhury, who was listening with avid attention. "Is there someplace we could have a chat, Dr. Rees? Is there a canteen in the hospital?"

"Yes, lowest level," Chowdhury answered. Then a call light on the nursing station began to blink and with a muttered apology, he hurried off.

"Why don't we go downstairs for a coffee," Kincaid suggested to Rees, who still looked alarmingly blank.

The doctor seemed to pull himself together a bit as they made their way downstairs to the bright coffee shop in the basement. While Kincaid chose a table in a quiet corner, Doug fetched drinks from the enormous vending machine. "Too bad the police station doesn't have one of these things," Doug muttered to Kincaid as he brought the drinks to the table. Then his mobile vibrated and he moved away to take the call.

Grasping his paper cup, Rees cleared his throat. "Can—can you tell me what happened? I still—I can't take it in. Sasha, murdered. How?"

"Someone stabbed her as she walked across Russell Square yesterday evening," Kincaid answered quietly.

"Stabbed?" Rees's cup jerked. "You mean, like some sort of gang killing? Here in Bloomsbury?"

"From the information we have so far, it seems to have been a lone individual. That's all I can tell you." Kincaid took out the little notebook he always carried in his jacket pocket. The use of pen and paper seemed to calm witnesses in a way that typing into a phone or tablet did not, and he found it helped him think. "Do you mind if I ask you some questions?"

"Of course." Rees blinked. "I mean, of course I don't mind. But I don't see how I can help."

"We'd like to know as much as possible about Sasha's work, and about anything going on in her life."

"You don't think she was . . . targeted?" Rees's question ended on a squeak. "But surely it was some deranged person?"

"That's certainly a possibility, but we have to explore every avenue," Kincaid said. "Could we begin by getting your full name and contact details?"

"Oh, yes, of course. It's Owen Rees. Dr. Owen Rees. I'm a consultant here." He gave Kincaid a phone number. "But I don't see how—"

"Bear with me, Dr. Rees. Mr. Chowdhury said you were the senior consultant on the ward. Does that mean you supervised Sasha Johnson?"

"I—yes. I supervise all the trainee doctors who come through on rotation."

"Was she a good doctor?"

"Yes. Yes, she was." Rees cleared his throat. "Exceptional, really. But I don't see what this has to do—"

"Were you on friendly terms, then?"

Rees's eyes widened. "It was a professional relationship, Superintendent," he snapped.

So the man had noted Kincaid's rank. "I merely thought that if you worked closely together, you might have an idea if there were any problems in Sasha's personal life."

"If there were, she wouldn't have shared them with me. That would have been inappropriate," Rees answered. "Sasha . . ." He drummed his fingers on the tabletop, as he had upstairs on his tablet. "Sasha was a very self-contained young woman."

"Did she get on with her colleagues?"

Rees's fingers went still. "Of course she did."

"It's just that Mr. Chowdhury gave the impression—"

"The man's a twat," Rees spat with such sudden venom that Kincaid felt a spray of saliva. "He's a troublemaker and a gossip. Sasha was a good doctor, better than most of the juniors that come through here. Chowdhury's a petty despot and he resented her." He pushed away his untouched coffee and stood. "Look, I have to get back to my rounds. I don't know what else I can tell you." As he walked away, he swiped the back of his hand across his cheek.

Considering, Kincaid watched him go. But before he could formulate his thoughts, Doug ended his call and strode towards him.

"That was Sidana," Doug said, "with the p.m. results. And here's an interesting thing—Sasha Johnson was pregnant."

—

Kit's knees went weak. His first thought was of Betty, Wesley's mother, who like Wes had been a comfort and an anchor to him. "Your mum, Wes. Is your mum okay? What's happened?"

But Wes was shaking his head. "Not M-Mum," he managed to say, his voice breaking. "My—our . . . it was our friend. More like a cousin. Sasha. She—me and my sisters, we grew up together. Always in and out of each other's p-pockets." He choked back a sob. "Sorry, man. I just can't believe it."

There was a muffled curse as Otto lunged for the cooker, extinguishing the flame under the chip fryer. Garlic was burning, too, in the big sauté pan, the charred, bitter smell catching in Kit's throat, making him cough. "Here, let me help," he called to Otto.

"No, no." Shuffling pans, Otto waved him off. "I can manage. See to Wesley."

"I can—" Wes started to rise, then sank back down onto the stool. "Just give me a minute."

"I'm so sorry, Wes," Kit said awkwardly. "What happened? Was it an accident?"

"No! She was killed!" Wes shot to his feet this time, his fists balled. "Someone just killed her, for nothing!"

"This morning?" Kit asked, shocked.

"No, no. It happened last night. But my mum just rang me, she heard the news from the family this morning. Sasha had—" Wes stopped, blinking hard. "She—she'd finished her shift at the hospital and she was just walking across Russell Square. Someone stabbed her." His voice broke.

Otto turned back to them. "You must go home, Wesley. Kit and I can manage the lunch."

But Wesley wasn't listening. He'd gone very still, and his expression made Kit step backwards instinctively.

"That little shit," breathed Wes. "If he got Sasha caught up in something, I'll kill him, I swear I will."

Alarmed, Kit said, "Who? What are you talking about, Wes?"

"Her wanker of a brother. Tyler. Training up to be a little gangster, isn't he? Why else would someone stab Sasha? Maybe they meant to teach him a lesson—"

A light tread sounded on the stairs. Kit moved out of the way just as Bryony Poole reached the bottom and stepped into the kitchen. A tall, auburn-haired young woman with a pleasantly freckled face, Bryony was their vet, and Wes's friend. Or more than friend, Kit thought, but he wasn't certain.

"Oh, Wes, I'm so sorry." Bryony went to Wesley, placing a hand gently on his arm as she gave him a searching look. "Your mum rang me. Are you okay?"

"Yes. No. I don't know." Wesley looked suddenly more bewildered than angry.

Otto, on the other hand, looked vastly relieved to see her. "Bryony, you will take Wesley home, yes? Wesley, you will let me know Monday if you want to come in." He wrapped one meaty arm around Wes's shoulders for a moment in a half hug, then thumped him on the back. Stepping away, he said, "Now, go, both of you," and made shooing motions with his hands.

"Thanks, Otto." Bryony guided Wesley to the stairs with that same gentle touch.

When they'd disappeared, Otto wiped at his eyes with his

apron, then turned to Kit. "He is like a son to me, that one. But now we must cook."

"I'll just check on the tables," Kit mumbled, embarrassed by Otto's tears.

He was halfway up the stairs when the realization struck him. Wesley's friend had been stabbed. His father had been called out urgently last night to a homicide. Russell Square was in Bloomsbury, his dad's patch. What if this was his dad's case?

———

Having said a quick farewell to Louise, Gemma stepped out on the balcony to find Tam still standing by the door to his flat. With his balding head not covered by the usual worn, soft cap that had given him his nickname, he looked somehow defenseless.

"Tam, was that Andy?" Gemma asked. "I'm sorry, I couldn't help but overhear. Are you all right?"

"Nae, that I am not," Tam answered in his soft Scots burr. He wiped a shaking hand over his face. "The lad has lost his mind."

"He sounded . . . upset," Gemma temporized.

"He's gone and canceled the whole bloody Christmas tour. I dinnae know what's got into him. He says he wants to get back into the studio, doing session work. And Poppy wants to get on with her music degree. Her music degree!" Tam shook his head, an expression of astonishment on his weathered face. "Tell me why in the name of all that's holy does that girl, who has more talent in her little finger than most people are born with altogether, need a freaking degree? I ask you."

"Maybe they aren't getting along?" Gemma suggested. Maybe the chemistry the two had onstage didn't carry over into their personal lives.

But Tam was shaking his head again, frowning. "Nae, I dinnae think so. He said they'd decided this mad thing together. The lass is talking to Caleb now." Caleb Hart was Poppy's manager, and a bigger player in the music world by far than Tam Moran. Andy— and by extension, Poppy—had been the big success of Tam's career.

"They're not saying that they're breaking up altogether?"

"They want to *elevate their profile*, the lad says." Tam rolled his eyes. "Well, I have news for the wee buggers. The club circuit may be a bit rowdy, but it's called paying your dues."

"Maybe the dues have changed, Tam," Gemma said. "Look at Billie Eilish and her brother, recording hits in her bedroom."

Tam rubbed at his face again, but this time it was a more contemplating stroking of his perpetual stubble, and after a moment, he said more calmly, "That's a talented lass, I'll give you that."

"So is Poppy. But she's young, too. What is she now, twenty? It's got to be tough for her, life on the road, being away from her parents and her brothers. And Andy," she added a bit ruefully, "well . . . maybe he and Poppy both just need some time. Just think, you could have worse problems than musicians who want to take a break and improve their craft." She gave Tam a wicked grin. "Like sex, drugs—"

"And rock-n-roll." Tam sighed. "Could be you're right, lass. Maybe I should have given them a wee break."

Gemma patted his arm. "Talk to Caleb. You'll work things out, I'm sure. Now, I'd better run. Give Michael and the dogs my best, will you?"

As Gemma turned to go, Tam called her back. "Gemma, do you ken how things are with Andy's lass, Melody? He willnae talk to me, but he's like a bear with a sore head. Is it truly over between them?"

"I don't know, Tam. Melody's not much better, and she won't talk to me, either. But it seems pretty definite."

As she walked to her car, Gemma wondered whether she should tell Melody that Andy and Poppy would be in London, at least for the time being. But Melody had boundaries that Gemma wasn't sure she could—or should—breach. She had no idea if Melody and Andy could repair their rift, or if they both needed to find ways to move on with their lives.

Still mulling this over, and wondering if she had time to pick up cupcakes from the bakery in Columbia Road, she'd paused to admire the sun glinting off the copper paintwork of her Land Rover when her mobile rang. She fished in her bag for it, thinking it must be MacKenzie calling about Charlotte.

But it was not MacKenzie. It was Kit.

—

Taking a breath, Sidana pushed open the door to the viewing room. Lucy McGillivray sat perched at the end of a row of waiting-room chairs, handing out tissues and patting the hand of a middle-aged, fine-boned woman that Sidana assumed must be Sasha Johnson's mother. A large, bald man sat beside her, his head bowed, his arm around a sobbing young woman who bore a strong resemblance to Sasha.

The heavy blue curtains had been closed over the window into the morgue, and the room felt airless and overly warm. The scent of the lilies in a vase on a side table was nauseatingly strong.

McGillivray looked up and gave Sidana an imperceptible nod. The parents had confirmed the identification, then. "Mrs. Johnson, Mr. Johnson, Kayla, this is Detective Inspector Sidana," McGillivray said. The weeping young woman looked up. "The inspector will have a few questions for you all."

McGillivray stood up and moved away, taking up a position by the door, while Sidana took a chair and shifted it around so that she could face the family. The curtained viewing window seemed to loom behind her.

"It's Clements." The young woman blew her nose on one of McGillivray's tissues. "Kayla Clements." She must be younger than Sasha, Sidana thought, but there was a softness to her, a dulling of the features.

Sidana leaned forward with her hands on her knees so that she could look at them all directly. "Mr. and Mrs. Johnson, Mrs. Clements. First, let me say how sorry I am for your loss."

Wiping her eyes, Mrs. Johnson nodded. But it was Mr. Johnson—Peter, Sidana remembered from her notes—who spoke first. "Inspector, have you any idea who did this thing?" His voice was deep and well modulated, as befitted a school headmaster. "We can't understand—"

"Why?" broke in his wife with a wail. "Why our Sasha?"

Sidana felt the rawness of the woman's grief like a lash, but she said as gently as she could, "Our inquiries are ongoing. I know that's not much comfort to you now, but I promise you that we will find the person responsible for your daughter's death. Can you tell us if Sasha had fallen out with anyone recently?"

"You think someone who knew her did this?" Mrs. Johnson's eyes widened in shock. "That's not possible. Everybody loved Sasha."

Sidana exchanged a glance with McGillivray, who was listening intently. As a police officer, Sidana had seldom found that statement to be true. "I'm sure they did," she soothed. "But is it possible that someone loved her . . . too much?"

Mrs. Johnson stared at her. "I don't understand what you mean."

"Could Sasha have had a jealous boyfriend?" Sidana asked.

Shaking her head, Mrs. Johnson said, "She——"

"Sasha didn't have boyfriends," broke in Kayla. "She said she wasn't dumb enough to throw her life away for a—" Kayla pushed herself away from her father's encircling arm and looked down at the wedding band she'd been twisting for the last five minutes. "Anyway, it doesn't matter now, what she thought, does it?"

"Kayla!" Mr. Johnson's reprimand was thunderous. "Show some respect to your sister." His anger brought out a faint accent that Sidana couldn't quite place.

After a moment, Kayla shrugged. "Sorry, Dad."

Sidana broke the charged silence. "Look, I know this is difficult for you, and I don't want to cause you any more distress. But I must ask these questions." She looked at each of them in turn. "If Sasha wasn't seeing anyone, maybe someone was angry because she rejected them."

"Angry enough to stab my daughter in a public square? That is insane, Inspector." Johnson sat forward as if to rise, his handsome face creased with pain. "I think we should go home now. There's nothing more we can do here."

Holding up a hand, Sidana said, "I understand, Mr. Johnson. But there is one more thing. You see, Sasha was a few weeks pregnant. Are you certain you have no idea who the father might have been?"

CHAPTER EIGHT

It started with John Snow. She'd read about the pioneering Victorian epidemiologist in a school science class. It had been just a sketch describing how in 1854, twenty years before the invention of the microscope, Snow, an anesthesiologist in London's teeming and cesspool-infested Soho, had used scientific inquiry to discover the cause of cholera. Not that Snow would have called himself an epidemiologist—it was his methodical and systematic investigations that would become the foundations of the discipline. If cholera outbreaks were common in areas near open sewage, Snow surmised, there must be some connection.

On a map, he plotted the cholera cases in Soho's Golden Square neighborhood, including the area's three pumps. When it became apparent that more cases were clustered near the pump in Broad Street, he began interviewing the families of the victims. When he found that they had indeed used the Broad Street pump, Snow became convinced that it was the water that was the common factor, not foul air.

Snow's unraveling of the puzzle had been brilliant, and she wondered what it would be like to look at a problem and see the solution fall into place.

On her seventeenth birthday she took the bus into Central London on a pilgrimage of sorts. Standing at the site of the Broad Street pump, she knew she wanted to follow in Snow's footsteps.

—

"What the hell were you thinking?" Kincaid asked, failing to keep his voice level. Shouting at his team was not his style, but he was furious.

Jasmine Sidana crossed her arms over her starched white blouse and shrugged. "It seemed the opportune moment."

The team had assembled in the Holborn incident room, Kincaid standing, the others sitting at workstations littered with used mugs, empty crisp packets, and paper coffee cups. Someone had apparently eaten Coronation Chicken for an early lunch, as the room reeked of curry.

Kincaid wished he could open a window to get some air, but the open-plan room had no outside access. He ran a hand through his hair and tried to tamp down his irritation. "Telling the Johnsons that they'd lost a grandchild, when they'd just viewed their daughter's body," he snapped at Sidana, "is not what I'd call opportune. Not only was it insensitive, it should have been my decision if and when to share that information with the family."

In the last few months, he'd thought his working relationship with the prickly DI had improved. He knew she'd resented his taking the job she'd hoped to be promoted into, but he'd also come to see why that advancement had not been forthcoming. Sidana was ambitious and hardworking, but her interpersonal skills left something to be desired.

He'd apologize to the Johnsons. At least when he spoke to them again, they would have had time to absorb the news.

Sasha Johnson's pregnancy was an unexpected complication to the case. He glanced at the photo of Sasha displayed at the top of the incident room's whiteboard. It was an enlargement of the canal-side photo he'd seen on her sister Kayla's Facebook page. He wondered again at Sasha's distant expression, and about the relationship between the sisters.

Now, however, he had to deal with Sidana. "But what's done is done, so let's move on," he said, giving her one more pointed glance as he went to the whiteboard and picked up a marker. "As you've all just heard, Sasha Johnson was four to six weeks pregnant, according to Dr. Kaleem. This may or may not have any bearing on her attack, but it's interesting, as her flatmate told us that Sasha wasn't seeing anyone."

"There were no signs of recent sexual intercourse," put in Sidana, "so maybe it was a one-off. I wonder if she used regular birth control."

"And if she knew she was pregnant," said Doug, "as she was having a glass of wine in the pub just before she was killed."

Sidana looked startled. "What pub? And how did you know about the wine? Rashid—Dr. Kaleem—said she'd had a small amount of wine shortly before she died."

"Because we saw her," explained Doug. "In the Perseverance, in Lamb's Conduit Street. Me and the guv, we were having a drink, but she left just after I got there. To tell the truth, I didn't really notice her." He gave a shrug of regret. "I wish I had."

Simon grinned. "Good that you two can alibi each other."

Kincaid was not amused.

Nor was Sidana. "Why didn't you say that you'd seen her? Was she on her own?"

"Yes, she was. According to her flatmate, Tully Gibbs, Sasha was supposed to meet Gibbs's brother at the pub, but he didn't show up. She then texted Gibbs and arranged to meet her at a coffee shop near the British Museum, which is presumably why she was walking through Russell Square. The fact that Doug and I saw her in the pub wasn't relevant except that we could confirm Tully Gibbs's account."

"What about her family?" asked McGillivray. "Did they mention a relationship?" The young DC, Kincaid was learning, was often a tension diffuser.

Sidana's defensive expression relaxed a little. "They said she wasn't seeing anyone, had no interest in relationships. Or kids."

Simon frowned, swiveling his chair back and forth as he thought. "Is there a possibility that the pregnancy could have resulted from a sexual assault? One she didn't report?"

"But she was a doctor," Sidana protested. "She'd have known exactly what to do. And how important it was to report an assault immediately."

Kincaid thought of the charged atmosphere on the hospital ward. Would Sasha have wanted any hint of a sexual assault reaching her colleagues?

"Besides," Sidana continued, "you'd think she'd have taken the morning-after pill."

It was a good point, Kincaid conceded. But still, they had to consider the possibility. "Simon, check the system. Make sure we haven't missed a report connected with Sasha. And see if there were any anonymous reports that would fit in the time frame, as well. Jasmine, check with Rashid. Ask if he noticed any indications of a previous injury or assault."

Kincaid made a note on the board's action list, then turned back to the team. "Now, Simon, anything useful from the cameras or the house-to-house?"

Not that the inquiries had been literally house-to-house, but they'd had uniform interview the staff at the café in Russell Square, as well as employees at local businesses near both square entrances.

Simon shook his head. "No. It was dark and wet and people were hurrying. Most of them had their faces in their mobiles. One woman did say someone bumped into her, hard, but she was texting and couldn't even say if it was a man or a woman."

"Where was she?" Kincaid asked.

Turning, Simon checked his computer. "Just coming in the north entrance to the square. She works in the HSBC branch just opposite and was on her way home."

Kincaid thought about this. Sasha Johnson had been walking south. Could they assume that her attacker had been heading north? Of course he—or she—could have been following Sasha, if she'd been a deliberate target. But in either case the killer had exited the square from one entrance or the other, and would most likely have been hurrying. "Have someone reinterview your witness. See if she can pinpoint the time. Maybe that will jog her memory." He added the action to the list, then tapped the marker against the board as he considered how to delegate the tasks.

"Jasmine, I want you to oversee opening Sasha Johnson's locker at the hospital. Simon's requested a warrant, and I want that followed up as soon as possible.

"I want a background check on her work colleagues, particularly Neel Chowdhury and Dr. Owen Rees. Simon, that's in your court. I also want any background on the flatmate, Tully Gibbs. We're going to want to talk to her again.

"First, however, I want a word with her brother, the bloke who apparently stood Sasha up in the pub. Doug, you're with me on this one."

He saw the flash of disappointment on Jasmine Sidana's face. He was going to have to have a word with her, one-on-one, if he wanted to keep his team running smoothly, but he wasn't going to call her into his office in the midst of a briefing. It could wait.

—

Kincaid had ducked into the glass-walled cubicle of his office for a quick sandwich, courtesy of the station vending machine, when his mobile phone rang. Seeing that it was Gemma, he set the limp triangle of egg and cress on its plastic packaging and took the call. "What's up, love?" he asked, swallowing a bite of sandwich. "Where are you?"

"I'm in Columbia Road. I've been visiting Louise, but I wanted to speak to you before I started home."

"What's wrong?" he asked. "Is Louise okay?"

"Louise is fine. But Kit just rang me. When he got to Otto's this morning, he found Wesley distraught. It seems the girl who was murdered last night is a family friend."

"Oh, damn and blast." Kincaid rubbed a hand across his jaw. "I should have seen that coming."

"You knew about this?"

"Not definitely, no. But when I was at the parents' flat last night, I thought I saw Betty in a group photograph with them. I wasn't certain it was a close connection, and to tell the truth it slipped my mind. It didn't occur to me that Sasha and Wesley might have been close. Christ."

"Kit guessed it was your case. He feels horribly awkward. He didn't say anything to Wes."

"He shouldn't have to. I'll have a word with Wes and Betty myself, as soon as I can man—"

"There's more," Gemma broke in. "Kit said"—there was a rustle of paper and Kincaid guessed that Gemma was consulting a note—"Kit said that Wesley seemed to think that the assault might be connected with her brother."

"Sasha's brother? Why?" Kincaid glanced at his own notes, refreshing his memory.

There was another crinkly sound before Gemma continued. "Sorry. All I had handy to write on was a Tesco receipt. Anyway, Wesley said the brother was a little gangster, and that maybe somebody meant to teach him a lesson. Because it was a stabbing."

That wouldn't have been extreme for one of the serious London gangs, but they didn't usually operate outside their own territories. They depended on the intimidation of locals, and examples were made where they would have the most impact.

"We'll look into it," he said. "Sasha's sister came to the mortuary viewing with her parents, but there was no sign of the brother." He filled her in on the results of the postmortem.

"Pregnant? But that's dreadful. And how awful for her parents."

Kincaid suddenly had a very unwelcome thought. "Kit said Wesley was really upset," he began, then hesitated. Surely he was borrowing trouble. But this was Gemma, and if he was completely bonkers she would set him straight. "Is it possible that Wes and Sasha were more than family friends?"

—

By the time Kincaid ended the call, Doug was waiting outside his door, occasionally glancing up from his mobile to peer through Kincaid's blinds. Kincaid tossed the remains of the soggy sandwich in the bin without too much regret and went out to Doug.

"I've signed out a car," Doug informed him, dangling a fob. "But I didn't want to interrupt your call."

Kincaid debated telling him about his conversation with Gemma, but decided he didn't know enough to share that information yet. He followed Doug down to the station car park and slid into the passenger seat of the silver Vauxhall Astra, which might as well have had UNMARKED COP CAR emblazoned on the side panels.

The bright sky of the morning had faded to a dull haze, tarnishing even the marquees of the Shaftsbury Avenue theaters and the bright paper lanterns of Chinatown. When they reached the Soho address Tully Gibbs had given them for her brother's club in Archer Street, Doug propped the POLICE placard inside the windscreen where it was clearly visible to traffic wardens, or any wandering vandals from the nearby primary school. The street was quiet, and there was no sign of activity at the club premises. Elegant lettering on the building's facade read BOTTLE.

The flat light reflecting on the door and windows made it hard to see inside, but Kincaid thought he could make out sofas, tables, and at the far side of the room, movement. "There's someone here," he said.

But there was no response when he knocked on one of the windows. After a full minute, he rapped again, hard enough to rattle the window frame. This time he gave it thirty seconds, but just before his knuckles touched the glass, one of the double doors swung open.

"Oi!" The young man in the doorway glared at them. "Can you not read? We don't open until two." He started to shut the door again but Doug had already insinuated a foot across the threshold and was holding up his warrant card. "Police. We need a word. Are you Jonathan Gibbs?"

"What if I am?" said the man, but after a moment he gave an

exasperated grimace and stepped back. "Whatever it is, make it quick. I've got to finish setting up for service."

As they followed him inside, Kincaid's eyes adjusted and he got his first good look at Tully Gibbs's brother. Early thirties, slender, but with muscles that showed beneath a snug white T-shirt and fashionably faded jeans. Gibbs had light brown hair, worn gelled and short, and a slightly elongated face in which nature had taken his sister's pleasantly ordinary features and rearranged them just enough to make the resulting visage arresting.

The club's interior looked more like a large, upscale sitting room, with plush sofas and velvet poufs arranged in groupings around low, candle-adorned tables. There were a few two-tops along the sides of the rooms and in the front windows. High-backed gray velvet stools lined a long bar at the far end of the room, and behind it, the club lived up to its name.

Glass shelves held row after row of bottles in every hue, the colors mirrored in the huge floral arrangement that rested on a tall table in the room's center. The scent of flowers hung in the still air. Kincaid heard faint voices and an occasional bang and clatter from somewhere out of sight.

When Doug had introduced them, Kincaid said, "We'd like to talk to you about Sasha Johnson."

"I just spoke to my sister. She said Sasha was murdered. Is it true, then?"

"She didn't stab herself in the middle of Russell Square," said Doug acidly.

Gibbs's shoulders gave a convulsive little jerk. "I thought—I hoped—well, that maybe Tuls got it wrong."

Doug frowned. "That's not the sort of thing you make a mistake about. Why would you think your sister wasn't telling the truth?"

Kincaid cleared his throat. "Do you think we might sit down?" he said, his tone deliberately conversational. "And then perhaps you can tell us why you didn't meet Sasha last night."

"Wait. How did you know—" Gibbs stopped, then shrugged. Grudgingly, he pulled a third chair up to one of the two-tops in the front windows. He sat, leaving Kincaid and Doug to take the other two chairs.

Doug answered him. "We know because Sasha told Tully. That's why Sasha was crossing Russell Square. When you didn't show, she asked Tully to meet her. Apparently she really needed to talk to someone."

"Oh Jesus." Gibbs looked genuinely shocked. "You're not saying it was my fault Sasha was killed?"

"Why don't you tell us what happened?" Kincaid asked.

"One of our deliveries didn't show up. It was manic, Friday evening. I had to hit the cash-and-carry myself in order to keep the bar stocked. I'd already told Sasha that she couldn't have picked a worse time, but she insisted. And then honestly, I just forgot." Gibbs shrugged again. "We were slammed, you know? I never imagined—" He shook his head. "How could I have known that would happen? I still can't believe it." His voice had softened, his slight West Country accent more noticeable.

"Why did Sasha want to speak to you so urgently?" Kincaid asked.

Gibbs hesitated, then sighed. "It was something about Tyler. Her brother."

"Why talk to you about her brother?" asked Doug.

"Because he does odd jobs for me, and sometimes on busy nights he works the door."

"You mean as a bouncer?" Doug glanced around at the upscale ambiance. "Why would you need a bouncer for a place like this?"

"We stay open late. We serve alcohol." Gibbs rolled his eyes. "I shouldn't need to tell you that punters can get stroppy, even if they're paying fifteen quid a cocktail."

Or maybe *because* they were paying fifteen quid a cocktail, Kincaid thought. He said, "So he's on the payroll here."

"Seriously?" Gibbs shook his head. "Are you going to grass me out to the Inland Revenue now? It's just a bit of cash in hand. If Tyler had been here last night, I'd have had him do the stock run."

"Why did you hire him if he wasn't reliable?"

"Favor to Sasha."

"So were you and Sasha an item?" Kincaid asked, wondering if Gibbs might be a candidate for the father of Sasha's baby.

"God, no." Gibbs looked horrified. "Look, Sasha is"—he blinked—"Sasha was a stunner. But no way would I get myself involved in something with my sister in the middle. Even if Sasha had been interested, which she wasn't, okay?"

"Was she seeing someone else?"

"I haven't a clue. If anyone should know, it would be Tully." Gibbs shifted impatiently, pushing his chair back. The noise level from the back of the club was rising. "Look, if that's all—"

Kincaid held up a restraining hand. "Was Tyler Johnson supposed to be working last night?"

"Yeah. Like I said, Friday nights can be bonkers. I like him to circulate, help out the waitstaff a bit."

"I thought you said he was a bouncer."

"I never said he was a bouncer." Gibbs eyed Doug. "*He* did. Ty's a cool kid. Hip, you know? Charms the punters. And he's got a bit of muscle when it suits."

"Did he give you a reason for the no-show?"

"Hasn't returned my texts," Gibbs said with a flash of irritation. He gave a quick brush to the knees of his jeans, then scraped his chair back and stood. "Look, I don't know what else I can tell you. I've—"

"Just one more question," Kincaid interrupted. "Do you know where we can find Tyler?"

"No idea. I think he lives in university digs. I'm sure his family can tell you."

—

"What a poseur," said Doug as he fastened his seat belt. "Who does he think he is, James Dean?" He frowned. "Or was it Paul Newman who wore the white T-shirts?"

Kincaid grinned. "Maybe you're thinking of Brando."

Easing the Astra back into traffic, Doug said, "Whatever. I still think Mr. Jonathan Gibbs is a tosser. I don't believe he didn't know exactly what Sasha wanted to talk to him about last night. Or anything else he said, for that matter."

Kincaid considered this. He trusted his sergeant's instincts, although he found Doug's instant dislike of the man perplexing. "I don't think Gibbs is telling us the whole truth, I agree. He'd have denied knowing anything about meeting Sasha if he didn't know Tully had already told us. We should take a closer look at both the Gibbs siblings. And Tyler Johnson." Kincaid thought for a moment. "I'd like to know more about what goes on at Gibbs's club on a busy night."

"Well, we can't check it out in person," said Doug. "What about asking Melody?"

"Probably not a good idea, on the off chance that Tully Gibbs frequents the place. Tully would recognize her." Kincaid could ask Sidana to do it, but on his life he couldn't imagine her fitting into the trendy club scene. Did she even own any clothing other than white blouses and dark skirts?

McGillivray might do, but she was too new to be tasked with a job that probably wouldn't be sanctioned by the brass. Simon Gikas could do it—he had quite the man-about-town persona—but Kincaid didn't want to pull Simon away from his computers.

To tell the truth, there was only one person he trusted to read a situation as accurately as he could himself—his wife.

CHAPTER NINE

Sometimes, when the work wasn't going well, Tully would close her eyes and imagine a fine wire running from her brain down through her hands, so that the spark of an idea was transmitted to the form taking shape on her wheel. But today piece after piece grew lopsided and collapsed, ugly and deformed.

Clamping her lips on a sob, she scooped the clay back into its bucket and snapped the lid shut, then stood and went to the sink. When she'd washed her hands, she checked her mobile, hoping Jonathan had rung back. She hadn't meant to tell him over the phone, but when he'd finally picked up, she'd blurted, "Sasha's dead. She was murdered last night."

The silence had lasted for so long she'd started to think he'd disconnected. But then he'd said, "This is not bloody funny, Tuls, not funny at all." His voice snagged on the last bit, a rough little hiccup.

"I'm sorry," she said, instantly contrite. "I should have waited, told you in person—"

"This is not happening again. Not here. Not now. Look, I've got to go." And he'd hung up.

Tully stared at the now-blank screen on her phone. Had Jon been . . . crying? The last time she'd heard him cry had been—well, she didn't want to think about that. Especially not today.

—

Useless. At loose ends. As Tully walked, she thought of phrases that meant you had nothing to do and nowhere to be. What anchored her in her life now, she wondered, what kept her from floating away like an untethered balloon? She had had Sasha, and Sasha was gone. And Jon, but Jon had just slammed the door in her face.

There was the gallery, of course. When she'd left the studio she'd popped her head in to check with David. But, his back turned, he'd been explaining the difference between thrown and hand-built ceramics to a customer, and Tully had eased herself out again without speaking. He didn't need her, not really. Anyone that could manage the till and memorize the catalog could take her place.

Looking up, she found she'd reached Queen Square Gardens, with the bulk of Great Ormond Street Hospital looming to her right. Suddenly she thought the weight of it might crush her. She gasped, trying to move air into her lungs. Her vision blurred. She grasped the square's railing, felt the bite of the cold iron against her palm.

Had Sasha reached out for something as she fell? Had she had time to know that she was alone? That she was dying?

A cyclist brushed past her, too close. Tully realized she was blocking the pavement, but she couldn't make herself let go of her support. Her knees were jelly, her chest wouldn't expand.

"Are you all right, love?" said a woman's voice.

Tully blinked, focused on a kind face surrounded by a dark hijab. Breathe, she had to breathe. Nodding, she managed to whisper, "Fine. Thanks."

"Are you certain? You look unwell. I can get you some help."

"No, no, I'm okay, really." Tully forced air into her lungs. "Just a little woozy for a moment. I'll be fine." When the woman looked unconvinced, she added, "I just live round the corner." It was only then that she realized she'd been going home.

Except it wasn't—or it wouldn't be.

She gave the woman what she hoped looked like a smile, loosened her grip on the railing, and set off, trying not to wobble.

Why had she never noticed how much the flat smelled of Sasha? Tully thought as she let herself in and sagged against the door. There was Persil, from the scrubs that were always in washing rotation, the tropical scent of the conditioner Sasha used on her hair, and a very faint and elusive spiciness.

In the bathroom, Tully lifted Sasha's towel from the hook on the back of the door and held it to her face, breathing in the sweetness of coconut and lime. Sasha had been vain about her hair, and it had taken the array of taming products that lined the little shelf over the basin to keep her perfect twists from frizzing.

Tully sank onto the floor, still clutching the towel. She supposed she should start packing up Sasha's things for her parents—that at least would be useful. But she sat, letting the tears slide down her face, until at last she pulled off a wad of loo roll and blew her nose. As she tossed the tissue in the bin, a bit of plastic caught her eye. The shape, even half disguised by its paper wrapping, was unmistakable. It was a pregnancy-test stick, and when Tully eased it from the paper, she saw that the two little bars in the clear window were red.

—

The dogs greeted Gemma as if they'd been abandoned for a week. When she'd rubbed Geordie's silky ears and let them both out into the garden, she checked to see if the cats had destroyed anything in her absence. Sid surveyed her from his perch on the back of the sofa. Then, yawning, he tucked his head under his paw and went back to sleep. There was nothing like a cat to put you in your proper place, Gemma thought.

That left the Terrors, Rose and Captain Jack. The kittens that Kit and Toby had found in the garden shed last winter were full-grown cats now, but still climbing curtains. Rose, however, was stretched out in a patch of sunlight on Gemma's baby grand piano. Jack, she assumed, must be upstairs in his favorite spot, the laundry basket in the children's bathroom.

She made a cup of tea and sat down at the piano, noodling a bit at the piece she'd been working on, "Underneath the Lovely London Sky" from *Mary Poppins Returns*. Humming, she let her mind drift. Was Louise's idea completely mad? What would a weekend be like if she were free of some of the weekly drudgery?

The insistent ring of her phone pulled her from a pleasant daydream. "Bugger," she muttered.

When she saw it was Duncan, she put the call on speaker and the dogs tilted their heads at the sound of his voice.

"Have you spoken to Wesley and Betty?" he asked.

"No. I thought you were going to talk to them first. Officially, or at least semi-officially." Gemma retrieved her cooling tea.

"I will, as soon as I can get away. But in the meantime, something's come up."

"You're not going to make it home for dinner," Gemma said, resigned.

"Um, it's not that, exactly." Sounding a little hesitant, he outlined what he had in mind.

Gemma swallowed a sip of tea the wrong way, triggering a coughing fit. Recovering her breath, she gasped out, "You're saying you want me to go clubbing? In Soho? On a Saturday night?"

"Well, yes, I was. Unofficially. What do you think?"

She thought it sounded infinitely more appealing than getting through dinner with tired and fractious children. "You'd have to be home with the kids."

"I'm sure I could manage that." He sounded amused.

"I couldn't go on my own," she said. "Not to a posh club."

"What about asking Kerry Boatman? I wouldn't want to involve someone not in the job."

Gemma's friend Kerry was a DCI, currently assigned to the Kensington and Chelsea Station in Earl's Court Road. "Her husband might not appreciate that, but I'll give her a try. Hang on while I text her."

But Kerry's reply, which came within seconds, was disappointing. *Sorry, hubs away on business. Daughter down with flu. Raincheck?*

"No joy," Gemma told Kincaid. "Why don't you ask Sidana? It is her case, too, after all."

———

Sidana was still seething as she waited in the hospital lobby for the locksmith. It had taken her an hour to get the warrant sent through from the magistrate, a job one of the DCs could easily have done. It was bad enough that Kincaid had given her a bollocking in front of the team without him giving her an action beneath her rank.

She'd used the time to leave a message for Rashid Kaleem asking about a possible previous assault on the victim, but when a man came through the lobby doors wearing a brown zip anorak with the locksmith company's logo, she breathed a sigh of relief.

"Kevin," he said when she'd introduced herself. "But you can call me Kev. Always glad to be of service to the fuzz."

Just her luck, Sidana thought as she shook his proffered hand with ill-concealed distaste, to get one of the bluff and hearty types. And who actually said *fuzz*?

Kevin was balding with a too-many-pints spare tire and an accent that was practically east of Essex. Sidana stepped back with a nod and led the way to the lifts.

She hadn't been up to the ward yet—she'd thought it better to show up with warrant and locksmith in hand, in case there were any interesting reactions among the staff. Kincaid had told her that the charge nurse was called Neel Chowdhury, so when she and Kevin reached the ward, she needed only a glance at the name tag worn by the man behind the desk.

"Mr. Chowdhury, I'm Detective Inspector Sidana, Holborn CID. I'm here about Sasha Johnson's locker." She handed him a copy of the warrant.

Chowdhury pursed his lips disapprovingly. "This is a search warrant? I was expecting something more, I don't know, official-looking."

"Sorry to disappoint you." Sidana tapped the paper. "It's duly signed by the magistrate, as you can see." For a moment, she thought he was going to be really obstreperous, but then he shrugged and, coming round the desk, led them down one arm of the Y corridor.

"Not going to catch anything, are we?" muttered Kevin. "Hospitals give me the heebie-jeebies."

Chowdhury heard him and threw him an exasperated look. "You'd like them well enough if you were ill." With a sniff, he walked on and opened a door.

The staff room smelled, like staff rooms everywhere, of a mix of stale coffee, overheated air, and human sweat.

Kevin gave a little whistle as they entered. "Nice lockers."

Following his gaze, Sidana saw only an ordinary-looking bank of metal lockers lining the back wall. "How can you tell?"

"I've worked on this make before. Antibacterial coating. There's an antifungal in the paint as well, so you don't get mold inside them. I've seen some nasty cases, believe me," he added with relish, "where things have been locked up for years. You don't want that stuff coming after you."

Chowdhury didn't look amused. He pointed at a locker on the right-hand side. "That's it. That's Sasha's." For the first time, there was a hint of some emotion other than annoyance in his voice.

"Nice locks, too," said Kevin, nodding towards the combination locks fitted on the locker doors.

"How are you going to open it?" Sidana asked, wondering if he'd finesse the lock or just take the door off the hinges.

But Kevin reached into the satchel he carried over his shoulder and pulled out a pair of wrenches. "The hospital should have had a master key, but no one seems to be able to find it. So"—he grinned—"I get to work my magic." He placed a wrench on either side of the hasp and gave it a twist. The hasp snapped cleanly off and the lock popped open. "Easy as pie," he said with satisfaction, and for a moment Sidana envied him his job.

She was already pulling on her nitrile gloves as Kevin stowed his wrenches and gave her a jaunty salute. "At your service, ma'am. Call us anytime." Calling out a thank-you, she squeezed the latch and opened the locker door. She could sense Chowdhury hovering behind her, but then his pager buzzed and he followed the lock-smith out.

Sidana was glad to be able to concentrate on the locker. She hadn't seen Sasha Johnson's flat and she had no sense of the victim as a person.

Hanging from one of the locker's top hooks was a lightweight waterproof anorak in dark blue. Sasha had been wearing a heavier, more fitted coat with a fur-trimmed hood when she was killed. A second hook held a white doctor's coat on a hanger, a stethoscope draped over the neck in a creepily lifelike way. A third hook sported a haphazardly hung woolen scarf and a red bobble hat.

Sidana moved on to examine the floor of the locker. An old gray cardigan had been tossed carelessly on top of a pair of white train-ers, the shoes Sasha must have worn on the ward. Beside the shoes lay a clean and folded set of pale green scrubs. And beside them, a battered brown leather satchel. "Bingo," muttered Sidana as she pulled it free.

The contents, however, were disappointing. There was a light-weight laptop, which Sidana opened, just in case, but the battery had died and there was no power supply. Perhaps Sasha had left that in her flat. A makeup bag held the usual; lip gloss, mascara, blush, all good quality but not terribly expensive high-street brands. An unopened box of tampons. There was a small vial of paracetamol, but nothing that required a prescription. At the very bottom of the bag was an energy bar, past its sell-by date, and a withered apple.

Sidana sat back on her heels, considering. It was all evidence of a perfectly ordinary and unexceptional life, and Sidana thought there had to be more. Levering herself to her feet again, she started through the pockets of the hanging items. The anorak yielded nothing but an Oyster Card receipt dated six months previously, and a Kit Kat wrapper.

The left-hand cardigan pocket was empty. From the right-hand pocket, Sidana, happy to be wearing gloves, fished some used and balled-up tissues. Then she felt something crinkle under her fingers. There was a bit of paper beneath the tissues. It was crumpled as well, but as she pulled it out and smoothed it, she saw that someone had scrawled THIS HAS TO STOP across it in heavy black ink.

—

Once back at Holborn, Doug saw that he'd missed a call from Tully Gibbs. Telling Kincaid that he'd be up shortly, he found a quiet corner in reception and returned it.

"Oh, hi. Thanks for getting back to me," Tully said when he'd identified himself. "It's just that—I wondered if we could talk."

"Of course. Is there something you've remembered?"

Again there was a moment of hesitation, as if she regretted whatever impulse had led her to call. "No, it's just that I—look, can we speak in person?"

"Are you at the flat? I can come round."

"No. I mean, yes, I am, but I don't really want to talk here. It's just . . . it feels weird."

"Okay, how about we meet for a coffee?" He considered the place where he and Kincaid usually met, but decided that it was too small and too close to the station. Instead, he suggested a coffee shop nearer Guilford Street, Redemption Roasters.

The walk took him less than five minutes, but Tully was already waiting. She gave him a tremulous smile. "Thanks for coming."

The brassy sky of earlier in the afternoon had faded to a dull, purplish gray, and just as Doug looked up a fat raindrop splashed on the lens of his glasses. "Come on, let's get inside," he said, opening the door. An intoxicatingly fragrant waft of warm air met them. At the counter to the right, the big espresso machine rumbled and hissed in a comforting undertone.

Spying an empty table for two in the back, Doug guided Tully to it, then went back to the counter to place their orders. Once he had their coffees in hand, he slid into the seat opposite her. She'd taken off her coat and draped it over the back of her chair. He saw that while she was dressed much as she had been yesterday, in a plain jumper and dark trousers, today her clothing had a few splashes and smears of something light gray.

Following his gaze, Tully looked down and brushed ineffectually at her top. "Sorry. Clay. I dressed for work but ended up in the studio instead. I had on an apron, but sometimes . . ." She trailed off, looking around her. "Sasha liked this place, but I've never been in."

"Was this a bad choice?" Doug asked.

"Everything is a bad choice right now. But I have to start somewhere." She wrapped her hands around her cup, as she had the mug of tea he'd made her last night.

"This must be really difficult for you. Is there anywhere else you can stay for a few days? Maybe with your brother?"

"It's just a studio flat." With a ghost of a smile, she added, "And the only way you can live above a bar is to keep bar hours, which I can't do because of work."

"We spoke to your brother earlier."

"Already? But he—Was he okay?"

"He didn't seem terribly upset, if that's what you're asking." When he saw her eyes widen in surprise, he gave a rueful grimace. "I'm sorry. That was rude of me. I don't know your brother and I shouldn't have made assumptions."

"It's okay. Jon can be . . . a bit difficult to figure out sometimes."

"Do you think he had feelings for Sasha?"

Tully stared into the fern-shaped foam on the surface of her coffee. "I honestly don't know. I'd have said no. Sasha was so not his type." Looking up at him, she added, frowning, "Jon likes party girls, and Sasha's"—she swallowed—"Sasha was definitely not that."

Doug thought he needed to tread carefully. "You said you *would* have said no. Past tense. Did something make you change your mind?"

Tully rotated the coffee she still had not tasted. The espresso machine burbled. A tattooed young man dropped his backpack on the floor with a thump and scraped back a chair at the next table.

Doug thought about his boss, who had the knack of not filling the silences in an interview, and pressed his lips together, determined to wait out this awkward pause. At last, when he thought he couldn't bear the tension a moment longer, Tully sighed and said, "I thought I knew her. I thought we shared stuff, you know? But this afternoon, I found this." She opened the shoulder bag she'd kept cradled in her lap and pulled out a small clear baggie. "Why didn't she tell me?"

Doug had seen enough TV adverts to recognize a positive pregnancy test result when he saw it. "So she knew. We wondered if she did."

"You knew she was pregnant?" Tully said, surprised.

"From the postmortem. I'm sorry," he added, seeing Tully's wince of distress. "Can you tell me where you found this?"

"In the bin in the loo. Wrapped up. I only saw it when I was putting some tissues in myself."

"Any idea how long it had been there?"

Tully frowned. "We usually tidy up at the weekend, but if the bin gets full one of us will empty it. So I'd think not more than a couple of days. Is it important?"

"I don't know. At this stage of an investigation, anything might be."

"I told you she wasn't seeing anyone." Tully finally took a sip of her coffee, which Doug thought must be stone cold by now. "I feel a right idiot. Obviously she was, unless it was an immaculate conception."

"Or a sperm donor."

Tully nearly spat her coffee. "Seriously? Why on earth would she do that?"

He shrugged. "Maybe she wanted a child without the bother of a relationship." He thought of the Facebook photo of Sasha with her sister. "Maybe she was jealous of her sister's baby."

But Tully was already shaking her head. "Sasha had plans. Big plans. She wanted a different posting, a different hospital."

"Any idea why?"

"That charge nurse on her ward, for one thing. She'd worked with him before and he was a total shit."

"You mean Neel Chowdhury?"

Tully nodded. "That's him. I saw him once when I'd walked with Sasha to the hospital. She crossed the street to avoid him."

"Any idea what the problem was between them?"

Frowning, Tully sipped more coffee before continuing. "I got the impression that she blamed him for something that had gone wrong. And that maybe the feeling was mutual."

Doug made a mental note to add establishing Chowdhury's whereabouts at the time of Sasha's murder to his action list. Maybe Chowdhury's dislike had gone beyond making life difficult for Sasha on the ward. The man was a medical professional. He'd have known where to put in the blade.

But Doug had a hard time picturing Chowdhury's petty nastiness escalating to real violence. He also wondered if Chowdhury had the height and the upper body strength to deliver such a blow. "Was there anyone else Sasha didn't get on with?"

"I don't know. She said all the staff gossiped, and Chowdhury encouraged it."

"Was there anything different about her behavior recently?"

Again, Tully took her time answering, and Doug began to think that this was more than shock. Tully Gibbs didn't dive into anything without due consideration. "She had been home more lately," Tully said at last. "And I can see now that she must have been worried about something. I should have realized. We lived together." She looked at Doug expectantly. When he didn't seem to be following, she added, "Women tend to synchronize, you know?"

It took a moment for the light to dawn, then he felt himself color. "I didn't know that."

"So I should have realized when she didn't get her period," Tully went on. She slipped off her heavy-framed glasses and blew her nose on a napkin.

Pushing his empty coffee cup out of the way, Doug leaned forward earnestly. "Don't beat yourself up. We don't know that Sasha's pregnancy had anything to do with her murder."

"I hate that she didn't feel she could talk to me." Tully's gray eyes swam with unshed tears. "I might have helped. Somehow."

—

When Melody came out of the Yard into Victoria Embankment, a fine mist hung over the river, softening the outline of the London Eye on the far bank. Her head ached from too many hours spent staring at a screen, and a pang from her stomach reminded her that she'd skipped lunch. She decided that a walk and fresh air would do her good, so she turned left along the river, feeling her cramped muscles ease as she got into her stride.

With only the regular hum and swish of cars passing on the Embankment and the cold dampness against her face, Melody began to relax and consider the information she'd found.

When she reached Charing Cross, she grabbed a salad and a coffee at Pret a Manger. Feeling more human when she'd finished both, she'd pulled out her mobile to ring Gemma when the tabloid abandoned at the next table caught her eye.

The paper had been folded over at the entertainment section, and there, in a tiny photo, was a familiar face, an elfin young woman with short, spiky ginger hair. The caption read, *Overnight singing sensation Poppy Jones cancels tour dates to spend time with Oxfordshire family.*

Melody stared, then read it again. Andy wasn't mentioned at all.

CHAPTER TEN

The little black dress was too much. Jeans and jumper were not enough. The weather wasn't conducive to anything very skimpy. Gemma slid the hangers in the cupboard back and forth, hoping something perfect would jump out at her. It had been so long since she'd been out for a proper evening that she wasn't even sure what was fashionable. And she might be worrying for nothing, as she didn't know if Jasmine Sidana had agreed to Duncan's scheme. She was relieved when her mobile buzzed, delaying any momentous wardrobe decisions.

She'd been expecting an update from Duncan, but it was Melody's name on the screen.

"Hi, boss," said Melody when Gemma answered. "I'm not interrupting anything, am I?"

"Just wardrobe trauma." Gemma sat down on the bed and explained the plan for the evening. When she'd finished, Melody was silent a moment, then said, "I don't think Tully Gibbs will turn up. I could have come with you."

"Yes, but on the off chance—"

"And I don't imagine she'd recognize me even if she did."

Gemma very much doubted that anyone who'd met Melody Talbot was likely to overlook her on a second occasion. "I think you underestimate your impact," Gemma said mildly. "And Duncan agreed he'd organize it with Sidana."

"That should be interesting," Melody muttered.

"Not you, too," Gemma said, exasperated with Melody's negative tone. "I'll agree the woman isn't exactly warm and fuzzy, but she's good at her job. Which is what this evening is about."

"Sorry, boss."

"Are you okay?" Gemma asked. She could hear traffic noise in the background, and an occasional honk. "Where are you, anyway?"

"Charing Cross. And I'm fine. It's only—" Melody paused, then blurted, "I just saw something about Andy and Poppy in a stupid tabloid. It says Poppy canceled their winter tour dates. Do you think it's true?"

Oh, dear. Gemma debated how much to say. Should she repeat what Tam had told her? But if Melody had seen the news in a tabloid, Tam must have been the last to know, and he hadn't sworn her to secrecy. "I was at Louise's this morning," she said. "I heard Andy arguing with Tam. He told Tam they wanted to take a break from touring."

After a long moment, Melody said, "But the tour, the success—it was what he always wanted. Why would he give it up?"

"Listen, if you want to talk about it, come over for a coffee in the morning."

But Melody said, with sudden briskness, "No, no, I don't want to interrupt your weekend. Sorry to have bothered you."

Gemma had opened her mouth to protest when Melody added, "Oh, I almost forgot. I spent the morning at the Yard, going through knife-crime reports. Maybe it's nothing, but I found an odd case from about six months ago, in Paddington. A Dutch tourist was walking back to her hotel after dark when someone knocked into her."

"She was stabbed?"

"Yes. A pretty deep laceration to her side. She thought the assailant had been after her bag. By the time she realized she was injured, there was no sign of him."

"Him?"

"Well, not necessarily. She wasn't sure if the assailant was male or female. She only had an impression of a dark jacket and a hood or cap."

"And nothing stolen?"

"No. That's not saying it wasn't a failed robbery, however."

"True," agreed Gemma. "But we should check into it. Are there contact details for the victim?"

"Yes, in the file. She was treated at St. Mary's Paddington so we might be able to get an opinion as to the weapon used."

"I'd pass it on to Duncan, then. Let his team follow up on it."

"Any progress on their end?"

"I'm not really in the loop." Gemma glanced at the clock and swore. "Bugger. I've got to pick up Charlotte and Toby. But listen. If you're not busy in the morning, let's do that coffee. I'll fill you in on the club scene. And—" She hesitated, afraid she was overstepping Melody's boundaries, then plunged on, "if you're worried about Andy, why don't you just give him a ring?"

—

Kincaid studied the plastic-encased scrap of paper that Sidana had placed carefully on his desk. THIS HAS TO STOP, it read in all capitals, incised so sharply that in some places the paper was almost torn. "Stop what?" he wondered aloud. "Before we assume that this note was intended for Sasha, we'd better be certain she didn't write it herself."

"In that case, would she have left it in her locker?" asked Sidana, who sat on the edge of one of his two visitor's chairs. Outside the glass door of the office, the CID room hummed with activity.

"Maybe she wrote it, intending to give it to someone, but never had a chance."

Sidana looked thoughtful. "I suppose that's possible. Maybe someone was stalking her."

"Or bullying her. Or even blackmailing her," Kincaid suggested. "On the other hand—" He stopped, as there was a rap on his office door and Doug opened it a few inches. Kincaid motioned him in. "You need to see this, too." Doug took the other chair as Kincaid filled him in and handed him the note.

"What about Neel Chowdhury?" asked Sidana. "From his attitude today I'd say there was definitely no love lost between him and Sasha Johnson."

"That might be an understatement," put in Doug. "I've just come from meeting with Tully Gibbs. She says Sasha wanted to change jobs so that she wouldn't have to work with Chowdhury."

"Any idea what the problem was?" Kincaid asked.

"Tully said they had a mutual blame fest going over something that happened at work. But that's not all she told me. She found a positive pregnancy test in the bin in the flat. She says it couldn't have been there more than a day or two."

"If Sasha had just confirmed she was pregnant, that would fit with what Rashid—I mean Dr. Kaleem—found in the postmortem," said Sidana. "But it doesn't tell us whether that had any bearing on her death."

"It could just be coincidence," Kincaid agreed, "but I don't like coincidences. Jasmine, did you get an answer from Rashid on whether Sasha might have been previously assaulted?"

"Not yet. I left him a message this morning."

"Follow up if you don't hear back soon." He thought he caught an expression of discomfort on Sidana's face, which surprised him. Ordinarily, bulldog was her middle name.

But she merely said, "Right, guv," and made a note on her mobile. What was up with his DI today? He hoped the accommodating mood would extend to his suggestion for the evening, but before he broached that subject, he needed to line up other actions.

"Let's get back to this note. We need a sample of Sasha Johnson's handwriting before we go off half-cocked with theories. Doug, can you ask Ms. Gibbs if there's anything round the flat we can use for comparison? If you can turn up something, get it off for forensic handwriting analysis, and put a priority on it." He turned to Sidana. "Jasmine, light a fire under the techies. We need access to that laptop and her mobile phone. And get a full employment history from hospital administration. I want to know where and when she worked with Neel Chowdhury.

"But in the meantime," he added, "there's something else I'd like to follow up. Doug and I interviewed Tully Gibbs's brother, Jonathan, this afternoon, the bloke who was supposed to meet Sasha in the Perseverance. According to Tully, Sasha wanted to talk to him about her brother, who works part-time at Jon Gibbs's club."

"Gibbs says he doesn't know what Sasha wanted to discuss, and he was cagey about what Tyler Johnson actually does for him," broke in Doug.

"He also says that he forgot he was supposed to meet Sasha

for a drink," Kincaid continued, "in part because Tyler Johnson didn't show up for work and couldn't make a cash-and-carry run, which Gibbs then had to do himself. Before we interview Tyler Johnson, I'd like to get a feel for what is really going on at Gibbs's club."

"The thing is," Doug put in, "that he's seen both of us."

Sidana stared at them. "You have got to be absolutely taking the piss," she said, then gave a little bark of a laugh. "Are you telling me you want me to go undercover?"

—

He'd been certain that Jasmine Sidana would refuse, but when he'd explained what they had in mind, she'd merely said, "Tonight? You must think I don't have a life."

"I thought we should take advantage of the weekend—" he began, but she was already shaking her head.

"Don't panic. I can do it. I didn't have plans." After checking the location of the club, she added, "Tell Gemma I'll meet her outside Piccadilly Station Underground at a quarter to eight. We can walk over together. Or give me her number and I'll text her."

When she and Doug had both left his office, Kincaid glanced at the time and realized that if he was going to speak to Wes and Betty Howard, he was cutting it fine. He tidied his desk, grabbed his coat, and slipped out of the CID room before anyone caught him up.

He flagged a taxi in Theobalds Road. Less than half an hour later, the taxi trundled down Pembridge Road. It was already almost dark, the twilight accelerated by the overcast sky and intermittent drizzle. The market would be breaking down, and as they passed the end of Portobello Road he could see the throngs of shoppers heading back towards Notting Hill Gate. Light shone cheerfully from the big windows of the Sun in Splendour on the corner.

When the taxi reached Westbourne Park Road Kincaid got out, paid his fare, and stood gazing up at the multihued terraced houses. It seemed every other one was covered with scaffolding these days. But Betty Howard and her son, Wesley, had so far managed to hold on to their third-floor flat, which had been in Betty's family since her parents had emigrated from Trinidad. Betty and her late husband had raised their children here. The five girls were all on their own now and only Wesley, the youngest and only boy, still lived in the flat with Betty.

Glancing up, he saw that all the flat's windows were lit. With a last glance at his watch, he rang the bell.

Wesley's voice came over the intercom with a crackle. "Who is it?"

"It's Duncan. Can I come up?"

The street door lock buzzed and Kincaid released the latch. As he climbed up the steep and narrow stairwell, he wondered how the residents had ever got furniture up and down it. When he reached the top, the door was ajar, and it was Betty, not Wesley, who greeted him.

"You'd better come in," she said, stepping back. She was bare-headed, and Kincaid, accustomed to her usual cheerfully colored and patterned headscarves, was surprised to see that her short hair had gone quite white. Her eyes were red-rimmed, her lips pale and clamped together tightly.

Her grief hit him with a jolt.

"I'm sorry to disturb you without ringing ahead," he said, when Betty had taken his coat. "But I wanted to speak to you about

Sasha Johnson. Kit told us that you know the Johnsons well. I'm very sorry for your loss."

"Is it your case, then?" asked Betty. "We thought it might be." She rubbed her hands against her forearms in an agitated gesture. "Sasha was a good girl. Why would someone do such a terrible thing to her?"

"We don't know yet. But we will find out, I promise you. Have you spoken to her parents?"

"Just on the telephone. I'm making some food for them now."

"I'm sure they'll appreciate that. I spoke with them last night."

Betty looked at him closely. "It was you who had to break the news? That must have been hard." She sighed and shook her head. "You should sit. I'll make us some tea."

"Thank you, Betty. I could use a cup."

"Go on, then." She shooed him towards the sofa. "Take a load off while I put the kettle on. I know how you like it."

Settling into the down-filled cushions, Kincaid breathed a sigh of relief. The sofa was covered in a fine deep-plum cotton, a counterpoint to the bright colors in the rest of the sitting room. It was Betty's work, he was certain. Trained as an upholsterer under her father, she had a reputation for the quality of her pieces. Her sewing machine had pride of place under the sitting room's front window, and the room was filled with bolts of cloth in brilliant hues.

Kincaid was wondering why Wes hadn't appeared when Betty returned from the kitchen, carrying a tray with two bright yellow mugs and a plate of flapjack.

Nodding at the buttery oat bars, she said, "I made these for Dorothy and Peter, but there's more than enough.

Kincaid accepted gratefully. The flapjack was delicious, the tea strong and malty, and Betty, taking the pretty printed chair across from him, seemed pleased to see him eat.

"You're a good friend, Betty," he said when he'd finished all but the crumbs and settled back with his tea, "and I'm sure the Johnsons will appreciate your thoughtfulness."

She sighed again. "It'll not be much comfort to them. Nothing will. Losing any child that way would be hard enough, but Sasha—Sasha was their pride and joy."

"Have you known the family long?"

"Since Sasha and Wesley were in primary school. The Johnsons moved from Kentish Town when Peter was taken on as assistant head at the sixth form college. Dorothy transferred her counseling practice and they bought the flat in Elgin Road."

"So Wesley and Sasha were at school together?" Kincaid asked, resisting the urge to swipe up the flapjack crumbs with his finger.

Betty nodded. "Sasha was always the serious one even then, top of every year. It was an odd friendship, I suppose. Wes loves the neighborhood—Sash couldn't wait to get out of it. On to bigger and better things, you know." The sharpness in Betty's tone made Kincaid think that she hadn't viewed Sasha Johnson with unbridled adoration.

"I wanted to speak to Wes, too."

"He's on the telephone with Des. She rang just as you came in."

Destiny, Kincaid remembered, was Wesley's next older sister. "She was friends with Sasha as well?" he asked.

"They had their little group, the younger lot. They were the terrors at church, always in trouble for their noise."

"We were, weren't we?" said Wes, coming into the room. He nodded at Kincaid. "Did Kit speak to you?"

"He guessed your friend's murder might be my case. He was

worried about you. But I wanted to speak to you myself, to say how sorry I am for the loss of your friend."

"Sorry won't bring her back." Wes stopped just outside the grouping by the sofa and armchairs, rocking on the balls of his feet. "You must have some idea who did this."

"As I've just said to your mum, Wes, we are doing everything we can to find out who killed Sasha. I thought you might be able to help me."

"Wesley Howard, stop looming and sit down this minute," Betty snapped. "Where are your manners?"

Wes looked like he might retort, but then he dragged over a spare chair and sank down just on the edge of its seat. "Sorry, Mum. Sorry, Duncan."

"I know this is hard," Kincaid said. "Your mum says that you and Sasha were close." When Wesley nodded but didn't speak, Kincaid went on. "I wondered if you'd spoken to her recently. I thought you might know if she was having any problems."

This time Wes shook his head and cleared his throat. "I don't know. She hadn't really been speaking to anyone lately, not me, not my sisters." He frowned. "I thought maybe she was just busy, you know, with her training. I should have made more of an effort. If I'd—"

Kincaid cut him off. "Stop, Wes. You can't hold yourself responsible for what happened to Sasha. But you can tell me if you have any idea why she'd become withdrawn. Was she getting on all right with her family, for instance?"

Wes closed his eyes for a moment, then looked at his mother. "Mum, Des just spoke to Kayla. Sasha was pregnant."

"Oh Lord, no." Betty put a hand to her mouth. "That's dreadful. Poor Dorothy, poor Peter."

Wesley turned to Kincaid. "But you'll know that. Kayla said it was the police who told them."

"We learned that this morning, yes. Have you any idea who the father may have been?"

"No. And I'm not surprised she hadn't told her family after all the grief she gave Kayla when Kay got pregnant."

"She didn't approve of her sister having a baby?"

"Said she was wasting her life. Things hadn't been great between them since then."

"Were they close when they were younger?"

"Kayla worshiped the ground Sasha walked on. But I think it was always going to end in tears—you can't keep up that sort of adoration and live your own life."

"Surely Sasha had boyfriends before," Kincaid said, going back to the paternity issue. "Any of them still around?"

"There were a couple of boys at school. I don't know after that. She didn't share personal stuff, really."

Kincaid decided he was going to have to push a little harder. "What about her relationships with the rest of the family?" He caught the frown Betty gave her son. "Listen," he added gently. "I know they are your friends and you don't want to speak ill of them, especially in these circumstances. But—"

"I don't see how airing the Johnsons' dirty laundry can possibly help you find the person who did this," Betty protested. "It must have been someone completely mad."

Wesley sat forward, one heel bouncing against the carpet. "There's no point in not saying anything, Mum. I'm sure Duncan will get onto it sooner or later. And if *he* is involved in some way, wouldn't you want the police to know?"

"He?" Kincaid queried, catching Wesley's emphasis.

"Sasha's brother." Wesley grimaced. "Tyler."

"Dorothy's been frantic," Betty said with a sigh of resignation. "He hasn't been returning their calls about Sasha. Peter went to see him at his university housing today and it looked like he'd moved out. Apparently he hasn't done any of his coursework, either."

Kincaid was recalling the frightened look on Dorothy Johnson's face last night. It wasn't Sasha she'd been worried about. "Has he been in some sort of trouble?" Tyler Johnson didn't have a record, they'd checked. But that didn't mean he hadn't been warned for an offense.

"It's only a matter of time," said Wes. "I've seen some of the blokes he was hanging with round here, even when he was still at school. Then a month or so ago, I saw him one night in Soho. He was tricked out, trainers cost more than I make in a month." Wesley gave a disgusted snort. "Proper little gangster, I'm telling you. Got picked up by a blacked-out Range Rover."

"Did Sasha know he was into questionable stuff?" Kincaid asked.

"I tried to talk to her. She wasn't having it. Told me to mind my own business. That was the last time we spoke."

"Do you have any idea where Tyler was living?"

Wes shook his head. "No clue, man."

"Any names for these people he was hanging out with?"

Wes looked horrified. "No. And I don't want to know."

"Do you think these people would have hurt Sasha?" Kincaid asked.

Wesley shrugged. "Maybe. Maybe they meant to scare Ty for some reason."

"I don't suppose you remember the index number of the car that picked Tyler up?" Wes was a photographer; he had an eye for details.

"No. I did look, but the tag was muddy. I remember thinking it was odd for London on a dry day."

"Sasha's flatmate told us that Tyler was working part-time at a club in Soho. Know anything about that?"

"Tyler, working?" Wesley laughed. "Fat chance. But I can tell you that if Tyler has something to do with this place, it's bad news."

CHAPTER ELEVEN

Having decided to walk home from the Howards', Kincaid headed toward Portobello Road. It was fully dark now, the buskers had packed up, and only the muted strains of Sinatra drifting from the CD stall vied with the clang of vendors' awnings coming down and van doors slamming. The tarmac, slicked with moisture and iridescent ribbons of oil, glistened. A few straggling pedestrians raised umbrellas and risked the stallholders' ire by darting between the vans.

Kincaid skirted the overflowing rubbish bins, the detritus of a busy market day. As he neared Elgin Crescent, he caught another more pleasant scent—the lingering aroma of grilled meat and onions from the German sausage stall. Next Saturday, he thought, he and Gemma would bring the kids and grab lunch.

Of course, he might still be mired in this case, which he was liking less and less by the moment. After talking to Wesley, he wasn't thrilled at the idea of sending Gemma to poke around at

Jonathan Gibbs's club. They could investigate the club, and Tyler Johnson, through more legitimate means.

Reaching Otto's Café, he glanced in the window. The small place was busy and Kit, wearing a white apron over his jeans, was clearing tables. Kincaid suddenly realized he was seeing his son as a stranger might. Kit looked self-assured and confident, balancing stacks of plates and chatting to the patrons with a friendly smile. He looked, in fact, not like a boy at all, but like a young man, and a handsome one at that.

Kincaid had meant to stop in, but now he felt that the intrusion might not be welcome. He sent a text instead, saying he was passing if Kit was ready to go home. The answer was swift.

Helping Otto until closing.

Kincaid felt an unexpected sense of loss. But a moment later, his mobile dinged again.

But thanks, Dad. See you later, okay? A row of smile emojis followed.

He walked on with a lighter step.

When he reached home, Charlotte and the dogs greeted him with unalloyed delight. Tess and Geordie danced about his ankles and Charlotte threw herself at him with a squeal. He picked her up and she wrapped her arms and legs around him, clinging like a limpet.

"Oof," he said, giving her a kiss on the cheek. "You're so heavy today. Have you been eating rocks again?"

Charlotte giggled. "No, silly. People don't eat rocks."

"Chickens do. Maybe you're a chicken. I think I'll eat you up." He made snorting sounds and Charlotte shrieked happily until he put her down.

"Mummy says Nando's." Charlotte tugged at his hand. "We're going to eat chicken at Nando's and you're coming, too."

He was glad he hadn't disappointed her. "I am indeed." He looked up at the sound of a quick tread on the stairs.

"Hello, love," said Gemma, the heels of her boots clicking on the tile as she came into the hall. Peering past him, she added, "No Kit?"

"He's going to stay until closing. I'm sure he'll text." Kincaid stared at his wife. Her coppery hair was loose, brushing her shoulders, and she wore a silky, shoulder-baring black blouse with very tight jeans. Clearing his throat, he managed to croak, "You look lovely. New top?"

"MacKenzie loaned it to me. I have the feeling she didn't think my wardrobe was up to snuff. Which it isn't." She kissed him on the cheek, then rubbed the spot with her thumb. "Sorry. Lipstick."

Kincaid leaned in again to catch the scent of her favorite Jo Malone cologne, but she'd turned away to check over her handbag.

"I've told the kids you'll take them for chicken," she said, snapping the bag shut. "The restaurant will be choc-a-block, so be forewarned."

"Mummy, I want you to come, too." Charlotte's voice wobbled.

Gemma bent down to her. "I know you do, lovey. But you and Toby are having a very special date night with Dad. No mummies allowed. Now, give me a kiss, then go tell Toby to wash his hands and get ready."

Charlotte ran off and they could hear her climbing the stairs with great exaggerated stomps.

"It'll be fun," Gemma assured Kincaid, flashing him a grin as she turned to the coat rack. "And I'd better be off. The longer I stay, the more likely the meltdown."

"Gemma, wait." He'd been going to say he wasn't sure this evening was a good idea. But now that he'd seen the sparkle in her eyes, he put his chances of talking her out of it as highly unlikely.

Instead, he said, "I think you should be careful," and repeated what Wesley had told him. "If Wes is right, these people could be pretty ugly customers."

"All the more reason we should get an idea what's going on." She slipped into her good wool coat. It was the color of goldenrod and set off her hair to perfection. With a pointed glance over her shoulder, she added, "And I am a police officer, in case you've forgotten."

With that, she opened the door and stepped out, leaving Kincaid standing in the hall with only a swirl of damp, cold air.

—

When Kincaid and Sidana had left the incident room, Doug rang Tully Gibbs. He'd almost disconnected when she picked up, sounding out of breath.

"Tully? It's Doug Cullen here. Sorry to bother you again but something else has come up."

"It's okay. I'm in the studio. Had clay on my hands."

"That's too bad." Realizing how that sounded, he amended, "It's just that we need a sample of Sasha's handwriting and I was hoping there might be something in the flat."

"Oh. Well, I can have a look when I get—wait, hang on a sec." There was a clatter as she put her mobile down. He heard rustling, then Tully picked up the phone again. "I remembered I had something in my backpack. Sasha gave me a shopping list. I never minded picking things up for her if she was busy. Sometimes her shifts made it hard—Oh God, I just can't get used to it . . ." She sniffed, then after a moment she sighed and said, "Why do you need her handwriting?"

"Look, how about if I come round and pick up the note?" Doug patted his jacket pocket to make sure he had an evidence bag. "It won't take me fifteen minutes to get there. I'll explain then."

Ringing off, he left the station, walking quickly west on Theobalds Road. Night had fallen since he'd met Tully for coffee, and while the moisture in the air wasn't heavy enough to justify an umbrella, the drops beaded annoyingly on his glasses.

He was as good as his word, turning into Museum Street just shy of the fifteen minutes he'd estimated. When he reached the studio he stopped to dry his lenses with the handkerchief he kept in his pocket, then rang the bell. This time the door buzzed open immediately and he found Tully waiting for him at the open studio door, wiping her hands on a towel.

"Hi," she said. "I wasn't expecting to see you again so soon. I've put the kettle on." She looked younger, softer somehow, and it took him a moment to realize she wasn't wearing her heavy glasses. In place of the jumper and trousers she'd worn at the café, she was dressed in clay-spattered denim overalls with a blue striped fisherman's jersey beneath it.

"Thanks. I won't say no, but I hate barging in on your evening like this." He took off his damp jacket, hanging it on the hook Tully indicated by the door.

Tully turned her back to him as she filled mugs from the kettle. "It's not like I have anything else to—oh, shit." She swung round, clapping her hand to her mouth.

"What?" Doug asked, concerned. "Did you burn yourself?"

"No. It's just—that sounded horrible. Like I'm feeling sorry for myself when Sasha's—" She shook her head. "You must think me a self-centered cow."

"I think"—Doug crossed the room and took a mug from her—"that you've had a horrible experience and that you shouldn't be so hard on yourself."

Unlike the cheap, chipped china mugs he'd used to make tea in the studio the previous evening, the cups Tully had chosen were obviously her own work. They were rounded with comfortably shaped handles, and the ice-blue glaze ran down the sides of the mugs in a pattern that made him think incongruously of melting ice cream.

"Thanks." Tully leaned back against the sink, holding her own hot mug gingerly. "They must teach you tact in the police."

"My middle name. Tell me, what would you ordinarily have been doing on a Saturday night?"

"Actually, probably this." She waved a hand at the potter's wheel and the cluttered worktable. "That's not as sad as it sounds. I don't mind spending time on my own, at least not when I'm working. It's just me and the clay, you know?" One of the shoulder straps of her overalls slipped down as she gestured, but she didn't bother pulling it up.

"Still, it doesn't seem like you should be on your own, after something like this." He didn't mention her brother. "You're not from London, are you?"

She gave a little eye roll. "And here I thought I'd conquered the West Country burr. I hate sounding like something out of *The Hobbit*."

Doug laughed. "You don't. And I like it. There's a softness to it that you don't hear in London. Where in the West Country?"

"Somerset. Near Glastonbury, so you can add weird Wiccans to the Hobbits. Anyway," Tully went on with a shrug, "I'm not a total social disaster. I do go out with friends. And if Sasha isn't"— she winced—"wasn't working, we'd have a meal, maybe watch a film or something. Although lately . . ." She frowned. "I guess we hadn't done that in a while. It seems obvious now, that she was seeing someone. But why didn't she tell me?"

"Did she normally share personal stuff?"

Tully considered. "She was never . . . effusive, I guess you would say, about her life. Kept herself to herself, you know? But she was a good friend, supportive if you needed a boost or had a problem."

Deciding to probe a bit more, Doug said, "So how'd you end up in London, you and your brother?"

"I came for uni. UCL. I did a BA in fine arts at the Slade. But I wasn't quite eighteen when I came up and Jon didn't think I should be on my own." Her lips quirked in an affectionate grimace. "Cramped my style a bit, I can tell you, having big brother checking up on me."

"What about your parents, then?"

Tully's smile vanished. "Our dad left when I was little. I've no idea what happened to him. Mum died when I was sixteen. Cancer. So Jon considers himself in loco parentis."

"Oh, I'm sorry about your mum. That must have been tough." More than tough, Doug thought. Had he been underestimating Tully Gibbs? It must have taken real gumption to get into a good degree program after such a loss—not to mention a great deal of talent.

He realized that of the two women, he'd assumed Sasha was the driven one. He hadn't considered that Tully might be a serious artist, with real credentials, and as determined in her own goals as Sasha had been in hers. He looked round with more interest at the finished and unfinished pieces in the studio. "So is this what you want to do, full-time?"

"Play in the mud, you mean?" Tully said, her tone sharp. "You think grown-ups should aspire to something more important?"

"No, no, of course not, it's just that with your degree, and working at the British Museum—"

"I should be more interested in cataloging ancient Chinese porcelain than in making coffee mugs? Let me tell you something." She jabbed a finger at him for emphasis, her cheeks flushing. "My mum worked in an insurance office her whole adult life. She was a responsible person. She had two kids to support and a mortgage to pay.

"But what she really wanted to do was paint, and there was never enough time. What do you think she regretted, those last months?" Without giving Doug a chance to respond, she continued, "Well, that's not going to happen to me, I can promise you." She sloshed the dregs of her tea in the sink. "Let me get you that note." Tully swiped up her glasses from the kitchen worktop, shoving them into place with a forefinger.

Doug followed her to the cluttered worktable, wondering if he should apologize. Then he stopped, staring, as he saw what she must have been working on when he'd interrupted her. A clay head, smaller than the palm of his hand, sat on truncated bare shoulders. It was so lifelike that for a moment he was unnerved. Then he remembered where he'd seen something similar—the dolls on the shelf in Tully and Sasha's flat.

But while those dolls had been odd, he didn't remember that they had been grotesque. This doll was different. Its hair sprang out from its head in a halo of tiny twists. The eyes were wide and staring, the nostrils flared, the mouth stretched in what might have been a scream.

"Christ," he said. "Is that Sasha?"

"I couldn't stop thinking about what it must have been like for her." Tully reached towards the head, then drew her hand back.

"Those dolls in your flat." Doug frowned in an effort to better recall the small faces. "Are they all like this? A sort of therapy?"

"No. Most are just drawn from interesting faces I've seen. This was . . . different."

"I thought you made pots and bowls and things." He gestured towards the potter's wheel with the mug he still held.

"Oh, I do. But that's thrown pottery. This is a different technique, hand building. It makes for a nice change, and they sell well in the gallery."

Doug couldn't imagine wanting a doll like this staring at him in his house. Forcing his eyes away from the agonized visage, he saw that Tully had retrieved a folded scrap of paper from the worktable. "Is that Sasha's list?"

"You still haven't said why you wanted it."

"We found a note in Sasha's work locker. We'd like to know if it was written to her, or by her."

"What sort of note?"

He considered showing Tully a copy. But he hadn't cleared it with Kincaid, and he didn't want to be subject to the sort of dressing down Sidana had got earlier. Better to err on the side of caution. "We're not certain yet."

He took the paper Tully handed him by its edge. It was just what she'd said, a scrawled shopping list. *Oat milk, tofu, teabags, loo roll, apples.* It might have been torn from a generic scratch pad. The writing was a messy cursive, and if asked to hazard a guess as to whether the same hand had printed the locker note, he'd say no.

He'd slipped the list into an evidence envelope when a door on the gallery side of the room banged open, making him jump. A tall, sandy-haired man looked in at them.

"Tully. What are you doing here? I thought you were off home for the day."

"I couldn't bear the flat," said Tully, then added as the man looked at Doug, "David, this is Detective Sergeant Cullen. He's investigating Sasha's . . ." She stopped, shaking her head. "Anyway, Doug—Detective Cullen—this is David Pope. He owns the gallery."

Doug had stepped round the end of the worktable, intending to offer his hand, but Pope's gaze had fixed on the clay head. "Ah, a new piece, good." Coming into the room, he reached out and ran a finger over the little clay cheek. Tully flinched but he didn't seem to notice. "Nearly dry, too. As soon as it's glazed and fired, I'll have a buyer for it."

"No," said Tully.

Pope looked up at her. "What do you mean, no?"

"I mean no," she said, her voice rising. "It's personal. I didn't make this for anyone else."

"But it's perfect. Really exceptional work. A collector will—"

"I don't care. I said it's not for sale." Tully took a gulping breath. "Not at any price."

CHAPTER TWELVE

Melody stood at the living-room window in her flat, gazing down at the market stragglers meandering along Portobello Road towards Notting Hill Gate. She hadn't changed from the run she'd taken to try to clear her head, and she could feel sweat still trickling down either side of her spine.

Her view was one of the things she'd always loved about her flat. The building faced on Kensington Park Road, but her flat overlooked Portobello. Tonight, however, watching a couple go by laden with shopping, she felt as if everyone had someplace to be, and someone to be with—except her. The highlight of her evening would likely be a takeaway, a bottle of wine, and *Strictly Come Dancing*. Seriously pathetic.

She glanced at the mobile phone on the kitchen table. Gemma's words echoed in her head.

If you're worried about Andy, why don't you just give him a ring?

But Andy had made it clear he didn't want contact with her.

She could understand that, she knew she'd been stupidly in the wrong—but she couldn't understand why he was suddenly giving up his tour with Poppy. What had happened? Why would Andy walk away from the life he'd always dreamed of?

Slowly, she crossed to the kitchen table. Her fingers hovered over the mobile, then touched the screen. But when the contact opened and Andy's face appeared, she froze.

Shaking her head, she tapped the contact closed and opened another.

—

The damp and chilly weather had done nothing to discourage the throng gathered round the statue of Eros in Piccadilly Circus. Gemma stood on the monument steps, nudging burger wrappers and crumpled paper cups out of the way with the toe of her boot. She hoped the girls in matching sparkly T-shirts who were snapping giggling selfies didn't fall over backwards and do themselves an injury. All she needed was a hen party gone wrong.

Standing on tiptoe, she scanned the crowd, her gaze passing over a dark-haired woman in a pretty scarf crossing Regent Street. Then she did a double take. That curve of dark hair fell across a familiar cheek. She'd never seen Sidana with her shoulder-length hair loose, and the transformation was dramatic. "Jasmine," she called, and waved as she started down the steps. "Over here."

When they met at the bottom of the steps, Sidana gave her a brisk nod and Gemma felt surprisingly reassured. At least she knew the detective hadn't undergone a personality transplant.

"Gemma." Sidana gave her an assessing look as they fell into step and started up Shaftesbury Avenue. "Nice coat. That's a good touch."

"I've no idea what one wears to go clubbing these days." Gemma could see that Sidana wore makeup as well, expertly applied. "You look great."

"Thanks. I thought it important to look the part," Sidana said. "I rang but they don't take bookings, so we'll hope we can get in."

"I suspect it's early for the usual punters," Gemma ventured as they turned into Great Windmill Street. Music and laughter drifted from the roof garden at Ham Yard, the boutique hotel. The anticipation she'd felt earlier was fast turning to a flutter of nervousness. "My hair's frizzing, I can feel it," she muttered. "They're going to think I'm someone's granny."

Sidana laughed, a throaty chuckle. "Don't worry. Just imagine you've gone all Pre-Raphaelite. I envy you that. My hair won't hold a curl to save its life."

Gemma's shock at the girl talk got them all the way to the Archer Street address. She looked up, taking in the discreet font of the bar's name on the frontage and the welcoming glow of the windows. Candles flickered inside and she could just make out small groupings of tables.

"Not a dive then," said Sidana. "Good. We won't be overdressed." She touched Gemma's arm. "We should have a story. Old schoolmates?"

"Haven't seen each other in yonks," Gemma agreed. "Leyton Comprehensive."

"What do you do?"

Gemma thought a moment. "Hairdresser. And God forbid I turn into my sister."

"I'll be a dentist, then," said Sidana, with a wicked grin. "And you'd better hope I don't turn into mine." She pulled open one of the double doors and motioned for Gemma to precede her.

They stepped into a small foyer with a row of coat hooks ranged across the back. Gemma had serious reservations about leaving her expensive coat in such an accessible area, but she slipped it off and tucked it behind a faux-fur jacket while Sidana hung her raincoat up as well. Sidana, Gemma saw, wore silky, wide-legged black trousers and a fitted top in a brilliant jewel green that set off her glossy dark hair. She looked stunning.

"Ready?" Sidana murmured. When Gemma nodded, they stepped into the club proper. Gemma took in the clusters of small gray velvet sofas and matching armchairs, the marble-topped tables, the warm lighting. Before she could get a good look at the other patrons, a young man advanced towards them.

Tall and slender, he moved with practiced ease between the tables. His slightly elongated features made his good looks more interesting. The smile he gave them, however, did not reach his eyes.

"Ladies. Welcome." The greeting seemed oddly formal from a man wearing a simple white shirt with the cuffs rolled back. "If you'll give me your name, I'll see if your table is ready."

Sidana looked taken aback. "Our table?"

He frowned. "You do have a booking?"

"I rang earlier," said Sidana. "The woman I spoke to said we didn't need to book, that you wouldn't be busy this early."

Their host, whom she assumed was Jonathan Gibbs, cast an annoyed glance towards the bar, where a young Black woman with hair in elaborate coils was energetically shaking a cocktail. "That will have been Trudy," he said. "She thinks reservations are an elitist tool."

Gemma laughed, as she was meant to. "And what do you think?" she asked.

"I think I don't like disappointed patrons. I'm Jon, by the way," he added, holding out a hand to Gemma, then Sidana. "And while disappointed patrons will be inevitable later on, I think I can find you a spot now. Do you mind sitting in the window?" He gestured to a small table at the very front of the room, which offered a clear view of the foyer and to Gemma's relief, her coat. It would also get a draft every time the front door was opened, and that no doubt explained why it wasn't filled.

They accepted readily, and when they were seated he left to fetch menus. "Well, he's interesting," Sidana said quietly. "Strictly in a professional information-gathering sense, of course," she added, completely deadpan.

But Gemma was becoming accustomed to this unexpectedly mischievous side to Detective Inspector Jasmine Sidana. "Absolutely," she agreed. "Nothing to do with the cheekbones. It's essential that we investigate thoroughly."

Menus in hand, Jon Gibbs stopped for a whispered word with the young woman behind the bar, but if he was berating her she merely rolled her eyes and went on with her precisely executed pour.

"Take your time, ladies," Gibbs told them when he returned. "If you have any questions, Marie or I will be happy to answer them." His gesture indicated the tiny blonde who was serving a table of four young women who didn't look much above drinking age. Most of the other patrons looked young as well, closer to twenty than thirty.

"I feel ancient," Gemma muttered to Sidana. "And that bunch should be out at a rave, not sipping cocktails."

"It's early, as Mr. Gibbs said. Who knows what they'll get up to later?"

Gemma looked down at her menu and gasped. "Bloody hell. How can they"—she flapped a hand in the general direction of the other tables—"possibly afford this stuff?"

"City jobs. Trust funds," hazarded Sidana. "Or maybe they just still live at home." Her tone was oddly mocking. "We'd better order."

Charming line drawings of cocktails were sprinkled among the exotic menu items. "What on earth is *forced carrot*?" Gemma asked. "And why is it in a drink?"

Sidana was frowning over her own menu. "That sounds more appealing than *falernum*. Look, here's one with vodka and tea, which doesn't sound too bad until they add cream and prosecco."

Gibbs materialized beside their table. "Any questions, ladies?"

Gemma was not about to risk total humiliation. "I'll have this one." She tapped the menu with her fingertip. "With the gin."

"A good choice." He turned to Sidana. "And what can I get you?"

"I'll have the Compton," she said, with breezy confidence. "How could I resist?"

It was, Gemma saw, the most expensive drink on the menu.

Gibbs smiled as if he meant it this time. "Very appropriate. And it's our most popular drink. A celebration of the neighborhood. Something to nibble?"

"Give us a few more minutes." Sidana flipped her menu over and Gemma realized there was more on the other side.

"I'll start your drinks." With a nod, Gibbs left them to it.

"We'd better get something to soak these drinks up," Sidana murmured. "There aren't any handy potted plants to help us out. What?" she added, catching Gemma's expression. "Did you think I didn't drink? I am vegetarian, though, so that makes the food an easy choice." She set the menu aside.

There were only two entrees, a meat and cheese charcuterie plate, and a vegan charcuterie plate. Gemma shrugged and said, "I'll have the other one, then. And we'll hope for lots of bread for sopping."

Marie, the blond waitress, brought their drinks and took their food orders. The gin drink was on ice, garnished with a wedge of grilled pineapple and a sprig of fresh basil, while Sidana's cognac-based cocktail came in a coupe, with a paper-thin sliver of lemon floating atop the amber liquid.

"Well, cheers." Sidana lifted her glass and Gemma followed suit.

"Cheers." Gemma took a tentative sip, her eyes widening as the gin hit the back of her throat. She coughed. "They don't skimp on the alcohol, that's for sure."

"Good thing we're not driving," Sidana said, her eyes widening as she tasted hers.

"Do you do this sort of thing often? Clubs or cocktail bars, I mean."

"Not often, no." Sidana gave a rueful shrug. "To be honest, my idea of excitement these days tends to be meeting one of my sisters for a glass of wine."

"Sisters? You have more than one?"

"For my sins. A dentist, a neurologist, and a cardiologist. I'm the black sheep. And the youngest. What about you?"

"One sister. The hairdresser. I suppose you could say I'm the black sheep as well. My parents don't approve of the job."

"And I'm the disappointment to an entire clan of doctors. And the dentist." Sidana took a bigger sip of her drink. "Cheers to black sheep."

"I'll drink to that." Gemma felt a warm glow beginning in her middle. "So, where did you grow up, with your multitude of sisters?"

"Hounslow, of course, the heart of the Indian diaspora." Sidana smiled. "When I first moved away, I'd wake in a panic at four in the morning imagining some worldwide disaster because I couldn't hear the morning jets coming into Heathrow."

"You get on with your sisters, I take it?"

"Most of the time. What about you?"

Gemma sighed. "Not so much, unfortunately."

"Your sister's younger?" When Gemma nodded, Sidana said, "Maybe she's jealous."

Frowning, Gemma considered this. "I can't imagine why."

"Can't you?" Sidana's glance was quizzical.

Before Gemma could work this out, the lights noticeably dimmed. While they'd been talking the music had grown louder, as had the hum of conversation in the room. There were no empty tables now, and both Gibbs and Marie were busy serving. Another bartender had joined Trudy and their cocktail shakers danced up and down in sync. There was a definite buzz in the atmosphere now.

"Things are heating up, I think." Gemma scanned the room. None of the new patrons fit the description Kincaid had given her of Tyler Johnson.

Turning back to her companion, she said, "Is that where you live now? Hounslow?"

Jasmine Sidana gazed into her drink, running her fingertip along the edge of the coupe. When she looked up, all traces of mischievousness had vanished. "Promise me you won't go sharing with *him*." It was clear from the emphasis that she meant Kincaid. "Or anyone else on my team."

"Okay," said Gemma slowly, hoping she wasn't putting herself in an awkward position. "Sure."

Sidana took a breath, blew it out. "I do still live in Hounslow. I live in the house I grew up in, with my parents. And my granny." Gemma's face must have shown her surprise, because Sidana went on. "Oh, I haven't always. I had a flat in Earl's Court for a good few years. Lovely place." She shrugged. "Anyway, some things . . .

happened. Long story. I moved back home for a bit and"—she shrugged—"I'm still there."

Cradling her drink, she sat back in her chair. "Now you can tell me how you ended up in Notting Hill. That's a pretty posh address for a girl from Leyton."

"Oh, that's a long story, too." Gemma took refuge in her gin for a moment, then added with a sigh, "I'd rather not think about it, to tell you the truth. It makes me feel very . . . precarious." She was saved from further revelations by the arrival of Jonathan Gibbs with their food.

The platters were stunning, the food composed as artistically as paint on canvas. Sidana's vegetarian array was particularly jewel-like, and there was bread as well, a sliced artisan loaf that gave off an enticing aroma. Kit would be in heaven, Gemma thought.

Wanting to keep Gibbs's attention, she said, "This looks amazing. But I wondered why you don't do any hot food."

"Kitchen's small, for one thing. Our chef makes the pickles, relishes, and garnishes in-house. Everything else we source from local producers. We want the focus on the drinks."

"They are brilliant," Gemma said, hoping flattery would get him to open up a bit more.

But Jon Gibbs merely cast a practiced eye at the level in their glasses and asked if they needed anything else. When they demurred, he gave them a pleasant nod and moved on.

"He thinks we're trying to chat him up," Gemma grumbled. "I feel an idiot."

Sidana nibbled on a glossy green olive. "Well, we are, just not in the way he thinks. And I'm sure he's accustomed to it."

"That doesn't make me feel any less like an awkward sixth former. I don't think I'm cut out for this undercover lark. While you, on the other hand, are bloody good at it. Have you ever done it for real?"

"No. But I've thought about it. What it must be like to get completely out of your life. But I suspect that if it came down to it, I'm not a big enough risk-taker," Sidana added with a sigh.

Gemma frowned at her. "Yet here you are. And you like it. I can tell."

"Not much risk here other than alcohol poisoning." Sidana finished her drink. "I'll just see if I can get Mr. Gibbs back with the drinks menu." But before she could catch Gibbs's eye, her mobile rang. She answered quickly, pressing her hand against her other ear to damp down the rising noise of the bar. "Hi. Thanks for getting back to me. Sorry about the din. The din," she repeated more loudly after a moment. "Hang on, can you?" With an apologetic glance at Gemma, she stood and went into the foyer.

Through the glass, Gemma watched her as she listened, occasionally nodding. Gemma assumed it was a work-related call, but when Sidana disconnected and returned to the table, she looked surprisingly pleased with herself.

"Is there a break in the case?" Gemma asked.

"Oh, no. That was Rash—Dr. Kaleem. I'd left him a message asking if there was anything that might suggest that"—she paused and leaned closer—"our victim might have suffered a previous sexual assault. But he says no, and that in any case any slight bruising or tearing would probably have healed by this time."

"So not even a positive negative." Gemma wondered if she was getting a tiny bit scrambled.

"Unfortunately." Sidana scanned the room until her gaze lit on Jonathan Gibbs. "If she was seeing him, why keep it a secret from his sister?"

"Assuming he's single."

Sidana glanced at Gemma, then gave an awkward little twitch of her shoulder. "Speaking of single, you're pretty good friends with Dr. Kaleem, right?"

"Rashid?" Gemma stared at her, perplexed. "We've worked together a good bit. He's a great guy."

"I would think he'd be quite a catch if he's not already attached. Nice-looking, good job. Although the cutting-up-bodies bit might be a little off-putting."

Gemma stared. "You're asking if Rashid is single?"

"Is that a crime?"

"But—" Gemma stopped. Jonathan Gibbs had appeared at their table and was regarding them with an amused expression.

"Ladies. How is everything?" When they'd assured him that everything was fine, he held out the menus again. "Another drink?"

Gemma saw that there were now half a dozen people waiting outside. If she and Sidana were going to stay, they were going to have to order something else. "Um, how about the milk-washed Ford's gin with Earl Grey, salt, and . . . biscuit?"

"A good choice." He was definitely amused now. She wondered if it was the buzz of the busy room that had relaxed him. "I can tell you know your gins."

Sidana got his attention with a full-wattage smile. "I think I need something a little less . . . intense . . . Can you make a suggestion?"

Moving to stand beside her, Gibbs ran a finger down her menu. "If you want to stick with the darker liquors, you could try the Irish whisky with sherry and chocolate bitters."

"Oh my." Sidana threw Gemma a slightly panicked glance, then shrugged. "I'll take your word for it, then."

"Coming right up." Gibbs gathered their menus and threaded his way towards the bar.

"You'd better tell your husband we had to take one for the team," Sidana murmured, rolling her eyes. "I'll expect a medal."

"I'm surprised they haven't thrown us out yet for not keeping our end up."

A high-pitched giggle came from a nearby table, where the four young women Gemma had noticed earlier had been downing cocktails faster than the staff could clear them. "And I'm not sure we're any further forward. Except that you've made a conquest."

Sidana's protest was interrupted by the entrance of three men. Gemma put them in their forties, older than most of the punters in the club, and the only group made up solely of men. Although they wore suits, there was a certain swagger to them that made Gemma's antennae quiver. "Interesting," she said to Sidana, whose back was to the door, and gave a little nod towards the group while keeping a bland smile in place.

"Not our person of interest?" Sidana said softly.

"Too old."

Marie ushered the men to a table near the bar, and as they passed the tipsy young women there was some jostling and more titters from the girls.

"I'm thinking someone needs to have a word with the management about overserving." Sidana glanced at the girls.

"Not us, not tonight, unfortunately," said Gemma. "Maybe we should pay our tab, be ready to pour those girls into a cab if we can. I don't like the idea of them—"

She looked up to find that Jon Gibbs had materialized at their table again, drinks in hand. "Ooh, lovely," she said, with what she hoped was an imitation of the neighboring table's giggles. Taking a little sip, she found that it was actually quite nice—and, she suspected, much stronger than it tasted. "Where do you get your ideas for these?" she asked, gazing up at him and all but batting her eye-lashes.

But Gibbs merely said, "It's all down to Trudy, and Manuel, our other bartender."

"What makes it foamy? Egg whites?"

"No. That could be a problem for our vegan patrons. We use something called aquafaba. It sounds fancy, but it's basically the liquid from tinned chickpeas."

"You don't say." As she widened her eyes in feigned astonish-ment, Gemma could feel Sidana smirking at her.

Jon Gibbs gave this inane comment the mere flicker of a smile it deserved. "Will there be anything else? Coffee?" His attention had already wandered to the foursome and Gemma wondered if he meant to ease them out as well.

Then a blast of cold, damp air hit them as the foyer door swung open and a young man pushed his way inside. Gemma's first thought was that he'd jumped the queue. Next, she registered the baggy, expensive-looking suit, worn with a tight T-shirt, the twists of hair so like his sister's, but tipped with blond, the almost too-pretty face. Then she heard the sharp intake of Jonathan Gibbs's breath and, glancing up, saw his contorted expression.

If looks could kill, Tyler Johnson would be dead.

CHAPTER THIRTEEN

"You're late," said Melody Talbot as Doug reached the table nearest the fire at the Jolly Gardeners, the pub just across the road from his house in Putney. She'd draped her coat over the second chair, a precaution against chair-snatching by other patrons. The place was heaving with Saturday-night punters, and he was surprised Melody had managed to get a table, much less keep it.

The pub, with its cheerful garden sheds in the forecourt and its comfortable, open interior, had been one of the unexpected benefits of his move into the small terraced house not far from the rowing clubs along Putney Reach. He ate here once or twice a week, usually with his laptop for company, when he couldn't face another microwavable ready-meal.

"Sorry," he said as Melody retrieved her coat and he slid into the vacated chair. "Train was delayed." He was still puffing a bit from his half jog across Putney Bridge and up the hill to Lacy

Road. Melody, he saw, was halfway down a glass of white wine, but before he could ask if she was ready for another, the waitress appeared at their table with a brimming pint for him and a sharable platter of the pub's signature halloumi fries.

Cocking an eyebrow at her, he said, "What's the occasion?"

"I thought you'd need sustenance. And I was starving."

He wondered why Melody was buttering him up. Still, he wasn't going to turn down a pint, especially after the day he'd had. He took a sip and had to resist the urge to smack his lips. "That's good. Thanks."

Melody, he thought as he examined her critically, looked as if she was the one who needed sustenance. Last night in Tully's flat she'd still been bundled into her coat and scarf, but now he could see that her face was too thin, and the jut of her collarbones showed beneath the soft knit of her cream-colored sweater.

"So what brings you to the wilds of Putney?" he asked, not quite managing to keep the edge from his voice.

Melody shrugged, a bit too casually. "I thought we should catch up."

"And you didn't think I might be busy on a Saturday night?"

"Well, were you?" When he didn't answer, she shook her head. "Seriously, Dougie, we're a couple of sad tossers, the pair of us, and we should just face up to it."

"Speak for yourself," he retorted, but her attitude worried him. He wondered how long she'd been waiting for him, and if this was only her first glass of wine.

"I've missed you, you know," she said, but without the expected trace of mockery, her gaze steady.

He was so taken aback that it was a moment before he could speak. "Well, I've been around," he finally managed, "and my social calendar is not usually packed. As you so kindly pointed out." Taking one of the hot cheese sticks gingerly, he searched for a neutral topic. "How's the new job?"

"I think it would be right up your alley. Collating reports, analyzing data patterns. Massaging strategic initiatives while prioritizing targets." She took a gulp of her wine while he tried to work out if he'd been complimented or insulted.

"But?"

Melody sighed. "I hate it. I never thought I'd miss Brixton, but I do. If this job is a step up the ladder, I'm not sure it's one I want to climb."

"Have you talked to Gemma?"

"No. She pushed for my transfer because I said that's what I wanted. I'd feel a right cow, throwing it back in her face."

Doug had the impression that Gemma had jumped at the chance to do a little actual policing tonight. "Maybe you should speak to her. Maybe she's not cut out to be a desk jockey either. At any rate, I'm sure she'd understand how you feel."

Melody's chin came up defensively. "I'll figure something out. In the meantime, you have a real knifing case, not just a bunch of statistics on knife crime."

"Get you another?" He nodded at her now-empty wineglass. "What are you drinking?"

"The Picpoul. Let's order while you're at it." She nibbled a bit more of the halloumi, then pushed the platter towards him to finish off. "I'll have the veggie-bowl thing."

"You just want to make me look bad," he teased as he stood, hoping to lighten the atmosphere.

When he returned with the drinks, she gave him an overly bright smile and said, "Ta. So is there any progress on your stabbing case? Gemma told me about her undercover outing tonight."

"There are more things we don't know the answer to, if you want to call that progress."

Melody sat forward, elbows on the table, face intent. "Such as?"

Doug began ticking things off on his fingers. "Why was Sasha Johnson so determined to talk to Gibbs? What did it have to do with her brother? Who was the father of her baby, since everyone swears she wasn't seeing anyone? Who——"

"Wait. She was pregnant?" Melody looked appalled. "Gemma didn't tell me that."

"Four to six weeks, according to Rashid. Also this morning her flatmate found a pregnancy test in their rubbish bin."

Frowning, Melody said, "That would explain the sudden urgent need to talk to Gibbs, if he was the father."

"He and his sister both say absolutely not, that there was nothing between them."

Melody took a sip of her wine while she thought about this. "Why so adamant on her part?" As their food arrived, she added, "Maybe Tully didn't want to share him."

"Bollocks," he protested. "I didn't get that impression at all. In fact——" He stopped suddenly. Was it a bit odd that Jonathan Gibbs had followed his sister to London when she'd taken up her university placement? Being an only child, he didn't really know what constituted normal sibling closeness. Nor, he reminded himself, did Melody.

"In fact, what?" she asked, still watching him.

He cracked the crisp batter on his fish and watched the steam rise. "In any case, that wouldn't explain the note."

"What note?"

"The one we found in her work locker." Pulling out his mobile, he showed her the photo of the scrap of paper. "We're checking it against her handwriting, just to make certain she was the recipient and not the writer. Then there's the possibility that she had some sort of history with the charge nurse on her ward, a fellow called Neel Chowdhury."

Raising an eyebrow, Melody said, "And you know this how?"

"Tully Gibbs said that Sasha almost didn't take the job when she found out she'd have to work with Chowdhury."

Melody pushed some of the charred broccoli around in her bowl. Then she put her fork down and looked at him very directly. "Doug. You do realize that except for the note, every single thing you think you know about this case has come from Tully Gibbs."

"But—"

"Have you got access to Sasha's mobile phone yet?"

"No, it's with Tech. But—"

"Has it occurred to you that the one person who knew Sasha would be walking across Russell Square at that moment was her flatmate?"

Doug stared at her, the chip on his fork forgotten. "You can't seriously be suggesting that Tully lured Sasha across the park so that she could stab her. That's bonkers. You didn't see her face when I told her Sasha was dead."

"You've never seen a good actor before?" Melody leaned forward again, knocking against her wineglass hard enough to send the liquid sloshing. "I know she's an artist, but those dolls in her flat look like little detached heads." She shuddered. "All I'm saying is, remember you're a cop. Don't let things get too personal."

But Doug recollected all too well how Melody had met Andy Monahan, in the midst of a case in which Andy had been a person of interest. Suddenly furious, he jabbed his fork at her. "You're a fine one to talk, Melody Talbot."

—

"Excuse me," Gibbs muttered, pushing past their table. But before he could reach Tyler Johnson, two couples who had been waiting in the queue piled in behind him.

"Hey, man, we were first," one of the men complained.

Tyler smiled at him. "Chill, mate. I'm staff," he said, and with a nod at Gibbs, slipped past and headed towards the bar. Gibbs had little choice but to deal with the punters jamming access to the front door.

By the time Gibbs had sent the couples back outside, Tyler was circulating through the room, backslapping or fist-bumping the men, cheek-kissing some of the women. A little ripple of interest followed him—as did more than a few admiring glances.

Sidana said, "Two pretty boys, then, Johnson and Gibbs. You'd think they'd get up each other's noses."

But Gemma had seen Johnson casting worried glances in Gibbs's direction. "I don't think Tyler is nearly as cool as he appears."

Tyler had almost reached the bar, but his path was blocked by a cluster of girls emerging from the toilet. Gibbs advanced towards him.

Gemma tensed. If there was a punch-up in the middle of the bar, they'd have to intervene. She slipped her mobile from her bag, ready to call 999 if things went pear-shaped.

Gibbs put a hand on Tyler's shoulder and shoved him against the bar, saying something Gemma couldn't make out. Heads began to turn and the people nearest the pair edged away. Tyler shook his head and held his hands up in a placating gesture, then winced as Gibbs appeared to tighten his grip.

"Okay, that's enough," murmured Gemma, starting to rise, but just then Trudy came round the bar and pushed in between the two men, shaking her head disapprovingly at Gibbs. She pulled Tyler into a hug, patting him on the back. Then Marie arrived from the kitchen, balancing three platters and shooting Gibbs a scowl.

Gibbs seemed to realize that everyone was staring. Slowly, he dropped his hands. Then he turned, slipped past Marie, and disappeared into the kitchen.

Gemma sat back, expelling a breath she hadn't realized she'd been holding. "Well, that was interesting."

"Not exactly what I'd call a sympathetic reception for a bloke who's just had his sister murdered," agreed Sidana.

"Why is Jon Gibbs so angry with him? Does he think Tyler had something to do with Sasha's death?"

"And why did Tyler show up here, when he should be at home with his family? If it were one of my sisters, I'd be—well, I don't even want to think about it."

"Shock takes people in different ways. But I think it's more than that." Gemma watched Tyler out of the corner of her eye. He was moving from table to table, chatting to the customers, making it impossible for Gibbs to confront him without making another scene. When he reached the four girls, he leaned down to whisper in the blonde's ear, brushing his fingers across her bare arm. She gazed up at him, laughing, but her eyes were unfocused. Tyler murmured something else, nodding towards the table with the three men. One of them raised a glass to her, miming a drink, then beckoned Marie as she passed his table.

"What the hell?" muttered Sidana. But Tyler had moved on, stopping at the next table, and now he was approaching them. By unspoken consent she and Gemma leaned closer together, raising their drinks, and Gemma laughed as though Sidana had just said something amusing.

Then Tyler Johnson was beside their table. "Ladies," he said, "how are you enjoying Bottle tonight? First time, yeah?"

"It's *won*-derful." Sidana flashed him the same blinding smile she'd given Jon Gibbs. "It's our new fave, isn't it, darling?" She clinked Gemma's glass with hers, sloshing most of what was left of her drink. Gemma wished she'd been quick-witted enough to do the same.

While Sidana was mopping up the spilled liquid with her napkin, Gemma turned to Tyler. "Such a cool place," she gushed. "Are you the manager?" It was over-the-top flattery. Even with the posh suit, Tyler Johnson didn't look old enough to be managing anything more high-end than a McDonald's.

But she saw the quick little puff of pride before he said, "Oh, no, I'm just a friend of the management. Let me get Trudy to make you something really special." He turned, and if Gemma hadn't seen his earlier moves, she might have thought he was signaling the bartender. But it was the unattached men he looked at, and she saw the slight shake of the head from the same bloke who had mimed a drink to the blond girl.

Tyler turned back to them. "I'll just send Marie over, yeah? You enjoy."

"Oh, but can't you at least give us a hint what's in the special drinks?" Gemma touched his arm before he could move away. He looked down at her, a tiny frown between his perfectly shaped eyebrows now, beads of moisture glistening at his hairline.

She caught it then, the rank smell of fear. The kid was terrified.

Sidana's eyes widened and Gemma realized Jon Gibbs had come up behind her. He scooped an arm round Tyler's shoulders in what might have been mistaken for a friendly gesture and steered him towards the door.

Gibbs had Tyler through the foyer and out onto the pavement before Gemma could take a breath. The street was empty. Apparently the impatient punters had given up, and she wondered if

Gibbs had waited to eject Tyler until there were no witnesses—or at least only her and Sidana.

Once outside, Gibbs pushed Tyler up against the wall beside the doors. "What the hell have you done?" Gemma heard him snarl. She couldn't make out Tyler's mumbled reply. Sidana leaned towards the window, but Gemma got up and slipped into the foyer. When the interior door closed, the cacophony of sound from the club was instantly muted.

Gibbs's voice carried clearly through the glass. "You little shit. I listened to her voicemail. What the hell did you get her into?"

"I didn't—" A thump rattled the doors, and Gemma caught a glimpse of Gibbs as he shoved Tyler again. She turned to her coat and began to dig through the pockets as if hunting for something.

"I only—" Tyler's voice rose on a sob. "I never meant—I didn't know who else to ask—"

"And what did you drag my club into? I've seen your mates in here before." There was another thump. "This is Soho—Do you think I don't know gangsters when I see them? If you got Sasha involved with them—"

"I didn't. I don't know what happened to Sasha, I swear."

"If you—"

The interior door swung open on a wave of noise. It was the four young women, one of whom—the blonde—looked decidedly green. She stumbled into Gemma and pawed at the coats.

"I'm going to be sick," she mumbled as she clutched the faux-rabbit jacket.

"Outside, love, outside," said another of the women, sounding reassuringly sober. "Get my coat, will you?" she snapped at the others as she hustled the blonde towards the outer doors. "And call an Uber."

Then, after a flurry of coats and a blast of chilly air, Gemma was alone in the foyer. When she peered out the glass doors, she saw Gibbs supporting the blonde as she vomited in the gutter. He had, she noted, managed to steer her away from the doorway.

Of Tyler Johnson there was no sign.

———

Kincaid lay full-length on the sitting-room sofa. The central heating had long since switched off but the black-and-white cat stretched across his thighs had kept him warm. Sid, the black cat Kincaid had adopted a few years earlier, glared at the interloper balefully from the top of the armchair.

Geordie lay on the floor beside the sofa, exactly where Kincaid's feet would go if he tried to stand up. "Surrounded by beasts," he muttered, scratching the cat under the chin, then checking his mobile phone once again just in case he had somehow missed a text from Gemma.

Having given up on the latest television crime drama, he picked up a novel about magic police in London that Kit had left on the coffee table. To his surprise, he found the actual policing portrayed in the book to be more accurate than anything he'd seen on the telly. But it was late and it had been a very long day. Soon, the book slipped from his fingers.

Then someone was shaking him and an icy hand touched his cheek. Starting awake, he found Gemma leaning over him, her fingers cold on his brow and a concerned expression on her face. "You were moaning in your sleep," she said. "Are you okay?"

He blinked, trying to focus as he sat up. "I was dreaming about ghosts." The cat was gone and his legs were cold. "What time is it? You didn't ring."

"Sorry. Jasmine and I were chatting in the cab."

This brought him wide awake. "Jasmine? You mean Sidana? What happened at the club?"

She pulled him to his feet and slipped her arms around him. She smelled faintly of alcohol, of rain and wet wool, and her eyes were bright. "Nothing that won't keep until the morning."

CHAPTER FOURTEEN

She'd been ringing their home number for a week. At first the calls had gone to voicemail. At the sound of his voice, she'd had to take deep breaths to steady her breathing. Waiting for a return call had been worse.

Then the message changed to "mailbox full." Her emails to him bounced. There was no landline to try calling—he'd had it disconnected before she'd left for Africa.

On day six, a message informed her that his mobile number was no longer in service. She was frantic now. There was no one else she could ask to check on her daughter. How could she explain what he was like to anyone? What she was afraid he'd done?

She'd thought that some time away might give her some perspective, that perhaps she'd see that she was blowing his behavior out of proportion, especially when she would be comparing her life to that of people truly in need.

But she had been wrong, and now she was frightened. She would have to go home, would have to face telling him she wanted

a separation—no, a divorce—and then she would have to face the
consequences.

—

A faint rattling sound gradually penetrated Kincaid's conscious-
ness. Blearily, he forced open one eye. The room was dark except
for the faint glow of the night light. Gemma lay with her back
pressed against his side, her shoulder bare where the duvet had
fallen away.

He lay, listening to her deep and regular breathing. The evening came back to him in little fragments. Gemma had been
tipsy—well, maybe more than tipsy—and he hadn't objected to
her lowered inhibitions. At all. Smiling, he rested one hand on
the curve of her hip and with the other adjusted the duvet so that
it covered her again. With a sigh, he sank back towards contented
sleep.

Then the rattling began again. No, not rattling, buzzing, like
an angry insect. This time he came fully awake, eyes wide. His
mobile, left facedown on the bedside table in his haste to get un-
dressed, was vibrating against the hard surface.

Swearing under his breath, he grabbed the phone and eased out
of bed. He swore again as the cold air in the bedroom puckered his
bare skin in a wave of gooseflesh. Reaching the bathroom in two
strides, he pulled the door closed and slipped, shivering, into his
dressing gown. Only then did he peer at the phone screen. It was
half past six. And every missed call said *Simon Gikas*. His heart
sank.

Sitting on the edge of the tub, he rang Simon back.

Simon picked up on the first ring. "Boss. Sorry to wake you at
such an ungodly hour on a Sunday morning."

"What's happened?"

"There's been another death, possibly a stabbing. Soho Square this time. An early morning dog walker noticed a man lying in the gutter and found him unresponsive. He called it in. Uniform is on the scene."

"ID?"

"I believe you interviewed him yesterday, at the hospital. A Neel Chowdhury. A mate at Westminster rang me when the name came up in their system. I'd put Chowdhury's name in HOLMES as a person of interest in the Johnson case."

Wide awake now, Kincaid surged to his feet. "Get Doug. And Sidana. Who's the pathologist on the rota?"

"I've rung Rashid."

"Good man." Kincaid rubbed his hand over his stubbly jaw. "I'll be there as soon as I can."

When he padded into the bedroom a few minutes later, he found Gemma just sitting up in bed. Switching on the bedside lamp, she pushed her tumbled hair from her face and blinked at him. "What's up, love? I heard the shower."

"Another death. This time in Soho."

"Not another young woman?"

"No, a man. The charge nurse on Sasha Johnson's ward, in fact. Doug and I interviewed him yesterday." He pulled on a cotton T-shirt, then a button-down, layering for warmth. "We meant to speak to him again today."

"Oh no. This is going to be bad, isn't it?"

"Undoubtedly." He sat on the bed while he knotted his tie. "Did you and Sidana learn anything last night?"

"Tyler Johnson showed up at the club. Jon Gibbs was furious with him—he seemed to think Tyler was somehow responsible for what happened to Sasha. And Tyler was frightened, but not of

Gibbs. There were some other men there and it looked like Tyler was setting up girls for them."

"Pimping?"

Gemma frowned and twisted her hair up, the duvet falling away from her breasts. "Not exactly. The girls were just ordinary punters, and drunk."

"Did they rumble you, Gibbs or Johnson?"

"Rumble?" Gemma snorted. "I thought that was something they did in *West Side Story*. But if you mean did either of them know we were cops, I'd say we were quite convincing as old friends having a girls' night out."

He shrugged into his tweed jacket. Soho Square was only a few blocks from the club in Archer Street. Was there a connection?

Their bedroom door creaked as Geordie pushed it open with his long nose. "I've got to go," he said to Gemma. "But here's someone to keep you company." He leaned across to give her a quick kiss, but lingered for a moment with his lips against hers, caught up in the memory of the night. Then he sighed and stood. "I'll ring you when I can."

—

London in the early hours of a Sunday morning seemed alien, a ghost city, the only traffic delivery vans. A strobe of blue lights lit the Tudoresque folly in the center of Soho Square as if it were a stage set. Kincaid could see that the gates of the small park were still locked.

Only a stone's throw from Oxford Street, the square provided an oasis for a stroll or a picnic lunch. The little hut at its heart actually dated from the '20s, built to mask the aboveground entrance to the Charing Cross Electricity Substation.

Rounding the square, Kincaid passed the Catholic church and eased his car into a parking space. A panda car, lights flashing, blocked access to the south side of the square, and a uniformed constable stood sentry in the street. Kincaid raised a hand in greeting and produced his warrant card.

"They'll be waiting for you, sir," said the constable, nodding towards the figures clustered between the park railings and a row of large black council rubbish bins.

Drawing nearer, Kincaid made out the one person not in uniform—Simon Gikas. His case manager was bundled into a waterproof anorak over an old university sweatshirt. His dark hair looked merely finger-combed and his chin sported a heavy, dark stubble.

"Guv. I thought someone should hold the fort other than the plods," said Simon, nodding towards the uniformed officers. "The others are on their way."

Soft gray daylight was seeping into the square now, providing enough illumination for Kincaid to see a dark shape on the ground between the black bins and the curb, but he didn't go any nearer. "Who reported the body?"

"A Mr. Quirk." Simon gestured towards one of the panda cars and Kincaid saw someone in the back. "I've asked him to wait for you. He tried to rouse what he thought was a drunk sleeping it off. When it was obvious there was no rousing to be done, he called 999."

"Another good Samaritan. Two in as many days."

"He said he was up for early Mass." Simon nodded at the church. "He lives nearby."

"Medics?" Kincaid asked.

"Been and gone. They disturbed the body as little as possible."

"What about cause of death?"

"There was a good bit of blood, but they didn't examine the wounds."

"We'll have to wait for Rashid, then," Kincaid said.

As if summoned, headlamps rounded the square and a car pulled in beside Kincaid's. A moment later Rashid Kaleem came loping around the corner, bag in hand. He looked as disheveled as Gikas. "I'd prefer my corpses at a more civilized hour," he said by way of greeting.

"Late night, Rashid?" Kincaid asked with a grin.

Rashid rolled his eyes. "Not doing anything pleasant, I'm afraid. Elderly neighbor fell and broke his hip." As he spoke, he pulled on his Tyvek suit, then added paper boots and a mask. He fitted a small headlamp over his hood, then slipped on his gloves. "Let's see what we've got, then."

Donning gloves and boots, Kincaid followed. As he stood near enough to observe without disturbing the scene, he was suddenly aware that his hands and feet were cold. The still, damp air magnified the odor of dog urine and of rotting rubbish from the bins. Beneath those, he caught the faint tang of blood and human excrement.

He could see now that Chowdhury lay on his side, his back against the center bin. Had he fallen or staggered there? Or had the paramedics moved him in order to get an ID? Using his phone torch, Kincaid examined the pavement, finding a few dark spots. "Is that blood?" he asked.

Rashid crouched down between the droplets and the body. "Spatter, possibly."

Kincaid saw nothing else on the pavement other than a few cigarette ends and an abandoned paper poppy.

"He's quite cold," Rashid said as he began his examination. "Rigor is well advanced. His clothing is damp but the ground beneath him is dry, so if there was a shower in the night that will help pinpoint time of death."

"I'll check," put in Gikas.

"From a preliminary look," Rashid continued, "I'd say he's been dead at least four hours, but probably not more than six or seven."

"After midnight, then," Kincaid said.

"Something's broken his glasses," Rashid added, loosening the twisted wire frames and placing them in an evidence bag. "Maybe from a struggle."

As the daylight increased, Kincaid could see that Chowdhury had been wearing some sort of dark waterproof coat over light-colored trousers.

Rashid eased back the coat, revealing the garment underneath. "This looks like a uniform tunic."

Frowning, Kincaid said, "What the hell was he doing in Soho in the middle of the night, still in uniform?"

"Drinking, for one thing. I can still smell the alcohol. Unless, of course, someone spilled it on him. I can tell you for certain once I've opened his stomach."

"I've got his wallet here." Slipping on gloves, Gikas removed it from an evidence bag and flipped it open. "The address on his driving license is listed as Dean Street, an upper number, so not too far from here. He could have been on his way home."

"We spoke to him at the hospital yesterday morning. Surely he can't have still been on duty near midnight last night," Kincaid said.

"There's a receipt stuck in here, folded over his credit card." Gikas smoothed out the paper. "From a place called Bottoms Up, just a couple of blocks from here. Must be one of the clubs that stays open into the wee hours."

Opening the victim's splotched tunic, Rashid said, "He's a bit of a mess, unlike your Russell Square victim." The pathologist's headlamp played over Chowdhury's exposed chest. "I think there are two wounds—punctures, not slashes. It's possible they were made by the same weapon, but the blows were not as cleanly executed." Rashid glanced up. "He didn't die straightaway."

Kincaid thought of Chowdhury lying alone in the cold gutter as his life drained away, and shook his head. "What about his hands?" he asked. "Any sign of defense wounds?"

"There's a smear of blood on his right index finger, but from the position of his hands, it's very likely his own." Chowdhury had clutched at his chest as he died, then, Kincaid thought.

"There's not much more I can do here." Rashid began packing things back into his bag. "I'll let you know as soon as he's ready for the table." A flash of lights heralded the arrival of the crime-scene van. "Ah, that's good timing," he added as he stood.

Kincaid turned at the sound of footsteps behind him.

"Boss," called Jasmine Sidana as she hurried towards him. "Sorry I'm late. My car wouldn't start this morning." She wore her customary dark trouser suit and looked even more pale and severe than usual. Hangover, Kincaid deduced. Then her face lit in a smile. Kincaid was so surprised that it was a moment before he realized the smile was not meant for him.

"Inspector," said Rashid. The pathologist had stepped away from the body, removing his mask and pushing back his hood. Only Rashid, Kincaid thought, could look dashing in a bunny suit.

"Dr. Kaleem," replied Sidana, all business again, but there was still a telltale crinkle at the corners of her eyes.

—

Doug arrived as Rashid departed. Like Sidana, he looked a bit hollow-eyed.

"Late night?" Kincaid asked, eying him. It seemed he had been the only one to spend a quiet evening.

"Not exactly," Doug mumbled, his lips pinched. He nodded towards the SOCOs now setting up around the body. "Simon said it was Chowdhury, the nurse. Is it true?"

Kincaid filled him in, then added, "We'll need to check out this club, but I don't expect we'll be able to find anyone about at this hour."

Simon looked up from his mobile phone. "I've just checked. The bar doesn't open until ten p.m., but I'll see if I can track down a contact you can speak to earlier."

"That at least gives us a window on Chowdhury's arrival at the place." Kincaid considered for a moment. "We'll need to start with the hospital staff this morning, but first, I want to see his flat." He'd had the keys, bagged and tagged, from the SOCOs, in the event that Chowdhury had lived alone.

His first instinct was to take Doug with him to the place on Dean Street. But he hadn't had a chance to get the full story of the previous evening from Sidana, and besides, it wouldn't hurt to mend fences after the bollocking he'd given her yesterday. "Doug, take one of the constables and see who you can roust at the hospital. Jasmine, I'd like you to come with me to check out Chowdhury's flat."

Before Doug could protest, a uniformed constable approached.

"Sir." She was young, fresh-faced, with red hair pulled back tightly beneath her cap. "It's the dog walker. He'd like a word."

"If you could take his details—"

"I have done, sir. He—Mr. Quirk—says he needs to speak to

the officer in charge." She took a breath. "And if I may say, sir, he's been waiting ages. He'd probably like a wee and some breakfast." Her accent was straight out of Bow Bells.

Kincaid smiled in spite of himself. "I suspect you're quite right. Tell him I'll speak to him in just a moment." Before she could turn away, he added, "What's your name, Constable?"

"Hawkins, sir. Emily Hawkins."

"Good job, PC Hawkins."

"Future commissioner, that one," Sidana said in his ear as the constable hurried away.

The dog walker in question had climbed out of the panda car and was peering at them from the far side of the SOCOs' cordon.

Kincaid approached with a smile. "Mr. Quirk, I'm Detective Superintendent Kincaid. It was good of you to stop to help this morning. I'm sorry the outcome wasn't better."

"The poor soul." Quirk's voice was tremulous, although Kincaid didn't put him much past his sixties. He was a small, neat man, his sandy hair going gray, and he wore a jacket and tie beneath his anorak.

"You were out early this morning," Kincaid said. "It must have been—"

"Just after six. I attend early Mass on a Sunday, and of course Wallace needs his walk first."

"Wallace?" Kincaid asked, then the light dawned as the scruffy brown terrier's ears pricked up at his name. "That's a big name for a small fellow." Kincaid bent down to give the dog his hand to sniff, then fondled his ears.

"After William, you know. Wallace is brave for his size."

"I don't doubt it. Mr. Quirk—"

"It was Wallace, you see. I'd have walked past, I think—one doesn't like to interfere." Quirk grimaced. "But Wallace was quite beside himself, whining and pulling at the lead. Of course, I thought it was someone who'd had too much to drink. But when I tried to rouse him, he was . . . cold. Quite cold. And—" Quirk stopped, tugging at the knot on his tie. Swallowing, he went on. "And when I saw his face, I realized that I knew him."

CHAPTER FIFTEEN

Kincaid had certainly not been expecting this revelation. "I think you'd better explain, Mr. Quirk."

"Oh, of course. I didn't mean I knew him as a friend. Not even as an acquaintance, really. It's just that he lives"—Quirk swallowed—"lived in my building. I only know his name from the bell plate. It's Chowdhury."

"Why didn't you tell us this sooner?"

"I—it was dark and he was—his face didn't look . . ." Quirk trailed off. "You'll think it ridiculous but I've never seen anyone dead before . . ." He gave a little apologetic shrug. "So I didn't want to look foolish, you see, if it was only someone with a resemblance. But the more I thought about it, and about Wallace being so determined to go to him, the more certain I felt."

"Did he like dogs?" Kincaid asked.

Quirk considered this. "No, I don't believe he did. He never stopped to speak to Wallace, and Wallace never met a stranger."

He glanced fondly down at his dog, who had settled down on the cold pavement as if ready for a nap, then looked back towards the SOCOs now setting up their blue-backed privacy shields around the body. "Was he—when I tried to rouse him, there was blood." Absently, he rubbed the fingers of his right hand with his left.

Kincaid wondered how much the man and his dog had contaminated the crime scene. "Mr. Quirk, I'm afraid my crime-scene officers will need to take some samples from you and from Wallace here." At Quirk's dismayed look, he hastened to add, "Don't worry, it won't be painful, and it will only take a moment. We'll need a signed statement from you as well, but we can send a constable round to your flat for that. You live in Dean Street, I take it?"

Nodding, Quirk gave him the address. "He—Mr. Chowdhury— is Flat 2. I'm the floor above."

"Does Chowdhury live alone?" Kincaid asked.

"As far as I know. I've not seen anyone else coming or going regularly. But—" Quirk broke off and Kincaid turned to see Sidana, accompanied by one of the scene techs, coming towards them.

"I think they're ready for you," Kincaid said. "Thanks for your help, Mr. Quirk. We may need to speak to you again."

—

A half hour later, having detoured via the Starbucks in Wardour Street, Kincaid and Sidana nursed their paper cups of coffee as they walked back towards Dean Street. It was too early for the street sweepers, and little eddies of rubbish had collected on the pavements. The narrow alleyway they'd cut through smelled so strongly of urine that Kincaid's eyes watered.

As they walked, Sidana gave Kincaid a brief—and he suspected edited—version of the previous evening. "I think Tyler Johnson is in some sort of serious trouble. Whether it has anything to do with his sister's murder, or with Chowdhury's killing, I don't know."

"We do know that Johnson was in Soho last night, thanks to you and Gemma. What time did he leave the bar?"

"Tennish, I think."

"What happened after Johnson left?"

"Gibbs came back into the club, looking like thunder. I thought he was going to speak to those men, but he got called to a table and by the time he was free, they'd left."

"And after that?"

"Gibbs disappeared into the back and the waitress presented us with the bill. It was leave or make a scene. We circled back an hour or so later, just to see if Johnson had come back. Gemma said she'd lost her mobile." Sidana smiled at the memory. "She was quite good. A proper damsel in distress. Unfortunately, the only audience was Marie, the waitress. No Gibbs, no Johnson."

Kincaid frowned. "What did you do in between?"

"We had a drink, so we could debrief. At the Soho Hotel, as a matter of fact." Sidana gestured towards the narrow mews entrance they'd just passed.

So, they had been just a few hundred yards from Soho Square and the site of Chowdhury's murder. He didn't like this at all. "You're sure you didn't see Gibbs or Johnson again?"

"Positive," Sidana said sharply. "I'd certainly have noticed. And if you're trying to place either of them at the murder scene, Rashid said Chowdhury was likely killed after midnight, by which time we were well tucked up at home."

Kincaid, checking the street numbers, saw that they had reached their destination. They were just shy of the Pizza Express and its renowned basement jazz club. There was a corner shop, a traditional pub specializing in pies, a newsagent's, and a hairdresser's—the last of which bore the street number on Chowdhury's ID.

Above the ground-level frontage rose three stories of a narrow building in brown brick, the white frames of its windows slightly chipped and peeling. It was certainly the least gentrified of its neighbors—one of the few not covered in the ubiquitous scaffolding of renovations.

Taking Chowdhury's keys from the evidence bag, he unlocked the main door. As they stepped in, he slipped on gloves before switching on the lights. The flooring was a mustard-patterned lino reminiscent of the '70s, the stair carpet a worn but serviceable jute.

When they reached the first floor, he said, "We'd better knock, in case Mr. Quirk was wrong about a flatmate."

Sidana rapped sharply on the door, but the only response was a muffled yip from above—Wallace the terrier, Kincaid assumed. "Hello! Anyone home?" she called out. After a beat of silence, she unlocked the door.

Once they were inside, Kincaid stopped, surveying the flat. It opened directly into a sitting room that faced the front of the building. Dust motes swam in a weak shaft of sunlight, but the rest of the room was shadowed. He found the light switch, and a ceiling fixture threw the room into sharp relief.

It took him a moment to sort the visual jumble of too much furniture in too little space, all of it seemingly brown. Two sofas faced each other with a long coffee table squeezed in between. Newspapers were spread across the coffee table, splattered with yellow stains from an empty takeaway container—curry, from the smell.

This, Kincaid had taken in in a glance. It was the rest of the room that held his attention. Cheap bookcases filled every available wall space. Their shelves were crammed, not with books but with pair after pair of china dogs. Two tables on the other side of the room were similarly filled. One dog lay faceup on the coffee table, its black painted eyes staring blindly at the ceiling.

"Good God," said Sidana, stepping forward to stand beside him. "What is all this rubbish?"

But Kincaid had moved to the nearest bookcase and was examining the figurines more closely. Some were chipped, or cracked and re-glued. The small faces had distinct personalities—even within a pair, there were minute differences. Most were King Charles spaniels, but at the end of one shelf Kincaid spied a pair of Dalmatians, rather crudely executed.

He turned back to Sidana. "Not rubbish, I think. These are Staffordshire, and I don't think they're reproductions. If I'm right, some of them"—he gestured towards the Dalmatians—"are worth a good bit."

—

Gemma fed Toby and Charlotte boiled eggs with toast soldiers, then bundled them into warm jackets and took them out into the communal garden. It was dry enough for a good game—fetch for the dogs and football for the kids, although who was chasing what got a bit confused. The exercise and the damp, chill air cleared the last of the hangover fog from her brain.

A half hour later, the children were red-cheeked and willing to go inside without too much protest. She lit the sitting-room fire, settling them with projects, then sat down at the dining-room table with her laptop and a pot of tea to tackle the work she'd neglected yesterday.

Kit slouched through on his way to the kitchen, hair tousled, and waved a hand in greeting. A murmur of voices told her that Charlotte had joined him, and soon there came the rhythmic sound of a knife on the chopping block. Gemma's eyes began to droop and her hands, poised over the keyboard, felt disconnected from her body.

The unmistakable scent of hot spices and frying onions woke her from an upright doze. She jerked awake, blinking. Her laptop screen was dark. How long had she been asleep? And what on earth were the kids cooking?

She carried her mug and the old Brown Betty teapot into the kitchen. Kit and Charlotte stood side by side in front of the Aga, Charlotte on her stepstool, stirring something in the big frying pan. "That smells heavenly," said Gemma, peering over their shoulders. "What is it?"

"Samosas," Charlotte answered, drawing out the middle syllable.

"Charlotte missed them," Kit explained. "That's the filling. Red onion, cauliflower, and peas." He was cutting sheets of filo pastry into little squares, ready to be filled with the mixture.

"We should do things like this more often, and you are a love to think of it," said Gemma. She gave his shoulder a squeeze and was about to ask what she could do to help when the doorbell rang.

"Expecting anyone?" she asked over the racket of the dogs barking, but Kit shook his head.

Frowning, Gemma walked to the door. Wesley Howard stood on the porch, hunched into a gray hoodie, his face absent his usual friendly smile. "Wes, come in," she said. "We were just in the kitchen."

"I don't mean to interrupt your Sunday. I just wanted a quick word."

Leading him into the hall, she said, "Let me put the kettle—"

But Wes was shaking his head. "I won't stop. I wondered if I could speak to Duncan."

"I'm so sorry, but he's not in. He was called out early this morning." She paused, then added, "I heard about your friend. I'm very sorry."

Wes just nodded, and she saw that he was trying to keep his composure. After a moment he swallowed and said, "Could you give Duncan a message for me?"

"Of course."

"I was a bit short yesterday when he came by the flat. I wanted to apologize."

"I'm sure he understands that. You and Sasha were close?"

He frowned. "We didn't see each other much these days. But she's always been in my life, and in my sisters', since we were kids. Lately, though . . ."

Gemma heard the hesitation, and waited.

After a moment, Wes went on. "But lately, I don't know. She'd been different since she took that last job. Distant. And a couple of months ago, my sister Des saw her in a restaurant in Covent Garden. She was with some guy, and they were obviously having a row. When she saw Des, she cut her dead. That was totally weird."

"I don't suppose Des gave you a description of the guy?"

"*Intense*, she said. That's not much help." Wes sniffed the air. "Is that Kit cooking?"

"He's making samosas. Are you sure you won't stay?"

"I promised my mum I'd go with her to the Johnsons'. I'd better dash. Tell Kit I'll see him tomorrow at the café, yeah?"

"Maybe Charlotte and I could stop and see your mum after we drop Toby at rehearsal this afternoon, if you think she'll be home then."

"We're only taking over some food. And she'd love to see you."

On impulse, Gemma reached out and gave Wes a brief hug. "You know we want to help in any way we can."

As she watched him walk away, hands in his pockets, she saw a familiar bright-blue car turn the corner from Lansdowne Road. It looked like Melody had taken her up on her invitation for a morning chat after all.

—

"Seriously?" Sidana stared at the little dogs in disbelief. "People pay for these?"

"Collectors do, apparently. Our antiques-dealer friend had a pair on his stall recently similar to those Dalmatians. He was asking a thousand pounds." Kincaid gestured round the room. "So if you put all of these together . . ."

Sidana turned in a circle, staring. "But these aren't displayed like a collection. They're just a jumble."

"Maybe he sold them on eBay," Kincaid suggested.

"Maybe." Sidana frowned. "But it feels like—I don't know— some kind of weird obsession. And if he was obsessive about one thing . . ."

"It certainly wasn't washing up," Kincaid said with a glance at the coffee table. He remembered the staff room at the hospital with its unwashed mugs and coffee rings.

He made a note to call Alex Dunn to see if he could arrange an appraisal of the Staffordshire dogs. Then they began a methodical search of the flat.

There was surprisingly little else of a personal nature. A flat-screen TV was squeezed into a space on top of one cabinet. There were no family photos, no diplomas, no artwork or souvenirs. The computer on a small desk in the bedroom was password-protected, so no joy there, and the post piled beside it seemed only the usual bills.

Chowdhury's clothes, other than uniforms, had been ordinary and not expensive. The only reading material seemed to have been the antiques catalogs beside the bed.

"No indication of next of kin?" Sidana asked when they met up again in the sitting room.

"None that I saw. At any rate, the hospital HR will have it. We'll see what Doug turns up there, and get forensics started on the computer."

"He didn't cook," Sidana said. "I can tell you that. There's nothing in the fridge and the freezer's packed with cheap ready meals. Oh, and there's no alcohol other than a couple of bottles of beer, so he wasn't a habitual drinker."

Kincaid considered this. "That makes it odder yet, the bar visit—assuming he was really as drunk as he smelled. We'll need Rashid to tell us that." He glanced at Sidana. "Do you want to take the postmortem?"

"Yes, of course," she said briskly. If he hadn't been looking he'd have missed the little twitch of satisfaction at the corner of her mouth.

"We're not much further forward until we know whether Chowdhury's wounds were caused by the same weapon used on Sasha Johnson," Kincaid said. "Then—" He stopped. There was a soft rap at the flat's door.

When Kincaid opened it, Mr. Quirk stood there, knuckles raised to knock again. "Ah, Mr. Kincaid. I hope I'm not interrupting, but I've remembered something." With obvious curiosity, he peered past Kincaid into Chowdhury's flat. "If you have a moment . . ."

Kincaid wasn't going to invite him in. "Why don't we come to you, Mr. Quirk, if it can wait a few minutes."

"Of course, of course." Quirk's quick nods reminded Kincaid of a bobbing bird. "I'll just put the kettle on, shall I?" With one last glance into the flat, he turned and retreated up the stairs with a surprisingly lively step for a man in carpet slippers.

"You go," said Sidana when Kincaid had closed the door. "I'll stay here and organize SOCOs."

"This shouldn't take long."

"Enjoy your tea," she called after him, and he heard the amusement in her voice.

—

He supposed he'd been expecting Quirk's flat to be fussy, but when he'd greeted Wallace the terrier, he gazed in at something very different indeed.

Light filled a sitting room that seemed airy despite its small size. The white walls held a series of bright, contemporary paintings, giving the space a gallery-like feel, and the furniture had been kept neutral so that it didn't distract from the art. The ceiling was higher than in Chowdhury's flat, and the kitchen had been opened up to the living area so that the spaces flowed together.

"Would you care for tea?" Quirk asked as he ushered Kincaid in. "I can make coffee if you prefer." But Kincaid saw that the glass-topped coffee table already held a teapot, two cups, and a plate of biscuits.

"Tea is fine," Kincaid said. "And thank you." He took the seat Quirk indicated on the porridge-colored sofa. Quirk sat in the opposing chair, and Wallace, after circling on a dog bed in the room's corner, sank down with a gusty sigh.

"A long morning for Wallace—and for you," Kincaid commented as Quirk poured a stream of deliciously malt-scented tea into deep, glossy blue cups. As Kincaid took his, he noticed that the coffee table also held some interior-design books and a stack of the *Radio Times*. Quirk was either an avid telly viewer or a devotee of Radio 4.

"I still can't quite believe it." Quirk wrapped thin fingers around his own steaming drink. It was an odd coincidence, Kincaid thought, that Chowdhury's body had been discovered by his nearest neighbor.

"Do have a biscuit," Quirk urged with a nod at a carefully arranged plate. "I make them myself."

Obliging, Kincaid was pleasantly surprised. The biscuits were ginger nut—dark, crunchy, and spicy enough to make his tongue tingle. "Are you always out so early, Mr. Quirk?"

"I don't sleep as well as I used to," Quirk said, "so we are out before daybreak most mornings. But not as early as on a Sunday. Wallace needs his walk before I go to Mass, you see." He sipped his tea, frowning. "I've seldom missed a Sunday Mass in twenty years. I imagine Father Donovan will be round to check I haven't been taken ill."

"Have you lived here twenty years, then?" Kincaid asked.

"Twenty-five, now. But I wasn't as regular at Mass the first few years. My work used to take me away from the city fairly regularly."

"What was that—your work?"

"I was with Sotheby's for more than thirty years, mostly doing estate appraisals."

Ah, Kincaid thought. No wonder Quirk had stared so curiously into Chowdhury's flat. "I suppose you know porcelain, then?"

"I mostly dealt in twentieth-century paintings." Quirk gestured at his walls. "As you can see, they're my passion, especially work by Winston Branch."

Kincaid wasn't familiar with the name, but if these paintings were an example, he liked the artist's work.

"You can't help but absorb a bit of everything, however, in the business," Quirk went on. "Were those really Staffordshire dogs I saw downstairs?"

Kincaid took another biscuit. "Yes. I'm certainly no expert, but I think some of them might be quite valuable. Had you any idea that your neighbor—I'm not sure 'collected' is the right word—"

Quirk shook his head. "I've seen some strange accumulations in my line of work, but I had no idea that Chowdhury had such an interest. Although"—Quirk tapped a finger against the side of his nose—"come to think of it, he did get regular packages."

"Did he have many visitors? Buyers, perhaps?"

"None that I ever saw. At least not until the other night. That's what I wanted to speak to you about."

Kincaid took out his small notebook. "Which night was this?"

"Not last night, and not the night before, so it must have been Thursday. Rather late. The ten o'clock news was just finishing so I was surprised when I heard the entry phone buzz. I looked out the window, but she must have already come inside the building."

"She? You're sure it was a woman?"

Quirk leaned forward, hands on his knees. "Oh yes. You see, I was just about to take Wallace out for his last little walk—half-ten, it would have been. That's our usual time. But when I opened the door I could hear a woman arguing with Chowdhury in the hall-way outside his door. I didn't want to intrude, so I went back inside until I heard the front door close."

"How long did you wait?"

Shrugging, Quirk said, "Five minutes, perhaps."

"This woman, did you see her when she left?"

Quirk turned his mug in his hands, then glanced towards the window. "I'd hate for you to think I'm a nosy parker. But I did just look. I didn't want to have an awkward moment on the stairs, and I wanted to make sure she had really gone."

"Of course. That's very understandable," Kincaid agreed. "Did you get a good look at Chowdhury's visitor?"

"No, I'm afraid not. She was walking away, so I never saw her face. But her hair was dark, curlyish. It was a damp night, and it sparkled in the light from the sodium lamps. I remember thinking she should pull up the hood of her anorak. It was one of those puffer jackets, with the fur trim."

CHAPTER SIXTEEN

"So you think it was Sasha Johnson who came calling here on Thursday night?" asked Sidana.

"From Mr. Quirk's description, it's certainly a possibility," Kincaid said. "It's too bad he didn't get a look at the woman's face." They were standing outside the Dean Street building, waiting to hand over the keys to the PC who would take charge of access for the SOCOs.

According to Quirk, he'd heard only two voices in the brief moment his door had been open, but he'd recognized Chowdhury's. "You could tell he was trying to keep his volume down," Quirk had recounted. "But he said something like, 'You can't just walk out and expect me to cover for you.' Then she said something I didn't catch, and he said, 'What about the supplies, then?' in a sneering kind of way."

"That's all?" Kincaid had asked.

Quirk had shrugged apologetically. "I was closing the door, but

I think she told him to leave her alone. Well, that's not exactly what she said," Quirk continued with a twinkle, "but you get the drift."

"What about CCTV?" Sidana asked when he'd filled her in.

"The bank at least will have a camera over the cashpoints, but it may not be close enough to give us anything useful," Kincaid said, surveying the street. "We'll have uniform check the other businesses once they're open." The smell of dough baking was already beginning to waft from Pizza Express, although it was at least an hour until opening time.

"If your Mr. Quirk is right about the conversation, and if it *was* Sasha, it sounds like Chowdhury was threatening her."

"That's a lot of ifs," Kincaid said. "Based on a description of her hair and coat, and a reference that might apply to a hospital ward. But if it was Sasha, something must have happened that day."

"What about the note in her locker?" Sidana asked. "Maybe he sent it—or gave it—to her."

"We haven't had a result from the handwriting expert yet. Until then, we can't be certain she didn't write it herself."

"Who writes a threatening note and carries it around in a pocket?" Sidana argued.

"Maybe she wrote it and changed her mind," Kincaid said, "although I agree it's unlikely. But if someone else wrote the note, what did they want her to stop? Could she have been taking some sort of hospital supplies? Not drugs, surely—they're too carefully monitored." He shook his head. None of it made sense.

"What if getting the note made her cry?" said Sidana. "That would explain the crumpled tissues in the same pocket. I keep thinking she'd just found out she was pregnant." She turned and looked up at Chowdhury's windows. "Let's just say that Sasha was here on Thursday night. Friday morning, she goes to work, and when she gets off, she texts Jon Gibbs and says she has to see him urgently about her brother. But what if it was really about the pregnancy test and he didn't want to admit it?"

Kincaid considered it. "He says they weren't an item."

"There are lots of reasons people hide relationships." There was something in her tone that made Kincaid give her a sharp glance, but she was focused on the small notebook she'd pulled from her jacket pocket.

A familiar silver Vauxhall nosed its way up Dean Street towards them. It was the pool car that Lucy McGillivray had driven on their Friday night visit to the Johnsons', and she was again behind the wheel. A uniformed constable occupied the passenger seat. As they climbed out of the car, McGillivray said, "Boss. I was on my way to the Johnsons' and thought I'd do chauffeur duty."

"Has Tyler Johnson come home?" he asked.

"Not by the time I clocked off last night. You can tell his parents are worried sick about him, on top of everything else." McGillivray's cluck of disapproval sounded very Scottish.

"Well, let me know right away if he does turn up, or if they hear from him. And if you can—gently—quiz the parents again about where he might be."

"I don't think they're very keen on having me there, but I'll give it a shot. Oh." She patted a pocket and fished out a scrap of paper. "I have a message for you from Simon. He says there's someone at the club—the one that was on the victim's receipt—that can talk to you this morning."

—

Doug Cullen had never been keen on hospitals, but since he'd broken his ankle last year, even a whiff of hospital smell made him queasy. Or maybe, he thought as he took the lift up to Chowdhury's ward, that was the hangover. His dinner with Melody at the Jolly Gardeners had not ended well, and when she left he'd propped up the pub bar until closing.

As the lift doors opened, he reached to straighten the tie he hadn't worn, then pushed his glasses up on his nose instead. He wished he'd stopped for a coffee.

Entering the ward, he saw a woman in a dark-blue tunic at the nurses' desk. She looked up with a frown. "Can I help you?"

Doug produced his warrant card as he approached the desk. "Detective Sergeant Doug Cullen, Holborn CID. I need to speak to whoever is in charge of the ward."

The woman's frown deepened. "That would be me. Allison Baker. I'm the ward manager today. Is this about poor Sasha?"

Doug lowered his voice. "Only partly. I'm afraid I have some bad news about another of your colleagues. Is there somewhere we could speak more—"

"Just tell me what's happened." It was a command from someone used to giving orders.

"It's Neel Chowdhury. He was found dead this morning."

"Chowdhury?" Allison Baker's shoulders slumped in what looked like relief. "I was afraid you were going to say it was another of the young women." Then her pleasant, middle-aged face colored. "Oh. That sounds dreadful. Of course I'm sorry to hear that about Mr. Chowdhury, but after Sasha . . . I had visions of someone stalking the female staff. What happened to him?"

"All I can say is that we're treating his death as suspicious. We'll need to contact his next of kin. Would you have that information?"

"Well, technically you should go through HR, but I suppose I can find it for you." Baker hesitated, then said, "I'm due a break. Let me get someone to cover the desk and I'll meet you in the canteen with Mr. Chowdhury's details."

It was as broad an invitation to gossip as Doug had come across, and he wasn't about to turn it down.

—

A bacon roll and a strong cup of coffee improved Doug's outlook. By the time Allison Baker appeared in the canteen entrance, his hangover headache had receded to a manageable level. He'd grabbed a table in a corner, well away from the other patrons, where he thought their conversation would be masked by the low hum of voices and the rattle of china and cutlery.

Standing, he pulled out a chair and offered to get the nurse a coffee. She declined, however, saying she'd grab a cup of tea from the buffet. "I have to ration the hard stuff," she added with a smile.

He studied her as she fetched her tea. She was perhaps in her late forties or early fifties, sturdy without being fat, her short brown hair dusted with a sprinkle of gray. This was a woman who radiated "dependable."

A few moments later she deposited her cup and saucer on the table and sank down opposite him with a sigh. "I'm still trying to take it in. I should have realized something was wrong when he didn't turn up this morning. The supervisor called me in—it was my day off. I tried ringing his flat, but there was no answer." She drew in a sharp little breath. "He wasn't—he wasn't found there, was he? I hate the thought of the phone ringing and him lying there . . . Maybe if I'd called someone—"

"No, no." Doug saw no harm in reassuring her. "He wasn't at home when he—when it happened. There was nothing you could have done."

Baker shook her head and drank some of her tea. "I was off

yesterday as well. I only heard about Sasha when one of the other nurses on the ward rang me." There was a glint of tears behind the lenses of her glasses.

"You were fond of Sasha, then?"

"Oh, yes. A lovely girl. Young woman, I should say. And she had the makings of a very good doctor."

"When we spoke to Mr. Chowdhury yesterday morning, we got the impression that he and Sasha didn't exactly get on."

Allison Baker set her cup down hard enough to rattle her saucer. "I know you shouldn't speak ill of the dead, but Neel Chowdhury was just downright poisonous. He made life difficult for everyone he worked with, but he seemed especially to have it in for Sasha. He'd use any excuse to report her."

"Did they have a history?"

"Not that I'm aware," Baker said thoughtfully. "But that would explain a lot." Baker tilted her head to one side and gave him a look that reminded him of Matron at his boarding school. "Do you think his death is connected with Sasha's? He wasn't killed in the square as well?"

"No, he was not," Doug said, as firmly as he could manage under her penetrating stare. "Do you know of anyone who might have had a grudge against Mr. Chowdhury, Nurse Baker?"

"Other than anyone he ever worked with, I really can't say." She pulled a folded piece of paper from her tunic pocket. "This is what we had on file for his next of kin. Perhaps they can help you."

After glancing at the note, Doug said, "One more thing, if you don't mind. Can you tell me what time Mr. Chowdhury left the hospital last night?"

"If he worked a twelve, plus paperwork, I don't think he'd have been later than about eight o'clock. I can check with whoever was on the rota with him yesterday, if you like."

Doug handed her his card. "Here's my mobile number, if you could let me know."

They both stood, but then Baker grimaced. "Look, I'm sorry. I think I've sounded a right cow. It's all a bit of a shock."

"I understand this is all very upsetting. But as you seem to have been close to Sasha, do you know if she was seeing someone? In case there's someone else we should speak to."

"A boyfriend? Not that she ever mentioned to me. And I think I've said quite enough."

—

After writing up his notes and finishing the dregs of his coffee, Doug took the lift up to ground level. When the lift doors opened, he found himself face-to-face with two white-coated figures. The man was Owen Rees, the doctor he and Kincaid had met the previous day. After a blank moment, Rees gave him a nod of acknowledgment.

"It's Inspector . . ."

"Detective Sergeant Cullen," Doug filled in the pause. "Dr. Rees, isn't it?" There was an awkward moment when Doug expected Rees to ask about the investigation into Sasha Johnson's murder, but Rees merely stepped aside to allow him to exit the lift, then blocked the closing lift doors.

The other doctor, a woman, put a proprietary hand on Rees's elbow and said, "I'm Lauren Montgomery. Owen's wife. Are you here about the murder? Such a terrible thing."

"Do you work on the same ward?" Doug asked. He had the strong sense that he'd interrupted an argument.

"No, although I'm occasionally called in to consult. I'm a cardiologist." She was an attractive woman with a square face and sharply styled blond hair, a contrast to Rees's slightly rumpled and brooding dark looks. There was a brittleness to her, however, that even on such a brief meeting Doug found off-putting. Her accent reminded Doug unpleasantly of his mother's garden-club friends.

"Is there any news?" Rees asked, still holding the lift doors open. Doug imagined the frustrated button pushing happening on other floors.

"I'm afraid the investigation is still in its early stages," he said. He debated mentioning Chowdhury, but he wasn't in any hurry to start rumors flying around the hospital. Not that it would take long, but the sooner the news got out the sooner the media would pounce on it.

Dr. Montgomery shook her head and gave him the sort of disapproving look he imagined her bestowing on patients who kept smoking or slacked off on their rehab. "I would think the police would give the murder of a young woman in a public place their top priority."

"We are, ma'am, I assure you," said Doug, although he didn't consider murder in a private place any less heinous.

Rees stepped all the way into the lift. "If you've finished instructing the inspector in his job, darling, I do have a patient to see."

Montgomery gave him an exasperated look but followed him. "Nice to meet you, Inspector," she called out as the doors began to close.

"And you," Doug answered. "And it's Ser—" but the doors closed in his face.

—

After a moment's thought, Kincaid decided that he'd check out the bar himself. He and Sidana walked as far as Soho Square together.

"I think you're going rogue," she said before she left him. "That sort of interview is a constable's job."

"Either that or I want my shot at the club scene."

That earned him an exasperated eye roll. But the truth was that he wanted to see Chowdhury's last route for himself. The wispy morning clouds had dissipated, and over the rooftops the sky was the deep crystalline blue that meant autumn was leaching into winter.

The day was fine and it would do him good to walk. Standing at the corner where the square met Greek Street, he consulted the map on his mobile phone. The club in which Chowdhury had run up his credit card was practically spitting distance as the crow flies but a bit farther on foot. A covered passage off Greek Street led him into what his map told him was Manette Street. This, however, was a misnomer, as it was merely a narrow pedestrian walk with wire fencing to one side and the ubiquitous construction hoarding on the other. Halfway along, a short side alley turned into a heavily graffitied dead end.

He passed a discreet sign advertising massages, then, when he could see the traffic moving on Charing Cross Road at the lane's end, he reached the club. The front windows were papered over with signs reading NO UNDER 18S, ALL NIGHT HAPPY HOUR, and BAG SEARCH—all good indications that it might be a familiar stop for the local patrol officers. It took him a moment to spot the camera tucked into the corner of one window.

Since the signage also said OPEN 10 P.M.–3 A.M., Kincaid assumed the door was locked, but when he raised his hand to knock, it swung open and a man looked out at him.

"You the detective?" the man said. "I was keeping an eye out."

"Thanks." Kincaid produced his warrant card. "Duncan Kincaid, Holborn Met."

"Darrell Cherry." He gave Kincaid's hand a firm shake as he ushered him in. "Can I do you a coffee?"

Cherry had an inch or two on Kincaid's six-foot height, and considerably more muscle under his tight, short-sleeve T-shirt. His graying blond hair was swept back in a ponytail, and what Kincaid could see of his arms was covered in full-color, beautifully detailed ink. "Boyfriend owns a studio," said Cherry, following Kincaid's glance.

"Nice work," Kincaid said with genuine admiration. He'd never had any desire for a tattoo, but he could appreciate the art. "And I'll take you up on that coffee, if you don't mind. I appreciate you taking the time to speak to me."

"I've got a cleaner and a prep cook out, so I was going to be here anyway."

Kincaid noticed that a hoover stood in the center of the room, its cord snaking towards the back, and that Cherry had a tea towel tucked into the waistband of his jeans. "You do food here as well as drinks?"

"Late-night bar snacks, limited menu. Chicken fingers or scampi and chips, in a basket."

"Very retro, then," Kincaid said with a grin.

Cherry chuckled. "You won't find any gastro pub grub darkening this place." He turned away. "We can chat in my office."

As he followed, Kincaid scanned the room. While not as posh as Jon Gibbs's Bottle, the place was clean and cozier than he'd expected. A small stage anchored one end of the room and framed posters showcased jazz greats. "You do music here as well?"

"A bit of cabaret, Sundays and Thursdays. Brings in the punters on the slow days."

Cherry took Kincaid down the white-tiled stairs to a small room tucked to one side of the kitchen. A drip coffee maker with a full pot stood on top of a gray filing cabinet. When Kincaid had taken the folding chair on one side of the cluttered desk, Cherry went into the kitchen and returned with two clean mugs. "Milk or sugar?" he asked Kincaid as he filled the mugs.

"Black is fine, thanks." Kincaid accepted his drink, then had to find a place to set it on the overflowing desktop while he took out his mobile phone. "I believe it was my sergeant, Simon Gikas, who spoke to you?"

"He said you had some urgent questions about one of last night's customers." For all Cherry's easy manner, Kincaid sensed an alert intelligence.

"A man was found dead in suspicious circumstances near here. He had a receipt from your bar, dated last night."

"Dead?" Cherry frowned. "One of my customers?"

Kincaid had snapped a photo of Chowdhury's driving license. Now he zoomed the photo in until only Chowdhury's face was visible, then held the screen towards Cherry. "Do you recognize this man?"

Cherry leaned closer for a better look, then sat back, nodding. "Yeah. He was here last night, all right. I was helping out on the floor and one of the servers complained about him. She cut him off and he was quite stroppy about it."

"What time would this have been?"

"Two, half-past maybe. Well before last orders. He came in not too long after opening and had been steadily putting away the vodka martinis."

"Was he with anyone?"

"Nah. Took a two-top by the stage, his back to the wall. He was an odd duck. Kept his coat on, so I thought he might try to do a runner, but he ponied up his card once I'd convinced him he wasn't having another drink."

Considering Cherry's size and his hamlike arms, Kincaid wasn't surprised. "Did he speak to anyone?"

"Not that I saw, and I was behind the bar most of the time. But there was something . . ." Cherry's gaze lost focus for a moment, then he looked back at Kincaid. "We see all kinds. You learn to recognize all the little clues. I can tell an alcoholic who's stretching out a drink from a regular punter who's just enjoying it, all from the way they hold the glass. This guy, he was working at it. He meant to get drunk. But . . ." He shook his head. "I'd say he wasn't a regular drinker. It was more like he was, I don't know. Spooked."

"I saw you have CCTV. Was it working last night?"

"Yeah, we keep it in good nick. It's on a twenty-four-hour loop, so last night's footage should still be there." Cherry pulled out the center drawer in his desk and rummaged, then held up a small plastic package triumphantly. "Spare USB, if you want me to copy it over for you."

"Thanks very much. If you could let DS Gikas know when it's ready, he'll have someone pick it up." Kincaid stood and handed him a card. "And if you remember anything else about last night, you can get in touch with either of us."

Cherry studied the card for a moment before putting it on his desk. "Will do." He fixed Kincaid with a sharp glance. "You didn't say you were a detective superintendent. Who the hell was this guy that he rates a superintendent doing the footwork?"

—

After tea with Gemma, Melody stopped at her flat to change into something more presentable than ratty leggings and a jumper. Jeans, her favorite cherry-red cardigan, and a swipe of lipstick later, she set out, not for the Yard but for the *Chronicle* offices just off Kensington High Street.

Her spirits rose as she came out of High Street Kensington tube station into the Sunday bustle of the street. Across the way, the bells in the tower of St. Mary Abbott's chimed one o'clock. The midday sun lit the Great War Memorial, still bedecked in fading poppy wreaths. The flower stall in the church forecourt was doing a brisk business, and Melody decided she'd treat herself to a bouquet of something bright on the way home, red tulips, perhaps.

But first, a little research. When she'd checked in at the paper's security desk, she took the lift up to the top floor. The newsroom never slept, of course, but the paper always felt quieter to her on a Sunday.

When she was a child, she'd been awed by the clatter and roar of the presses under Fleet Street, but those days were gone, with the presses moving first to Wapping in South London, and now to a huge plant in Broxbourne, in Hertfordshire.

In the newsroom, the clack and ding of typewriters had long since given way to the soft taps of keyboards, but her father kept a collection of vintage typewriters on the sideboard in his office. She had been fascinated by them, and the first thing she'd ever typed had been on his mint-green portable Olivetti. No one had wanted typewriters then—now they were worth a small fortune.

Settling herself in her father's Aeron chair, she started with the basic publicly available information—the Gibbs siblings' dates and places of birth. Jonathan Gibbs was three years older than his sister, Tully. Both had been born in a maternity hospital near Glastonbury and had lived in a village near Shepton Mallet, where their mother had worked in an insurance office. Their mother had died when Tully was sixteen and Jonathan nineteen. The father had not been listed on the tax rolls for the house, and it appeared that the house had been sold in the year following the mother's death.

Next, a troll through social media. She found Tully quickly enough, with her unusual name. Her Facebook profile showed her as having a BA from University College London, but any other information was locked.

There were dozens of Jonathan Gibbses, however, and not having met him, Melody couldn't narrow the possibilities by photo. She could, however, winnow by age and location, but an hour and a headache later, she'd struck out on potential candidates.

That in itself was weird, she thought. Why would an early-thirties, trendy nightclub manager not have a social-media presence? She had to assume that he had no criminal record, as Holborn CID would have checked and either Doug or Gemma would have mentioned it.

Sitting back, she tapped a pencil on the desk, then placed her hands once more over the keyboard. She tried the club, but found only its official website and reviews on different entertainment sites, mostly positive. She didn't think there was any way Jon Gibbs could have funded the operation himself, so the place must have backers, but ferreting out their names would take a trip to Companies House.

Next, she logged into the paper's data aggregator but had no luck there, either.

But a newspaperman's daughter was not so easily discouraged. After snagging a cup of coffee from the newsroom, she settled in for the slog. How many local Somerset newspapers could there be?

Quite a few, as it turned out, and some of them still in the twentieth century as far as their search engines went. The light had faded outside the office windows by the time she stopped, stretched, and sat back with a satisfied smile. No wonder Jon Gibbs had no social media.

Doug Cullen was going to owe her a big, fat apology.

Her mobile had dinged a few minutes earlier, but she'd been so engrossed in her reading that she'd hardly noticed. Now she picked the phone up and idly checked the screen.

What she saw drove all thoughts of Doug Cullen or Jonathan Gibbs from her mind.

CHAPTER SEVENTEEN

Gemma accepted a steaming mug of tea and settled into Betty Howard's plum-colored sofa with a sigh of contentment. She loved Betty's sitting room. The flat was small, but it always felt warm and welcoming. She thought about Wesley and his sisters growing up here, how crowded it must have been with six children crammed into the same amount of space she and her sister had shared like settlers in separate armed camps.

"You look a bit frazzled, love," said Betty, coming back from the kitchen with a plate of sliced cake. "This will fix you right up. It's lemon drizzle."

"I want cake," piped up Charlotte from her spot at Betty's worktable. "With drizzles." Betty had set her up with two pieces of pretty floral fabric, a large needle, and a thimble. It was meant to be a duvet for Bob, Char's stuffed elephant.

"Are you sure she's old enough to use a needle?" Gemma had whispered.

Betty had snorted in dismissal. "My papa had me using the sewing machine by the time I was four. Char is a bright thing, and the fabrics, they're in her blood."

That was true enough. Charlotte's mother had been a renowned fabric artist and Charlotte had loved Betty's bright bolts of cloth and bins of trim and buttons since the very first time she'd visited the flat.

"Remember your manners," Gemma said now, giving Charlotte a stern look.

"May I have some cake, pretty please?" Charlotte obliged with a giggle. "A biggest piece."

"Of course you may, love," Betty told her, sliding a thick slice onto a small plate. "But make sure your fingers aren't sticky before you go back to your sewing. Rule number one: don't muss the fabric."

Gemma rolled her eyes at the size of the cake slice. "You'll spoil her, Betty."

"A little spoiling never hurt a child." Betty handed Charlotte her cake along with her favorite daisy mug, filled with very milky tea. "At least, not this sort of spoiling," she added, frowning as she sank down on the other end of the sofa.

It was Betty who seemed exhausted. Her skin had an ashy tinge, and she had forgone her usual colorful headscarf. Gemma saw that her hair, which she kept shaved down to a fuzz, had gone more white than gray.

"Are you all right?" Gemma asked. "I'm so sorry about your friends' daughter."

Betty sighed. "Duncan will have told you. It's a very hard thing. I wish I could do more for them. This morning we took more food, but no amount of cake is going to ease that grief."

"And the daughter, Sasha, she was going to have a baby, I

understand," Gemma said softly, glancing at Charlotte. But Charlotte had put down her cake after only a bite, wiped her fingers carefully on a cloth napkin and picked up her sewing again, completely absorbed in pushing the needle in and out. "That must make it doubly hard."

"They told them at the hospital. Some policewoman. Can you credit that? Kayla said she thought her mum would collapse from the shock."

So Jasmine had told the family. It sounded as if she'd been less than tactful, too. Gemma knew Duncan would have wanted to tell the parents himself, and she bet he'd been livid. No wonder Jasmine hadn't mentioned it over their drinks last night.

"Kayla is Sasha's sister?" she asked. "Were they close?"

"Not so much, the last couple of years." Betty sighed. "Kayla has a baby, and you know how that is. Sometimes you barely have time to eat and sleep."

Betty would know, if anyone did, Gemma thought. "But Kayla will be some support to her parents?"

"I'm sure she'll do her best, but that doesn't make up for the other one. That Tyler," Betty added, shaking her head. "He's the youngest, spoiled rotten by his sisters and his doting parents, and I don't mean the good sort of spoiling. You'd think with Dorothy being a psychologist, they'd have known better, but maybe you can't see the rotten apple in your own basket." She shook her head. "And Peter wanted a boy so badly, he could see no fault in him. It didn't help that Tyler was the most beautiful child, even prettier than Sasha."

Gemma chose her words carefully. "I take it Tyler has been . . . difficult."

"Difficult!" Betty exclaimed. "That doesn't begin to cover it. He hasn't even rung his mum. Now they're worried something bad has happened to him, too."

Gemma suddenly found herself in a very awkward position. She couldn't very well say that Tyler had been fine when she'd seen him at ten o'clock last night. Well, maybe not fine, she amended, thinking of his scuffle with Jon Gibbs, but at least alive. "I'm sure he'll turn up," she offered. "He doesn't still live at home?"

"He's supposed to be at uni, at UCL, but when Peter went to his rooms, this other boy said he didn't stay there anymore."

"Maybe he's at a friend's. Or a girlfriend's," Gemma added, wondering if this was an angle Duncan's team had checked. Tyler had seemed quite friendly with Trudy, the bartender, last night, but it hadn't struck her as that sort of relationship. "Or maybe a boyfriend?" she suggested.

Tilting her head to one side, Betty considered this. "A boyfriend, no, I don't think so. He's had the girls hanging on him since he hit puberty, and the feeling seemed to be mutual."

"What about Sasha?" Gemma asked. "Was there a boyfriend?"

Betty snorted. "Unless there was an immaculate conception, I'd say there must have been. Or at least a man, but in either case she certainly kept him to herself." She levered herself up from the sofa and came back a few moments later with a fresh pot of tea.

"I spoke to Wesley this morning," said Gemma, when Betty had refilled their cups. "He came by the house. He told me that Destiny saw Sasha with a bloke, in rather odd circumstances."

Betty's eyebrows rose. "I don't know anything about that. Do you think it's important?"

"I don't know. And of course it's not my case," Gemma hastened to add. "But it might be helpful to know exactly what happened."

Retrieving her mobile from the sewing table, Betty swiped it open. "Let's find out, then." She switched the phone to speaker and Gemma heard the ring tone, then Destiny's voice.

"What's up, Mum? You okay?"

When Betty explained, Destiny said, "Yeah, all right. Hi, Gemma."

"Hi, Des. I hope you don't mind me asking about this."

"No prob." Destiny's voice was muffled against a background babble of voices. "Sorry, out for a late Sunday lunch at the pub. Let me go outside." The noise faded into a hum and Destiny began again. "So I was at this sushi place in Covent Garden, grabbing a quick lunch with my mate from work, and I see Sash across the room, with a bloke. A fine-looking guy, too, but they were rowing—you could tell.

"Then Sasha looked up, straight at me. I gave her a wave and she looked right through me, like she'd never seen me before in her life! Cut me dead. I couldn't believe it. I'd known this girl since she was in nappies. I was so pissed off, I was going to march right over and give her what-for, but my mate talked me out of it." Des sighed. "Maybe Sash had her reasons."

Destiny, Gemma guessed, was not used to being ignored under any circumstances. As exuberant as Wesley was reserved, she worked in Wardrobe at the Royal Opera House and always looked as if she'd just stepped out of a fashion shoot. "When was this, do you remember?"

"A couple of weeks ago, two, maybe three? When I think what's happened, that it was the last time I'd ever see her . . ." Even the unquenchable Destiny sounded subdued now.

"What was he like, this guy?"

"A white bloke, but not fair-skinned, you know? Late thirties, maybe early forties. Well fit. Brown hair, cut short."

"Is there anything else you remember? His clothes, for instance?"

"Just ordinary stuff, you know. Shirt, a jacket, I think. Business casual."

It was pretty vague as far as descriptions went, thought Gemma, but it could fit Jon Gibbs. "Do you think you'd recognize him from a photo?"

"Yeah, I think so. Do you know who he was?"

"Just an idea, but it's worth a try. I'll see what I can come up with." Last night, Jasmine had waved her phone around at the restaurant with what had seemed casual abandon. But now Gemma wondered if Jasmine had managed to get a photo of Gibbs. "Can I text you?" she asked Destiny.

"Sure." Destiny rattled off her mobile number, then added, "Give me yours, in case I remember anything else. We should do lunch sometime, now that we're connected and all."

"I'd like that," Gemma responded. "Des—" She paused and glanced at Charlotte, but Betty had joined her at the sewing table and they were deep in consultation over the button box. "Do you have any idea where Sasha's brother Tyler might be?"

"That little scumbag," spat Destiny, rattling the phone speaker. "I have no idea, but if you find him, I want to know about it. He borrowed fifty quid from me and I never saw a penny back."

—

Kincaid's meeting with his boss, Chief Superintendent Thomas Faith, had not been a pleasant one. Two murders in two days was enough to make any station commander out of sorts, but two potentially high-profile deaths was enough to call Faith away from his Sunday golf, adding insult to injury.

The fact that Chowdhury's murder was actually on Westminster's patch rather than theirs only served to complicate things further. Kincaid had spoken to his opposite number at Westminster, a detective chief inspector named Trevor Pine, and they'd agreed that Kincaid's team would take the lead as long as it looked like Chowdhury's death might be related to Sasha Johnson's.

"Press conference at eight in the morning," Faith had finished, "and by then I expect us to know whether we've got some mad bugger targeting hospital staff. In the meantime, I don't want anything leaking to the bloody press about the Chowdhury case."

Kincaid had hastened to impart the same directives to his team, now gathered in the CID room. Taking his place at the white-board, he said, "Doug, any luck getting Chowdhury's next of kin?"

Doug checked his notebook. "According to his hospital records, it's a cousin named Nira Gupta. Lives in Willesden. The nurse I spoke to was pretty broken up about Sasha Johnson but not so upset about Chowdhury. It sounds like he was a bully and that he targeted Johnson in particular, but I'm not sure that gets us much further forward. If Sasha had killed him, maybe she'd have had motivation, but . . ." He shrugged.

"There is another possible connection between the victims," Kincaid said, and outlined what Howard Quirk had told him. "We don't know for certain that it was Sasha who visited Chowdhury on Thursday night, but I want any CCTV from Dean Street tracked down and gone over with a fine-tooth comb." This elicited groans.

"We should also have CCTV coming from the bar Chowdhury visited last night. Simon?"

"On it," said Gikas. "Courier's picking it up now."

"The bar manager," Kincaid continued, "says Chowdhury was not a regular, and that he drank alone until they refused to serve him a little after two a.m. This narrows our window for Chowdhury's murder. My guess is that Chowdhury walked from the bar straight to Soho Square, where he was killed. That might have taken ten minutes, maybe longer, considering that he was very drunk.

"My question is whether his killer was waiting for him, or if he—or she—followed him from the club. Unless, of course, we have two random fatal stabbings, but I'm inclined to think that strains probability."

"My contact at the hospital says Chowdhury would normally have left the hospital not long after eight p.m.," put in Doug. "If that was the case last night, where was he between eight and the time he showed up at this bar?"

Kincaid nodded. "Good point. The manager thought Chowdhury arrived not long after opening at ten, but we should be able to clarify that from the CCTV. If he went home, his neighbor didn't hear him, and he was still in his work clothes when he was found, so I'm guessing he didn't. Mr. Cherry, the bar manager, says Chowdhury never took off his coat. Maybe he didn't want to be seen drinking in his uniform tunic."

"Or maybe he didn't want to be recognized," said Sidana.

Kincaid considered this. "That's a possibility. He was nowhere near the hospital, but not that far from his flat, so he could have been avoiding someone he knew in Soho." There was a large, much-pinholed map of Central London on the wall beside the whiteboard, and Kincaid turned to study it.

"In that case, why turn down Charing Cross Road rather than continue along Oxford Street to Soho Square?" asked Doug. "That would have been his most obvious route home."

"We don't know enough to hazard a guess." Kincaid turned to Sidana. "Jasmine, as you're taking the postmortem, it would be helpful to know when and what Chowdhury last ate. Maybe he stopped off for a meal somewhere, or met someone, nearby."

Sidana made a note, then glanced at her watch. "I'd better go soon, boss. Dr. Kaleem just texted that he's setting up. I don't want to keep him waiting."

"Right. Update me as soon as you've finished. Our top priority is learning whether or not we're dealing with the same weapon and the same perpetrator."

When Sidana had gathered her things and left the room, Kincaid turned back to the group. "Here's another loose thread that needs following—Sasha Johnson's wayward brother, Tyler Johnson. Sasha was on her way to meet her flatmate, Tully Gibbs, when she was killed. She had arranged to meet with Tully's brother, Jonathan Gibbs, at the Perseverance, to talk about Tyler, but Jon Gibbs didn't show.

"Sasha then arranged to meet Tully at a café near the British Museum. Her route from Lamb's Conduit Street to the café took her through Russell Square, where she was killed." He made a rough timeline beneath Sasha's photo on the whiteboard, then continued. "When Doug and I interviewed Jon Gibbs at the bar he manages in Soho, he said Tyler did odd jobs for him, but didn't turn up on Friday evening. Gibbs said he had no idea why Sasha wanted to discuss her brother, and that he didn't meet her because he had to run the errands on which he'd normally have sent Tyler."

Here he paused. He hadn't previously shared what he'd learned from Kit or Wesley Howard with the whole team. Nor had he mentioned Sidana and Gemma's expedition to Bottle. He needed a less complicated version—one that preferably left out his wife and son's connection.

"Meanwhile," he continued, "we heard a rumor from another source that Tyler might be involved in some criminal activities. We also learned that he hadn't been in touch with his family since his sister's death, although they've tried to contact him. DS Cullen and DI Sidana and I decided it might be a good idea to learn more about this club, so last night DI Sidana paid a visit to Bottle."

Doug kept a poker face, but Simon Gikas looked astounded. "Are you saying that the DI went there undercover?"

"Exactly." Kincaid was glad Sidana wasn't there to be offended by Simon's reaction. "The club seemed tame enough until Tyler Johnson showed up. Then all hell broke loose, apparently. Gibbs accused Johnson of getting Sasha killed—"

"This gets better and better," Gikas interrupted.

Kincaid gave him a quelling frown, but said, "It does indeed. Tyler Johnson appeared to be setting up some of the female customers with male punters. Gibbs threw him out."

Doug, who was hearing an account of the evening for the first time, said, "And Gibbs didn't know?"

"According to Jasmine, he said, 'You little shit, I listened to her voicemail.' Maybe Sasha told Gibbs what Tyler was doing."

Lucy McGillivray raised her hand. "Sir, if you're right, how did Sasha find out?"

"That," he said, "is a very good question. One that we can ask Tyler Johnson when we find him."

———

Like all dorms in Doug's experience, the residence hall in Gower Street smelled of sweat, floor cleaner, and old ramen noodles, with barely perceptible undertones of vomit and weed. The joys of the student life. Still, for all the hall's lack of glamour, Tyler Johnson's parents had paid good money for a room their son had apparently abandoned, although his name was still on the little card in the door.

Doug knocked sharply, waited, then knocked again. A voice yelled, "Hold your horses, will you?"

The door swung open, revealing a boy with an array of acne

across his pink cheeks, and straw-colored, stringy hair. The boy stared at him, taking in the suit. Even without a tie, Doug was overdressed for a lecturer.

"Can I help you?" the boy asked, his accent Northern, Yorkshire or maybe Lancashire, Doug thought.

Doug held up his warrant card. "I'm looking for Tyler Johnson."

"He's not here," said the kid, and started to close the door.

"Not so fast." Doug stepped forward just enough to block the door with his foot. "I'd like a word. Are you Porter?" Raymond Porter had been the other name on the door tag. "Raymond Porter?"

"Ray," Porter corrected. "Nobody calls me Raymond."

"Can I come in?"

Porter hesitated in the way that meant he was wondering if he could refuse, but then he shrugged. "Yeah, okay, I guess." He stepped back, but Doug saw his eyes dart towards the desk on one side of the room. Worried about his stash, Doug guessed, or porn, but there was no sign of drugs on the desk's surface and the computer monitor showed only a *Star Trek* screen saver.

"Thanks." Doug took his time surveying the room. The walls, or at least the portions not covered by anime posters, were a revolting dirty mauve, but the single window was high and let in a flood of waning afternoon light. There were two beds at right angles, one unmade, the other covered with discarded clothing, papers, and books. A second desk shoehorned into the only other available wall space held more books, a high-end gaming console, and a small flat-screen TV.

Ray Porter, thought Doug, wasn't expecting his roommate back anytime soon.

"Nice setup." Doug nodded towards the game console. "What are you playing?"

"Assassin's Creed," Porter said, then winced. "That doesn't sound right. I heard what happened to Ty's sister. His dad was here, looking for him. He said she was stabbed. That's awful, man."

Doug blinked back the sudden image of Sasha Johnson's still face, damp with rain, against the grass in Russell Square. "Yeah," he said, "it is. So how long has it been since you've seen Tyler?"

Porter shrugged. "I don't know. Couple weeks, maybe. He's in and out, like."

"More out, I take it." Doug glanced at the cluttered bed.

"Well, the last couple of weeks, yeah, more out."

"Has he been in touch?"

"Nah. I texted him, after his dad was here, but he didn't answer."

If that was true, Doug thought, Tyler Johnson really had gone to ground. Except for his appearance at Jon Gibbs's club last night. "Any idea where Tyler's staying?"

"Nah. We didn't hang, you know?"

From what he knew about Tyler, Doug wasn't surprised, but he merely said, "What about the club where he worked, in Archer Street? What do you know about it?"

"Ty worked at a club?" Porter frowned. "What kind of club?"

"It's called Bottle. It's a fancy cocktail bar."

Porter picked absently at an acne scab while he digested this. "Not my scene, man. He never said anything to me about it. I did wonder where he got the dosh for his clothes. But when I asked him, he told me to—well, never mind." Red blotches bloomed on his cheeks. "Look, I've got to—"

"Did Tyler leave any of his clothes here? Or anything else?"

"Nah, don't think so. But he was like, tidy," Porter divulged with obvious astonishment. "So I'd been back from lecture for hours before I realized it was all gone. Laptop, clothes, everything. Poof. Well, almost everything," he amended. "He left some of his books." He gestured at a stack of textbooks teetering on the edge of the desk that also held the gaming console and an open jumbo-size bag of prawn-cocktail-flavored crisps.

"May I?" When Porter nodded, Doug carefully nudged aside the crisps, then rifled through the heavy-looking tomes on economics and business studies. He found nothing more interesting than the occasional outbreak of yellow highlighter. "He didn't need these for his coursework?" he asked.

Porter's shoulder twitched in another shrug. "I don't think Ty went to lectures much after the first few weeks of term. He said you didn't need a degree to make money, just brains."

"What about Tyler's friends? Who did he hang out with?"

Porter shook his head. "He never brought anyone back here. We weren't on the same course, so I never saw him in lectures or study groups. Basically, he just slept here. But . . ." He hesitated, then said, "Why are you asking about Ty, anyway? It was his sister got killed."

"Just routine," Doug assured him. "We like to speak with the family. And his parents are concerned about him."

"Yeah, his dad was pretty bent out of shape. My dad would go spare if something happened to my sister and I'd buggered off uni. Doesn't seem right. You don't—" His glance was sharper than Doug expected. "You don't think something's happened to Ty, too?"

"We'd just like to make sure he's okay," said Doug, "so if there's anything that might help us find him . . ." Doug made himself leave the statement dangling.

Sure enough, after a long moment, Porter filled the silence, blurting, "There's this girl. I saw him chatting her up a couple of times in the student center." The flush stained his cheeks again. "She's a babe. Well fit, you know, and blond. I don't know if they had a thing, but . . ."

"Great. Do you know how we could get in touch with her?"

"She's in one of my lectures. I think her name's Chelsea."

—

The walk from Paddington Station disoriented her. The lights reflecting on the rain-slicked streets were dizzying after months in the Congo's tent city; the zoom and swish of passing cars made her heart thump with panic.

The house, when she reached it at last, was dark. She hadn't told him she was coming. Perhaps they were out. But she stood watching for a long time, gripping the handle of her little roller bag as if it were an anchor, hoping to see a flare of light, or a shadow behind the drawn curtains. Her need to see her daughter consumed her like a fierce thirst.

And yet. She told herself it was ridiculous to be so afraid. What could he say that could hurt her, unless she let it?

She would go back to her life, her job, and she would make a new home for her little girl. She could deal with this.

Taking a breath, she climbed the steps and rang the bell. Then, she shook her head in disgust. It was her own house, too, for God's sake. There was no reason why she couldn't let herself in, but her hand shook as she tried to fit the key in the lock.

It didn't turn.

Perhaps in the dark she'd used the wrong key, although she knew the shape of them with her fingers as well as she knew her face. Fumbling with her key ring, she tried the other key, but no, that was the key to her building at the college, she was sure of it. She tried the house key again. It didn't budge.

She stood back, panting now.

He must have changed the lock.

Shakily, she moved away from the door and sat down on the wet stairs. Where were they? What had he done? Pulling out her phone, she took a deep breath and rang his number. When the no-longer-in-service recording kicked in, she hung up.

Exhaustion swept over her. She hadn't slept well in days, hadn't eaten since she'd started for the airport in Kinshasa.

Tonight, she'd have to find a place to stay. Get some sleep. Tomorrow, she would deal with whatever the day brought.

CHAPTER EIGHTEEN

"I've done the messy bits," said Rashid Kaleem. He glanced up at Sidana, and it surprised her to realize how well she could read his expression, even though he was wearing full protective gear. "I never see why anyone else should have to deal with stomach contents."

"Much appreciated." Sidana returned the smile. "I have to admit it's not my favorite thing." She was masked and gowned as well, but she could already feel the mortuary cold beginning to seep through her clothing layers. Forcing her gaze away from Rashid, she looked down at the naked corpse on the gurney. Neel Chowdhury did not inspire the same gut clench of regret she'd felt looking at Sasha Johnson. Still, there was something piteous and vulnerable about this middle-aged man's body, laid bare in all its undignified flaws. No one, no matter how unpleasant, deserved to have their life snatched away and their remains exposed to this clinical regard.

Rashid had closed up the Y incision, the stitching as neat and regular as zipper teeth. There were two wounds beneath Chowdhury's left breast. Like the blow that had killed Sasha, they were smaller than a pencil eraser.

The one nearer the left side of the chest was shaped more like a teardrop than a circle, however. "This seems to have been the first blow," said Rashid, touching the teardrop with the point of a long pair of tweezers. "It glanced off his fifth rib and nicked the pericardium, but in all likelihood would not have been fatal, assuming he'd got help pretty quickly. Now, this one"—he touched the tweezer points to the other, more circular, wound, nearer to the center of the chest—"this one was more problematical, deep and delivered with considerably more force. It missed the rib altogether and penetrated the right ventricle. Still, he might have survived, but not for long unaided."

Leaning in for a closer look, Sidana examined the second wound. "It looks slightly darker around the puncture. Is that bruising?"

"Well spotted," said Rashid, as if she were a prize pupil. "That's one of the indications that death wasn't instantaneous."

"But it looks regular. Almost like a pattern."

"Well spotted again. Have a look at this." Rashid turned to the computer on one of the work benches and pulled up a photo of the wound. A few clicks of the mouse enlarged it until it filled the entire screen. The pattern was now more evident.

"It's almost a daisy shape," said Sidana. "What could have made that?"

"I'd say it's the hilt of whatever made the puncture. It was a deep thrust. We'll see what the lab comes up with."

Stepping back to the body, Sidana gazed at it. "What do you think, Rashid? Are we looking at a double murder?"

"The lab will have more precise measurements, but I think it's more than likely that the weapon was the same one used on Sasha Johnson—although I'd say the method of attack was different."

"How so?"

"The placement and angles of the wounds. The first victim, Johnson, was stabbed by someone facing her. Like this." He picked up the long tweezers again, wrapping his fist around the instrument. Holding it at chest height, his elbow cocked, he mimed pushing it forward. "I think he—or she—got lucky with that one. It was a calculated risk. If the blow had missed or only injured her, your perpetrator would have just disappeared into the crowd. The thrust wasn't that deep—it was bad luck on Johnson's part that it happened to nick the aorta.

"But this one," he continued, tapping Chowdhury's corpse with the tweezers, "this one was different. Look at this." He touched Chowdhury's neck just beneath the right side of his chin. "It's a bit harder to see with the beard stubble, but there's some faint bruising here. Combine that with the angle of both stab wounds, and what you get is this."

Rashid gripped the tweezers again in his right hand, but this time he mimed reaching around with his left arm until his left fist was under his jaw, then stabbing in and upwards with the tweezers.

"Chowdhury was attacked from behind?"

"Indeed. And held while he struggled. But considering his blood-alcohol level, he wouldn't have been able to put up much of a fight."

Sidana imagined the dark square, Chowdhury walking unsteadily, the killer waiting until his victim was shielded from the street by the bulk of the rubbish skips, then grabbing Chowdhury around the neck. Hoping Rashid hadn't seen her shudder, she said, "He's an opportunist, then, this killer, if it is the same person. But not someone targeting young women."

"No." Rashid looked at her, the concern in his dark eyes evident even behind the face shield. "Are you okay?"

The openness of his expression stopped her from shrugging off her reaction. "It's just that I met him yesterday, at the hospital. It's . . . unsettling, seeing him like this."

"That's understandable. We can finish in my office—"

"No. It's okay, really." Frowning, she looked back at Chowdhury's still form. A sprinkling of dark curly hair on the chest, the beginnings of a spare tire around the waist, the shriveled genitals . . . She transferred her gaze to the face, but it looked naked as well, without his glasses. They'd been found broken at the crime scene, she remembered. Now she saw that there was an abrasion across the bridge of his nose. "Did this happen in the struggle?" she asked.

"Possibly, but it could have happened when he fell."

Had Chowdhury's killer waited for him? But how would anyone have known he'd be staggering home at that hour of the morning? "Was he a regular drinker?" she asked.

"There were no obvious signs of habitual alcohol use. The labs will tell us more."

Remembering Kincaid's admonition, she said, "What about his stomach contents? Had he had a meal recently?"

"Not unless you count olives. I'd say he hadn't eaten since breakfast yesterday."

Sidana shivered again. The cold was getting to her.

"You're freezing," said Rashid. "I've bagged and tagged everything I removed from his pockets, so unless there's something else you'd like to see here, let's get you warmed up."

Rashid twitched a sheet over Chowdhury's body with practiced ease, then collected a plastic bag filled with smaller labeled bags from a cart near the door.

Ten minutes later, having removed their protective gear, they were ensconced in his office and Rashid was making them both coffee. Sidana was surprised by how comfortable it felt. He'd slipped a white coat over his scrubs and she was glad of the professional veneer. She could, however, just see the top of his T-shirt in the scrub tunic's V neck, and she couldn't help wondering what this one said.

"That should help," he said as he handed her a mug and she wrapped her hands around it. "I'd prefer that my live visitors not turn blue. I don't need the extra work," he added with a grin.

"I'm sorry. It's just that I had a short night." To her surprise, she found herself telling him about her visit to the Soho club with Gemma. "I thought we might have a lead on Sasha's murder," she concluded, "with the brother and his friends. But now I can't see how any of that ties in with Neel Chowdhury's murder."

"The only connection between the victims is that they worked in the same hospital?"

"As far as we know. But now it looks like Sasha Johnson might have visited Chowdhury at his flat the night before she was killed."

Frowning, Rashid rummaged through the large evidence bag he'd placed on his desk. "I did find one odd thing," he said as he removed a clear bag the size of an A4 sheet of paper and handed it to her.

Sidana examined the contents. A standard, white envelope bore Chowdhury's name but no address. "Laser printer," she muttered. The envelope was creased as if it had been folded in half. Beside it was a square of newspaper.

"The clipping was inside the envelope," Rashid said. "The lab will run prints on both."

The newspaper clipping was an obituary, Sidana saw, the print tiny and slightly smudged. Rashid handed her a magnifying glass.

"You're a regular Scout," she said, accepting it gratefully. The obit was dated a month previously. Sandra Beaumont, LN, aged fifty-three, survived by a daughter and grandson. No cause of death was given.

"Another nurse." She looked up at Rashid. "This was in his pocket?"

"Of his anorak, yes. There was nothing else out of the ordinary—keys, wallet, a packet of chewing gum, a handker-chief."

"He wasn't a pocket pack rat, then," mused Sidana. "Which makes it likely that he'd just received it, maybe only yesterday."

"But not in the post."

"No." Sidana thought about Chowdhury's building. "It could have been put through the letter box at his flat. He'd probably have checked his post on the way out the door yesterday morning."

"If the clipping was some sort of threat, it might explain the empty stomach," Rashid said. "Maybe he didn't eat because he was worried."

"It could also account for the uncharacteristic drinking." Sidana regretfully finished the last sip of her coffee and then took a close-up of the clipping with her phone before handing the evidence bag back to Rashid. "Can you make a proper copy of this and email it to me, as well? We'll need to get started tracking down this nurse in Brighton. And extend our search for CCTV coverage of Chowdhury's building to cover the early hours of yesterday morning." Standing, she added, "Thank you for the coffee. I may have to invest in one of those machines."

Rashid stood, too, then hesitated. "DI Sidana—"

"I think you can call me Jasmine."

"Okay, Jasmine, then." He smiled and she felt a little hitch in her breathing. "It's been a long day for both of us. I don't know about you, but I'm starving. I wondered if you'd like to grab a curry with me."

—

Doug stood outside the residence hall, irresolute. Ray Porter had given him the name of the teacher whose lectures the mysterious Chelsea attended, but there was little likelihood he'd be able to track down the professor on what was fast becoming a Sunday evening. The sun that had lit Porter's room had dropped below the roofs of the university buildings—dusk would not be far behind.

He started walking back to Holborn Station, but as he neared the British Museum, it occurred to him that if Tyler were seeing this girl, Sasha might have known her—and Sasha might have mentioned her to Tully. He checked his watch—it wasn't quite five.

It was only a bit out of his way to stop at the gallery, and when he turned into the pedestrianized section of Museum Street, he saw that the gallery lights were still on. When he opened the door, a bell jingled faintly but no one appeared.

Thinking Tully might have popped into the studio through the connecting door, he looked around with interest. The ceramics were beautifully displayed on open white shelving and simple white tables. Discreet tags identified the artists, and one area featured a number of Tully's dolls with their uniquely individual faces. Having seen the tags on some of the other work, the prices on the dolls shouldn't have surprised him, but still he whistled under his breath.

He was examining a deep-blue bowl, the first thing he'd seen that he could actually envision having in his flat, when he heard voices. Behind the till, a door—he assumed it was the door connecting to the studio—stood slightly ajar.

Doug had started to call out when a man's voice said clearly, "That was the deal you agreed to. You use the studio and kiln, your work supports the gallery." It was the gallery owner he'd met yesterday, David Pope.

"You know how much it costs to run the bloody kiln," Pope continued. "I've got to make that up."

"I never agreed not to make things for myself. That's just bollocks, David. You have no right to take my work without my permission." That was Tully, her voice high and strident.

"I don't think you realize what you have with your place here. You have the chance to make a name for yourself, your reputation as a potter. Do you think you're going to get that anywhere else? But if you don't appreciate working here—"

"Are you firing me, David? When I don't even know that I have a place to live?"

"Calm down, Tully. You're overwrought—"

"I've a bloody good reason to be overwrought, so don't use that patronizing tone with me." There was a muffled thump.

"It's not going to help either of us if you break all the product."

"I don't bloody care," Tully said on what sounded like a sob.

Doug thought it was time to intervene. He walked back to the door and swung it open with enough force to make the bell jangle loudly. Then he called out, "Hullo? Tully? Is anyone here?"

After a moment, David Pope emerged from the studio. "Can I help you? We're actually closed." Then he frowned in recognition. "Oh, it's you. Sergeant—Sorry, I don't remember your name."

"Doug Cullen. Detective Sergeant. Is Tully about?"

Pope turned his head to call into the studio. "Tully, the police are here for you." He made it sound as if uniform had come to arrest her.

Doug stepped past Pope and peered into the studio. "Do you have a minute to talk?"

Tully stood at her worktable, surrounded by open boxes and a drift of crumpled newspapers.

"Is it okay if I come in?" Doug asked.

"Sure. Okay." She wiped the back of her hand across her cheeks. "Just close the door behind you."

Doug was glad her glare didn't seem to be directed at him. "Are you okay?" he asked when he'd shut the door firmly. "Or is that a stupid question?"

That earned him a ghost of a smile. She scrubbed her hands on the front of her spattered overalls. "I'd say I was having a very bad day, but I don't want to sound overwrought."

"I'm sure you're not. Is there anything I can do to help?"

"I—Look, can we not talk here?"

Doug remembered the pub he'd seen just a few doors away, the Plough. "You look like you could use a drink." Then, with only a fleeting thought for Melody's criticism of the night before, he added, "Why don't you let me buy you one."

—

Kincaid had sent Sidana home when she'd returned from the Royal London. She'd seem unusually abstracted, but he'd put it down to her late night and suggested she get some rest.

Doug hadn't come back from his visit to Tyler Johnson's university lodgings. Simon was going through the CCTV footage that Darrell Cherry had sent round, as promised, but it was a slow business. Lucy McGillivray had just returned from another visit to the Johnsons in Westbourne Grove and was fidgeting in a way that indicated she was waiting for an opportunity to speak to him.

Glancing at his watch, he saw that it was past five. "McGilli-vray," he called out. "I'm going to pay a call on Mr. Chowdhury's next of kin. Are you up for driving?"

"Certainly, sir." She straightened her jacket and tucked a stray wisp of hair into her tidy bun.

"The address is in Willesden. You can drop me off home after-wards and bring the pool car back, or take it home, whichever suits you."

"Right, sir."

Once they were traveling west in the silver Astra, a trail of red taillamps ahead of them, he glanced over at her. "Now. Tell me what's going on with the Johnsons."

After a moment, she said, "Maybe I'm not doing the job prop-erly, but they don't seem to want me there at all. I understand that they're grieving, but this just seems . . . odd."

"In what way?"

"Well, they're always finding excuses to send me out of the room. And when their daughter, Kayla, is there, I hear them whispering, then as soon as I come back in, they stop. It's like the bloody veil of silence has descended—oh, sorry, sir."

Kincaid smiled. He thought he could glimpse her flush of em-barrassment even in the car's dim light. "Do you have any idea what they're talking about?"

"I've heard the brother's name mentioned. I knew they were worried that he hadn't been in touch, but now I'm wondering if they know he's involved in something criminal. Or if they even think he had something to do with Sasha's murder. And, then"—she paused to indicate as she smoothly changed lanes—"this afternoon, a man called round looking for Tyler. I answered the door, and when I told Mr. Johnson, he said to send the bloke away. It was after that the Johnsons turfed me out."

"Can you describe the man?"

"Mid-forties. White. Stocky build. Hair buzzed so short I couldn't really tell what color it was. Brown going gray, maybe. A London accent, I think."

Curious, Kincaid asked, "Do all Londoners sound alike to you?"

"As in, not Scottish?" McGillivray answered with a grin. "Well, DI Sidana is a Londoner, definitely. DS Cullen is slightly posh, so that makes his harder to place, but I'd guess somewhere in the Home Counties." She glanced at him. "I don't think you're a native Londoner, though, sir, if you don't mind me saying so. There's something a bit Northern to yours."

"Good call," Kincaid said, impressed. "It's Cheshire, actually, but I've been in London twenty years now."

"Anyway," McGillivray continued, "this bloke, he was off, you know? I've seen his type often enough when I was on the beat. If he hadn't made me as a copper—and I felt sure he did, even though I wasn't in uniform—I thought he might have forced his way in."

Kincaid remembered Sidana's mention of the male punters in the club. "Run his description by DI Sidana in the morning, see if she ties him to the men she saw at Gibbs's place."

They were on his home turf now, having passed the Ladbroke Grove Sainsbury's, where he or Gemma usually did their weekly shopping, and the darkness on their left marked the Kensal Green Cemetery.

A few minutes later they reached a street near the Willesden Sport Centre and pulled up in front of a vaguely faux-Tudor semi-detached house. All the on-street parking spaces were taken—unsurprising at six o'clock on a Sunday evening—so McGillivray pulled into the property's paved-over forecourt behind a motorbike and an aging Renault hatchback.

As they climbed out of the car, he saw that the forecourt's front wall needed a new coat of white paint, as did the house's trim, but the place looked otherwise clean and decently maintained. He and McGillivray both straightened their jackets, then McGillivray rang the bell. From inside the house, he could hear the familiar theme of *The Six O'Clock News*.

The woman who answered the door did not look pleased. "You can't park there," she said. "And whatever you're selling, I don't want any. Now, bugger off before I call the police." As she started to shut the door, McGillivray stepped into the doorway.

"Mrs. Nira Gupta?" McGillivray held up her warrant card. "We *are* the police. May we come in?"

Kincaid put Gupta in her mid-forties, near enough the same age as Neel Chowdhury. She was thin, with bony wrists and shoulders, and her clothes gave off the distinct whiff of stale tobacco.

She stared at them blankly, then her hand flew to her chest. "My husband! Has something happened to my husband?"

Once they'd reassured her, she invited them in. The sitting room was cluttered but comfortable, with pride of place taken by the large flat-screen TV, which Mrs. Gupta muted.

She motioned them to seats on the black mock-leather sofa and cleared a basket of laundry so that she could sit in the matching armchair.

They'd agreed that McGillivray would lead. "Mrs. Gupta," she began, "I'm afraid we have some bad news about your cousin, Neel Chowdhury. He was found dead this morning, near his flat. You were listed in his hospital records as his next of kin."

Gupta's dark brows drew together in a puzzled frown. "Neel? Dead? Oh my goodness. But how? Was it an accident?"

"I'm afraid not, ma'am," said McGillivray. "We are treating his death as suspicious. We'd like to ask you a few questions, if you don't mind."

Blinking, Gupta shook her head. "I'm sorry. I just need a moment to take it in." Her fingers strayed to the cigarette-packet-shaped outline in the pocket of her gray cardigan, which she patted before returning her hand to her lap. From the lack of an ashtray on the coffee table, Kincaid assumed that she didn't smoke in the house.

"Perhaps a cup of tea, ma'am," offered McGillivray. "If you'll point me towards the kitchen, I can—"

"Oh no." Gupta pushed herself up from the armchair. "Where are my manners? Please, sit. I'll just put the kettle on." Before McGillivray could offer to help, she'd disappeared through the doorway that led to the kitchen. Kincaid heard the click of the switch on the kettle, then the rattle of crockery, then the bang of a door.

"Should I help, sir?" whispered McGillivray.

Kincaid shook his head. "Smoke break. Give her a bit."

A few minutes later, Gupta returned with a tray holding three mugs of milky tea, the Tetley's bags still in, and a plate of custard creams.

"I just can't believe it," she said as she sank down on the edge of the armchair. "Neel, dead. We're the only ones left on that side of the family. Our mums were sisters. We were only a few months apart, so we always had to play together as kids."

Kincaid noticed the phrasing. "Did you and your cousin not get on?" he asked, accepting one of the mugs.

Gupta pulled a face. "It sounds dreadful to say it, but Neel was always a right little shit, even as a child. A tattletale and a stirrer, you know. But still, I wouldn't have wished him . . . dead. Can you not tell me what happened to him?"

"Mr. Chowdhury was attacked by person or persons unknown." He did not want anyone, relative or not, spreading word of a second stabbing. "Do you know of anyone who might have wanted to harm your cousin?"

"Oh." Gupta's eyes widened. "No, not really. I mean, I can't imagine anyone caring enough to—" She put a hand to her mouth. "That sounds dreadful."

"No girlfriends? Or boyfriends?"

"I don't think he liked women much. But on the other hand, I never had the impression that he fancied men, either."

Kincaid thought of the bizarre collection of Staffordshire dogs in Chowdhury's flat. The man had liked something, at least. "We noticed that he seemed very fond of china dogs. Staffordshire, I believe."

"Oh, that." Gupta sighed. "That's from our Welsh granny, I suppose. She had half a dozen of those creepy things. Neel was fascinated by them when we were children, but he wasn't allowed to touch. She'd smack him with a ruler if she caught him near them. I don't know what happened to the dogs when she died. Maybe Neel got some of them."

"Had you seen your cousin recently?" asked McGillivray. She had unobtrusively brought out her notepad.

"Not since his mum's funeral, so that would be two years ago. Honestly, our lives just didn't intersect much. I suppose I'll be needing to make . . . arrangements for him?"

Kincaid handed her his card. "We'll be in touch, once funeral arrangements can be made, and once our investigators have finished with his computer and documents. You don't happen to know who his solicitor was?"

"I can give you the name of the man our mums used, Mr. Jenkins." She rifled through the things on the coffee table looking for a scrap of paper until McGillivray tore a page from her notebook.

When she'd copied the solicitor's name, Kincaid said, "Thank you. You've been very helpful, Mrs. Gupta. But one more thing, if you don't mind." He unfolded the copy he'd made of the obituary clipping found in Chowdhury's pocket. "Do you know if your cousin had a connection to this woman, Sandra Beaumont?"

Gupta frowned as she studied the clipping. "Her name sounds familiar, but I don't—oh, wait. I know where I've seen her name. It was in the newspaper story after that big stink at Neel's last hospital. That's why Neel left his last job, I always thought, because of the bad publicity. She"—Gupta tapped the clipping—"was one of the other staff on the ward." Both Kincaid and McGillivray must have looked blank, because she shook her head impatiently. "You know, when there was all that fuss about the Ebola case."

CHAPTER NINETEEN

The pub was classic—unadorned wooden furniture, Sky Sports on a mounted flat-screen television, a video-game machine, lots of etched glass and brass behind the bar. But best of all, it was quiet enough for a conversation. Doug bought a pint for himself and a glass of Pinot Grigio for Tully. Her choice was an uncomfortable reminder of Melody's usual white wine, but he determinedly shoved that thought away.

"Thank you," said Tully as she raised her glass to him. "You shouldn't have, really." Some of the stiffness had gone from her shoulders and the high color had receded from her cheeks.

They'd settled at a corner table and Doug had given Tully the banquette, even though it left him with his back to the room, always an uncomfortable feeling. "You've had a very tough weekend. I just wanted to make sure you were okay."

"Tough doesn't half cover it." Closing her eyes, Tully rested her cold glass against her cheek for a moment. "I keep thinking I'll wake up and it will all have been a really bad dream." She sniffed and attempted a smile. "Hasn't happened yet."

"No." Doug took a sip of his beer. "I can only imagine."

"It's horrible being in the flat. Everything reminds me of Sasha, and I keep expecting her to walk through the door." Her eyes filled and she sniffed again. "I thought I'd feel better in the studio. I wanted to get some things in the kiln. But that didn't exactly work out. As you saw."

"You seemed a little upset back there." He nodded towards the gallery. Not wanting to admit he'd been eavesdropping, he added carefully, "I got the impression your boss was being a bit shirty."

Tully snorted. "Of all the days to pick to complain about the cost of running the kiln, and whether I'm earning my keep, so to speak." She rolled her eyes. "Wanker. It's not that the kiln's not expensive, I'll give him that. But he has family money. You'd think he was running the gallery on a shoestring, the way he goes on, but he can bloody well afford a few extra pounds on a firing."

"How did you end up there?" Doug asked.

"It wasn't that long after I'd got the job at the museum and moved in with Sash. David came into my department and said he was looking for an experienced potter who might want to pick up some extra hours as a sales assistant, and there was studio space available. I jumped at it. I didn't mind working weekends and our department usually finishes early on Fridays, so I could get some extra hours then, too.

"I hadn't had access to a studio since I finished at uni, and to find something not just in Central London but practically across the street from the museum"—she shook her head—"well, no way was I going to pass that up."

"No, I can see that." Doug liked hearing her talk about what she did—it gave him a sense of her that wasn't colored by the tragedy of Sasha's death. Tully Gibbs might not be exactly pretty, but when her face lit up with enthusiasm, it was hard to look away.

"What about you?" Tully asked.

Startled, he realized he'd been staring at her for longer than was polite. "Me?"

"Yes, you. We've talked about me, me, and more me, and I don't know anything about you. Other than your job, obviously." Her mouth turned down at the corners but she took a determined gulp of her wine.

"Oh. I'm not very interesting, I'm afraid. I grew up in St. Alban's. Went to boarding school. Went to university. My dad expected me to get a law degree and join his chambers. But"—he shrugged—"I saw a recruitment advert for the Met, and I went for the interview on a whim. I knew my dad would be disappointed, but I saw his life spread out before me, with the bridge clubs and the chambers infighting and the boring petty cases, and I knew I couldn't bear a single day of it."

His skin prickled with embarrassment. He'd never told anyone why he'd joined the service. No one had ever asked, other than the Met interviewer, and then he'd spouted the usual bollocks about *using his talents to make a difference.*

"Not that there isn't enough of infighting and petty boring cases in the police," he added, "but at least I've escaped the bridge club."

"Your dad must have gone spare," said Tully.

Doug winced. "That is an understatement. 'The best public school education wasted on social work for the riffraff, blah, blah.'"

"Ouch. I'll bet he reads the *Telegraph*."

Doug laughed. "Sometimes I think he dips into the *Daily Mail*. But only in secret."

Tully smiled back, and he liked the way her eyes crinkled at the corners. "So, you did the unexpected, you're a rebel," she said. "How is that not interesting? What else?"

He shrugged. "Not much, really. Last year I bought a little house in Putney. I like to row, although I wasn't tall enough at uni to make a college boat. I keep a little scull at Putney Reach."

She studied him over the rim of her wineglass. "No pets? No girlfriend?"

He felt himself flushing again. He was going to sound like a sad case if he answered honestly, but he felt she deserved it. "No to both. The job makes it difficult. I wouldn't mind having a dog, but I work long hours and I never know when I might not be able to get home."

"You could have a cat. They're much more forgiving. We always had cats when I was growing up. I miss them." She sounded sad again, caught up in a memory.

"How about another round?" Doug asked, and when she nodded, he scooped up her now-empty glass with one hand and his pint with the other.

When he came back from the bar, he thought Tully looked as if she'd freshened up. It never failed to amaze him what women could do with a bit of lipstick and face powder—the traces of her earlier tears had vanished. He put down their drinks and a couple of packets of crisps. "I thought you might need a boost."

"Ooh, sea salt and vinegar. My favorite," Tully exclaimed. But although she tore open the packet, she didn't take a crisp. Instead, she pleated the torn-off paper strip between her fingers, then looked up at him with an expression he couldn't read. "It was very kind of you to rescue me," she said. "But I don't imagine you came by the gallery looking for a damsel in distress."

Doug felt a bit wrongfooted by this, as if he'd lost control of the interview—if interview it was. "I was happy to help. But, actually,

I did have a question. It's about Sasha's brother, Tyler. We'd like to have a word with him but he seems to have disappeared."

"Tyler?" Tully's eyes widened in surprise. "He'll be at his parents', I'm sure—"

"They haven't heard from him. They're a bit concerned. I thought you might have some idea where he stayed when he wasn't at college, that Sasha might have mentioned it."

She shook her head. "No, not that I remember. But my brother might know."

Doug frowned. Surely she knew they'd questioned Jon Gibbs about Tyler. "Tully, have you spoken to your brother?"

"Not since yesterday, when I told him . . . about Sasha. He texted today and said he'd meet me for lunch tomorrow, when the club's closed. I can take an hour on my break from the museum."

Doug couldn't mention her brother's altercation with Tyler Johnson, as he had no legitimate way of knowing about it. Instead, he said, "Did you ever get the impression that Tyler was involved in some . . . risky activities?"

"You mean like drugs?" Tully didn't seem too surprised. "Not specifically, no, but whenever Sasha talked to him lately, she seemed out of sorts afterwards, and I know how she felt about drug use. She said she'd seen the results too often in A and E. If she suspected . . ." Frowning, she added, "I wish I'd never suggested Jon might give him some work at the club. He doesn't need that sort of trouble."

It seemed to Doug that Tully was very protective of her brother. "Are the two of you close?" he asked. "I'm an only, but I always wished I had a brother or sister."

"Yeah. We are." Her expression softened and she picked up her wineglass. "I don't know what I'd have done when Mum died, without Jon. But . . . yesterday you said you didn't think Jon was

upset about Sasha. That's not true at all. It's just . . . complicated."
She set her glass down again and twirled it by the stem.

"Complicated how?"

Tully looked up and met his gaze. "The year before our mum
died, my best friend disappeared. The police questioned Jon."

———

"When is Dad going to be home?" Toby stood, shifting foot to
foot, right in Gemma's path between the chopping board and the
fridge.

"Soon." He'd texted an hour ago to say he had one last interview,
in Willesden, and would be home after that. Nudging Toby, she
said, "Move it, kiddo. Make yourself useful, why don't you?" She
nodded towards the cutlery drawer. "Set the table, please."

"I want to show him my new step." Toby did a little shuffle tap.
Mary Poppins Returns had been playing on repeat ever since they'd
returned from his rehearsal, and he'd been trying to imitate some
of the dances.

In the sitting room, Lin-Manuel Miranda's clear voice sang "Underneath the Lovely London Sky." Humming along, Gemma finished cutting up salmon fillets for a red curry and coconut stir-fry.

It had taken her some practice to learn to use the boiling
plate on the Aga for quick, hot cooking, but she'd perfected the
technique—it was all in the prep, so that every ingredient was
ready to go in the pan. She'd shooed Kit out of the kitchen for the
evening, as he had a maths exam the next morning and needed
to study.

A car door slammed in the street, followed by a volley of barking and then Charlotte shrieking, "Papa!"

A moment later Kincaid came into the kitchen, dogs still

dancing round his feet, Charlotte and Toby tugging on him from either side.

"Give your dad a moment to breathe," Gemma told the children as she kissed his cheek. His hair was damp, and he smelled, faintly, of cigarette smoke. "Was that your new DC?" she asked, nodding towards the street. "You should have invited her in."

"I suspect she was glad to be rid of me," Kincaid said. "Long day."

"Papa, I've been sewing," piped Charlotte. "Come see my fabrics. It's got flowers—"

"No, Char, he doesn't want to see your silly sewing," Toby interrupted. "Dad, I learned a new dance. You have to see it—"

"Enough." Gemma put her hands on her hips and glared. In her best she-who-must-be-obeyed voice, she added, "No show-and-tell until after supper. I mean it, both of you. Go wash up, turn off the telly, and call your brother."

Go they did, although not without some whining. Kincaid scooped Rose from a kitchen chair and sank into it while Gemma poured him a glass of wine from the bottle in the fridge. "You're not going out again?" she asked as she handed it to him.

"I bloody well hope not. And thank you." He tugged off his tie and stuffed it into his jacket pocket with a sigh of relief.

"They've missed you today," Gemma said with a nod indicating the kids. "I suspect you spoiled them rotten last night."

Kincaid looked round as if suddenly aware of an absence. "Where's Kit?"

"Studying. I hope you're not worried about my cooking," she added with a smile.

"Your cooking is top-notch." He raised his glass to her. "If we're not careful they'll be auditioning you for *Master Chef*." After a sip of wine, he said, "It's just that I haven't had a chance to talk to

him about Wesley. When he came in last night I was busy putting
the little ones to bed, then by the time I'd finished he was on the
phone." Frowning, he added, "About last night, Sidana said—"

There was a shout, more barking, and the clatter of feet on the
stairs. All three children burst into the kitchen.

"Oi," said Kit, snagging Toby in a headlock, "those are my earbuds you've got. Dad, tell him to give them back."

Gemma tossed the salmon into the hot pan and called out,
"Three minutes. Chairs, you lot. Now."

—

After supper, Kincaid had overseen baths while Gemma did the
washing up. Then he'd read a chapter of *The Wind in the Willows*
to Charlotte and Toby. His mother had recently sent him the copy
he and Juliet had read as children, with its original Ernest Shepard
illustrations.

Kit, who was supposed to be studying, had come in quietly, removing his earbuds as he folded himself into a seat on the floor just
inside Charlotte's doorway.

"Mum read it to me," Kit said afterwards, when the younger
children were tucked up in their beds and just he and Kincaid stood
in the hallway between the bedrooms. "I remember thinking that
it had been written just for me, that it was *my* river, and that if I just
looked hard enough I'd see Rat or Mole or Toad."

Until his mother's death when he was eleven, Kit had lived in a
cottage in the Cambridgeshire village of Grantchester. The back
garden had sloped right down to the River Cam, and Kit had spent
every spare moment in the water or on the riverbank. "Mum used
to call me Water Rat."

"You miss it," Kincaid said, a statement rather than a question.

Kit shrugged. "Not so much this time of year."

But Kincaid had seen the flash of grief in his son's eyes. "We should visit soon."

"Nathan and I have been writing letters," Kit said.

Kincaid stared at him in surprise. "Letters? You mean actual *on-paper* letters?"

"Nathan says you can't formulate a view of the world in an email. Or, God forbid, a text." Kit's mimicry of their friend Nathan Spring was so spot on that Kincaid laughed, but Kit continued, "And he says that if I'm to make a mark in life, I need to learn what I think, and how to express it."

"That's very good advice," Kincaid said, touched that Kit had shared this with him. "He's a good man, Nathan. And I'm sure he considers himself fortunate to be your friend." Dr. Nathan Spring, lecturer in biology at Cambridge, had been Kit and his mother's neighbor in Grantchester.

"He says maybe I can come up for a couple of days over the Christmas hols."

"Not until after the ballet," Kincaid said, raising his brows in mock horror.

"No way." Kit grinned and shrugged himself away from the doorjamb he'd been leaning against. "Well, back to maths." He disappeared into the boys' room, earbuds already back in place, and Kincaid realized he still hadn't spoken to him about Wes. It would keep.

When Kincaid at last reached the kitchen, he found Gemma seated at the table, tea steeping in her Clarice Cliff pot.

"Cuppa?" She raised one of the two mugs she'd set out.

"I think I'll pass. Too much caffeine today as it is." Fetching a glass, he poured himself a scant finger's worth of his latest Scotch Malt Whisky Society acquisition, a treat reserved for special occasions—or very long days. He added a tiny splash of water and sank gratefully into a chair. Taking a sip, he closed his eyes for a moment as the warmth spread through him.

When he blinked, he saw that Gemma was watching him, her expression concerned. "Start from the beginning," she said.

So he did. As he spoke, he saw that Gemma had conjured a pad and pen and was scribbling quick notes. He told her about the crime scene, about Howard Quirk, and about his visit with Sidana to Chowdhury's flat. When he reached Chowdhury's strange menagerie of Staffordshire dogs, Gemma looked up.

"My mum had one when we were kids—it sat on the mantel above the electric fire in our sitting room. It came from her granny, but I've no idea what happened to it."

"You should ask. It might finance their retirement."

Gemma snorted. "Fat chance, that. It probably went to Oxfam years ago. So do you think this Chowdhury was running a stolen-china-dog ring?"

He smiled. "Stranger things have happened. I've asked Alex Dunn if he can have a look at them." It had been Alex, their antique dealer friend, who'd given Gemma the Clarice Cliff teapot. "Have you heard how Wesley and Betty are doing?"

"Wes called by this morning, to see you. He wanted to apologize for being abrupt yesterday—"

Kincaid shook his head. "He needn't. He had every reason to be upset."

"We talked a bit about Sasha. I got the impression that she was . . . troubled. Not just at work, but personally. It sounds like she might have been having an affair."

"With a married man, you mean?"

"Maybe. Or at least with someone she didn't want to introduce to her friends." She told him about her visit to Betty's and her conversation with Des Howard. "I thought I'd check with Jasmine in case she managed to snap a photo of Jon Gibbs last night. I could have Des take a look at it." Swirling the dregs of her tea, she added, frowning, "Although as far as we know, Gibbs isn't married, but I suppose there could be other reasons she was sneaking around with him."

"Something to do with Tyler, would be my guess," Kincaid said. "Any chance either of you got a photo of the punters in the club last night? Lucy McGillivray, the DC who dropped me off, has been acting as family liaison to the Johnsons. She says that while she was there this afternoon, a man came looking for Tyler. Reeked of gangster, from her description. I wondered if it might have been one of Tyler's mates."

"Sounds like the burly white guy, the one Tyler seemed most afraid of." Gemma stood and emptied her teacup into the sink, then sat down again and poured a splash of his whisky into her cup. Before Kincaid could caution her, she took a swallow, then coughed until her eyes were streaming. "Bloody hell. How do you drink this stuff?" she spluttered when she could get her breath.

"Add a bit of water." Kincaid grinned. "And take very small sips."

"I'll stick to my gin, thank you very much."

"Remind me not to take you to the whisky society—you'd disgrace me," he said, still smiling, then he grew serious. "Jasmine said the two of you went back to the club last night with some ruse about your losing your mobile. That could have been dangerous. Whoever is committing these murders is ruthless, and I don't like the idea of you two wandering around Soho—"

"We weren't wandering." Gemma tipped a splash of water into her cup with more force than necessary. "And we have had some training, in case you've forgotten."

Kincaid was beginning to regret putting Gemma and Jasmine Sidana together, but he was curious. "She was all right last night? Jasmine?"

"She was brilliant. She's not nearly as starchy as you think, you know."

"So I'm beginning to gather."

"And you don't know that either the first or the second killing has anything to do with either Jon Gibbs or Tyler Johnson." More thoughtfully, Gemma added, "Still, from what we saw last night, Tyler is obviously in some sort of trouble." She took a much more tentative sip from her teacup. "I'd say the only reason Tyler showed up at the club last night was because he was afraid not to. He could be in real danger."

Kincaid sighed. "I don't want another body on my watch. But we can't protect him if we can't find him. I had a text from Doug. Tyler's cleared out of his rooms at the residence hall. The only remote lead Doug found is the first name of a girl he's been seen with around the university. Following that up will take wading through miles of university red tape, and for all we know there are dozens of girls in their system named Chelsea."

Gemma's brow furrowed in the way it did when she was thinking through a knotty problem, and Kincaid knew the expression well enough to wait. He was rewarded when, after a long moment, she said, "If I were you, I'd have a word with Trudy, the bartender at the club. I definitely had the impression that she and Tyler were close."

—

Melody stood in Oxford Street, just outside the Tottenham Court Road tube station, unable to move forward, unable to get a breath.

The pedestrians parted around her as if she were a boulder in a stream bed. A large man bumped her shoulder and swore as he pushed past her, but still she stood, buffeted by a tide of memories.

To her left lay Hanway Place and Andy's flat. To her right was Denmark Street, where Andy had first taken her to hear him play—the night she'd gone home with him afterwards.

And now, almost two months since that awful September day when he'd told her they were finished, she was going to see him again.

When she'd left him a message that morning, it had been her final straw, her attempt at some sort of closure that would allow her to get on with her life. She hadn't expected to hear back.

And then he'd texted her. *We should talk.*

He'd sent her the name of the taco place in the food arcade at Centre Point, and a time, seven o'clock.

His territory.

She checked her watch—it was still too early. What if she sat in the restaurant and he didn't come? But when the lights changed, she let the crowd surge carry her into the zebra crosswalk, and then she kept going along New Oxford Street until she reached the arcade entrance.

There were several restaurants in the open-plan food hall, but the taco place was easy to spot. It was busy, too, and at first she didn't see Andy.

But then there he was, at a table near the bar, in his navy pea-coat. His head was down as he studied something, and the bright lighting burnished his blond hair.

Then he looked up, his eyes widening as he saw her. He didn't smile.

It took all of Melody's willpower to thread her way through the tables until she reached him. He stood and they kissed cheeks, a ritual social greeting, but her skin burned where his lips had barely skimmed it.

"Thanks for coming," he said as she slid out a chair and sat.

"Thanks for asking me." Oh God, she sounded an idiot. But she couldn't take her eyes from his face. He looked exhausted, his eyes shadowed, the blue irises so dark that they looked almost black. His shaggy hair needed cutting and he had at least a day's worth of stubble.

She hadn't had any idea what she would say to him—she'd rehearsed a dozen openings and dismissed them. But now she blurted, "Are you okay? I saw in the paper, about you and Poppy canceling your tour. I was worried about you."

This earned her a crooked smile. "I'd no idea we'd make the important news. Let me get you something to drink." He gestured to a server passing their table, but the girl apparently suffered from voluntary blindness.

The place was pulsing, the noise level rising in just the few minutes she'd been inside. When a party of four squeezed into the table next to them with loud apologies, Andy pushed his chair back and stood. "Let's go somewhere else." Dropping a five-pound note on the table, he gestured to Melody to lead the way to the door.

When they came out of the arcade into the cool dampness of Oxford Street, he immediately turned right, propelling Melody along with a light touch of his palm on her back. "That was a bad idea," he said, once they could hear again. "I thought it would be someplace we could talk."

He set a quick pace down New Oxford Street, and when Melody spotted the triangular redbrick building with its distinctive green spire, she guessed where they were going. "The Bloomsbury Tavern," she said. It was one of the oldest pubs in London, and reputed to be the last stop on the route to the hangman's noose at Marble Arch. She hoped that wasn't an omen.

Welcoming light spilled from the pub's distinctive leaded windows, and when Andy opened the door they were met with a wave of warmth and the comforting smell of chips frying. Once in the long, narrow room, they squeezed into the corner of a banquette. Andy slipped out of his coat and went to the bar without asking what she fancied.

This gave Melody a chance to observe him, and she didn't like what she saw. He'd always been slight, but now his shoulder blades looked sharp beneath the fabric of his long-sleeve T-shirt, and there was a hunched defensiveness to his posture.

Returning with a glass of white wine for her and a pint of ale for himself, he slid into the chair facing her.

"Thank you," she said into an awkward silence.

Andy lifted his glass in a slightly mocking salute. "You're welcome."

They looked at each other, the silence stretching, and then they both said at once, "I'm sorry."

Andy gave a snort. "All right. You first, then."

Melody swallowed. "I'm sorry I didn't tell you about my parents."

He scowled. "You were ashamed of me. Of where I came from, and what I do."

But she was shaking her head before he finished. "No, no, that's not true at all. I wanted you to lo—" She stumbled over the word, frowned, and started over. "I wanted you to *like* me for myself, not as an extension of them. Not for what influence they might have." Seeing him start to protest, she hurried on, entreating. "By the time I knew you well enough to realize that those things didn't matter to you, it got more and more awkward to explain. I'd never even told anyone at work about my family, and it had sort of got to be a habit, not sharing that. Even now, it's only Doug and Gemma and Duncan who know. I was going to tell you—I just couldn't work out how."

Andy stared at her for a long moment. Then, at last, he shrugged and his mouth relaxed. "Maybe I was . . . hasty. But I felt"—he winced—"dismissed. And left out."

Melody reached out, brushing his hand with her fingertips. "I never meant to hurt you."

She'd been protecting herself. But she saw now that it had been cruel as well as thoughtless. She knew Andy's story, knew how vulnerable he was beneath his tough guitar-boy exterior. "It was stupid of me, keeping things from you. And selfish."

This earned her another crooked smile. "I might have to agree." But he turned his hand up and grasped her fingers for an instant. The warmth lingered on her skin even after he released her.

Clasping her hands together to stop herself touching him again, she leaned across the table and said quietly, "You trusted me, and I let you down. I don't know if you can forgive me."

He looked away, but not before she'd seen the glint of tears in his eyes. "Honestly, I don't know if I can, either." His voice was hoarse.

Melody didn't trust herself to speak again. She wouldn't beg.

She'd steeled herself to make a graceful exit when he met her gaze again and said, "But it looks like I'll be around, at least for a while."

Not certain what he meant, she asked gingerly, "What happened? With you and Poppy, and the tour."

"That was bollocks." He shook his head. "They threw us out there, Tam and Caleb. Some of those bookings were fucking snake pits." Grimacing, he took a gulp of beer as if to wash away a bad taste.

"Not as glamorous as it's cracked up to be, the rock-and-roll life," Melody said, attempting lightness.

He didn't smile. "I never wanted the sort of attention we got, the tabloid bollocks. I just wanted to make music, but I wanted to make it on my own terms."

"You and Poppy haven't"—she hesitated over the term—"broken up?"

"No, we haven't split up. But Poppy wasn't ready for life on the road. She's too bloody young for that—she'd never been away from her family, never even lived away from her parents. I could see the toll it was taking. She wanted to go home, finish her music degree at college, see her brothers. And we want to get back into the studio, put together an album. Then, when we're ready, we'll choose when—and where—we play."

He was leaning towards her now, both hands on the table, and Melody realized how much she'd missed this, his passion for what he did. Then, he grimaced again and sat back. "Now I'm the one not being honest. That's not the whole truth. It wasn't just about Poppy."

Melody braced herself for bad news, but he surprised her.

"*I* wasn't ready to play the gigs," he said. "I—whenever we were onstage, if there was a noise, a disturbance, or just someone hanging about in the back of the room, I'd—" He stopped again, wetting his lips before he said, "I'd just . . . freak, you know? I'd see the grenade flash, and the smoke. The smell." He shook his head. "I kept telling myself that if I could just keep playing the gigs, it would get better. But it didn't. I can't—" He stopped and looked round, as if suddenly aware of a threat even here, in the cozy confines of the pub.

Following his gaze, Melody saw that he was looking at two girls at a nearby table, and that they were staring back, whispering.

"Bugger," he said, pushing away his unfinished pint and rocking the table as he stood. "Come on," he said, his voice rough. "I don't need this shit. Let's get out of here."

Shrugging into her coat, Melody let him pull her to her feet, felt his arm come round her hard as he hustled them to the door.

But even in the confusion of their exit, she caught, on the edge of her vision, the flash of a mobile phone camera.

CHAPTER TWENTY

She was burning up. Blisters, her skin was blistering from the heat. The sun—or was it a fire? Moaning, she tried to kick away the weight on her legs. Was it the tent? Had it fallen on her? She gasped and her eyes flew open.

Not the tent.

A room. An ordinary room. An ordinary bed, with the coverings half on the floor. A desk, a wardrobe, a bedside table, a streetlamp illuminating a gap in the curtains. Pushing her matted hair from her face, she struggled into a sitting position and fumbled for the switch on the lamp.

This was her room, she remembered now, the hotel room she'd taken last night near Paddington Station, when the house had been locked.

Locked.

Why was the house locked? She couldn't remember. They would be waiting for her—no, that wasn't right. She was cold now, shivering, her teeth beginning to chatter. She lunged for the dressing gown that was still bunched at the foot of the bed and managed to shrug herself into it, but the room was swimming and she was horribly, ragingly thirsty. Unsteadily, she stood, balancing for a moment before staggering into the bathroom.

But she couldn't drink, not yet. There, in her toilet bag, the old-fashioned mercury thermometer she always carried. She slid it under her tongue and only then did she look in the mirror. Eyes red, skin white but blotched with fiery pink. Closing her eyes, she tried to count the minutes, but the room tilted ominously and she pulled the thermometer out and squinted at the mercury line.

Oh no. It couldn't be. But this thermometer didn't lie.

When she drew a deep breath, her throat hurt. Dear God.

"No, please," she whispered. She'd been screened at the airport in Kinshasa. No fever then, no symptoms. But she must have carried the virus in her system, waiting. Incubating. She sipped a little water from the bathroom cup, then held the coolness of the glass against her cheek as she fought the sudden surge of nausea.

She knew how this progressed, all too well. She had to get help, and soon. But she couldn't risk exposing anyone, not the desk staff at the hotel, not a cabdriver or an ambulance crew.

The hospital wasn't far. She would walk. While she could.

"Budge up, budge up," Doug muttered as he squeezed his way onto the tube train. Any weekday-morning commute into Central London was bad enough, but on this damp and dreary Monday his fellow passengers seemed grumpier and more distracted than usual. It had been drizzling and still fully dark when he'd crossed Putney Bridge on his way to the tube station, the river an inky gulf beneath the parapet.

He'd stood looking over that same parapet last night, hoping that a few minutes of communing with the dark swirl of the Thames would clear his head and help him decide what to do about Tully. It was not as if she'd sworn him to secrecy—she would know he had to follow up on her story. Still, she'd confided in him and he felt he owed it to her to do a little digging before he took the information to Kincaid.

The summer Tully turned sixteen, her best friend had walked out of her parents' house on mid-summer eve and simply vanished. Pushing aside her wineglass, Tully had taken a photo, creased with wear, from her wallet.

Doug had gazed at the two laughing girls, their arms round each other's waists. Tully seemed hardly to have changed. The other girl, Rosalind Summers, was pale-skinned and dark-haired, with a tiny silver ring in one nostril and a flirtatious cast to her smile.

There had been no sign of foul play, Tully said, but no trace of the girl had been found in the weeks and months that followed. Tully and her brother had been questioned repeatedly but had both been at home with their mother and had no idea what had happened to Rosalind.

Then Tully's mum had been diagnosed with cancer, and by the time Tully finished school, her mother had died. Tully took up her place at university and Jon moved to London as well. Neither sibling had been back to the village since.

Understandable, Doug supposed, given their mother's death. But what if it was more than that? What if Gibbs had been responsible for the disappearance of Tully's friend?

What if Tully and her mother had lied to protect him?

What if he had come to London not to look out for his sister but to make certain she kept what she knew to herself?

And what if Sasha had somehow found out the truth about the missing girl?

The train lurched as it slowed for Holborn Station. Doug couldn't shake the image of the two girls, arm in arm on a green summer day, a stick of candy floss held up between them. Not even the smell of wet wool emanating from the pinstripe-suited man crammed into the carriage beside him could quite banish the scent of strawberries and spun sugar from his imagination.

He needed to talk to someone from the Somerset team that had investigated Rosalind Summers's disappearance, but he could hardly do that without informing Kincaid. What he really needed was someone skilled at researching newspaper archives. In other words, the one person he couldn't ask for help.

—

The press conference had gone as well as could be expected. The chief super assured the public that the police did not think Sasha Johnson's death was related to gang violence, nor did they believe they had a modern-day Jack the Ripper stalking young women in Bloomsbury. They were following a number of leads and would continue to keep the press, and the public, informed. Kincaid had then stepped in to ask members of the public to come forward if they had seen anything suspicious in Russell Square on Friday evening, and that had been that.

The press had not yet, thank God, got wind of the Chowdhury murder, but it was only a matter of time.

Kincaid slipped out of the conference room, avoiding the knot of journalists still chatting—and his boss, if the truth be told. Loosening his tie, he took the stairs up to the CID room.

Simon Gikas turned from the whiteboard, where he'd been putting up photos. "How'd it go, boss?"

"I don't think we're making headlines in the *Sun*. Yet. Which is the good news. But we'd better be making some progress going forward." Kincaid saw that Simon had traded last week's cherry-red trainers for a pair in neon green. "What have you got for us?"

Simon pointed to the first of two photos. "I've been going over the CCTV footage from Manette Street. A man left the club not long after Chowdhury. As you can see here"—he tapped the second photo—"he looks quite similar to this bloke leaving Russell Square by the north gate on Friday evening."

Kincaid crossed the room to study the photos. Both showed a man in a dark anorak with a hood. Both were blurry, and neither showed the wearer's face, even in profile. And that was assuming it was a man, because in the bulky, anonymous clothing, even that was up for grabs.

"I know, I know," said Simon, anticipating Kincaid's comments. "But have a look at the videos."

Kincaid followed him to his workstation, where, with a tapping of keys, Simon pulled up two different videos on his large side-by-side monitors. The left-hand screen showed the Russell Square exit. "This was about ten minutes before the first 999 call," Gikas explained.

It was the usual after-work crush, people hurrying with hoods up or umbrellas unfurled, a good many of them looking down at what he assumed were their mobile phones. Most would be heading for the Russell Square tube station just round the corner. The hooded figure that Simon had singled out moved out of frame, gone in a blink, and the loop began again.

Kincaid focused on the right-hand screen next. The camera outside Bottoms Up in Manette Street had been tightly focused on the area just in front of the club's door, and angled slightly towards Charing Cross Road. On the screen, the club's door swung outwards and a man appeared in the video frame. Dark hair, an overcoat bunched up tightly around the chin, a glint as the light caught the lens of his glasses. Then he turned right, swayed, steadied himself against the wall before disappearing in the direction of Greek Street, but in that instant the camera had caught him full-face. Chowdhury.

Simon held up a finger. "Wait for it."

Then, on the screen, the door opened again. A figure filled the video frame. A dark anorak this time, the deep hood pulled up. Without an instant's hesitation, the figure turned right, in the direction Chowdhury had taken, but, unlike Chowdhury, this figure kept its head down, the face obscured by the deep shadow of the hood.

After watching both videos loop again, once, twice, Kincaid nodded at Simon, who froze the feeds. "Two things," he said. "No, make that three things. The subject in both these instances is a man." Even in those short bursts, there had been something indefinably male in the way the figure moved. "And it's the same man, I'd wager all of you a round at the pub on it." There was a murmur of agreement from the other detectives, who had gathered round to watch as well.

"The third thing?" Simon asked.

"The shielding of the face is deliberate. He's aware of the cameras and doesn't mean to be seen."

"If he was there for Chowdhury," put in Doug, "did he meet him, or did he follow him?"

"It's worthwhile someone having another word with Darrell Cherry at the nightclub. See if he remembers any other men on their own that night, and if so, did they pay with a credit card?" Turning back to Simon, Kincaid said, "What about CCTV from Dean Street? Any luck there?"

"No joy there, boss, unfortunately. The angle was wrong from the bank, and no one else had working cameras."

For the city of Big Brother surveillance, thought Kincaid, it was surprising how hard it was to get a good image when you needed it. "Good job, Simon, thank you. Let's move on." He took up his position at the whiteboard again. "Doug, tell everyone what you turned up at the university yesterday."

"Tyler Johnson seems to have moved out of his residence digs lock, stock, and barrel. I gather from the roommate that Tyler thought uni was for plonkers and that he had bigger plans. The roommate also said that Tyler seemed to have a thing for a girl named Chelsea who attends his—meaning the roommate's—lectures. The lecturer is a Dr. Hawkins."

Kincaid noted the names on the board. "Simon, can you start the bureaucratic wheels turning at the university? We may be able to get the girl's full name and details from records, without having to track down this Professor Hawkins. Also, can you have a word with Human Trafficking? See if they've run across an operation like the one Jasmine describes going on at Gibbs's club." He turned to McGillivray.

"Lucy, if you could give Simon a description of the man who came to the Johnsons' flat yesterday, then compare that to Jasmine's description of the men at the club. See if there's a match there. I'd also like to know more about Tyler Johnson's entrepreneurial ambitions, but it sounds to me as if he's got in over his head."

"He'd be very small-fry," Sidana said thoughtfully. "I'm not sure I can imagine these blokes, as unsavory as they were, killing Johnson's sister to make a point."

"I'm inclined to agree. But we'll follow it up, nonetheless. We'll need to have another word with Jon Gibbs, as well, but I think we'll wait until we've followed up Doug's lead on the girl. And until we've explored the other matter," he added with a nod to Sidana.

He'd caught her as he came into the station before the press briefing and asked if she'd managed to get a photo of Jon Gibbs on Saturday night.

"I did, actually," she'd said, "although it's not great." By unspoken accord, they'd moved away from the lift doors and into a quiet corner of reception. Taking her mobile from her bag, she flicked through the photos, and in one Kincaid caught a glimpse of Gemma, laughing, her glass raised, and wondered when he'd seen her look so relaxed.

"I couldn't risk a full-on shot," Sidana had continued, "so a half profile when he was seating another table was the best I could manage." She tilted the screen towards him. The image on it was slightly fuzzy but still recognizable as Gibbs.

"Can you send that to Gemma?" He explained about the friend who'd seen Sasha Johnson arguing with a man in a Covent Garden restaurant. "She'll pass it along and we'll see if we can ID Sasha's companion."

"What's your feeling about Gibbs?" he'd asked when Sidana had shot off a text. "From what you saw the other evening. Do you think he and Sasha were an item?"

She took her time considering her answer. "I'd say he was genuinely upset."

"More upset than you'd expect someone to be on hearing of the violent death of a friend and your sister's flatmate?"

Sidana shrugged and slipped her mobile back into her very organized handbag. "Possibly. But if he was responsible for that death, he could be putting on a very good act all round."

Now, Kincaid wondered what Gibbs had really been doing

when he'd failed to meet Sasha in the Perseverance. He turned back to Simon. "What about Gibbs's alibi for Friday evening?"

"We've checked the cash-and-carry. They do show an order picked up for Bottle on Friday evening." Swiveling in his chair, Simon crossed his one ankle over the other knee, showing the green trainers to full advantage. "If it *was* Gibbs," he went on, "he'd have had his car, or maybe a van. He could have parked near Russell Square, either going to or coming from the cash-and-carry."

"And just nipped out of the car to stab Sasha?" Sidana shook her head. "That sounds pretty far-fetched. And how would he have known where she was, exactly? Unless she called or texted him."

"Ah." Looking pleased, Simon swiveled back to his keyboard. "I was just getting to that. Tech hasn't done the laptop yet, but they did access the phone. All work and no play, was Sasha. Most of her texts and emails seem to be work- or family-related. There are no regular texts between her and Jonathan Gibbs. She did call him, however, or someone listed in her contacts as 'Jon,' on Friday afternoon at 2:02. The call lasted less than a minute, so I think we can assume she left a message. She then texted him twice, at 5:15 and again ten minutes later, saying, 'Where the hell are you?'

"Shortly after that, she sent a text to Tully Gibbs. It said, 'Can you meet me usual place ASAP? Was meeting J re Ty but no show. Need to talk.' To which Tully replied, 'OMW.' On my way." Simon looked up from his computer screen, his dark eyes without their usual twinkle. "Sasha's text to Tully was her last communication."

Kincaid could see it all so clearly. As illogical as he knew it to be, he still felt that he might have somehow, some way, prevented what had happened to Sasha Johnson.

"What about her brother?" he asked. "Had he been in touch?"

Simon grinned and tapped his screen. "Spot-on. She had a call from Tyler on Thursday just after noon. It lasted about ten minutes."

Kincaid thought back to his conversation with Howard Quirk. If Chowdhury's visitor on Thursday night had been Sasha, Quirk had heard Chowdhury say something about "covering for her." Had he meant that day? "I'd like to know if Sasha left the hospital after that call. Doug, you have a contact there now. See what you can find out, will you? Are we any further forward on Chowdhury's movements on Friday evening?" he added.

Doug shook his head. "I haven't heard back from Nurse Baker. I'll just pop over and have a word now."

"There is one more thing," Simon said as they'd all begun to gather their things or turn to their computer screens. "Sasha Johnson got a text from what looks like a burner phone, on Wednesday last week. It read, 'You fucking slut. Stay away from him or you'll be sorry.'"

—

Gemma's Monday had not begun well. Somewhere in the wee small hours of the morning, Charlotte had cried out with another nightmare. Slipping into her dressing gown, Gemma padded down the stairs in her bare feet. She found Charlotte curled up on the first step above the children's landing, her arms round Geordie, who was whining and trying to lick her face.

"Oh, lovey." Gemma slid down beside her. Charlotte was never able to articulate what monsters inhabited her dreams, but her terror was real. Pulling the child into her lap, Gemma held her, rocking gently, until the sobs had subsided into sniffles. "Come on, lovey, let's get you back to bed."

So it was that Gemma had awakened a few hours later, stiff and cramped in Charlotte's narrow bed, one arm pins and needles from resting under Charlotte's damp head. The clanking of the radiators told Gemma that it was after six and the heating had come on.

Having roused the children and let the dogs out, Gemma had gone upstairs to find Duncan, showered, shaved, and just tying his tie. "You're not dressed," he said when he saw her. "Are you all right? I thought you were up already."

"You might have noticed I wasn't in bed half the night." When he looked at her, startled, she waved her hand at him. "Never mind. Long story."

"I'm sorry, love. I've got to—"

"I know. Press briefing. Go on, then."

This left Gemma to rush three cranky children through breakfast and into the car for the school run. By the time she'd accomplished that, then driven to Met headquarters in Victoria Embankment, she was nearly as cross as the children.

A cup of bad coffee later, she was cheered by a text from Jasmine Sidana that included a photo of Jon Gibbs. She sent the photo on to Des Howard, as promised, but afterwards she stared at the photo for a few minutes, thinking about the evening and how good it had felt to actually be doing some investigating.

She'd turned back to her computer with a sigh when Melody approached her workstation, looking flustered. "Sorry I'm late, boss." Melody looked as if she'd dressed in a hurry—the buttons of the white blouse under her suit jacket were misaligned and her hair was uncharacteristically tousled.

"Are you okay?" Gemma tapped her own blouse, then nodded at Melody.

"Oh, bugger," Melody muttered after a glance at her shirt. "I'll fix it in the loo. Overslept," she added by way of explanation, and turned to go.

Then, at the door, she hesitated. "Boss, about your case—I mean Duncan's case, I suppose. I did a bit of research on the Gibbses."

Gemma gave a noncommittal nod. She thought Melody had a bee in her bonnet about Tully Gibbs. "And?"

"A decade ago, they were involved in the disappearance of a sixteen-year-old girl in Somerset."

"What do you mean, *involved*?"

"Neither of them was charged, but they were questioned, repeatedly. It was Tully's best mate who went missing, a girl called Rosalind Summers. Jonathan Gibbs had been seen talking to her earlier that day. A witness said he was chatting her up."

Gemma frowned. "But he'd already know her well, if she was his sister's best friend."

"Doesn't mean he wasn't coming on to her. Maybe she met him later and things got out of hand . . ." Melody shrugged.

Raising an eyebrow, Gemma said, "So you're saying you think Jon Gibbs killed this girl but was never arrested?"

"His mother and sister swore he was at home with them, watching a film. And . . ." Melody shifted from one foot to the other, then added reluctantly, "He didn't have a car. So if he'd disposed of her body, it would have had to have been in the immediate area, and no body was found. Still, you have to admit the whole thing is fishy. I thought you could pass it on to Duncan."

Gemma gave Melody the frown she seldom used on her friend. "First, if you think this is something the team need to know, you take it directly to Doug. I'm not going to play go-between here.

"And second, I've worked with Somerset CID, and they're a pretty competent bunch. If they didn't charge Gibbs, I suspect they had good reason."

Melody's eyes widened a fraction before she schooled her expression and said, "Right, boss."

She'd turned away before Gemma stopped her. "What was the name of this village in Somerset?"

"It was a place called Compton Grenville, boss."

CHAPTER TWENTY-ONE

Once Kincaid had achieved the seclusion of his office, made a decent cup of coffee, and eaten a doughnut—snatched from the greedy fingers of one of the data-entry PCs—he took out his mobile phone and scrolled through the contacts. When he found the number he wanted, he dialed, and after a few rings was rewarded by the sound of a very South-London voice saying, "Duncan Kincaid, well, I never."

"Lisa. How are things down there in the sticks?"

He'd met DI Lisa Gill on a command course at Hendon several years previously, and they'd got to know each other well enough to exchange Christmas cards and to catch up over a drink when opportunity afforded. She was a Peckham girl who'd taken a posting in the wilds of Brighton and discovered that she actually liked the place, in spite of what she referred to as the shocking lack of melanin in the citizens.

"Same old, same old," she said, but he could hear the note of curiosity in her voice.

"Kids are fine?"

"Jordan's doing his A levels this year. I can't believe how fast the time goes. But considering that it's not even ten o'clock on a Monday morning, my brilliant detective brain tells me that this is not a social call. What can I do for you?"

"I'm interested in a death on your patch a couple of months ago. A woman named Sandra Beaumont. I have an obit but no cause of death, and I wondered if it had come across your radar for any reason."

"Sandra Beaumont?" Gill's voice rose in surprise. "I'll say she came across our radar. She was a nurse, walking home from her shift at the hospital, up on the hill, you know? Someone stabbed her at the edge of the park, and made a messy job of it. A dog walker found her, called 999. They got her to A and E, all right, but she didn't make it. Lost too much blood, apparently."

"Was she able to say what happened, or describe her attacker?"

"No. She was in shock and barely conscious. They'd only started treating her when she went into cardiac arrest. Horrible for the staff there, too, as of course they worked with her."

"Any luck finding the perpetrator?" he asked, although he thought he already knew the answer.

"What do you think? It was eleven thirty at night. Just luck that a man taking his dog for a final pee happened to find her. There was no one else in sight."

"CCTV?"

Lisa Gill gave a snort. "Chance would be a fine thing."

"What about the weapon used?"

He heard the tapping of keys, then Gill said, "Some sort of thin blade. I'll send you the pathologist's report. What's going on, Duncan?" she added, her voice sharp now. "What's your interest in Beaumont?"

"We've had two stabbing deaths in the past three days. Both worked in the same hospital. The second victim had Sandra Beaumont's obituary in his pocket. According to his cousin, he and Beaumont had worked together." He explained their theories about the envelope and how it might have come into Chowdhury's possession.

"You think someone sent him Beaumont's obit as a threat?" Gill asked, her skepticism evident. "Her death wasn't exactly news. She was killed in early October."

"I thought it was worth exploring. We're clutching at straws here. Did her family or colleagues know if she'd had anything similar? Our other victim also had a note in her pocket, but that one was handwritten and I'm not sure the two are connected."

"She hadn't had any threats or problems that I know of. By all accounts, Sandra Beaumont was a happy woman. She was well liked at work and a doting grandmother to her only daughter's seven-year-old son. The daughter's in London. Her details will be in the file I'm forwarding to you."

"What about a husband?"

"Divorced. Amicably, apparently. He seemed gutted when I interviewed him. And he was out of the country on business when Sandra was killed, so he was a non-starter as far as suspects." Gill paused, then added, "I hope you catch the bastard who did this, Duncan, and not just for my clear-up rate. And keep me in the loop, okay?"

When he'd rung off, Kincaid gazed absently at his email inbox as he waited for Gill's report to come through. Until he'd mentioned it, he'd forgotten about the note found in Sasha Johnson's pocket. Could there be a connection between that scribbled scrap and the envelope found in Chowdhury's pocket? He stood up from his desk and opened his office door.

"Simon, did we ever hear from the forensic handwriting expert?"

—

The hospital had begun to seem familiar to Doug, which was not, to his mind, a happy state of affairs. The receptionist in the main foyer even gave him a smile and a wave as he headed for the lifts up to the now equally familiar ward.

Allison Baker, however, seemed less than thrilled when she glanced up from the nursing station and saw him coming through the ward doors. "Detective Sergeant. I haven't had time to ring you. We're still short-staffed and I've been rushed off my feet."

Deciding that placation was his best strategy, Doug said, "I haven't come to scold you, Nurse Baker. I know how busy you must be. But we've had some new information and I was hoping you could shed some light on it."

Baker peered at him over the top of her glasses. "Convincing, I'll give you that much. And even possibly true." She sighed. "Come in the staff room, then, and I'll get someone to cover me for five."

When she'd summoned a young nurse called Esther, Allison led him into the room where he and Kincaid had first spoken to Neel Chowdhury. It looked quite different on her watch—clean cups and saucers were neatly laid out on a tea towel, the magazines were organized into tidy piles, and the moisture-ringed coffee table had been scrubbed as clean as elbow grease could make it.

Allison switched on the kettle, then waved a mug in Doug's direction. "Tea? If I'm going to take a break I might as well get my cuppa in."

"Don't mind if I do, thanks," agreed Doug, although he'd been hoping to get through this interview quickly so that he could concentrate on researching Tully's story.

When Allison had filled two mugs and passed him one of them, she sank onto the utilitarian sofa and stretched out her legs with a sigh. "My feet are going to be the size of rugby balls by the time this shift is finished. And I'm on again tomorrow, as there's no one else to cover the rota until the hospital manages to shuffle some staff." She blew across the top of her cup, then fixed her level gaze on Doug. "Now, to answer your question from yesterday, no one I've spoken to could remember seeing Neel Chowdhury after his shift finished on Saturday.

"In fact, Esther, whom you met, said that he didn't update all of the patient files before he left, which was very remiss of him. She also said that he was distracted and even more short-tempered than usual." With a grimace, she added, "Not that he was sunny on the best of days."

Doug frowned. If this meant they could assume that Chowdhury had left the hospital around eight o'clock on Saturday night, where had he been between then and his arrival at the club at ten?

Allison cut his deliberation short. "Now, what else did you want to ask me?"

"A few questions about Sasha, if you don't mind." Doug looked round for a place to put his teabag, then decided he'd drink the tea stewed. "Or at least partly about Sasha," he amended. "We now know that she had a phone call early on Thursday afternoon, and we have reason to believe that she might have left the hospital for some period of time afterwards."

Looking startled, Allison said, "Thursday? Why do you want to know about Thursday?"

"Was there anything unusual about that day?" Doug asked.

She took a breath as if about to protest, then frowned suddenly.

"Wait. There was a team meeting. But Sasha wasn't there. Of course, the junior doctors are in and out, that's not unusual. But it wasn't like Sasha to miss a scheduled meeting. Neel was very put out, if I remember."

"But Sasha came back?"

Allison sipped her tea, thinking. Finally, she said, "Yes, I'm sure she did. I remember—" Her eyes widened and her face took on a deliberately neutral expression. "I remember seeing her," she continued, setting down her mug and making a bit of a production of checking her fob watch. It was the old-fashioned kind, not one of the newer silicone types he'd seen on some of the staff. "Now, I'm afraid I must get back on the ward—"

"What struck you just now, about Sasha?" Doug leaned forward. "And why didn't you want to tell me?"

"I'm sure it's not important," Allison said, but not before he'd seen her hesitation.

This was a woman used to being in charge, and used to keeping confidences, Doug thought. He needed to handle this carefully, or she would clam up. Firmly, he said, "You can't know that. We wouldn't tell you how to do your job. You need to trust that we know how to do ours, too. Let me be the judge of what matters."

The silence settled. Allison picked up her mug again and turned it in her hands, studying it as if its daisy pattern might reveal a secret. "Of course I want to help the police," she said at last. "But this concerns another person, and I wouldn't like to . . . make things unnecessarily difficult for . . . them." Looking up, she met Doug's gaze. "But you're not going to give up on this, are you, Sergeant?"

"Sorry, but no."

Her shoulders slumped, and she gave an audible sigh. "All right, then, if you insist, but I feel an awful telltale. It was when I was going off my shift on Thursday night. I came in here to get my things from my locker. I was in a hurry and I didn't realize anyone else was in here." She touched her watch again, in what seemed to be an unconscious comforting gesture. "But . . . It was Sasha and . . . They were having a row. And it wasn't the first time I'd seen them in an awkward . . . situation."

"Awkward? As in—"

"Well, unprofessional in any circumstances," Allison said, with a return of some of her crispness. "But especially in this case, as he's married. And her supervisor."

—

Bottoms Up was definitely a cut below Bottle, Sidana thought as she turned from Charing Cross Road into the passage that was Manette Street and spied the club entrance. Still, she'd seen worse, and she supposed the neon martini glass next to the name might be a nice retro touch when it was lit. At least there were no triple X's festooning the windows.

She'd rung ahead, using the contact number the club's manager, Darrell Cherry, had given them, because of course the place was closed on a Monday morning. Cherry had agreed to meet her on the premises, and when she rapped on the door, it opened promptly.

A large, pony-tailed white man surveyed her. "DI Sidana, I presume?"

"Mr. Cherry? Thanks for seeing me. I know this can't be very convenient for you." She stepped inside, blinking as her eyes adjusted to the lower light.

"No problem. Always things need doing here."

She saw that, indeed, he seemed to have been in the process of unpacking the cases of lemonade and bottled beer that rested atop the bar.

While one expected to find a certain amount of seediness to a bar in its off hours, Bottoms Up looked clean and well cared for. And thank goodness such places no longer reeked of stale cigarette smoke, she thought. Music played faintly in the background, something surprisingly swingy with horns and drums.

"Can I get you something to drink?" Cherry asked. When she demurred, he pulled two of the stacked chairs from a nearby table-top and motioned her towards one of them. "Have a seat, then." He flipped the other chair round and straddled it with surprising lightness for a man his size. "Was the video helpful at all?"

"Up to a point." Sidana took out her mobile phone and pulled up the still photo Simon had sent her. It was a freeze-frame of the man who'd left the club after Chowdhury, but although it had been the best angle Simon could find, it still showed only the blur of shoulders and hood. "This man left only a minute or two after our victim, Mr. Chowdhury, and appeared to go in the same direction." She turned the phone's screen to Cherry. "Do you recognize him from Saturday night?"

Cherry took the mobile and studied the image for a long moment, then handed it back to her with a rueful grimace. "I'm sorry, but I can't say that I do. It's our busiest night, Saturday, and we were rushed off our feet. And it was wet out, so most of the punters would have been pulling on macs and putting up hoods or brollies as they left." He glanced at the photo again. "You're sure it's a man?"

"Not entirely, no. That's a best guess."

Nodding, he gestured at the club's entrance. "Would have to be a large woman, given the person's scale against the door frame here."

"This . . . person"—she took her mobile back and tapped the screen—"let's stick with 'he' for the moment—may not have been following Mr. Chowdhury at all. But as it's a possibility we have to consider, can you remember if you'd noticed any men on their own that night?"

"You mean other than your dead bloke?" Cherry nodded towards the far side of the room. "He was sitting just over there. I did notice him, as I told your superintendent, because there was something not quite right about him. You get a nose for it in this business, and I don't like weirdos in my bar." Sidana must have raised an inadvertent eyebrow, because Cherry laughed. "I know you're thinking, *Soho*, *bar*, and yeah, some of our punters are a bit odd. But this guy, sitting there sweating in his raincoat, looking like he was in some third-rate porn house—I don't tolerate *that* sort of weird. Went meekly as a lamb, though, when I had a word with him," Cherry added. "Poor sod . . ."

"Did you notice anyone else?"

"Well, now, let me think. As I said, it was a busy night." Cherry scanned the empty room as if that might trigger a visual memory. In the artificial light, his eyes were the faded blue of old denim, but they were sharp and Sidana thought it wouldn't do to underestimate Darrell Cherry.

Following his gaze, she tried to imagine the place with the lights low, tables packed, glasses clinking, music and conversation flowing. At least half the tables were two-tops, and they were close together, so ordinarily a person alone wouldn't have stood out.

"We get quite a few singles, mostly men," Cherry said, as if she'd spoken aloud. "Some regulars, some tourists wandering in off Charing Cross Road. Maybe . . ." He frowned, then shook his head. "I can't pinpoint anyone. But I can print you a list of the card charges, if you think that might help."

"Thanks. We can cross-check the names against any persons of interest."

"Righto, love. Back in a tick." Before she could object to being called "love," Cherry had jumped up and disappeared through a door near the end of the bar.

Sidana stood as well and walked around the room, examining the big band posters and, on one wall, a collection of fedoras. The music was still playing—was that "Cheek to Cheek"? She swayed a little, humming, and for a moment she imagined herself being swung round on the tiny dance floor in front of the stage.

Then she froze, flushing, when she realized who she'd conjured as her partner. God, she was a silly cow. After she'd stammered a refusal to Rashid's dinner invitation yesterday, she'd probably been put on his "professional politeness only" list. She'd been flustered as a schoolgirl, too, when he'd probably only meant to be nice.

"Here you go, love." Cherry's voice startled her out of her musings.

"Oh, thanks." She took the list, happy to mask her embarrassment, and quickly scanned it.

There was Chowdhury, all right, no surprise there. But there was no Gibbs, of either sex, and no Johnson, nor any other name that rang any bells at all. Still, she'd enter the list into the case file and, unless Darrell Cherry remembered something else, with that she had to be content.

—

According to Simon, the handwriting sample had proved helpful only to the process of elimination. Sasha Johnson had *not* written the note found in her cardigan pocket. There was still the possibility that Neel Chowdhury had been the author of the missive, but Kincaid hadn't been able to come up with a scenario in which that fit.

But who had been threatening Sasha? If the note had indeed been a threat. Kincaid wondered if they were trying to make two plus two equal five.

Or six, if they included the Brighton murder.

He drank the dregs of his cold coffee, grimaced, and scanned his action list again. He'd sent the file on Sandra Beaumont's murder to Rashid, with an urgent flag and an explanatory note. He'd tried the number for Beaumont's daughter, but the call had gone to voicemail. He left a message, explaining who he was and asking that she ring him back at her earliest opportunity.

Doug was still out, as was Sidana. Simon was contacting the cellular provider of the mobile phone that had sent the anonymous text to Sasha.

Had the text been sent by a jealous wife or girlfriend? It seemed an obvious assumption from the wording of the message, but if that were the case, how did Chowdhury fit into it?

Or Jonathan Gibbs?

Or the elusive Tyler Johnson?

Kincaid stood and opened his office door. "Simon," he called out, "any luck with getting the girl's name from the university lecture roster?"

Simon looked up from his keyboard. "Not yet. The lecturer is lecturing, believe it or not. I've left a message. I've also left a message for the university registrar's office."

"Good man." Kincaid closed his door again, but didn't return to his desk. He could see, through the half-drawn blinds of his office's exterior window, that the sun had come out. It was almost lunchtime, and the combination of doughnut and too much black coffee had conspired to give him a splitting headache.

He needed some fresh air.

Last night, Gemma had suggested he speak to the bartender at

Bottle. Having a word with her was certainly worth a try, and it would stop him twiddling his thumbs.

Snagging his jacket from the coat rack, he walked back into the CID room. "I'm going out," he said to Simon. "Text me if there are any developments."

—

He hopped a Number 19 bus right outside the station and rode it all the way through Holborn and down Shaftesbury Avenue to Piccadilly Circus. The wet morning had morphed into a perfect autumn day. The sky was porcelain blue, the air was crisp, and the white stone of the Regency buildings in Piccadilly seemed almost to glow in the sun.

By the time he stepped off the bus and headed up Great Windmill Street, his headache had abated and he was feeling distinctly more human. Even if the visit to the cocktail club turned out to be a dead end, he'd at least grab a decent lunch before heading back to the station.

Archer Street, with the tower of St. Anne's Church framed like a painting at its eastern end, seemed a quiet oasis after the bustle of Piccadilly. Only distant traffic and the faint shouts of children playing in the primary school yard disturbed the peaceful aspect.

The club was dark, the Closed sign prominently displayed on the glass doors, but he rapped on the glass as he'd done on his first visit.

It took three tries before he heard the sound of the inner door opening, followed by a muffled curse. The glass door swung open and a young woman stared at him, her expression none too friendly. She wore an apron over jeans and a T-shirt, and she held a large knife in one hand. "What the hell! We're closed, mate."

Kincaid held up his warrant card. "You might want to put the knife down," he said with what he hoped was a disarming smile. "I'd like a word, if you don't mind." He thought, from Gemma's description of the bartender's luxurious coiled braids, that he might have found just the person he wanted.

The feeling was obviously not mutual. "It's you. You were here the other day, talking to Jon. You and the guy in the Harry Potter glasses." She had a strong face with smooth, dark skin, wide cheekbones, and a firm chin that was at the moment thrust out in displeasure.

"Yes, we were. Is Jon here?"

"No. I'm just prepping the bar."

"Do you think he'll be back soon?" This was beginning to feel like pulling teeth.

"Look, I don't know." She blew out an exasperated breath. "He's having lunch with his sister, and I've no idea how long that will take, do I?"

"You must be the bartender, then."

"Bar manager," she said, glaring.

"I'll just come in and wait for a bit, shall I?"

He thought she might refuse, but after a moment she shrugged and stepped back. "Oh, all right. You might as well, as long as you don't stop me working. I'm Trudy, by the way," she added, with a glance over her shoulder as she led him inside.

"Duncan Kincaid. Nice to meet you, Trudy."

The tables, he saw as he followed her, were already set up, each adorned with a fresh candle and a small vase holding a single bloom.

When they reached the bar, Trudy gestured at the velvet barstools. "Have a seat."

Once she was round the other side, she began quartering limes on a cutting board, her knife flashing as she worked. She threw him a glance but the knife never stopping moving. "What do you want with Jon? You're not still thinking he had something to do with what happened to poor Sash?"

When Kincaid breathed in, the sharp, perfumed scent of the limes caught him at the back of the throat, making him cough.

"Here." Pulling a Collins glass from a rack, Trudy added a squirt of seltzer, then took a bin filled with ice from an under-counter freezer. She loosened a cube with a quick smack of an ice pick, then used tongs to add it to his glass, along with one of the lime quarters.

"Thank you," he said, once he'd drunk half. "That's much better. Actually, I came about Sasha's brother. Tyler. We'd really like to have a word with him, but he seems to have disappeared."

This time, Trudy stopped slicing, knife in mid arc. "Disappeared? What do you mean, disappeared?"

Kincaid knew he was toeing a fine line. He didn't want to reveal things he could only know from Gemma and Sidana's clandestine visit. "His family haven't heard from him since Sasha died," he said, "and he seems to have moved out of his residence hall. We also know that Sasha rang him the day before she was killed. If she felt threatened by someone, she might have told him."

Putting down the knife, Trudy drew her brows together. "Are you saying you think Tyler might know who killed her?"

"It's a possibility. We've also heard from family friends that Tyler could be in some sort of trouble. We'd like to assure his parents that he hasn't come to harm as well. They're terribly worried."

"Oh. I didn't think . . . Of course they must be frantic. How terrible." She went back to quartering limes, but much more slowly.

"We thought that since Tyler worked here, Jonathan might know how we could get in touch with him."

Trudy snorted. "Not bloody likely." Her ironic tone might have been lost on Kincaid if he hadn't known how Jon and Tyler had parted ways on Saturday night.

He raised an innocent eyebrow. "Oh? Why not?"

Using the blade of the knife, Trudy scooped her lime quarters into a plastic tub and snapped on a lid, pressing the seal with more concentration than the task surely required. Then, she picked up her knife again, but merely held it poised over a waiting bowl of lemons.

"Tyler was okay on Saturday night," she said at last. "He came into the club for a bit. He was gutted about his sister."

"You spoke to him on Saturday night?"

"Yeah. Barely. It was in the middle of service and he was—he and Jon weren't . . . getting on."

"Because of Sasha?"

"Well, I suppose you could say that. It's . . . complicated." She sighed. "So Sasha rang Jon on Friday. She said, did he know what sort of racket Tyler was running out of his club. She wanted to talk, like face-to-face.

"But Jon wanted to speak to Tyler himself before he talked to Sasha, see what was up. But Tyler didn't show up for service, Jon had to do the cash-and-carry, and then it was mad here. It wasn't until after closing that Jon thought to ask if *I* knew what Sasha was on about." She glanced up at Kincaid, then went back to rolling a lemon back and forth under the heel of her hand.

"And did you?" he asked.

She grimaced. "Not specifically. But I'd been keeping an eye on young Tyler. Some of the blokes he was palling about with, his *mates*, he called them, were total tossers." Rolling her eyes, she added, "I grew up on a council estate in Hackney, and I know bad news when I see it. These guys were throwing wads of fifties around like Monopoly money, swaggering about in the place, hitting on the female customers. Jon didn't see it." Her face softened. "He's a bit of an innocent sometimes, you know? Maybe they don't have gangsters in Glastonbury."

"I wouldn't count on that," Kincaid said with a smile. "So, did you tell Jon about Tyler's friends?"

"Mmm." Pursing her lips, Trudy cut smoothly into the lemon. "I had to, didn't I? He was right pissed off. With me, with Tyler.

"Then, next day, when we heard that Sasha had been killed, he went bloody ballistic. I told Tyler when he showed up on Saturday night that he'd better make himself scarce."

"And he left?"

"After Jon nearly gave him a drubbing."

So far, Trudy's story jived with Gemma and Sidana's accounts. He considered how to phrase his next question. "So, these unsavory friends were coming in, spending money. Was that a problem?"

Trudy shot him a sharp look. "I don't know. I couldn't prove anything, could I? But Ty would chat up the girls, and pretty soon these blokes were sending drinks to their tables. All aboveboard, but something was going on."

"And you didn't like it."

"No. In spite of being an arrogant little git, Ty is actually not a bad kid. There's no meanness in him, you know?" She shook her head. "But these guys . . . they were . . . hard. I hope Ty hasn't got himself into some real shit. And I hope to God his so-called *mates* didn't have anything to do with what happened to Sasha."

"What about other friends?" Kincaid asked. "His roommate at the residence hall said Tyler had been seen quite a bit with a girl. Name of Chelsea."

"He's been in with her a few times, yeah. In fact"—she frowned and dispatched another lemon with quick strokes—"I think he might have met her here, or maybe he recognized her from uni. She has a flat in the neighborhood. Rich daddy, didn't want his kid living in residence hall, apparently, where kids get up to all sorts. Daft, if you ask me. Girl can get into all kinds of real trouble living on her own."

"You don't happen to know where this flat is?" Kincaid dared to think they might have a viable lead on Tyler Johnson's whereabouts at last.

"Mmm." Trudy slid lemon quarters into another tidy tub, then began slicing a new victim. "Berwick Street, maybe? Or was it Brewer? Somewhere nearby. She's brought her laptop in a few times when we're slow in the afternoons, and we got talking. I can tell you that her last name is Traynor, though, with a *y*. From her charge slips. I haven't seen her in a week or so, though."

Kincaid made a note on his mobile. "Thank you. I'm sure we'll turn her up."

A door slammed in the street and Trudy glanced past him. Turning, Kincaid saw that a white Transit van had pulled up on the double yellows in front of the bar.

"Sorry," she said, wiping her hands on her apron and coming round the bar. "Delivery. And Jon will be back soon. I think he'll have had a hard enough day without being interrogated by the Bill. No offense. You seem nice enough." She gave him the first small smile he'd seen.

"I'll take that as a compliment."

As they reached the door, she stopped, touching his arm with light fingers. "I liked Sasha, too, you know."

He had noticed her easy possessiveness whenever she mentioned Jon Gibbs, and the way she talked about the bar with more than an employee's investment. "I take it Sasha and Jon weren't an item," he said as she unlocked the outer door.

"Better not have been, or he'd have me to answer to," said Trudy.

———

The lights were too bright, blinding. She blinked, trying to focus on the faces looming over her. Fuzzy. Her head swam. Another wave of nausea, roiling. "No," she managed to whisper. "No. Don't. Can't . . . touch—"

"Christ," said a voice. "She's burning up. Did someone just drop her off?"

"Ambulance crew found her collapsed in the bay." A second voice.

"Any ID?"

"No bag. But there's a hotel room key in her coat pocket."

"Ma'am." First voice. "Can you tell us your name?"

She tried to wet her parched lips. "Anne," she managed to croak. "So thirsty. I—"

"Don't worry, we'll get you sorted, love." Second voice. Kind. A woman. "Are you on any medications, Anne?"

She tried to shake her head but the room spun, then lurched horribly, like a ship in a swell.

Oh God. She was moving. A gurney. She was on a gurney. No. No, they mustn't take her.

"Anne, can you tell us your last name?"

"No. Get. A . . . way. Me." Her tongue was cotton wool, filling her mouth. "Snow," she mumbled. "It was . . . Snow. I wanted . . ."

"Anne Snow, is that it?" Second Voice.

"No, no, pump. It was . . . the pump," she whispered. She felt the tears leaking from the corners of her eyes. "I . . . wanted . . . Snow.

Congo. To . . . help." She tried to raise her hand, to wipe the tears away, but her arms wouldn't move.

Tied. She was tied. Why?

She wet her lips again, tried to force the words out. "Don't . . . tell. Him. He said . . . shouldn't . . . Sick. Going to be . . . don't touch—"

"Delirious," said First Voice. "Just my effing luck, end of shift."

"Never mind your shift." Second Voice, cross.

Then, closer, a face blocking the light. "Don't you worry, love. You'll feel better soon."

A cold prick in the back of her hand.

She . . . had to . . . tell . . . "No. Don't . . . touch . . . I went . . . Con . . . go. Con-tag-ious . . ."

The words swirled away in the enveloping darkness.

CHAPTER TWENTY-TWO

After her conversation with Melody, Gemma had managed to get through a morning's worth of email and a task force meeting. There had been the usual rash of knife crime over the weekend, peppered across the boroughs. The one fatality had been in Dalston, the perpetrator a thirteen-year-old girl, the victim a classmate. According to the report, an argument in the park over designer trainers had escalated.

While Gemma supposed she was happy enough not to have to deal with the bereaved families, if it were her case at least she'd be *doing* something immediately useful, rather than making recommendations to the mayor's office that more funds be put towards placing youth workers in A and Es.

She snapped her laptop shut and stood up. Lunch would probably improve her outlook. But first, she checked her mobile for messages once more.

Nothing from Des. Nothing from Duncan. Nothing from

Melody. Had she made the right call on that? She didn't like whatever was going on with Doug and Melody, didn't like whatever was going on with Melody, full stop. A few months ago, she would have absolutely trusted Melody to do the right thing with the information she'd found. Now she wasn't so sure.

Then her mobile buzzed in her hand and Des Howard popped up on her screen.

"It's not him," said Des without preamble when Gemma answered.

"Are you sure?"

"Positively. Sasha's bloke was good-looking but not that hot. Darker hair, more Heathcliffy. Your guy's a real looker."

Gemma laughed. "We'll have to put 'Heathcliffy' in our official police descriptions. What does that mean, exactly?"

"Or maybe I'm thinking of Mr. Rochester. I always get those Brontë heroes confused. Anyway, this guy was more brooding, like."

"Okay. Brooding. Got it. Anything else?"

"I was focused more on Sasha. It's all kind of a blur now." Des was quiet for a moment. "His eyes were dark, I'm pretty sure. But I can't guarantee it. Slim, almost too thin. Harried-looking, you know?"

"Thanks, Des. I'll pass that along, and we'll get together for that glass of wine soon."

"I don't suppose you've got a phone number for the hot guy?" Des's voice rose hopefully.

"In your dreams," answered Gemma, laughing, and disconnected. At least she could give Duncan one result.

But there was no response when she texted him, so she headed for the canteen in search of lunch.

A half hour later she was back at her desk, mulling over this latest development. If they assumed that Destiny's failure to identify Jon Gibbs meant that he hadn't been Sasha's lover or the father of her baby, that still didn't rule him out as a suspect. What if Sasha had learned something about the missing girl back in Somerset? Could she have been threatening him? Or even blackmailing him? That could explain the note found in Sasha's pocket.

And what about Tully, the sister that Melody had taken such a dislike to? Could she have killed her own flatmate to protect her brother? Duncan had said they'd checked her movements, but Gemma knew there was almost always a bit of wiggle room in even the best alibis.

Neither of those scenarios accounted for the guy arguing with Sasha in the restaurant, however. Or the baby. Or the missing Tyler Johnson. Or what Neel Chowdhury had to do with any of it.

There was one non-official avenue she could explore as far as the Gibbses were concerned, however. She'd recognized the name of the Somerset village where the Gibbses had lived—she did, in fact, know it well. And who better than the parish priest, who also happened to be her cousin-in-law Winnie Montfort, to know all the local gossip?

—

As he walked away from Bottle, Kincaid was already ringing Simon. "Traynor," he said when Simon picked up. "The girl's name is Chelsea Traynor. With a *y*. Look for a Traynor connected with a property in Soho. Her father either owns or leases the flat."

Simon whistled. "Good on you, guv. I'm on it."

"No joy with getting her details from the university?"

"They have privacy concerns. I'm having to go up the food

chain on this. How'd you manage to winkle out that juicy bit of info?"

Kincaid filled him in on his interview with Trudy.

"The old charm. Works every time," said Simon. "You've put me to shame. You coming back in?"

"Not until I've had lunch," Kincaid told him, ringing off. He'd remembered there was an Italian deli that made amazing sandwiches on Old Compton Street, not five minutes away. That should be just the ticket.

As he walked, he gazed at the flats above the shops and restaurants, wondering if one of them belonged to Chelsea Traynor. Chelsea Traynor, who hadn't been seen in a week. Was she at risk, too?

When he reached Old Compton Street, he was glad to see that I Camisa and Son was just as he remembered it, down to the basket-adorned delivery bike stationed out front. As he waited in the sandwich queue, he breathed in the distinctive aroma of the place. Old cheeses. Cured meats. Coffee, fresh bread. And always the undertone of spices, some familiar—basil, fennel, oregano—some elusive. The place had been there a long time, long enough for the scents to seep into the very fabric of the shop.

But it was an efficient operation, and when his turn came at the counter, his order was filled quickly. With his ham, mortadella, mozzarella, and tomato on focaccia stowed safely in a paper bag and his coffee in a paper cup, he walked back into Old Compton Street. There he hesitated, his face tilted up to the sun. He'd meant to take his lunch back to Holborn, but the day was still fine and he had a better idea.

He rounded the corner into Wardour Street and was soon seated on a bench in St. Anne's churchyard, watching the pigeons as he ate and trying not to drip roasted tomato on his best suit trousers.

His mother, a great fan of detective fiction, had once told him that the author Dorothy L. Sayers's ashes were interred beneath the tower here, where she had served as churchwarden.

It was only when he'd finished his sandwich and brushed the crumbs from his lap that he checked his messages. He'd missed a text from Gemma.

Des says guy with Sasha NOT Jon Gibbs.

Well, that at least gave more weight to Trudy's assertion that she, not Sasha, was Gibbs's girlfriend. Did that mean that the rest of what she'd told him was more likely to be true?

He was about to ring Gemma when he saw that he'd missed a call as well as a text. Karen Sterling, Sandra Beaumont's daughter, had left a message. When he returned her call, she gave him an address in Clerkenwell and said she could see him straightaway.

—

Karen Sterling lived near St. James Church, not far from Kincaid's former boss, Denis Childs, and his wife, Diane. Like the Childses', the house was Georgian, in an elegant and well-maintained terrace.

As Kincaid paid off his cab, he saw that in the course of his journey a scrim of thin cloud had shawled across the sky. That afternoon's brief blaze of perfect autumn weather had been short-lived. Scarlet leaves drifted from the lone tree growing along the pavement, adding a splash of color to the sedate terrace's mottled brown brick.

He lifted the knocker on Karen Sterling's glossy black door and gave it a couple of gentle taps. The door opened so quickly that he thought she must have been watching for him through the slatted blinds.

"Are you Mr. Kincaid?" asked the woman who greeted him. She was white, slightly plump, with blond hair pulled up into a messy ponytail, and a pleasant pale face that looked drawn with exhaustion.

Kincaid showed her his warrant card. "Thank you for seeing me, Mrs. Sterling, especially on such short notice."

"Come in. And do call me Karen. I use Beaumont at work, so Mrs. Sterling always makes me feel like my mother-in-law." She ushered him into a black-and-white-tiled entry hall. To his right, he glimpsed a rather formal living room, papered in a green-and-gold William Morris print. Karen Sterling led him straight ahead, however, towards a descending staircase. "Let's talk in the kitchen, if you don't mind."

Like most terraced houses from the period, this one was tall and narrow, and Kincaid assumed that the old below-stairs servants' quarters had long since been repurposed as kitchen/living space. On reaching the bottom of the stairs, he found that the green theme from the ground floor continued. The walls were dark green, as was the kitchen cabinetry, but bright white metro tiles above the worktops kept the space from seeming gloomy. On the island, a bright scarlet vase held a spray of holly berries, reminding him that Christmas was creeping up.

"Tea?" Karen asked when she'd motioned him to a forest-green Harris Tweed sofa.

When he accepted, she busied herself with a glass tea kettle, giving him a chance to look round. It was a pleasant space, with French windows opening onto a small garden. A moment's examination told him that the Sterlings had at least one child, and he remembered Lisa Gill saying that Sandra Beaumont had been a doting grandmother. Feeling something poking into his back, he fished out a plastic robot that had been hidden among the cushions.

"Oh, sorry about that." Karen grimaced when she saw what he was holding. "Leo *will* hide the bloody things in the sofa."

"I have kids myself," Kincaid said, "so I'm used to surprises. Especially from the seven-going-on-eight-year-old."

"A boy? If you have any tips, please let me know. Although my mum only had me, she said a career in nursing had prepared her for anything boys might do. A scary thought, isn't it?" Karen filled a teapot, then brought over a tray, clearing a box of LEGO from the low table to make a place for the tea things. The tray was set, not with mugs, but with china cups so delicate they were almost translucent.

"These are beautiful," he remarked as she poured tea into his.

"My mother was always nagging me to use the 'good stuff.' It's called celadon, that pale green pottery. Chinese. She found these in a street market." Her eyes had filled with tears.

"I'm very sorry for your loss. She sounds a lovely person, your mother."

Sniffing, Karen pressed the back of her hand against the base of her nose for a moment. "Sorry. I never know when it's going to hit me. Yesterday I started crying in the biscuit aisle in the supermarket. Over chocolate Hobnobs, can you believe it? Her favorite." After another sniff and a resolute sip of her tea, she set her cup down. "But never mind me. You said on the phone that you had questions about Mum."

"I understand that before she moved to Brighton, your mother worked at a hospital here in London, in Paddington."

Looking puzzled, Karen said, "That's right. And I wish to God she'd never taken that job in Brighton. She'd still be—" She stopped, pressing her lips together.

"Was there any particular reason she left London?" Kincaid asked, keeping his tone gently conversational.

"As a matter of fact, there was," Karen said slowly, frowning. "She'd had a difficult experience at work. A patient came in, a woman, very ill. Mum was on the admitting team in A and E. It turned out that the woman had come from the DRC—the Democratic Republic of Congo—and that she had Ebola, but they didn't know either of those things in the beginning.

"When they realized what it was, everyone that had come into contact with the patient had to quarantine—as did their families. Mum had kept Leo the day after that shift, and she was horrified. We all spent days wondering if we would become ill.

"Afterwards, there were reprimands, and a lot of bad feeling among the staff. Mum said she didn't think she'd ever feel comfortable working there again. The DRC had been red-flagged and the team missed it, but she felt she'd been unfairly blamed for the failure of protocol. When the Brighton offer came up, she took it without much hesitation. She'd always wanted to live by the sea. The only drawback for her was not being nearer us, but it was only an hour on the train and we could bring Leo every weekend . . ."

"About the hospital in Paddington," Kincaid said, steering her back, "do you remember anyone she worked with there?"

"Not really. It's been a couple of years now, and Mum liked to keep her work and her personal life pretty sep—" Karen stopped, teacup poised in midair. "Oh, wait. There was a nurse she really disliked. What was his name . . . Chowdhury? Something like that. Mum didn't dislike many people and she didn't usually talk about work, so I suppose that stood out."

"Was he also involved with the Ebola case?"

"He was, yes, now that I think about it. I remember Mum saying that he should have caught it on the intake—the red flag. Instead, he faulted her for it. It was all very unpleasant."

"Does the name Sasha Johnson ring a bell?"

Karen thought for a moment, then shook her head. "No, sorry, I can't say that it does. But I don't understand what any of this has to do with some mad person knifing my mum in a Brighton park."

Kincaid set down his empty teacup and prepared to rise. If Karen Sterling hadn't seen anything in the news about Sasha Johnson's death, he didn't want to start her speculating. "It's just routine. Your mother's name came up in the course of another investigation. Would you happen to remember the name of the Ebola patient? We might need to speak to her as well."

Karen's eyes widened. "Oh, but you can't. You see, she died."

—

In the cab on the way back to Holborn, Kincaid thought about Ebola, and how easily he'd made the assumption that modern British medical care would be enough to save the woman's life. Such confidence had apparently been unfounded. Had the hospital team mishandled the case? Or had the virus simply been too wily for even well-equipped humans?

Was there some connection between Neel Chowdhury and Sandra Beaumont, other than the fact that they'd worked together on that particular case? He remembered Doug saying that Sasha had worked with Chowdhury before—could it have been at that hospital? Surely Sasha would have been a very junior trainee then. Still, it was worth hunting up the news story and checking with the administration at the Paddington hospital.

And hadn't Gemma said that a Dutch woman had been injured in an unsolved knife attack in Paddington? That was certainly a tenuous connection, but he'd add it to the action list.

His agenda was hijacked, however, when he reached Holborn and the CID room. Simon was on the phone, Sidana was focused on her computer screen, and Lucy McGillivray was watching the door as if waiting for him. Only Doug was missing.

McGillivray jumped up from her workstation. "Boss. I managed to get Dorothy Johnson on her own this afternoon. She admitted that Sasha called her on Thursday night. It was the last time they spoke. Sasha told her mum that Tyler was in real trouble, and that if anyone came looking for him not to tell them anything. Sasha told her parents she'd sort it, somehow. The Johnsons were afraid to say anything to us, but now that Tyler hasn't come home they're worried sick."

Kincaid thought again about Dorothy Johnson's panicked face when he and McGillivray had shown up at the Johnsons' flat. She'd been terrified for her son.

"I wonder if Sasha 'sorting it' had anything to do with her visit to Chowdhury later that night," Kincaid said. "Assuming that it *was* Sasha who called on Chowdhury. Any more luck with getting CCTV from Dean Street?"

Before McGillivray could answer, Simon ended his call and swiveled round in his chair. "Guv, that was my mate in Human Trafficking. She says there are some new players in Soho lately, running low-level drugs and some higher-end prostitutes. They've been recruiting kids from uni to sell the stuff to other students. It sounds just Tyler Johnson's cup of tea."

"True enough." Kincaid frowned. "But it doesn't explain what Tyler was doing at Gibbs's club, unless it was just looking for prospective buyers for the drugs. Or maybe looking for girls that could be recruited?"

"I think it was more than that," said Sidana, who'd left her desk to join them. "Those blokes . . . What they were doing with the girls . . . It was almost like it was . . . some sort of sport."

Simon, so usually unflappable, looked grim. "If the guys you saw were the ones running Tyler, they had easy access to prostitutes. Maybe they were looking for less willing girls." He glanced at Sidana for confirmation.

She nodded. "I can see that. And it would make sense when a financial motive didn't."

"We may be able to learn a bit more," said Simon. "I think I've found your Chelsea Traynor."

———

Melody packed up her laptop and escaped the Curtis Green Building. She walked west on the Embankment, as quickly as her skirt suit and sensible shoes allowed.

Once she reached Westminster Bridge, she ducked into the Caffè Nero on the corner, a familiar refuge. There, ensconced at a table in the back and fortified with coffee, she logged into the Met's secure system and slogged her way through the day's emails and reports. After all, the new Met headquarters at Curtis Green had been designed to encourage remote working, and if the top brass could log in from coffee shops, she bloody well could, too.

Concentration did not come easily, however, as much as she usually liked the comforting white noise of a busy coffee shop. She kept replaying the scene with Gemma, with more and more discomfort every time her mind wandered back to it. How could she have been so unprofessional as to try to dump the whole business of Doug and the Gibbses in Gemma's lap?

Gemma had been right—she was going to have to take what she'd found to Doug herself, but every time she pulled out her phone to ring him, she stared at the screen, then put the mobile back. She couldn't work out how to begin. Doug was going to be furious with her for digging into the Gibbses' background behind his back, and she couldn't very well say she'd just happened across the information. The fact that she appeared to have been right about their being dodgy would only make things worse.

She and Doug were, however prickly and unlikely it might be, friends, and she wasn't sure that friendship would survive another falling-out.

She'd only begun to realize how much that mattered to her.

With a sigh, she closed her laptop and stared out at the traffic moving on Westminster Bridge. At least worrying about Doug had kept her from constantly checking to see if Andy had messaged her. She couldn't think about last night. Not now. Not yet.

Once again, she took out her mobile and fixed her gaze on the statue guarding the bridge, Boadicea with her spear and chariot, as if the warrior queen might give her some encouragement.

This time, she dialed. After two rings, Doug's voicemail picked up. "Bloody hell," she muttered.

Then, at the beep, she took a breath and blurted, "Look, we have to talk. I found some things you need to know. I'll come to your end. Fitzroy's. The bar. As soon as you can."

CHAPTER TWENTY-THREE

Doug Cullen could have found his way round the University College area in his sleep. Before he'd bought his house, he'd lived in a gray flat in a gray concrete block where the Euston Road met Gower Street. He'd also had a girlfriend named Stella, and he regretted the loss of neither.

So when Allison Baker had given him an address in Endsleigh Street, he knew exactly where to find Dr. Owen Rees's surgery. It was a basement flat in a brown-brick terrace. Clattering down the iron staircase, Doug thought Rees must see any disabled patients elsewhere. He buzzed at the door, and when it clicked open he stepped into a small reception area that did not look as though it was meant to receive patients at all. There was an unoccupied desk piled with papers and two unappealing plastic visitor's chairs. The dingy yellow walls were only improved by the usual peeling NHS posters.

Before Doug could call out, an inner door opened. "Just put it on the des—" Owen Rees, his head round the door, stared at Doug in consternation. "You're not—I was expecting a delivery—" Then recognition dawned. "You're the detective. Cullen, was it?"

"Detective Sergeant Cullen, Dr. Rees. If I could have a word?"

Rees looked even more harried than when Doug had seen him on Saturday. His eyes were sunken and the flesh seemed to have melted away from his cheekbones. For a moment, he just stared at Doug. Then, he stammered, "I have . . . I have rounds . . ."

"This won't take long. If we could speak in your office? We don't want to be interrupted."

As Doug advanced, Rees stepped back reluctantly. "I don't know how I can help you." But he subsided into a battered chair behind a desk even more cluttered than the one in reception. Stacks of manila folders vied for space with dog-eared medical journals. Some of the files teetered precariously at the desk's edge, as if they might decide to leap. Taking the spare chair, Doug said, "Do you not see patients here?"

"I don't do outpatients." Rubbing his face with the heels of his hands, Rees added, "I have rounds at three hospitals as well as a lecture schedule."

Not sure if he was expected to commiserate, Doug made a non-committal noise, then said, "You don't share the surgery with your wife, then?"

Rees blanched. "God, no. Lauren's aiming for Harley Street. She'd never work out of a dump like this."

Having met Dr. Lauren Montgomery, Doug had no trouble believing either of those things. He'd also seen the bitter twist of Rees's lips when he mentioned his wife's name. He took that as his cue to plunge in. "So, tell me about your affair with Sasha Johnson."

Owen Rees didn't even bother to protest. His face crumpled and this time when he put up his hands, it was to cover his eyes. His shoulders shook and he gave a sound that was half moan, half sob. After a moment, he scrubbed his red eyes with the heels of his hands and took a gulping breath. "I'm sorry. It's just that I'm so tired."

Doug had spied what looked like a camp bed against the back wall of the office. A tartan blanket had been thrown across it, but there was still a dent in the rumpled pillow. The room smelled faintly of sweat and fried food. Had the man been living here?

Doug felt a spasm of pity for the man, but that didn't stop him from being a prime suspect in the murder of his lover.

"I haven't been able to talk to anyone," Rees went on, "about Sasha. How did you know?"

"You were seen together. On the ward."

"Oh God. You have to understand. Lauren and I were separated. Things had been . . . difficult. Lauren wasn't happy with my"—he made air quotes and his lips twisted again—"*career trajectory*. And I couldn't bring myself to . . . well, never mind." Rees examined his fingernails. "I had a bedsit in Mecklenburgh Place—it was all I could afford with the mortgage on the house. One night I ran into Sasha in Ciao Bella, you know, in Lamb's Conduit Street. We were both eating alone. We started talking. We had some wine. One thing led to another." He looked up, meeting Doug's eyes. "I know it was inappropriate. I know it could even have cost me my career, but I didn't care. Sasha, Sasha *admired* me. We could talk about things, and she didn't . . . cut at me all the time."

"And she felt the same way about you?" Doug asked, wondering if Rees had considered what the relationship might do to *Sasha's* career.

"I don't think she'd ever been serious about anyone before." Rees shifted uncomfortably.

From this, Doug gathered that Sasha had been besotted with him, and Rees had been—what? Bolstering his self-esteem?

Something must have shown in his expression, because Rees hastened to explain. "I felt like I was sixteen again. Giddy with it. We made plans."

"Plans?"

"You know. Get out of London. Set up a GP practice together somewhere, or work in a small hospital. Never enough doctors in the country."

Doug thought about everything he knew about Sasha Johnson. Her focus on her career, her disdain towards relationships, even towards her sister's baby. Had she changed that drastically? Or had she been indulging Rees in this pipe dream? He looked around the fetid room, then back at Rees. "So what happened?"

Rees had brightened a bit when describing their imaginary future, as if for a moment those things were still possible. Now his face fell, and he swallowed. "My wife . . . my wife found out."

"But you were separated," Doug said. "If you meant to divorce . . ."

"Oh, but that wasn't Lauren's plan. The separation was meant to be me coming to my senses, falling in with her agenda. She wanted me to give up teaching, go into private practice. Then we could afford to send the kids to the right schools . . . The whole success package."

"What happened when your wife found out about Sasha?"

Rees looked as if he might be sick. He swallowed again. "She—she said if I asked for a divorce, she'd say I abused her. She had pictures, from when she took a tumble on her bike last spring. Bruising. A black eye. She said she'd make sure I lost custody of the kids. She's very convincing. Mia's only six. Miles is eight. I couldn't—she's not always . . . kind . . . to them. I couldn't . . ." Rees closed his eyes.

Doug stared at him, remembering the way Lauren Montgomery had taken charge of the conversation when he'd met her, her pincer grip on her husband's arm as she steered him into the lift. This was a woman who had to be in control—what might she have done to make certain she stayed that way? "What did you do?"

"I gave up my bedsit. Moved back in."

"And what about Sasha?"

"I told her we had to stop. That I couldn't risk the kids. But she—" He shook his head.

"Did you write her a note?" asked Doug, remembering the crumpled scrap of paper in Sasha's cardigan pocket. *This has to stop.*"

Rees blinked and stared at him. "How did you know?"

"She kept it. We found it in her locker."

"Oh, Christ." This time, when Rees's eyes filled, he made no effort to stop the tears.

"Did your wife send Sasha threatening texts?"

"What?"

Doug thought his shock was genuine. "*Leave him alone or you'll be sorry.* From a burner phone."

"Christ," Rees said again, shaking his head. "I don't know. It's possible. Sasha—we didn't text, we didn't think it wise, but I suppose Lauren could've got her number from the hospital."

"You were very careful."

"I suppose I was always a bit paranoid."

Or you always intended to go back to your wife, Doug thought. "So when did Sasha tell you she was pregnant?"

Blanching, Rees took a shuddering breath. "On Thursday, when I did my evening rounds. We hadn't talked since I moved home. She said she had to speak to me. We went in the break room."

Doug waited, but no more seemed to be forthcoming, so he asked, "What did you say? When she told you."

"I said we'd sort something out. And I would have. Somehow."

"She meant to keep the baby?"

Rees nodded.

"Is there any way your wife could have found this out?"

"Lauren?" Rees frowned. "I don't see how. I only saw her for five minutes that afternoon, when she came through the hospital to check on a patient."

Doug wasn't so sure that Lauren Montgomery hadn't read something in her husband's face. Owen Rees broadcast his emotions like the big video screen in Leicester Square, and Doug couldn't believe that Rees's controlling and jealous wife wouldn't have sensed that something cataclysmic was up.

Something else was bothering him. "You said you'd moved home." He nodded towards the camp bed. "So why this? Sleeping here."

For a moment, Rees looked startled, as if it hadn't occurred to him that Doug might notice. Then, he sagged further into his chair. "When I found out Sasha was dead—had been killed, for God's sake—I couldn't face going home, couldn't face Lauren pretending to be sorry. When I saw you yesterday, Lauren had cornered me in hospital reception, trying to convince me to come home."

And yet, Sasha's death had solved what must have seemed an insurmountable situation to Owen Rees. "Where were you on Friday evening, Dr. Rees? Between five and six o'clock?"

Rees stared at him, his pupils dilating. "I was doing my rounds. At the Coram and UCL Euston Street. You're not suggesting that I—"

"I'm merely clarifying a timeline." But who better to have followed Sasha from the hospital, or from the Perseverance? Who better to have known just where to stab? Except, of course, the doctor's cardiologist wife.

———

Gemma had intended to leave work early in order to pick up Toby from his after-school club and take him to dance rehearsal. What she hadn't counted on was finding her seven-year-old son in tears. "Mum, my tights have a rip," he wailed as he climbed into the car. "No way can I go to rehearsal in them!"

"I'm sure they're fine," she said, putting the Land Rover into gear.

"No! It's a big hole. Like this big around." In the rearview mirror, Toby held up his hands, demonstrating a circle the size of a football. "It'll show my bum. Mr. Charles won't let me dance in them!"

Gemma shifted back into park. "What about your spare pair?"

"They're . . ." Toby mumbled something.

"What?"

"I sort of . . . lost them."

This time, Gemma twisted around in her seat so that she could look at her son. "Toby James, you are supposed to be responsible for getting your things together the night before. And how do you just now know about this, when your dance bag is in the car?" She'd watched him sling it into the cargo area that morning.

"I sort of . . . forgot. We were all rushed this morning."

Every good parenting tip ran through Gemma's mind. *Children need to learn responsibility. Children should be taught that their actions have consequences.*

But Toby was right. They *had* been rushed, and that hadn't been his fault. And although he might be tasked with getting his things organized, she should have double-checked last night.

Sighing, she resisted the urge to bang her head on the steering wheel and looked at the clock instead. "You know there's not a dancewear store nearer than Covent Garden. We'll have to see what we can find in the girls' things at Boots."

"But I don't want to wear—"

She gave him *the look* in the rearview mirror. "Do you want to dance?"

After a moment, Toby said, "Yeess." It was barely a mumble, but it would do.

"Okay, then. But just this once," she admonished.

Famous last words, she was sure.

—

She had delivered Toby to the Tabernacle, tights mission accomplished, with thirty seconds to spare, and was just contemplating whether she had time for a cup of tea in the Tabernacle café when her mobile rang.

It was Winnie Montfort, returning her call from earlier in the day. "Gemma, darling, so sorry to have missed you. I had parish visits this afternoon and never a moment to catch my breath. But it was so lovely to hear your voice."

"And lovely to hear yours," said Gemma. "How's little Connie?"

"Not so little. And not just walking, but running, as fast as her little legs can carry her."

"And Jack?"

"He's got a big project on in Wells, so we're juggling a bit between our schedules and the babysitter."

"I know the feeling," said Gemma. She could hear Constance babbling happily in the background.

Baby Constance had been an unexpected blessing in a late

marriage. "Are you still planning to come for the ballet? We've saved you tickets."

"We wouldn't miss it. And it will be a nice chance to see Rosemary and Hugh. Is there any problem with the arrangements?"

"No, no, it's all fine." Gemma had already booked both the Montforts and Duncan's parents into the two rooms offered by one of the pubs on Portobello Road. "We're so looking forward to seeing you. But I've an odd question for you, if you can spare a—" A loud clatter drowned her out. When it subsided, she said, "Was that pots?"

"Oh, sorry," Winnie answered, laughing. "She's into the cupboard now. I'll let her bang on for a bit."

"I'll be quick. Do you remember a girl going missing from the village, about ten years ago? Name of Rosalind Summers."

There was more clattering, then Winnie murmured, "Here, take the spoons instead, love." When the noise level subsided a bit, she continued, "Ten years . . . that would have been just before my time. Let me see . . . Oh, I know. That'll be Brenda Summers's girl, Roz."

"You know her? Rosalind?"

"I've met her, once or twice. She works at the supermarket in Street. She had a job at the Clarks factory before it closed down." The village of Street, Gemma remembered, had been the home of Clarks Shoes. "Are you certain this is the same girl?"

"Oh, it was quite the scandal, I recall now. Girl vanishes from her house on Midsummer's Eve. Except she turned up a couple of years ago, two kids in tow and no husband to be seen. Apparently, she'd run off with a lad from the traveling fun fair—gypsies, more or less. She was all of sixteen and had rowed with her parents. Couldn't bring herself to tell them she was pregnant, I suspect. Brenda Summers divorced her husband afterwards, turned out he'd been abusive, so perhaps he harmed his daughter as well. I'm not breaking any confidences here," Winnie added. "It was all the talk in the village when Roz came back. But at the time she ran away, everyone thought the worst."

And they had laid the blame on Jon Gibbs, who, with his sister, had left Somerset as soon as he possibly could. Had Jon and Tully known the truth even then? Surely, they'd have given up Rosalind's secret when Jon was thought guilty of murdering the girl. She wondered if anyone had told them that Rosalind Summers had returned from the dead?

But in any case, neither sibling had killed Rosalind Summers and disposed of her body, so there had been no secret for Sasha to discover, and no reason for her to be silenced. Melody's theory of a motive for Sasha's murder had dissolved like smoke.

—

The address Simon had found for one Robert Traynor, a property developer, was in Brewer Street. A little trawl through social media had revealed that Traynor did indeed have an only daughter called Chelsea, who had just recently celebrated her eighteenth birthday. From there, a little more searching had netted photos of a pretty blond girl. In one group shot, Tyler Johnson's arm had been thrown casually across her shoulders.

Brewer Street ran parallel to Archer Street—earlier that afternoon, Kincaid had been, quite literally, right around the corner. He might have bumped into Chelsea Traynor in the street, or in the deli queue, and not known it.

Kincaid and Sidana took Sidana's car, a recent-model Honda in spook black, and counted on the miracle of a parking space once they reached Brewer Street. As they sat in traffic on Shaftesbury

Avenue, Kincaid was beginning to feel a definite sense of déjà vu. Finally, they reached Great Windmill Street, then headed east again on Brewer.

They were in luck, and Sidana nosed the Honda into the first spot vacated by a delivery van. At almost five o'clock, dusk had faded to full dark and the light from the ground-floor shops and cafés fell in welcoming pools onto the pavement. Not all the premises were equally cozy, however, unless a massage parlor or a sex-toy shop counted as your cup of comfort.

The flat registered to Robert Traynor was on the third floor of a redbrick building near the intersection with Wardour. A trendy clothing boutique occupied the ground floor, with a hairstylist on one side and a bakery on the other. Having decided it would be best not to announce themselves, Kincaid and Sidana were contemplating buzzing multiple flats in hopes that someone would release the main door when it swung open. A helmeted figure carrying a padded pizza delivery box nearly cannoned into them, muttering, "Sorry, mate," as Kincaid stepped neatly into the breach.

"What are the odds," said Sidana as they climbed the stairs, "that if they're not going out, food is coming in?" The smell of garlic, perhaps left behind by the pizza box, lingered in the stairwell. A television blared from the flat on the second floor, but when they reached the third floor, it was silent.

With a glance at Sidana, Kincaid shrugged and said quietly, "Worth a try." Then he rapped on the door and called out, "Miss? Sorry, you've got the wrong pizza."

A moment later, the door swung open and a young woman looked out at them, frowning. "No, ours is fine—" She stopped, her eyes widening in shock as she took them in.

She started to close the door, but Kincaid had his warrant card out and his foot in the gap. "Chelsea Traynor? I'm Detective Superintendent Kincaid, and this is Detective Inspector Sidana. Metropolitan Police. We'd like a word." He wasn't sure he'd have recognized the smiling girl from the photos. Her blond hair was dirty and scraped carelessly into a ponytail. She looked thinner, her eyes were hollow, and a purpling bruise bloomed across one cheekbone. There was something else, too, a slight hunching in her posture, as if she were in pain.

"I don't want to talk to you," she said, but he caught her frightened glance to the left.

"This won't take long. If you're not comfortable speaking here, we can have our little chat at the station."

This caused another terrified glance. Kincaid could see the flat's bathroom just behind Chelsea, and could just glimpse a partially open door to the left—perhaps the bedroom. "I—are you arresting me?" Chelsea drew herself up a bit straighter.

"We'd just like your help with our inquiries," answered Sidana. Standard police-speak, but she'd made it sound reassuring.

"I don't know how I can—"

"Chelsea," said Kincaid, "you and Tyler are in trouble. We can help."

"How did you—" Chelsea began, but her eyes had filled and the color drained from her face. She swayed and Sidana stepped forward, putting a supporting hand on her shoulder.

"Let's get you sat down, shall we? And maybe a cup of tea?"

Chelsea let Sidana lead her to the right, where a combination kitchen/sitting room overlooked the street.

Following Sidana inside, Kincaid closed the front door and stood firmly in front of it, blocking any escape route. The flat looked expensive, but any style had been overcome by student-life chaos. Clothing was strewn across the back of the sofa and a pile of unfolded laundry teetered on the armchair. The open pizza box stood on the dining table beside an open laptop and a stack of books. A pair of trainers too large to be Chelsea's had been abandoned beneath the glass-topped coffee table.

Sidana, having eased Chelsea into one of the dining chairs, had busied herself in the open-plan kitchen with a kettle and tea things. When Kincaid caught her eye, she gave him a quick nod.

"Tyler," Kincaid called out. "We know you're here. You might as well come out. I don't think you want us to get a search warrant, but we will have a chat one way or the other." He waited a beat, then another.

Chelsea gave a little sob. "Ty, I can't do this by myself. Please."

After another long moment, the bedroom door creaked open and Tyler Johnson stepped into the hallway. In the flesh, his likeness to his sister Sasha was so strong that Kincaid felt discomfited.

"You can't bully her like that," Tyler said, but it wasn't much of an attitude display.

"We don't intend to bully her. Why don't you sit down and tell us why you've made your family frantic with worry."

"My family?" It came out a squeak. "You're not here about—"

"Oh, that's not the only thing we're going to talk about, don't worry. Now, sit." Kincaid made it a command.

Gone was the cheeky young man from the group photos. This Tyler looked very young, and very frightened. He wore a hoodie and tracksuit bottoms, but these were well worn, not fashion statements. Kincaid was forcibly reminded that these two were only a few years older than Kit, and had got themselves into a world of trouble.

Tyler gave him a sullen look, but joined Chelsea at the table, slouching into a chair beside her with what looked suspiciously like relief.

When Sidana had brought over a single mug of tea and placed it in front of Chelsea, Kincaid took the chair between the kids and the door. He didn't want Tyler changing his mind.

"I've put milk and sugar in," Sidana told Chelsea, then took the remaining free seat.

Tyler stared at her, frowning. "I know you from somewhere."

When Sidana glanced at Kincaid, he gave her a nod. No point in being coy with the kid—he would figure it out, and they were better off going for the shock value.

"Bottle, on Saturday night," said Sidana. Reaching up, she loosed her hair from its ponytail and shook it so that it fell to her shoulders. She smiled at him.

"Holy shit," Tyler gasped. His eyes might have been doughnut holes. "You. With the redhead. You're a cop."

Sidana put her hair up again. "Last time I looked."

"But—What were—"

Kincaid interrupted him. "This isn't twenty questions. Let's start with what we know, and then you can fill in the blanks."

"You were setting up those drunk girls with those three men," said Sidana. "And it wasn't the first time you'd done that, either. But you didn't want to be there on Saturday night, did you? You'd just learned your sister had been killed and you should have been at home, with your family. Instead, you were working the club. Why was that, Tyler?"

"You don't understand. I couldn't—I had to—They said they'd—" Tyler's eyes swam with tears.

Chelsea reached out and put a hand on his arm. Her chest rose as she inhaled, but when she spoke it was barely a whisper. "They said that next time they would do worse than rape me."

—

Between the two of them, the story came out in fits and starts.

It had all begun as a lark. Tyler had met the three men in a club in Leicester Square. They'd been flush, and when they'd offered him some ecstasy, he'd thought, why not?

When he'd met them a second time, they'd given him some tablets to sell. Of course he'd get a cut, they said, and for a while it had been okay. Extra cash, along with what Jon paid him for odd jobs at Bottle—he'd been cool. And he could afford to coast for a term, couldn't he? He'd make it up—he'd always been a quick study.

Only his cuts got smaller, and the volume they expected him to sell got larger, until one day they said he owed them more than he'd made. And then they'd shown up at Bottle.

That first time, they'd only ordered rounds of expensive drinks and sneered at the charcuterie. He'd relaxed, maybe shown off a little, chatting up the punters when he knew the blokes were watching. The next time, they told him to introduce them to some girls at one of the tables. The girls had been a bit squiffy, but Tyler hadn't seen any harm in it.

At this point, Tyler had thrown an anxious glance at Chelsea, his bare heel drumming on the carpet. The skin that had begun to form on Chelsea's untouched tea shivered with the motion.

"How often did this happen?" Kincaid asked. He'd closed the lid on the pizza box, but could still smell garlic and congealing cheese.

Tyler twitched a shoulder. "A few times. But Trudy"—he threw a glance at Sidana—"she's the bartender, yeah?—Trudy had started to notice." And in the meantime, he'd met Chelsea, and he'd started to think that maybe he was better off out of business with the three blokes.

Jesus wept, Kincaid thought, shaking his head. The kid really had been an idiot. You didn't go out of business with that sort.

"I told him," Tyler went on. "I said, 'I'm done, mate.' And he just . . . laughed." Tyler's expression said he hadn't found this funny at all. But he was staying with Chelsea by this time, and avoiding the uni campus, and he thought maybe the whole thing would go away. The only problem with this plan was the club, but he needed the money from the part-time work.

Then one night the blokes had come in when Chelsea had been there with a couple of girlfriends. "He—he told me to have Trudy send her a drink."

"He?" interrupted Sidana. "You keep saying *he*. Which one are we talking about here?"

"Mick. The white guy, buzzed head."

"Last name?"

Tyler shook his head vehemently. "No. No way. I don't know. I didn't *want* to know. But the other white guy's called Jerry. The Black bloke is Malcolm."

"I don't suppose they paid by card at the club?"

"Only cash, with big tips."

Sidana sighed. "Right. So what did you do?"

"I said fine, he was welcome to buy as many drinks as he liked. But she wasn't leaving with him." Chelsea had seen her mates off, then had helped Trudy behind the bar. Mick and his friends had left shortly afterwards, and that night Tyler and Chelsea had stayed until closing, then got a couple of the guys in the kitchen to walk out with them, to make sure there were no unpleasant surprises. "We were shit scared, honestly."

"But that wasn't the end of it," Kincaid said, his gaze on Chelsea, on the purple bruising on her cheek. The visible injury. "Was it, Chelsea?"

"I—" It came out a croak. She licked her lips, then picked up the mug and drank half the cold and scummy tea. She closed her eyes for a moment, took a breath, and began again. "I had evening lecture. Wednesday night. Ty was working. I was walking to the tube afterwards. A van pulled up. The back doors opened. I started to cross the street, to get out of the way in case they were unloading something. And then they just . . . scooped me up. Like a rag doll." Chelsea drank more tea. Sidana slid quietly from her seat and fetched a glass of water from the kitchen.

The girl accepted it with a nod of thanks before she continued. "They put something in my mouth. Oily. I can still . . . taste it."

They had driven her somewhere, not far, but echoey, as if the van was inside a space, a warehouse, maybe. "And then he—" She stopped, shook her head. "I'm sorry. I can't . . ."

"Take your time, love," Sidana said, very gently, but Kincaid saw that her fists were clenched. "You said 'he.' Did you see the man's face?"

"I saw . . . all of them."

"The same three men, from the club?"

Chelsea nodded. "They wanted me to . . . know."

Sidana glanced at Kincaid, then said, "Did all three of these men . . . assault you?"

"Just the one. Mick. The others . . ." Tears were sliding down her cheeks now. "The others . . . watched."

Tyler had been sitting with his arms crossed tightly over his chest, holding something in, or keeping something out. But now he leaned forward and thumped a fist on the table. "That's enough. Can't you see she doesn't want to talk about it?"

But Chelsea shushed him with a look. "I have to, Ty. I see that now." She turned back to Sidana. "Afterwards . . . they made me drink something. And then I—it's all blurry. I think I must have slept. When I woke up, I wasn't in the van. It was light. I was in a park. I was sick. But after a while, I could stand up. And I just . . . walked."

Eventually, she'd realized that she still had her mobile phone, and her wallet. There was traffic. She flagged a taxi and came home. Where she'd found Tyler, frantic.

They had sent him photos, along with the threat.

"You didn't call the police? Or go to A and E?" Kincaid asked.

She shook her head. "No. Ty—I thought they'd kill him. And my father, oh God. I couldn't tell my father. But I was . . . bleeding."

Kincaid thought through the timeline. "This was Thursday." He looked at Tyler. "Lunchtime by then. You called your sister."

Nodding, Tyler scrubbed his cheek with his knuckles. "I didn't know what else to do."

"Sasha came," whispered Chelsea. "She said I needed to go to hospital, but I couldn't."

So no rape kit, Kincaid thought, no DNA. But Sidana leaned forward and touched Chelsea's hand. "Sweetie, did you save any of your clothes? Your underpants?"

Chelsea nodded. "I wanted to throw them away. But Sasha told me to put them in a paper bag, in a safe place."

"Good girl. That was very clever. Are you willing to make a statement now? You'll need to be examined at a special forensic center, but I'll stay with you all the way."

"Does my father have to know?"

"You're an adult. It's your decision. But you're going to need help and support."

The girl thought for a moment. "But what about Ty? I don't want to get him in worse—"

"They can arrest me," broke in Tyler, with what sounded like hope. "I don't care."

Kincaid shook his head. "No, we can't. That's not how it works. We have no actual evidence that you've done anything illegal."

"But—what am I going to do? I can't go home. They know

where my parents live—they told me. And if they killed my sister—"

But Kincaid was already shaking his head again. "Tyler, these are very bad guys, and we'll do everything we can to hold them to account. But I'm not at all sure that they killed Sasha."

Because there was nowhere, in any part of this story, to fit the murder of Neel Chowdhury, and he couldn't shake his certainty that the two killings were connected.

—

It was going on five o'clock by the time Doug got back to Holborn. He'd listened to Melody's message—he had, in fact, walked right by the Fitzroy on his way back to Lamb's Conduit Street, and for a moment he'd been tempted to go in. But he wasn't ready to talk to her, not until he'd found out more about Tully's missing friend, and especially not with Melody being so bloody self-righteous. Who did she think she was, anyway, ordering him to a meeting like she was his boss? So he'd shoved his hands in his coat pockets and walked on, ignoring the lure of sharing what he'd discovered about Owen Rees and his wife.

When he reached the station, he found the CID room empty except for Simon and a couple of stray constables doing data entry.

"Ooh, the prodigal returns." Simon turned from his keyboard to shoot him a grin.

"Where is everyone?" Doug tossed his coat on the nearest empty chair.

"The boss and the DI are following a lead. I found an address for Tyler Johnson's girlfriend."

"What? The mysterious Chelsea? How?"

Simon filled him in on Kincaid's interview with Trudy, the bar-tender at Bottle. "After that, piece of cake."

"Shit," Doug muttered. He'd have wanted to be in on that in-terview, if they had actually found the girl, and possibly Tyler. But he had news, too.

Simon whistled when Doug had told him about Rees and Mont-gomery. "A jealous wife, one who knows where to put a blade."

"Could be the husband, trying to make the pregnant mistress go away. He was pretty quick to drop his wife in it, maybe shift-ing the blame." Although, Doug thought, if he'd been married to Lauren Montgomery, he might have dropped her in it, too, kids or no kids. "Either way, we'll get them both in for interviews in the morning. In the meantime, put in a request with her service provider, will you? See if Montgomery's registered phone just hap-pened to be anywhere near the burner when Sasha was sent the threatening text."

"Will do. I'm waiting for someone in records at the hospital in Paddington to get back to me anyway. But first"—Simon rolled his chair back from his workstation—"I'm going for coffee and a sandwich. Want anything?"

"No, but ta." Doug was already pulling up the case file on his own terminal. He wanted to be certain that no one else had run across the cold case in Somerset, although surely Simon would have mentioned it if they had. At any rate, he needed to enter his own notes from the day and make an action list for tomorrow.

He was scanning Sidana's notes on her interview with the bar owner, Darrell Cherry, along with the list she'd made of the bar's credit-card charges for Saturday evening, when he stopped dead.

What the hell was *that* name doing on *this* list?

CHAPTER TWENTY-FOUR

Tully joined the closing-time exodus from the British Museum, slotting herself into the throng moving down the steps into the grand forecourt. Discarded ticket stubs formed a mosaic on the damp pavement, and moisture hung in the air as if waiting for the perfect moment to condense into drops and splatter her glasses.

The weather certainly suited her mood. She'd dithered all through lunch with her brother, which they'd grabbed at the ramen place in Museum Street. At least Jon hadn't suggested the Plough, where Doug had taken her the previous evening.

Doug . . . She wouldn't exactly call Doug Cullen warm and fuzzy, but there was something solid about him that made her feel she could trust him.

But had that been any excuse to run her mouth last night and spill all the family secrets? Okay, so maybe she'd had a bit of a meltdown. Who wouldn't, given the circumstances?

Today, she'd rationalized her urge to confess. As hard as she and Jon had tried to put everything that happened in Somerset behind them, they were going to have to face reality. The police were bound to ferret out the old history. A preemptive strike, that's what she'd done, getting it out of the way. Better for them to have heard it from her.

So why hadn't she told Jon what she'd done?

Jon had been distracted, anyway, checking his mobile, not meeting her eyes. She'd assumed he was upset about Sasha, or worried about the investigation. Or worried about her, about what the hell she was going to do now. And it had been partly that, she'd learned, when he'd finally pushed aside his empty noodle bowl and looked up.

"I thought I should tell you," he said. "Trudy's moved in."

She'd stared at him. "Oh. That's great."

"Yeah. I think it is." There had been a note of surprise in his voice. The girls had always swarmed around Jon, and in turn he'd treated them all as equally disposable. Never, as far as Tully knew, had he considered any sort of committed relationship.

Tully had been pleased. She liked down-to-earth Trudy, who was kind to her, and who wouldn't put up with any bollocks from her brother. But she'd felt a little like the girl left standing on the doorstep when everyone else was inside at the feast. "Why are you just telling me now? Were you afraid I'd expect you to take me in?"

He'd had the grace to blush. "Well, what *are* you going to do?"

But she couldn't tell him, because she didn't know. Her job at the museum, as glamorous as it had sounded, was in reality poorly paid and a crashing bore. She spent her days cataloging old pottery and porcelain when what she wanted, what she'd always wanted, was to feel the live clay under her hands.

Which brought her to the gallery job, she thought now as she passed the chestnut seller huddled over his brazier in Great Russell Street. Was David really trying to fire her? And even if not, did she really want to stay? David had always been critical, even difficult, but yesterday had been downright weird. Putting up with David had been a trade-off she'd been willing to make for the use of the studio and the kiln.

Now she wasn't so sure.

Something else was niggling at her, too, but as she reached the gallery, the thought slipped away. Although it was just past five and the gallery was normally open until six, the Closed sign was displayed on the door. The lights were still on, but when Tully tried the door it was indeed locked. Double weird, she thought. This was the magic hour, when the gallery usually caught the tourists leaving the museum and eager to spend any funds they hadn't dropped in the museum gift shop.

Shrugging, she let herself into the next-door building and walked down the hallway to her studio door. She frowned as she jiggled the stiff lock, but it released with coaxing and she stepped inside the familiar, cluttered space. God, she would miss this if she had to give it up.

Maybe she would see if she could sort things out with David, assuming he was still in the gallery, but first she needed to check on the pottery she'd fired overnight.

It was such a crapshoot, firing. The most perfect pieces might not survive the kiln, and there was no way to predict which ones would emerge whole. Switching on the outside light, she went out the studio door into the small, enclosed backyard, which held the kiln shed. The mist swirled in the beam from the lamp, a sparkling fog that beaded her hair and her face.

She took a deep breath, as always, then unlatched the kiln and peered inside. Bowls, cups, vases, a delicate teapot still possessing its spout and handle, all intact, the glazes rich and glowing.

All, except for one thing—her little doll made in Sasha's likeness, and it had not cracked.

It had been smashed to bits.

—

Doug waited, staring at the monitor, holding a pencil over the scratchpad he kept on his desk, for a full five minutes. Apparently Simon had been going farther afield than the station vending machines for his sandwich and coffee or he'd be back by now. No one else had returned to the incident room, either.

Maybe the boss and Sidana had run down Tyler Johnson and were even now installing him in an interview suite. Maybe Tyler's thuggish friends had stabbed Sasha as an object lesson, and Neel Chowdhury's murder in the wee hours of Saturday night was just one of those cosmic coincidences. And maybe the name on Sidana's list of Chowdhury's fellow drinkers that night was a coincidence, too. These things happened. The world was full of all sorts of weird connections, and in policing you soon learned that most of them came to nothing.

But he still didn't like it. He didn't want to look like an idiot, however—the name on the list was surely common enough. Maybe he should have a word with Tully before he pursued the matter any further. Checking his watch, he saw that she would probably still be at the gallery. He could kill two birds with one stone.

Pushing his glasses up on his nose, he stood and shrugged back into his coat.

—

What had she been thinking, to suggest the Fitzroy? It had been the first place to pop into her head, Melody supposed, because she'd been here for dinner with her parents a few months ago. The restaurant had been getting good reviews and her father liked to stay on top of what was going on in the city. She realized, too, that the terracotta behemoth at the northeast corner of Russell Square must have registered on her subconscious when she and Gemma visited the square on Friday night.

When she'd glanced into the square as she passed, she'd felt an unexpected wave of melancholy. What had Sasha Johnson been thinking about as she'd hurried across the grassy expanse in the drizzle? Had she had any premonition that her life, with all its small joys and concerns, was about to be cut short?

Now, seated in the hotel bar, Melody gave herself a little shake and took a sip of her bitter drink. She'd ordered a Negroni, because the Fitz, as the bar was called, was the sort of place you drank a classic cocktail. Dark leather banquettes and club chairs, mood lighting, stained glass—it was the sort of place where, before the smoking ban, a blue haze would have hovered in the room like a low cloud.

It was *not* the sort of place where you told your friend he was about to seriously fuck up his career if he didn't get a grip, and she'd regretted her choice from the moment she entered the bar. She'd even thought about trying to catch Doug on the way into the hotel, but there were two entrances and she couldn't be certain he'd come in from Guilford Street. Swirling the ice cube in her glass, she checked her mobile once more for missed messages. The minutes were ticking by, and she was beginning to think she'd been stood up.

Surely Doug wasn't still ticked off over Saturday night? Maybe he'd been delayed by a development in the case. But even then, it wasn't like him not to let her know.

Another glance at the time decided her. He could call her a

busybody—or worse—but he had to know what she'd learned about Tully and Jon Gibbs. Ignoring the appraising look from the corporate type nursing a whisky at the bar, she signaled for the check.

Ten minutes later, she was pressing the buzzer of the flat Tully had shared with Sasha Johnson. But although a dim light could be seen through the front window, there was no response. Melody walked along the pavement until she could peer through a gap in the rack of Tully's clothing that served as a curtain. Nothing stirred in the flat, but she could just glimpse Tully's dolls on the shelf above the sofa bed.

Melody's uneasiness was growing. Holborn Police Station was just up the street. If Doug was in the incident room, there was no way he could avoid listening to what she had to say.

———

Kincaid and Sidana returned to Holborn to find the CID room empty except for an array of used paper coffee cups scattered across the workstations. "Bit early for everyone to have buggered off," Kincaid said, checking the whiteboard for any updates to the action list.

He'd not been entirely happy about leaving Tyler and Chelsea— he couldn't help but think of them as *the kids*—in the flat overnight. But he needed to arrange for someone from Charing Cross nick to sit in on Tyler's formal statement in the morning.

In the meantime, Tyler and Chelsea would probably be safe enough where they were, as long as they didn't let anyone in. *Not even pizza delivery*, Kincaid had stressed.

As for Chelsea, Sidana was on the phone now, setting up the girl's forensic examination for the morning. Sidana had promised to go with her, and afterwards they would bring her into the station for an official interview.

"We'll need to have uniform do house-to-house where Chelsea was picked up," said Sidana, who'd finished her call. "And we'll need to check CCTV in the area. I can't believe the bastards were able to snatch her right off the street in the middle of freaking Bloomsbury."

It had been smooth—and brazen—he had to admit. Had he been too quick to dismiss Mick and his mates as the possible perpetrators in Sasha's murder? He didn't buy that they'd killed Sasha as a warning to Tyler or Tyler's friends. Tyler was small potatoes, a part-time campus dealer with no gang connections to be intimidated by an example.

But what if they'd somehow learned that Tyler had told Sasha about Chelsea's rape? Self-protection was more credible. Still, he couldn't make the logistics work. These guys weren't omniscient.

Unless they'd had an informant . . . What if someone had told them that Sasha had taken an urgent call, then left the hospital with medical supplies?

What if that informant had been Chowdhury?

But how would Mick and his pals have known Neel Chowdhury? Maybe they'd been selling him stolen Staffordshire dogs. Kincaid snorted at the thought.

"Sir?" Sidana looked up from her desk.

"Just entertaining myself with far-fetched theories." He realized he'd been fiddling with the uncapped whiteboard marker and now had a smear of black ink across his fingertips. Snapping the pen closed, he glanced at the board once more. Doug Cullen was supposed to have been reinterviewing the hospital nurse this morning about Chowdhury's movements, but the item hadn't been checked off the action list. And where was Doug, anyway?

"Has Cullen filed a report today?" he asked Sidana.

"Doesn't look like it."

He'd pulled up Doug's number on his mobile when the CID room door opened and Simon edged in, a coffee in one hand and a paper bag in the other. The bag bore the logo of the Fryer's Delight, the legendary shop across Theobalds Road, and the smell of hot fried chicken oozed into the room like a tangible thing.

"Anyone want some chicken?" Simon asked. "I got extra. Chips, too." Opening the bag, he extracted one and waved it at them.

Kincaid ignored the temptation. "Have you seen Cullen?"

"He was here when I left. Didn't look as if he meant to bugger off." Simon gestured at Doug's workstation. "He was bursting with news. Turns out the doctor who was supervising Sasha Johnson was also shagging her—he flat-out admitted it. And it turns out the doc's wife is a doctor, too, a cardiologist, and not a happy camper about the affair."

Dr. Rees, Kincaid remembered, with the dark Welsh looks. He and Doug had met him that first morning, when Chowdhury had informed Rees about Sasha's death with what had seemed almost like relish. Kincaid had put the lack of sensitivity down to the man's general nastiness, but now he wondered if Chowdhury had known about the affair.

If Rees—or his wife—had killed Sasha, could Chowdhury have suspected? In which case, Chowdhury's murder would make sense.

What didn't make sense was Doug walking out of the station without filing a report or filling him in.

He'd started a text to Doug when Simon's internal phone rang. Carefully returning a chicken thigh to its cardboard box, Simon picked up, listened a moment, then said, "Right. Send her up. Thanks, mate."

He rang off and turned to Kincaid. "It's Melody Talbot downstairs, boss. The desk sergeant's sending her up. Oh, and boss . . ." Simon paused to wipe his fingers on a napkin before tapping on his keyboard. "The contact at the Paddington hospital called back while I was out. They've emailed the info you requested." As a file opened on his screen, he skimmed it and added, "It looks like Sasha Johnson, Neel Chowdhury, and Sandra Beaumont were all on the team that failed to follow Ebola safety protocol. Sasha would just have been starting her clinical rotations, I'd guess. That must have given her a black mark."

"What about the patient? Did they give you a name?"

Simon scrolled down the file. "Here it is. It was Anne—that's Anne with an *e*—Pope. Forty-one years old, a lecturer at St. Mary's. Epidemiology."

"That's a bit ironic," put in Sidana, who'd come to read over Simon's shoulder. "It says she'd been volunteering with an aid organization in the DRC. The country was red-flagged at the time. I remember seeing something in the news."

"That's all very well," Kincaid said, "but that was, what, four years ago? I don't see how—"

"Wait." Sidana went back to her own computer. "Pope. I've just seen that name. Where was it?" Frowning, she scrolled through documents on her screen, then her face relaxed. "It was on the charge-card list from Darrell Cherry's club. A David Pope." She looked up at Kincaid. "The name could be a coincidence. We haven't run across him in connection with Johnson or Chowdhury before this."

But Simon had pushed his chicken box aside, his fingers flying over the keyboard while they waited.

"Got it!" Simon swung round with a victory fist pump. "We have run across it. In Tully Gibbs's statement. David Pope owns the gallery where she works."

Just then, the CID room door opened and Melody Talbot, a visitor's lanyard round her neck, paused on the threshold. "Sorry if I'm interrupting." Her face fell as she scanned the room. "Actually, I was looking for Doug. Has anyone seen him?"

—

Tully stood, staring down at the shattered pieces of the doll's head, for what seemed a very long time. Then, she started to shake. Sasha. She had made her friend's likeness in the first surge of grief. It had been a way of holding on, and she couldn't re-create that moment.

With trembling fingers, she picked up one of the cardboard boxes she used to transport pieces from the studio to the kiln and very carefully placed the shards of clay inside it. She closed the kiln door gently, as if that might somehow mitigate the damage. With leaden legs, she let herself back into the studio, then carried the box through the connecting door into the gallery.

There was no sign of David in the front showroom, but then she heard a faint musical clink from his office in the back. This was a room she didn't enter often, as he'd made it clear early on that he considered it his private territory. She'd wondered if he'd thought she'd steal his liquor, as he kept a cocktail setup on a console table to one side of his desk.

The bottles were all high-end stuff, from what she'd seen— single-malt whisky, boutique gin, vodka that came in a fancy engraved bottle. He had the accoutrements to match, too; crystal tumblers, gossamer-thin martini glasses, an ice bucket and tongs finished in iridescent copper—all chosen as if they were objets d'art.

It was the ice she'd heard, she saw as she stood in the doorway, dropping into one of the crystal tumblers. The sharp, woodsmoke scent of peated whisky caught in the back of her throat. He'd offered it to her once, in one of his more garrulous moods, but she'd refused. She didn't like scotch, and she hadn't thought boozing with her boss a good idea, even then.

David turned, glass in one hand, tongs in the other, as if a sixth sense had told him she was there. "Tully. I didn't hear you come in."

"Why is the gallery closed, David?" she managed to ask, surprised to find that fury had left her voice steady.

He shrugged, gave a rueful smile. "We haven't had a single customer all afternoon, and I had some paperwork to take care of."

"Did you lock the front door because you were in the kiln shed?"

"What?" His brow creased in his familiar irritated expression. "Why would you think that?"

Reaching into the box, Tully scooped what was left of the doll into her palms and held it up. "This. Why would you do this?"

He studied her, tilting the liquid in his glass. "I'm not sure what you mean, Tully. Accidents happen in the kiln, as you very well know. Perhaps there was a fault in the making."

"There was no fault," she shot back. "I've built hundreds of these, and not a single one has ever exploded. This was deliberately smashed, and no one has access to the kiln but you. Is it because I wouldn't put it up for sale?"

David took an experimental sip of his drink before he spoke. "Are you seriously accusing me of something so petty?" He shook his head. "I'm disappointed in you, Tully. I thought our arrangement was to your benefit, but perhaps it's time we parted company."

Moving to the bar, he switched the tongs for an ice pick and lifted the top from the copper bucket. With one deft stroke, he split a chunk of ice, then turned back to her, the pick still in his hand.

"You can leave without notice, and with what you're owed, but I'm afraid I'll have to dock your pay for Friday afternoon."

The thing that had been niggling at Tully suddenly coalesced into a solid thought. Friday afternoon. The charge slips not filed, the cash drawer not emptied. Why had David, who was so obsessive about paperwork, not closed out the shop? Had he shut the gallery, early, the way he had today?

Then, as she focused on what he held in his hand, an absolutely horrible idea took hold, blossoming in her mind like a cancer. She made a little involuntary sound, almost a whimper, and when she looked up, something in his eyes had changed.

All she managed to whisper was, "Why?"

CHAPTER TWENTY-FIVE

"Why? I should think that would be obvious," said David. "I was counting on you, and you let me down. I can't have someone so irresponsible in charge of the gallery."

Tully swallowed against the lump that had formed in her throat. "I—it was an emergency." She tried to take another step back towards the door, but her feet seemed rooted to the carpet. Surely it was mad, what she was thinking, but she couldn't stop her spiraling brain. Or her mouth. "Where did you go on Friday afternoon, David? When I left to meet Sasha? You didn't close the shop properly."

In the distance, a phone rang. Hers, left in the studio. After a moment, it stopped.

David raised an eyebrow. "You're an employee, Tully—or I should say, you *were* an employee—and I don't see that it's any of your concern. I was counting on you to work until closing on Friday. I had other plans."

"Did you go to Russell Square?"

Tilting his glass, David gave the brown liquid another meditative swirl, then lifted the lid on the ice bucket and gave the ice a single tap with the pick. When he set the pick down in order to use the tongs, Tully saw that it was not the one she'd seen before, carefully arranged with the tongs and a cocktail spoon on the bar tray. That pick had been longer, with a carved wooden handle, a silver rosette at its base. This one was plain, the utilitarian sort you'd find at any supermarket or ironmonger.

When he'd added ice and another splash of whisky to his glass, David said, "Am I not allowed to walk to the tube station? That is usually the way I go home."

"No. Of course. I mean . . ." She should shut the hell up. Just walk away from this bloody gallery and David's sarcastic moods. She should just put the scenario she'd concocted down to the overactive imagination that had kept her from sleeping at night for years after Rosalind vanished.

David had met Sasha only a handful of times, after all, when she and Sash had met up at the gallery before an after-work drink or a meal. Had they even spoken, other than the usual pleasantries? It was beyond ridiculous to think he had left the gallery, walked to Russell Square, found Sasha, and stabbed her. Tully felt faint with the absurdity of it.

But if David hardly knew Sasha, why had he smashed the doll? Because Tully was absolutely certain that he had.

"You hated her. Sasha." Again, the words came out before she could stop them. "What I don't understand is why."

David's eyes narrowed. "I have no idea what you're talking about, Tully. But I think you had better give me your keys. I'll have your things sent to you—I won't be selling any more of your work, by the way—but I want you out of my gallery. Tonight."

He'd been leaning lightly against the console table, but now he straightened to his full height and there was something threatening in the way he loomed over her.

Tully tensed, fear prickling along her spine, but she had to go on. "You knew she was coming to meet me. You knew that coming from the hospital, she'd take the shortest route, across the square. And you must have known that if you left straight after me, you'd be likely to intercept her."

She couldn't take the words back. Time slowed, hung suspended, and still her feet wouldn't move. There was a tiny sound from somewhere, a mouse rustle of movement, but David didn't seem to have heard it. Her gaze strayed to his hands. Where had the ice pick gone? There one minute, gone the next, like a conjurer's trick. Had he put it in his pocket?

Slowly, he set his glass on the desk, freeing both his hands. She watched, mesmerized, as he brushed his palms together in an odd little gesture, as if disposing of crumbs. When he took a step towards her, she had to tilt her head to look up at him.

"You do know," he said, "that no one will believe you."

———

After leaving the station, Doug walked quickly down Theobalds Road, scanning the traffic in both directions for a yellow light atop a black cab. But every cab that passed was annoyingly engaged, even those with no visible passengers. "Bloody taxis," he muttered, thinking he'd look stupid jogging in his work brogues and his anorak, but he couldn't shake a feeling of urgency.

Then, as he swung around to check the traffic behind him once more, he caught a flash of red. A westbound 27 bus was trundling towards him. If he put some steam on, he might just make it. He broke into a dead run, brogues be damned. The bus pulled into the stop and Doug darted across the road through the oncoming traffic, jumping onto the bus platform just as the doors were closing. The driver gave him a scowl but opened the doors. His heart thumping, Doug scanned his Oyster card, then grabbed a hand strap as the bus lurched into motion.

Theobalds Road quickly merged into Shaftesbury Avenue and in just moments the bus reached the Museum Street stop. He hopped off when the doors whooshed open and headed briskly towards the gallery.

Smokers stood on the pavement outside the Plough, creating their own little clouds in the damp air. Doug detoured round them and was congratulating himself on having reached his destination in good time when he glimpsed the Closed sign on the gallery door.

"Sod it," he muttered, checking his watch. It wasn't yet six—had they closed early? The lights were still on, but the window shades were drawn. When he gave the door handle an experimental tug, it didn't budge.

Taking out his mobile, Doug tried Tully's number. After a few rings, he realized there was an echo to the sound coming from his phone speaker. He pulled the mobile away from his ear, but the call had gone to voicemail. Had the echoing ring come from inside the gallery? Or the studio?

He stood, irresolute, his uneasiness growing. Why was the gallery closed? Why, if Tully was inside, was she not answering her phone?

He needed to speak to David Pope, as well. The more he'd thought about a David Pope showing up on the list of customers who'd been in the Manette Street club the same evening as Neel Chowdhury, the less he liked the coincidence. Pope's name might be common enough, but two David Popes popping up on the fringes of these murders was two too many, even if he could see no obvious link between Pope and Chowdhury.

He'd try the studio, he decided. Going next door, he rang the bell. When there was no response, he pushed the buzzers for the other flats. After a moment, the front door's lock mechanism released with a satisfying thunk. People really should learn to be more security conscious, he thought as he slipped in and made his way down the hall to the studio.

He'd raised his hand to knock when he realized the door was not quite closed. He remembered Tully complaining about the door's failure to latch. When he gave it a gentle push, it swung open.

The studio was empty. A half-drunk mug of tea sat on the end of the worktable, amid a litter of crumpled newspaper and clay-spattered rags. And there, beside a tub of powdered glaze, Tully's mobile phone. He was about to call out a tentative hello when he saw that the door into the gallery was also ajar. Raised voices were coming from the room beyond. One was Tully, he was sure. The other was male—was it David Pope?

Some instinct kept Doug quiet. Taking out his own mobile, he made sure it was still set on silent, then he crossed the room as stealthily as he could manage. When he reached the open connecting door, he stopped and stood just inside it, listening.

"...you'd...intercept her," he heard Tully say, her voice unnaturally high. Pope—he was sure now that it was Pope—rumbled something in reply. Doug took another step. He was still—at least he hoped—just out of the line of sight of anyone in the gallery.

Tully's words were clear now. "What did Sasha ever do to you?"

"Your precious flatmate, the good doctor?" Pope's voice dripped disdain. "She killed my wife, that's what she did. She and the other incompetents in that hospital."

"Sasha? That's crazy. She would never have hurt anyone—"

"If my wife had got proper treatment, if they'd been doing their jobs, she would have lived. And then she wouldn't have let anything happen to Olivia."

"Olivia?"

"Our daughter. We were climbing, in the Cairngorms. A holiday to take Olivia's mind off things. But Olivia fell, because her mother wasn't there to look after her. Someone had to be held responsible. Surely you can see that." Pope made the proposition sound so reasonable, a simple eye-for-an-eye transaction.

"You shouldn't have meddled," he went on, his tone growing sharper. "Hiring you was a mistake, obviously, but it was a way to keep an eye on her."

"Wait." Tully sounded incensed. "Are you saying you hired me because of Sasha?"

"Of course. I turned all the other applicants away."

"You were . . . stalking us?"

"If you want to call it that. But now," Pope said with a sudden frightening briskness, "you've complicated things, Tully. What am I going to do with you?"

"I won't say anything. Really, I won't. No one could prove anything."

David Pope laughed. "I'm not stupid, you know." He paused, then added almost dreamily, "An intruder, I think. Yes, someone after the cash box. You will have left the kiln-yard door open. How often have I spoken to you about that?"

Doug realized he was holding his breath. What the hell should he do? This guy was mad as a hatter, and it was clear he meant to hurt Tully. Doug didn't see anything he could use as a weapon. He couldn't back out of the studio, and he couldn't call for help.

There was nothing for it but to go forward.

Easing another step into the gallery, he saw a second doorway. It must lead to a room he hadn't seen when he visited before. An office? Whatever it was, that was where the voices were coming from. He took another silent step. Now he could see a slice of the room past the edge of the door.

It was now or never. Doug took a deep breath, pulled out his warrant card, and stepped round the corner.

"Oi," he barked. "Police. What's going on here?" Two startled white faces turned to him in a blur of movement. It took an instant for his mind to process what he was seeing—Pope, advancing on Tully, something in his right hand. Then, Pope's left arm shot towards Tully in a wild grab that just missed. Doug charged, shoulder down like a rugby forward.

Something bright flashed in Pope's hand just as Doug cannoned into him. Together, they fell against a heavy desk, Pope taking most of the impact. Doug managed to scramble backwards, looking for something, anything, he could use to subdue the man. But Pope had recovered as well, and this time as he lunged, Doug saw the ice pick clearly.

He threw up his arm as he swung to one side and the thin blade caught in the sleeve of his anorak.

"You *bitch*," Pope hissed through gritted teeth. Doug stomped on his instep with all the force he could muster. When Pope gasped, his grip on the pick loosening, Doug kneed him in the bollocks.

"Run," he shouted to Tully. "Get help."

But Tully had other ideas. She raised both arms and smashed something against Pope's head with the force of someone twice her size.

David Pope's grimace relaxed into a disconcerting blankness, as if his personality had been suddenly sponged away. Doug just managed to step out of the way as the man crumpled to the floor. The ice pick fell from Pope's hand amid a shower of ice and bounced out of reach.

Panting, Doug gaped at Tully. "What the hell was that?"

"Ice bucket. It was all I could think of."

"Well, it was bloody awesome."

"Did I kill him?" she asked, inching closer. "I hope I did."

Gingerly, Doug sank to his knees to examine the unconscious man. Pope had fallen facedown, one arm beneath his chest, legs splayed awkwardly, but Doug could hear his breath whistling in a faint snore. Blood was seeping into the blond hair on the back of his head. "He's going to need medical attention, but he's breathing. I'm going to bind his hands, just in case he comes to."

Then he remembered that he'd left his cuffs on his desk back at the station, and he wasn't wearing a tie. He decided his belt would have to do. But when he reached for the buckle, his fingers brushed against something damp. One of Tully's ice cubes, he thought, lifting his hand curiously. To his astonishment, he saw that his fingers were red and sticky.

He looked down at the spreading dark stain on his white shirt and said, "Oh, bugger."

CHAPTER TWENTY-SIX

They had taken Sidana's Honda, Kincaid in the passenger seat, Melody in the back. Sidana drove efficiently and aggressively, although there was only so much time to be made on Shaftesbury Avenue.

Melody leaned forward. "He's still not answering calls or texts. I hope he hasn't got himself into a mess."

"I don't think he can have known about Pope's dead wife," Kincaid said. They'd found the words *Pope* and *gallery* scribbled on the pad by Doug's keyboard, joined by arrows and a question mark. But Simon told them that Doug had been logged into HOLMES, so they had to assume he'd seen Sidana's list from Cherry's club. "You never said why you were looking for him," Kincaid said to Melody, twisting round to glance at her.

"He was supposed to meet me for a drink. I was worried when he didn't show and he didn't answer his phone. He was . . ." Melody hesitated. "He was pissed off with me because I thought he was taking anything Tully Gibbs said as gospel. But now . . . If Doug thought Pope was involved in these murders, checking on Tully was the first thing he'd have done."

"We could be making mountains out of molehills," Kincaid said. "Stringing coincidences together." But putting his mobile on hands-free, he rang the direct number for Control and asked them to send an area car to the gallery.

"Five minutes out," the dispatcher replied.

"We'll be there sooner," Sidana told him as she overtook the 27 bus. She looped them around Bloomsbury Square and through the one-way system south of the British Museum, braking the car in Little Russell Street where it intersected Museum Street. "The gallery should be just along here," she said, pointing past the Plough as she pulled the Honda up on the double yellows.

Bollards closed off the pedestrianized section of Museum Street, but Kincaid could see what looked like a gallery a few doors along. He led the way, only his longer legs keeping Melody from outpacing him. The shop appeared to be closed, but lights were still on inside.

Kincaid tried the door, then banged on the glass with a fist. "Police. Open up," he called out. There was a flare of headlamps as the area car pulled up at the other end of the pedestrian plaza. He'd raised his hand to bang on the door again when he thought he saw movement through the semi-opaque window shades.

Melody peered past him. "Is that someone inside?"

Then the shape drew closer and Tully Gibbs threw open the door. "It's you. Thank God. How did you—I rang 999—an ambulance—"

"Where's Doug?" broke in Melody. "Is he okay?"

But Tully had already turned and headed towards the back of the shop. Kincaid and Melody followed while Sidana hung back to direct the uniformed officers.

Tully led them into a smaller room at the back of the gallery. A tall, fair-haired man lay half on his side, his hands bound behind him with a leather belt. He moaned when they came in and muttered something in a slurred voice.

A few feet from him, Doug Cullen sat propped against a desk, a wad of red-stained cloth pressed to his midsection. "Took your time," he said.

"Jesus, Dougie," burst out Melody. "What have you done to yourself?"

"It's a scratch. It's that one needs medical attention." He nodded towards the bound man. "Head injury."

"Make that two ambulances," Kincaid called out to Sidana. He looked at the belt, then back at his detective sergeant, and shook his head. "Doug Cullen. When are you going to learn to carry your bloody cuffs?"

—

It had taken Gemma three bedtime stories to get Charlotte to sleep, but that was merely the end of a chaotic evening. By the time she'd got the little ones home after ballet rehearsal and Charlotte's school pickup, she realized she hadn't bought anything for supper. The children were already fractious, and not even their favorite emergency meal of hastily heated frozen chips, fish fingers, and peas had helped. Toby had thrown a tantrum when she'd insisted he turn off his Spider-Man film on the telly.

Charlotte had tipped her peas onto the floor like a toddler, and Gemma's subsequent scolding had brought on a bout of inconsolable sobbing. When Charlotte had finally been pacified and the dogs had hoovered up the peas, Gemma's stone-cold food had gone straight into the bin.

Kit would surely have managed to whip up something delicious, but he'd come home after a shift at Otto's, given the fridge a disconsolate look, and gone straight upstairs to revise for his exam.

When the little ones were at last tucked in, Gemma had contemplated wine or bath, then chosen the bath. Kincaid had rung to say he'd be late—they had a suspect in custody. If she wanted to hear more, she had to be awake when he got home. So after a good soak, she put her favorite old cardigan on over her warmest pajamas and padded downstairs in her slippers. The silence of the house seemed alien after the turmoil of the evening.

As she opened the garden door to let the dogs out for the last time, she found the weather had changed. Cold air stung her cheeks and swirled round her ankles. Shooing the dogs in hurriedly, she lit the gas fire in the sitting room and went into the kitchen to make herself a cuppa.

She hated being out of the loop. It had been such a letdown, going into work that morning after her weekend involvement in Duncan's case. At least she'd been able to put Melody's mind at rest about Tully Gibbs and her brother. In between her domestic duties, she'd managed to send Melody a text. *Rosalind Summers alive and well in Somerset.*

A little yip from Geordie and the sound of the front door opening interrupted her musings. "Not a burglar, then," she said as her husband came into the kitchen with the dog dancing round his ankles.

"You shouldn't have waited up." When Kincaid bent to kiss her, his cheek felt cold and bristly against hers.

"Oh, I'm not going to bed without the full Monty on what happened tonight." She put the kettle back on the hob. "Tea?"

"Yes, please. It's been quite the evening. For starters," he added as he sank into a chair, "Doug is in hospital for overnight observation. When I left, Melody and Tully Gibbs looked like they might come to blows over who was going to sit with him. Melody played the police card in order to override the visiting hours."

"Oh my God. What happened?"

"He had a little run-in with an ice pick." When his tea had been poured and a dollop of whisky added to it, he proceeded to tell Gemma about the night's events.

"Is Doug going to be okay?" she asked.

"The A and E doc said the blade grazed a lower rib but missed anything vital. But it bled a good deal and they wanted to keep an eye on him."

"Our Doug was quite the hero, then."

Kincaid sighed and rubbed his forehead. "Idiot. I'd be angrier with him for rushing out on his own like that if it weren't for the fact that he probably saved Tully Gibbs's life."

Deciding this wasn't the time to share her little investigation into Tully Gibbs's history, Gemma said, "What about—what did you say his name was? Pope?"

"Concussed. No serious complications so far. He'd recovered enough to lawyer up by the time I left hospital."

"Do you think he killed the nurse, Chowdhury, as well?"

"Yes. And most likely the nurse in Brighton, too. All three were on the team that treated his wife when she fell ill with Ebola. He blamed them, rightly or wrongly, for her death. Apparently, he'd been plotting for a good while. We'll get into his house in Paddington tomorrow—the warrant's in progress."

"And neither Tyler Johnson nor Jon Gibbs had anything to do with the murders?"

"No, but young Tyler is another kettle of fish, one I have to deal with first thing in the morning." He stood and rinsed his cup under the tap. "After a day like today, I could do with a quiet one like yours."

Gemma thought he was quite lucky she didn't kill him on the spot.

———

"Does it hurt?" Melody asked, once she'd convinced the ward nurse to let her see Doug for a few minutes.

"Not much," he said, but his face looked drawn and he winced when he moved.

The plastic chair screeched on the linoleum as Melody pulled it out. She glanced round, afraid she'd attracted unwanted attention from the ward sister, but all was quiet so she sat down. "You are a complete muppet, you know. I mean, seriously, riding to the rescue like Sir Galahad. You could have been killed."

"Well, I wasn't, was I?" countered Doug with a return of his normal mulishness, but he looked pleased with himself. "Sorry I didn't turn up at the Fitzroy. What did you want to talk to me about?"

Melody had been dreading this, but she supposed it was better to get her confession over with. "I, um, I did a little research. I thought I'd found out something about Tully Gibbs and her brother that put them in the frame."

Doug stared at her. "The missing best friend."

Melody stared back. "You knew?"

"She told me. She wasn't trying to hide anything."

"But—I thought that if Sasha had found out that he—or they—had killed her—"

Doug shook his head, grimacing as the motion traveled down to his ribs. "You didn't trust my judgment. Or my common sense."

It was true, Melody realized. "I—I'm sorry. I was wrong. And it turns out the friend isn't dead at all."

"What?"

"Gemma's cousin-in-law, the vicar in Somerset, she knows the family. Rosalind Summers turned up again a couple of years ago, kids in tow."

"Did you tell Tully this?"

"No. How could I? That would have been a bit . . . awkward."

"Yeah. You could say that." Doug leaned back and closed his eyes. "I think that makes us even on the meddling, don't you? I need to get some rest now."

—

The day that followed David Pope's arrest was a long one for Jasmine Sidana. She'd begun, as she'd promised, by accompanying Chelsea Traynor to the forensic evidence facility. She'd then delivered Chelsea into the very capable hands of Lucy McGillivray, who would take her formal statement.

Midmorning, she'd met Kincaid at an address near St. Mary's Hospital in Paddington. The house was in an elegant Victorian terrace on a quiet square. The terrace's white stucco was pristine, the black wrought-iron railings gleaming. Most of the properties had been divided into flats, but David Pope's, in the center of the terrace, was still a single dwelling.

"Family money," Kincaid had said as they waited, bundled against the cold, for the arrival of the SOCOs and the locksmith. "Simon's done some research this morning. The Popes made their fortune in importing from Asia, and are the benefactors of a small private museum near St. Mary's with a fine collection of Asian pottery and artifacts."

"That's where the funding came from for the gallery?"

"And his expertise in ceramics, apparently. Whether he opened the place before or after he knew Sasha and Chowdhury were working in Bloomsbury, we don't know. The only family we've been able to contact so far is an aunt on the museum board. She confirmed that his daughter died in a climbing accident two years ago. She also said that David was a bit of a black sheep, always difficult. Dropped out of medical school, never turned a hand to anything successful. They were surprised when he wanted funds for the gallery. She also told Simon that the late Anne Pope was lovely and she'd always suspected Anne made that trip to Africa to get away from her nephew."

"Whoa. Nothing like having family in your camp."

The locksmith arrived and Sidana had followed Kincaid inside with a feeling of trepidation.

The place had looked abandoned, dust thick on the furniture in the main rooms. On the lower floors, only the basement kitchen had shown signs of habitation, the American-style fridge/freezer stocked with ready meals.

It was the child's bedroom on the second floor that got to Sidana. A little girl's room, with its pink-and-purple décor, stuffed unicorns, and a dollhouse. She'd quickly followed Kincaid up to the third floor.

This was clearly where David Pope had spent his time. There was a plain bedroom, and across the hall, a sort of study with a sofa and television.

"Holy shit," Sidana exclaimed in spite of herself as she took in the details of the room. One wall had been devoted to his "project." There were photos of Sasha Johnson and Neel Chowdhury, as well as an older woman that Sidana assumed was the nurse Sandra Beaumont. And there were others, faces she didn't recognize from their investigation, a Black man, a middle-aged woman with East

Asian features, a white man with thick white hair. There was also a full-sized human anatomy poster, covered with puncture marks. "He bloody practiced," she said.

"Look at this." With a gloved finger, Kincaid gestured at a long table taking up the adjacent wall. On it was a neatly arranged array of ice picks. One, with a carved handle and a silver base, was particularly striking.

"I think," he said, "that Mr. Pope is going to need a very good solicitor."

Now finished for the day, Sidana found herself driving east from Holborn, rather than west. She would be expected at home in Hounslow for dinner with her parents and grandmother. They would ask her about her day, out of politeness, but they would certainly not want to hear about it. And after that, she would go upstairs to her little suite of rooms on the top floor and face the long evening. Just the thought of it made her shudder, remembering David Pope's solitary lair.

She'd given up her Earl's Court flat and moved back in with her parents when she'd been ill, a temporary necessity. Why, she wondered now, had she let herself stay until she'd begun to calcify in place?

She passed Aldgate Station and continued east into Whitechapel Road. It was late, past six o'clock. He might have gone home to wherever he lived and whatever he did in the evenings. He might be out on a case.

She was still second-guessing herself as the bright scarlet flash of the Royal London's air ambulance on its helipad came into view. When she'd found a place in the car park, she locked the Honda and took the circuitous but now familiar route to the mortuary.

The cold struck her as she came out of the lift into the basement. She should turn back, she thought, shivering, before she made a fool of herself, but somehow she kept walking.

The door of Rashid Kaleem's office stood open. When she knocked, he turned from his computer, eyes widening in surprise. "Detective Inspector." He stood hurriedly, knocking a stack of papers to the floor.

"I'm so sorry," she said as he bent to retrieve them. "I didn't mean to startle you. I just stopped in on the off-chance." Which was ridiculous, as he would know perfectly well, but he motioned her into a chair with an agreeable nod. "It's just that I thought you might like to hear about the case," she went on, clasping her hands in her lap to keep them still.

"Duncan rang, and forensics have sent over the first batch of images of the likely weapons. But I'd love to know what happened last night. I got the impression it was quite the drama." He smiled at that, the corners of his eyes crinkling, and Jasmine Sidana felt something inside her uncoil like a loosening spring.

"Maybe," she said, swallowing, "I could tell you about it over a curry."

—

The hospital had insisted Doug stay off work for the rest of the week. He'd spent the time fretting, trying to focus on the gardening catalogues littering his coffee table, and waking with a panicked start whenever he dozed off. Often, when he was awake, a sudden memory of the ice pick's silver glint would catch him unawares.

He hadn't rung Melody, because he was still angry and he couldn't work out what to say to her.

He hadn't rung Tully, either, although she'd sent him several texts asking how he was faring. He'd wanted to tell her the news about her friend in person, so when he'd finished a checkup at the hospital outpatient clinic late on Friday afternoon, he found himself walking, albeit slowly, from the Russell Square tube station to Guilford Street.

To his relief, because his side was aching, a light shone in Tully's flat. When he pressed the buzzer, there was a twitch at the clothing rack in the window and a moment later the door released.

Tully threw open the flat door with a smile. "Doug! Are you okay? Should you be out and about so soon?"

"I've just come from hospital. They've said I can go back to work on Monday, as long as I take it easy. I wanted to see how you were." As Tully ushered him in, he took in the state of the flat. The small sitting room was littered with open cardboard boxes, some empty, some with clothing and kitchen items spilling out haphazardly. "Oh. You'll be packing up Sasha's things. That must be difficult."

He knew that Sasha's funeral was the next day and supposed her family would have made arrangements to clear out the flat.

"It was," said Tully. "Her mum came round yesterday."

"But—" Doug realized suddenly that all the pottery dolls on the shelf above the sofa were missing, as were half the clothes from the makeshift curtain rack. "Your things—have you found a new place?"

"It's a bit more complicated than that." Tully gave him a look he couldn't interpret. "Here, sit." She waved him towards the sofa. "I'll just put the kettle on."

She left him to look round the room and he could see now that it had been well and truly stripped. Tully's books were gone, as were the colorful prints and the fabrics and pillows that had festooned the sofa.

"I had so much to tell you," she said as she returned with two of her pottery mugs. She sat on the other end of the sofa, so that she could turn to face him, and for a moment it was like being back in the studio with her, chatting over tea. "But I didn't want to burden you with anything while you were unwell. Especially after what you did for me."

Doug shrugged at that. "I'm just glad I was there. You're really leaving the flat, then?"

"Yes. You know I couldn't stay on." She hesitated, turning the warm mug in her hands, then looked up and met his gaze. "I've given notice at the museum, too. They're not going to insist that I work out my two weeks, under the circumstances. It's kind of them."

"But—what will you do?"

"After the funeral tomorrow, I'm going home. To Somerset. Jon will bring my things in the club's van once I'm settled." She must have seen his shock because she went on hurriedly, "Your nice superintendent came to see me. He said he'd learned that my friend Roz is all right after all. She's come back."

"That—that's great news," Doug stammered, trying to mask his disappointment that he hadn't been the one to tell her.

"Isn't it?" Tully's face lit up, and it hit Doug that it was the first time he'd seen her smile untarnished by grief. "She—well, it's a long story. But I've been talking to Roz's mum. She has a spare bedroom, and I'm going to stay with her for a bit. There's an opening at a pottery co-op in Glastonbury, with use of the studio in return for teaching some classes." She took a breath. "I need a new start. Away from all of this." Her gesture took in the flat, the museum, the gallery. London. Him. But there was a note of entreaty in her voice, as if it mattered to her that he understood.

"Yes, of course. Of course you do. I can see that. It sounds the perfect answer." He managed a smile and set his mug down. As he stood, his side felt suddenly much more painful. "Thanks for the tea. I'd better leave you to get on. Best of luck with everything."

He'd reached the door when he heard her call out.

"Doug, wait." She darted into the kitchen, returning a moment later with something in a plastic carrier bag. "To remember me by," she said, thrusting it at him.

It wasn't until he was seated on the tube heading home to Putney that he opened the bag and looked inside. It was the mug with the pale blue glaze.

—

Kincaid attended Sasha Johnson's funeral on the cold and windy Saturday at the end of that long week. The service took place in the newly restored Dissenters' Chapel at Kensal Green Cemetery, and afterwards he followed the procession through the winding green tracks to the graveside. He'd come partly to pay his respects to the family, as was his custom when he worked a murder investigation, and partly to keep an extra eye on Tyler Johnson.

A much-chastened Tyler had been stashed in a safe flat while he helped Charing Cross CID with their inquiries into the drug and prostitution rackets run by one Mick Carney and his two associates, all three of whom Tyler had quickly identified from photos in the Met database. Tyler had been accompanied to the funeral by a plainclothes constable, but Kincaid wanted to make sure he was returned safely.

Chelsea Traynor, having given her statement and identified the same three men as those who'd kidnapped and raped her, had been whisked off to the Home Counties by her father. Once they had a DNA result from the clothing Chelsea had kept, Kincaid's team would have the pleasure of picking up Mick Carney and his mates on what they hoped would be the first of many charges.

Now Kincaid stood behind the mourners clustered round Sasha's open grave, far enough away that the words of the committal were snatched by the wind. Near the Johnsons stood Betty and Wesley Howard and the Howard sisters, none of whom he could keep straight except for the striking Destiny. Tully Gibbs stood a little apart from the family, her face blotched with tears.

How much damage David Pope had wreaked, in so many families, beginning with his own. From the interviews they'd conducted following his arrest, it seemed likely that his abusive and controlling behavior had driven his wife to flee to Africa. As for the daughter's climbing accident, a year after her mother's death, Kincaid had spoken to his friend Alun Ross in Inverness CID.

"Aye, we had our suspicions," Ross had said. "But we couldn't prove anything. There were no witnesses, and the injuries were consistent with a fall. But who takes an eight-year-old girl out in the Cairngorms on a trek like that, I ask you?" Ross had tutted his disapproval.

Kincaid spent far too long after that call staring at the photos of little Olivia Pope.

"Duncan," a voice called out, and he saw Betty Howard coming towards him. The service was over, the mourners scattering. "You look like you've seen a ghost," she added as she reached him. She gave him a searching look, then patted his arm. "You've done all you can here, love, and it is much appreciated. But now you need to go home and see your own children."

—

The end of November and the first two weeks of December passed in a blur for Gemma. In between work and ballet rehearsals, they'd managed to take the children to see the Christmas lights in Regent Street and for the obligatory visit to Hamleys. Gemma had found a wreath for the front door and collected some holly sprigs for the mantel. They'd bought a tree from the Christmas tree stall at St. John's Church and had managed to wrestle it into the cargo hold of the Land Rover for the short journey home.

Then, at last, it was the weekend of *The Nutcracker*. Gemma woke on Saturday morning to find the grass white with frost. "Snow, snow," Toby and Charlotte had chanted, but much to their disappointment the white icing had disappeared within the hour. There was possible snow in the forecast, however—Gemma just hoped it would hold off until after the performance.

By afternoon the family had begun to arrive—Rosemary and Hugh on the train from Cheshire; Jack, Winnie, and little Connie by car from Somerset. Lastly, her parents had come just for the evening from Leyton, her father grumbling about the tube, her mother looking frail but beaming with pride over Toby's debut.

The star himself, however, after weeks of vibrating with excitement, had gone strangely still and quiet. Gemma was afraid he'd come down with a sudden case of stage fright.

When she'd delivered him early to the Tabernacle, she walked as far as the bottom of the stairs with him, then stopped him with a hand on his shoulder. "Toby, lovey, are you okay? You know you're going to be just fine."

He looked up at her, his small face serious. "I know, Mum. I just don't want it to be over." Then he wriggled out from under her hand and flashed her a big grin. "An hour to curtain. Gotta go," he said, and bounded up the stairs.

An hour later, the small auditorium was packed and Gemma's heart filled as she saw how many of their friends had come. Wesley and Betty, Bryony Poole, Alex Dunn—even Otto was there with his two daughters. Kit had brought Erika. Louise had come, too, as she'd promised.

The lights went down, the curtain went up, and Gemma gripped Duncan's hand in the dark.

—

Two hours later, when the last strains of Tchaikovsky died away and the curtain fell for the final time, Gemma knew there were going to be decisions to be made. Even in a mouse costume, Toby had lit up the stage. She knew she was biased, of course, and that she was no expert on dance. But he had something that set him apart, in the way he moved, in his comedic timing, in the sheer joy he radiated on the stage.

As they joined the throng shuffling from the auditorium, Louise Phillips caught her eye. "Remember what we talked about," she murmured to Gemma, and gave her a brisk nod.

"What?" Kincaid asked as they reached the ground floor and the tables of refreshments organized for after the performance.

Now, Gemma thought, was as good a time as any. "We need to talk." She tucked her hand into his arm and steered him towards the front doors. "Let's get some air before everyone comes down."

The cold was a shock after the warmth of the auditorium, the air still and sharp, heavy with the scent that presages snow. "The kids may get their wish after all," she said, then turned to face him. "Toby was good, wasn't he? Really good."

Kincaid nodded, his expression puzzled. "He was. Are you not pleased?"

"Of course I am. But the thing is"—she took a breath—"his dancing is going to be a challenge for us. And there's an opening at Westminster for a DI. I've applied for it. I want to go back on an active team."

"But the kids—"

She shook her head. "We can't go on cobbling things together and hoping one child or the other doesn't fall through the cracks. It isn't working even now. We're going to need help. A lot of it."

—

Melody sat cross-legged on the futon, watching Andy sleep. For someone who seldom stopped moving when awake, his restless energy crying out for a guitar even when his hands were empty, he slept like an effigy, on his back, with his hands folded at his collarbone. Reaching out, she pulled the duvet up to cover a bit more of his shoulders. Bert the cat was curled up on his other side, against his knee. In their earlier hurry to get to bed they'd left the kitchen curtain open, and the streetlamp shone through into the sitting room now, limning Andy's slightly tilted nose, the curve of his cheek. She reached out again, brushing a strand of hair from his forehead, her touch like a feather.

Looking at him, she felt an almost physical pain deep in her chest. Was it supposed to be like this? Did Gemma feel this when she looked at Duncan? How did you live with it every day and not be consumed by it?

These last few weeks, she'd felt herself seeping away. She wasn't certain that the little core of what made her herself could survive this erosion, this subsummation by desire, and she was afraid.

With a last touch to his cheek, she eased herself from the futon, slipped into her clothes, and very quietly let herself out the door.

ABOUT THE AUTHOR

Deborah Crombie is a native Texan who has lived in both England and Scotland. She divides her time between the UK and Texas, where she lives in an old house with her husband, cats, and two German shepherds.

deborahcrombie.com
 deborah.crombie
 deborahcrombie
 deborah.crombie

EXPLORE THE DUNCAN KINCAID
& GEMMA JAMES NOVELS